PRAISE FOR
Declan Hughes, a Master of Suspense Fiction

"Relentless, wayward, compassionate, and all too human, Ed Loy is a classic hard-boiled private detective, more than worthy of a place among the great creations of Chandler and Hammett. Hughes is simply the best Irish crime novelist of his generation."
—John Connolly

"Mr. Hughes is a highly impressive noir newcomer to this field."
—Janet Maslin, *New York Times*

"Irish crime fiction, or Irish noir, is huge. The latest writer to join the growing ranks of Emerald Isle novelists finding an enthusiastic readership in North America is Declan Hughes."
—Paul Goat Allen, *Chicago Tribune*

"Hughes joins his fellow countrymen Ken Bruen and John Connolly in making an impact on crime fiction."
—Oline H. Cogdill, *Fort Lauderdale Sun-Sentinel*

"Declan Hughes is Ireland's Ross MacDonald."
—Carole E. Barrowman, *Milwaukee Journal-Sentinel*

"Declan Hughes has captured the spirit of Ireland in his series featuring the private detective Ed Loy. . . . He is a very fine writer."
—*The Daily Telegraph* (London)

PRAISE FOR
The Price of Blood

"Stellar. . . . Beaten up, warned off, and yet undaunted, Loy uncovers a horrible series of secrets, leading to a violent and labyrinthine conclusion. . . . This intelligent, often brutal thriller will have readers' hearts racing from start to finish."
—*Publishers Weekly* (starred review)

"Hughes's abilities to craft a 'Dublin noir' crime novel and to expand the character of Ed Loy combine to make this a welcome addition to an eminently readable new series. Highly recommended."

—*Library Journal* (starred review)

"Declan Hughes's detective novels . . . owe a literary debt less to Hammett and Chandler than to Ross MacDonald's Lew Archer books, family melodrama disguised as PI fiction. . . . Hughes's third go-round with private eye Ed Loy tips its narrative hat to Sophocles and other purveyors of Greek tragedy."

—Sarah Weinman, *Los Angeles Times*

"Brilliant. . . . [The] delight in telling stories, even tragic ones, reveals itself everywhere in *The Price of Blood* and leavens its sad, inescapable tragedy. Though the novel explores themes as ancient as tragedy itself, it also offers portraits of the newer Ireland: its horsey set, its failed entrepreneurs. . . . At its heart, though, Hughes's book is far more about old things than new."

—Peter Rozovsky, *Philadelphia Inquirer*

"*The Price of Blood* gallops along like a Celtic Lew Archer novel, and Hughes . . . deftly maneuvers Ed Loy around a plot as challenging as the trickiest steeplechase. . . . The dialogue snaps with ribald wit. . . . There's dash and spirit in Hughes's writing, [and] I'll gladly read his next Ross Macdonald redux."

—Eddie Muller, *San Francisco Chronicle*

"Tough, ironically self-aware, loyal, Ed is the perfect Chandleresque hero. The book's various twists . . . wrap themselves around a dense core of Irish authenticity, all the voices pitch-perfect, all the developments dark."   —P. G. Koch, *Houston Chronicle*

"Like Ireland itself, Loy is stuck between a pugnacious past, where bloodlines dictate loyalty, and a moneyed future, where business is business. Since Hughes suggests that those who remember Irish history are doomed to repeat it, it's no wonder his Dubliners are always after a drink: in Ireland, forgetfulness begets prosperity."

—Jake Tracer, *Entertainment Weekly*

"*The Price of Blood* is violent yet compelling. If it's Irish action you want, pick up this book and you'll be off to the races."
—Diana Pinckley, *New Orleans Times-Picayune*

"This dark mystery from the Emerald Isle manages to be quintessentially, unsentimentally Irish—and as twisty and nasty as *The Big Sleep* and *Chinatown*. . . . This is atmospheric and tough."
—*Booklist*

"If you're new to Irish thrillers, this is a good place to start."
—Allen Pierleoni, *Sacramento Bee*

"Loy is an exceptionally well-drawn character, strong but not unnecessarily violent, introspective without being angst ridden. The dialogue is spare and edgy, the pacing crisp; Hughes's sense of local color, and particularly his ability to impart it to his readers, is absolutely spot on."
—*BookPage*

"Declan Hughes's Dublin recalls Hammett's San Francisco and Chandler's 1940s L.A. . . . [*The Price of Blood*] is a rich mix, and the book's conclusion owes as much to Greek tragedy as to Chandler. . . . Hughes is not afraid to have a good time. Above all, he is not afraid of writing well."
—Anne Enright, winner of the Man Booker Prize, in *The Guardian*

"Hughes [is] a deeply atmospheric writer. . . . The discipline of his theater background has been put to fine use. His keen ear for the demotic, his sharp eye for the damning detail, make *The Price of Blood* a vivid, gripping, and occasionally chilling read."
—Claire Kilroy, *Irish Times*

© Patrick Redmond

About the Author

DECLAN HUGHES is an award-winning playwright and screenwriter. He is the cofounder and former artistic director of Rough Magic Theatre Company and has been writer in association with the Abbey Theatre. The first Ed Loy novel, *The Wrong Kind of Blood*, was nominated for the CWA New Blood Dagger and won the Shamus Award for Best First P.I. Novel. Declan lives in Dublin, Ireland, with his wife and two daughters.

THE
PRICE
OF
BLOOD

An Irish Novel of Suspense

DECLAN HUGHES

HARPER

NEW YORK LONDON TORONTO SYDNEY

HARPER

A hardcover edition of this book was published in 2008 by William Morrow, an imprint of HarperCollins Publishers.

HarperCollins books may be purchased for educational, business, or sales promotional use. For information please write: Special Markets Department, HarperCollins Publishers, 10 East 53rd Street, New York, NY 10022.

FIRST HARPER PAPERBACK PUBLISHED 2009.

The Library of Congress has catalogued the hardcover edition as follows:

Hughes, Declan, 1963–
    The price of blood : an Irish novel of suspense / Declan Hughes.
—1st ed.
      p. cm.
    ISBN 978-0-06-082551-5
    1. Loy, Ed (Fictitious character)—Fiction. 2. Private investigators—Ireland—Dublin—Fiction. 3. Horse racing—Fiction. 4. Missing persons—Fiction. 5. Dublin (Ireland)—Fiction. I. Title.

PR6058.U343P75 2008
823'.914—dc22   2007040667

ISBN 978-0-06-176358-8 (pbk.)

09 10 11 12 13 OV/RRD 10 9 8 7 6 5 4 3 2 1

To Alan Glynn

PART I

ADVENT

Depend on the rabbit's foot if you like,
but remember, it didn't work for the rabbit.

—R. E. Shay

The Turf, and long may we be above it.

—Jorrocks' Toast

ONE

Three weeks before Christmas, Father Vincent Tyrrell asked Tommy Owens to fill in for George Costello, who had been the sacristan at the Church of the Immaculate Conception in Bayview for thirty years until he was rushed to the hospital with inoperable stomach cancer. A lot of Father Tyrrell's parishioners were outraged, to put it mildly, since Tommy was known as a dopehead and a malingerer and a small-time drug dealer, one of the die-hard crew who still drank in Hennessy's bar, and not a retired Holy Joe shuffling about the church in desert boots and an acrylic zip-up cardigan like George Costello, God have mercy on him. And fair enough, the first time I saw Tommy on the altar in cassock and surplice, it was a bit like something out of a Buñuel film.

But what a lot of his parishioners didn't know was that Tommy had been one of Father Tyrrell's most devout altar boys until he was eleven, when the sacrament of confirmation had the unintended reverse effect of enfeebling his faith entirely, or that since Tommy's mother had dropped dead of a stroke a month ago, Tommy had been haunting the church, the only soul under seventy at ten mass every morning. Now he was standing by to clear the altar after eleven-thirty mass on the last Sunday in Advent as I stood and made the best fist I could of rejoicing with the rest of the congregation about Emmanuel's imminent arrival.

O come, thou Dayspring, come and cheer
Our spirits by thine advent here;
Disperse the gloomy clouds of night,
And death's dark shadows put to flight.

The altar cloths and hangings were purple; the tree was decorated and the great crib was installed in a side altar; the fourth candle on the wreath had been lit. Christmas hadn't meant much to me in a long while, never mind Emmanuel, but I had always liked Advent, the way the anticipation was so intense it could make you clean forget the inevitable letdown in store, just like a bottle, or a woman. Although when a priest sends for a private detective the day before Christmas Eve, the distinction between anticipation and letdown tends to blur; the only thing you can properly be prepared for is the worst.

Looking at Tommy, now he had stowed his vestments in the sacristy, I wondered if those graying parishioners streaming past me with their damp winter coats and their filmy eyes and their scent of lavender and pan stick and dust had revised their opinion of him; certainly he was a far cry from the goateed, stragglehaired ne'er-do-well of just a few months ago. The haircut and beardless chin came from the Howard case he had worked with me (a case he was in no small way the cause of; a case in which, not incidentally, he saved my life), but the rest of it—the multicolored acrylic jumper that was not a zip-up cardigan but may as well have been, the relaxed-fit cords, the soft-soled shoes—was close enough to George Costello to reassure even the most doctrinaire old biddy of the strength of his devotion. And of course, Tommy dragging his ruined foot—the result of a stomping from George Halligan for stealing his brother Leo's bike back when we were kids—surely completed the picture of harmless piety. To my eyes, it looked like nothing but the antic shades of mourning, the haphazard motley of confusion and grief.

Tommy came down the aisle toward me; I stood out from the pew and genuflected; he turned and I trailed after him to the altar, where there was another genuflection from us both, old enough to have had it bred into our bones. For all the Godless years I worked in L.A., people found it strange that I could never break the habit of crossing myself when I passed a hearse, or heard the tolling of a church bell. I still can't. I stepped up onto the altar to make for the sacristy, but Tommy turned left and exited through the side door. I followed out into the bright, cold morning and Tommy led me down a path to the rear of the churchyard. We stopped at a low metal gate beneath a row of bare sycamore and horse chestnut trees glistening with frost and Tommy, still determinedly avoiding my eyes, pointed over it to a redbrick Victorian villa fifty yards away.

"I know where the presbytery is, Tommy," I said. "Sure didn't we once have thirty sacks of pony nuts and four dozen bales of hay sent there, for the crack?"

"And Father Tyrrell knew it was us," Tommy said. "Down to the school the next day with him."

"He knew it was you," I said. "You know why? Because you gave the deliveryman your real name."

"I didn't," Tommy said. "I said Timmy Owens, not Tommy."

"Yeah. A mystery how he caught on to us, really."

"I never gave you up, Ed."

"You didn't need to, sure everyone knew we hunted as a pair. Jasus, the clatter he gave us."

"He went easy on you. They always did. They knew deep

down you were a good boy. You were just easily led, that's all, by tramps the like of me."

I laughed at that, my breath pluming in the crisp air, and Tommy's face creased into something like a grin. It was the longest conversation we'd had since the funeral.

"How're you making out with this sacristan thing, Tommy?" I said, half fearing he'd say something like "'Tis a great comfort," or "Sure 'tis the will of God," in reply.

Tommy grimaced, looked over his shoulder at the last of the 'oul ones straggling out of the church, shrugged and lit a cigarette.

"It's not exactly me, is it?" he said. We both laughed at that, furtive, back-of-the-class laughter in the chill noon sunlight.

"But yeah, it's keeping me out of trouble. Out of the house. I can't face the whole, all her clothes, her paintings, the whole gaff just reminds me of her. Feels like it's haunted. *You* know what I mean, Ed."

I nodded. I had come back from L.A. to bury my mother, and stayed to find out what had happened to my father, who had disappeared twenty years earlier. Now I was living in the house I grew up in; living and partly living. There were days it seemed more like all I was doing was dying there: the souls of the dead hovered in the rooms like smoke, until I thought I might suffocate. I spent the time I wasn't working in one pub or another, stumbling home when I could be sure I would fall asleep straightaway, and then leaving the house first thing the next morning and starting all over again. If I wasn't thirsty, I spent time in churches, too: they were warm and quiet, and no one thought you were unwelcome there, or at least no one made you feel as if you were. I knew what Tommy meant all right.

"And Father Tyrrell's a bollocks, this we know, but he's on the level, he doesn't expect you to pray with him or pretend to be a Holy Joe or anything. And he has the inside on the ponies, of course. I'm making a mint on the tips he's giving me, and Leopardstown comin' up."

I had three beaten dockets in the pockets of my coat, and more on the floor of my car, and the opposite of a mint in the bank, but before I could ask Tommy to share a few of those tips, or to explain why a Catholic priest should "of course" know so much about horse racing, the dark-clad figure of Father Vincent Tyrrell appeared in the doorway of the presbytery, a cigarette in his hand, the smoke coiling in a wreath above his head. Tommy held a hand up to the priest and bowed his head and stood aside as if he was presenting me at court, and I thought I saw a flicker in his face and something cross his eyes: not fear, nor hatred; maybe just the lingering ghost of both. Whatever it was, he dispelled it with a wink in my direction and a grin that didn't reach his eyes and hauled himself back toward the church.

Father Vincent Tyrrell was in his sixties now but still straight-backed at five five, with a white crew cut above a flushed drinker's face whose protruding cheekbones looked like they'd been inserted artificially: they overshadowed his narrow sliver of a mouth and tiny chin; above them popped saucer eyes of the deepest blue, completing the impression of a vivid, cunning animal. He greeted me with a thin smile and showed me into a study paneled in dark wood. The mahogany table had worn dull in patches: half of it was covered with books and paperwork; the other half had three place settings, silver candlesticks and condiments, an overflowing ashtray and the remnants of three breakfast plates, one with two cigarette butts stubbed out in bacon rind. A murk of fried food, cigar smoke and aftershave clung to the air.

"My apologies for the mess. I have a lady who does—it's just, on Sunday, she doesn't," Tyrrell said. He tidied the dirty dishes together with the ashtray and took them away. I stood and looked around the room: the bookshelves of philosophy, theology, poetry and art history, the wooden crucifix on one wall, the woven Bridget's cross above the door, the reproductions of Mantegna's *Crucifixion* and Poussin's *Last Supper* and Caravaggio's *The Taking of Christ*, the lost masterpiece that had shot to fame since its discovery on the disused parlor wall of a Jesuit retreat house in Dublin, where it had been living anonymously for years. I looked at the Caravaggio: the ever-approaching darkness, the soldiers clasping Jesus; the stricken face of the bearded Judas, already paid, and now paying, for his betrayal. When he hanged himself, having cast away the thirty silver pieces he was paid for his betrayal, the priests and elders wouldn't take back the coins, calling it the price of blood.

Tyrrell came back into the room with a bottle and two crystal goblets on a tray.

"Now Ed," he said, sitting down. "At a guess, I'd say you're not much of a sherry man. But most men who think they don't like sherry have a memory of some terrifyingly sweet liquid being forced on them by their granny. Many good reasons why they mightn't want to revisit such a traumatic primal scene. This is not cream sherry, it's Manzanilla, a salty fino, very refreshing."

He poured the yellow liquid and offered me a glass. I sat down opposite him and took a drink of the bone-dry wine, and the drink took me back to a dark-haired girl I knew in Los Angeles, a girl with Spanish blood who knew her Manzanilla from her Palo Cortado, and wanted to teach me the difference, until one day she stopped wanting to, although she didn't tell me that until it was too late. We had a child, a daughter with blond curls and the wrong kind of blood, who died before she was two, and my Spanish girl and me couldn't get past that, and maybe didn't want to, didn't really try. Now she was married again to a man she had never stopped seeing while she was married to me, and they had their own child, a son, and she had rung me last night to wish me a happy Christmas, perhaps, or to tell me about how the kid was getting on, maybe, or to taunt me with her happy life and her happy home and with how she had never really been mine and now never would be, possibly. I don't know; I saw the number come up on the caller-ID display and the answering machine wasn't on, so I waited until the phone rang off the hook and then

I waited until it did it twice more, and then I waited for another while, a long while, before I got to sleep. The Manzanilla was the first I'd tasted since my marriage, and it brought it all swirling back in a storm of memory and desire, of grief and regret and yearning. That's only the beginning of what a good drink can do.

I took another swallow and lifted my eyes and said, "Very good, Father Tyrrell. Nice bite."

"How are you, Ed? Are you all right?"

Was I all right? I'd received a lot of publicity on the Howard case: a journalist called Martha O'Connor cooperated with me in return for my story. She did her best to make me look good, but I could have done without the exposure: Dublin was a hard enough city to be a private citizen in, let alone a private investigator; people wanted their secrets kept, not sprayed all over the front pages. As a result, I was having trouble finding clients. I had fallen behind on repaying the mortgage my mother had taken out to fund the retirement she didn't live long enough to enjoy; I was cashing checks I didn't have the money to back up in any pub that would let me; the bank had run out of patience and was getting ready to cut me loose. The local Guards were taking pleasure in my plight, happy at DI Fiona Reed's bidding to feed pet journalists embellished sagas about my misdeeds. I was drinking too much because I had no reason not to, or because I was stressed out over my debts, or at any rate, I was drinking too much, and I was betting on the horses with the money I didn't have because every day around drink four I became momentarily possessed by the evident delusion that my luck was in. I looked at Father Vincent Tyrrell and felt a sudden urge to confess, to throw myself on the mercy of a God in Whom I didn't believe, to be embraced by a church I had rejected long since. How was I?

"Very well, thank you," I said.

"Only I gather things haven't been going so well for you recently. In the detective business."

"Tommy been talking, has he? You should know better by now than to listen to half of what Tommy says."

"Tommy hasn't said a word. I just hear things. And read the papers. Of course, the fact that the O'Connor woman was involved didn't help."

Tyrrell twinkled beadily at me with the nice combination of sympathy and malice that had kept his parish on edge for over thirty years. Martha O'Connor was known above all for her investigative work on clerical sex abuse and medical malpractice in Catholic hospitals, and it would not have been atypical of Tyrrell's sense of humor to classify me with culpably incompetent doctors and pedophile priests. I wasn't going to rise to his bait, if that was what it amounted to, although it was probably nothing more than habit. I shrugged and finished my drink.

"What can I do for you, Father?" I said.

His lips vanished into his wet mouth as he thought about this, and I almost smiled. It was always the same, and worse if they were used to being in control, the moment when I asked them what they wanted. Because however much they tried to conceal it from themselves, it wasn't want that drew them to me, but need: a need that family or friends, public officials, politicians or the police couldn't satisfy. Just like the need for a whore, and sometimes I took little more than a whore's bitter pride in my work.

"It's about a boy," he said.

I waited a long time for him to say something else.

"Patrick Hutton was . . . is his name."

There was another long silence, during which Tyrrell finished his drink and stared into his glass. He wore an open-necked black shirt and a black jacket, classic priest's mufti; the clothes themselves were finely cut, the shirt silk, but then it had always been clear not only that Vincent Tyrrell came from money but that he still had some; the crucifix on his lapel was inlaid with tiny diamonds.

"I'm sorry, I appreciate this isn't very helpful, but I'm afraid I can't tell you much more," Tyrrell said finally, the blue eyes glinting again, as if almost amused by his reserve.

"Much more? You haven't told me anything, Father. You've given me a name. I'm not overburdened with modesty about my abilities, but there's not a lot I can do with a bare name. Look it up in the phone book. But sure you could do that."

Tyrrell produced an envelope, opened it to reveal a sheaf of bills and laid it on the table between us.

"Five thousand. Just to get you going."

I stared at the money. It would sort out my mortgage debts and pay my bills and go some way toward keeping my head above water and the bank off my back until well into the New Year. There was need on my side too, and the thin smile spreading across Tyrrell's face showed he recognized it. I shook my head and stood up.

"This is a waste of my time. Maybe Tommy Owens has you thinking I'm some kind of charity case—"

"I told you, Tommy hasn't said a word. Or more accurately, I haven't listened to a single word he says. Even in grief, he does like to prattle. And I assure you, if this were charity, you'd hardly be a deserving beneficiary. Patrick Hutton. He was a jockey. His last known address—known to me, at least—is in the envelope. That's all I can tell you."

"But you know more," I said, suddenly seeing where this was heading.

"Yes, I know more, much more. But what I know was told to me in confession, Ed. You remember the rules about that, don't you?"

I nodded and sat down again. The sanctity of the confessional: the promise that sins confessed to a priest during the sacrament of penance will not be divulged, because of course the priest is merely the channel through which God's reconciling grace flows to the penitent; it is up to God to tell what He has heard, no one else. And God hasn't been talking much of late. Tyrrell stretched a hand toward me and patted the envelope of money on the table between us.

"Well, so do I. And even on the occasions when there are very good reasons to break them—and I fear this is such an occasion—the rules still apply. Maybe one day they won't, maybe one day the liberals' prayers will be answered, and the Church will transform itself as they believe Pope John the Twenty-third intended, and all manner of change will occur: women and homosexuals will dance together on the altars, and teenagers will copulate in the aisle, and obese children will make their first holy communions with giant hosts made of cheese-and-tomato pizza. Maybe one day the Church, like everything else on this rock of ours, will dwindle to a mere engine devoted to making us feel good. But that day will come too late for me. Thanks be to God."

Tyrrell's hand shot out suddenly and seized mine.

"I'm dying, Ed. They said I should do chemotherapy, and radiation therapy, but I don't want any therapy. I don't want to be healed. It's my time. I want to die. But not without setting a few affairs in order. Chief among them Patrick Hutton."

His hand felt like a claw; the bones shone ivory through flesh mottled like stained parchment. I couldn't think of anything to say, so I sat still and stared at his hand until he released mine. He poured another two drinks and passed me one, and held his glass up in a toast to—I don't know, to death by cancer, or to ordering his affairs, or to Patrick Hutton and the secrets Tyrrell and God were keeping.

"You'll take the case?"

"Patrick Hutton was a jockey," I said. "Tommy says you've been tipping him winners. Says you have insider information. How's that?"

"I don't," Tyrrell said. "But people always think I do."

I waited for him to explain. He looked surprised that I needed him to.

"I suppose the time you spent away means there are gaps in

your local knowledge, Ed. My brother is F. X. Tyrrell. We don't speak, haven't for many years. But people don't know that, or don't believe it."

Francis Xavier Tyrrell was the trainer of the winning horse I didn't back yesterday, and of most of the winners I hadn't backed in the days before that. He'd been doing it for a long time, and you didn't have to know very much about horse racing to have heard of him: he had been a national figure for decades, stretching back to his first Gold Cup triumphs at Cheltenham in the sixties.

"Must be in the blood then," I said.

"Francis had the true feel for it—I always said Saint Martin of Tours was watching over him; the horses liked him, they didn't know me—and I couldn't stand coming second. Pride has been my besetting sin. It'll see me broken on the wheel one day."

Tyrrell smiled at the prospect of this, and I had a flash of his instructing my class in the seven deadly sins, and what the appropriate punishment for each was: avarice would see us boiled in oil; gluttony and we'd be force-fed rats and snakes; pride would have us broken on a wheel. Father Vincent Tyrrell was quite the young firebrand in those days, his blue eyes bulging with cold fervor, his hands rapping an ominous tattoo on the blackboard as he talked us through the tortures of hell. We were nine years old.

Tyrrell was a fanatic and a bully and a snob, and my rational self despised all this, but part of me insisted on liking him, the part I had no control over, the part that drank whiskey in the morning and took the wrong woman home at night, liked him for his unflinching absorption in what used to be called the Four Last Things: Death, Judgment, Heaven and Hell. Because increasingly, these were the objects of my own devotions. The difference being, I didn't believe in Heaven.

He raised his glass and we finished our drinks and I stood up and nodded at him.

"How do you know I won't just take the money and tell you I couldn't find him?" I said.

Tyrrell's face clouded momentarily, the muscles quivering as if he were having a slight stroke; he controlled them by what looked like the angry force of his will, and directed his cold, penetrating gaze at me.

"I doubt if your footfall upon the earth is especially heavy as it is, Edward Loy. You would never act like that, never betray the only calling you have. You wouldn't do it out of fear. Profane fear: of the harm that would be done to your reputation. And spiritual fear: that if you acted so out of character, you'd run the risk of disappearing entirely."

The bells began to ring for the next mass. He drew his thin lips into a smile, and I found I couldn't meet his piercing eyes; I nodded at the floor to seal the deal. At the presbytery door he gave me a blessing I didn't ask for. Despite myself, I felt glad of it.

TWO

I wanted to ask Tommy some more about Vincent Tyrrell, but he was busy setting up for the next mass: there was a priest home from the African missions who needed minding. I couldn't wait until the mass was over; I was late already for another job. I didn't like to work more than one case at a time, but I didn't like being broke either; I wasn't in a position to turn anyone down. The car park was filling up as I walked toward the racing-green 1965 Volvo 122S that had been my father's, and that Tommy, wearing his mechanic's hat, had done up for me. I was by no means a petrol head, but looking at a roly-poly man and two boys in matching anoraks clustered around the car's bulky hood, I felt a stupid kind of pride. As I drew nearer, and they turned and looked at me and looked quickly away, I understood how stupid: what had caught their attention was not the car, but the damage done: the windscreen wipers had been torn off and laid in the shape of a cross on the hood; beneath them someone had scraped RIP. The man muttered something about not even church car parks being safe nowadays; I agreed and said that in my day, all we used to do was drink cider here and then break the bottles beneath the tires of the parked cars. He took off quickly after that, hustling his giggling sons into mass. I threw the wipers on the backseat, sat into the car and started the engine. At least it wasn't raining.

Heading south toward the Dublin–Wicklow border, I called George Halligan on his mobile.

"The fuck do *you* want?"

The tar-and-nicotine rasp was sandpaper harsh: he sounded like an emphysemic wildcat sizing up its prey.

"Nice talking to you too, George. Out and about, are you, taking a walk?"

"A *walk*? The fuck class of swish cunt d'you think I am? I'm in the parade ring at Gowran Park so I am."

"How'd you get in there, George? Do they not know who you are?"

"I'm here to see Jack of Hearts strut his stuff. Very sleek he looks an' all. And after that, I'll wander across and see him walk away with this little maiden hurdle. And I've Fish on Friday in the last race. What are you doing today, Ed Loy? Dole office not open on a Sunday, is it? Suppose that leaves the pub, if there are any left that'll give you credit. Or you could always stand outside mass with an accordion. If there isn't a Romanian there ahead of you."

"George. You told me you'd let me know when Leo got out."

There was a pause, during which all I could hear was the double-bass rumble of George Halligan's breath. When he spoke it was in as soft and careful a voice as he could summon up.

"Oh Jesus fuck. Friday. I forgot myself, to be honest with you. Why? What's he fuckin' done? Whatever it is—"

"Just some inventive damage to my car."

THE PRICE OF BLOOD | 17

"Send me the bill, Ed."

"That's not the point, George."

"D'you think I don't know that? I was supposed to have him picked up outside the Joy. He hasn't been in touch. He must've been sulking all fuckin' weekend . . . listen, Ed, I'm surrounded by cunts here, I'll have someone, eh, look into that matter, and I'll get back to you, all right my friend?"

George's natural Dublin accent had suddenly upped anchor and set sail for the mid-Atlantic. I pictured him: a known gang boss turned property developer and "businessman" hobnobbing with the Barbour Jackets and the Cashmere Coats in the parade ring. I reeled through the scene in my mind's eye for its incongruity. Nothing doing. George'd fit in nicely there: beggars on horseback all. Although I doubted if many of the other owners and trainers had a brother fresh out of Mountjoy Prison to worry about.

"We're not friends, George, and we never will be. And you be sure and get hold of Leo and remind him why it was a very good idea Podge went down, for the Halligans as well as the rest of us."

Podge Halligan was a murderer and a rapist, an unhinged, volatile nightmare of a man, but it was only when he began to set up secret deals with rival drug dealers, in the process compromising George's attempts to take the family business legit (not to mention stealing from the business before it had acquired that legitimacy), that George had moved against him. I worked the case that helped put Podge away, with George's assistance. At the time Leo had sent word from jail that Podge should do the right thing for the family; ever since, the drumbeat coming from the Joy was that I was to blame for Podge's fate, and that I would pay when Leo came out.

"I'll get the first fifteen on that one for you, yeah? Ciao for now."

"Just remember there, George: you can't buy respectability," I said.

George Halligan's voice dropped and his accent flashed back, a whip laced with salt: "Maybe not. But if you're too broke to make a profit from it, it's fuck all use to you, isn't that right Ed?"

He ended the call before I could respond. But George Halligan getting the last word was the least of my worries. Leo Halligan had gone away for a bullet-behind-the-ear hit on a nineteen-year-old drug dealer; he was thought responsible for at least another three murders, and possibly as many as ten, some of them drug-related, some because the victims had committed the fatal error of getting in his way, or on his nerves. He was smart like George, without craving legitimacy, and ruthless like his younger brother, Podge, without being mental: easily the most dangerous of the Halligan brothers, everyone said. And now he was on my trail, in the season of goodwill. Merry Christmas everyone.

I had avoided the N11 but traffic was thick on the old roads too. I turned on the radio to pass the time. The crime reporter on the news told me that the man's body found in a shallow grave near Roundwood this morning was being examined by the state pathologist, but that "early indications were that it bore all the hallmarks of a gangland killing." Fortieth of the year, if I was counting right. On a hunch, I called Detective Inspector Dave Donnelly at home. His wife Carmel answered.

"Hey Ed. Are we going to see you? Come up to the house on Christmas Eve, we're having a party."

"My invite must've got lost in the post."

"Why'd we waste an invite? You've stood us up the last three times. And Dave the only Guard in Dublin who'll talk to you."

Dave had been with Seafield Guards until the Howard case, when his work caught the eye of someone in Garda Headquarters and he was transferred to the National Bureau of Criminal Investigation. They used him on murder and organized crime investigations, and he used me, and did what he could to keep me out of trouble with Superintendent Fiona Reed and her merry band.

"Is Dave there?" I said. "I . . . I have a horse for him."

"Do you now? And have you lost his mobile number?"

"He's not there, is he?"

"Are you fishing, Ed? You have a horse for him."

"I do."

"Fuck off."

"All right, you've got me. I was calling to see if the coast was clear. I could be there in five minutes."

"Oh, Ed," she purred, her voice all husky. "You know what we could do."

"You tell me."

"You could mind Sadie, who has chicken pox, and pick the lads up from football and cook their dinner, and put two loads of washing through the machine, and I could nip over to Dundrum and do some last-minute shopping, then have a long lunch in Harvey Nick's."

"We could do all that?"

"And I'd never tell Dave. It would be our secret."

"I don't think I could do that to him, Carmel."

"Boys' club. You're all the same, just talk."

"I'm actually in Wicklow now, Carmel. Not far from Round-wood."

"He likes you at the moment, Ed. Don't go annoying him."

"Just wanted to know."

"Christmas Eve. That's tomorrow, Ed. Bring a date. Or I'll find one for you."

South of Bray I crossed the N11 and headed west into the hills, snow-topped in the distance, then cut off onto an old road flanked on one side by the pedestrian entrance to a sprawling local authority estate called Michael Davitt Gardens and on the other by a stretch of oldish semidetached houses with asbestos tile roofs.

I pulled up outside a house with three feet of trellis on top of its perimeter walls and six-foot-high wooden gates and got out of the car. Across the road the pavement widened to include a broad patch of grass running ten yards or so by a twelve-foot concrete wall before it swung into the council estate. My client, Joe Leonard, was concerned about the garbage being illegally dumped outside his house, an increasingly common problem now that most local councils had privatized their refuse collection service. I walked across to have a look. The grass was clogged with plastic and glass bottles, pizza boxes and chip papers, sacks of household waste, broken bicycles and scooters, disabled stereos and vacuum cleaners. How jealous the other PIs would be when they heard they'd missed out on this job.

I crossed the road and walked up the drive past the black SAAB 93 and rang the bell of number four. There was a purple-and-red wreath hanging on the doorknob and paper angels stuck on the inside of the glass. A girl of about six or seven opened the door. She had shiny new teeth that seemed too large for her Cupid-bow lips and dark hair in plaits and bright brown eyes. When she saw me she frowned in disappointment. I pulled a cross-eyed face in return, and she rolled her eyes and giggled.

"You're not Granny!" she said.

"I try to be," I said.

"You *can't* be. You're not an old lady."

"Well. I knew there was something," I said.

"Who *are* you then?" she said.

"My name is Edward Loy," I said. "What's yours?"

"Sara," she said. She pronounced it to rhyme with Tara. Just as I was about to ask her where her dad was, he appeared. Joe Leonard had sounded cross on the phone and he looked even crosser in the flesh: he had shaving rash and thinning hair ruffled up with gel to give the appearance of volume, and he wore those oblong Yves Saint-Laurent–style glasses young men in a hurry seemed to favor these days and a rugby shirt with the collar up and deck shoes and flared jeans that made his short legs look even shorter.

"Sara, I told you *not* to answer the front door. Go back inside please," he said.

The little girl pulled a cartoon face of appeasement at her father, which he greeted with an impatient flick of his hand. Turning to me, she drew the corners of her mouth down in mock panic, said, "Ulp!" and went back into what I guessed was the kitchen. There was room for two people in the hall, but I was still outside. Sara's father smiled at me thinly.

"Mr. Loy, Joe Leonard. Perhaps we should head over first and inspect the, ah, scene of the crime," he said.

"I've just done that."

"I've been having my battles with the council, and I can tell you, you may as well be talking to—"

"Joe."

A petite woman with short black hair and fine, almost elfin features had appeared in the hall.

"Annalise, this is Mr. Loy, the, ah—"

"Private detective. Why is he standing on the doorstep, Joe?"

Joe Leonard turned from his wife and stared past me grimly, his protruding lips pursed, as if I were a tradesman, a roofer perhaps, and he had been hoping to conclude our business without my having to cross the threshold.

"Come in, of course, Mr. Loy," he said, and retreated into the kitchen. I closed the front door behind me and looked at his wife, who raised her eyebrows at me and pulled a cartoon "Ulp!" face not unlike her daughter's, but with a leaven of irony, of malice, almost, as if her husband's moods were trivial and amusing, or as if everything was.

The kitchen was long and narrow and bright, with Velux roof windows and a pine table and chairs by the door and a pale wood floor; glass doors led to a small living room, where Sara and a small boy were grazing on bananas and watching cartoons on TV. A green tree with white lights and cards on the bookshelves above the television reminded us that Christmas was on its way.

We sat around the kitchen table and Annalise Leonard brought me a cup of black coffee; her husband went into the living room and turned the TV off; howls of protest followed him out of the door, which he closed behind him; his children pushed their wailing faces up against the glass, and his wife looked at him almost in pity, as if his stupidity was an affliction.

"They've been watching television all morning," Leonard said.

"Well, if you had got *up*—"

"I had a night out; you got a lie-in when you had *your* night out."

"And I didn't complain about the way you looked after the kids then."

"I didn't plonk them in front of the television all morning."

"You don't have them all day every day."

"And I didn't stay in bed until four in the afternoon."

"I didn't ask you to get up."

"You just said I should have."

There was a pause, and then they both turned toward me, embarrassed but strangely expectant, as if I might give them some cut-price marriage counseling. I put what I hoped was a genial expression on my face, intended to suggest that due to temporary deafness I hadn't heard any of their conversation, or that it had been conducted in a language I didn't speak, and made a show of looking at my watch. Annalise gave her husband a forced smile, went into the living room and turned the TV back on, settled the kids on the couch and came back out, pausing at the fridge. When she joined us at the table, she had a glass of white wine in her hand. Leonard flinched at the sight of this, and looked like he was going to finish what he'd started, and I decided I'd better start talking before the bell for round two sounded.

"You were saying you've tried to get the local council to sort the problem out," I said.

"They do clear it up fairly regularly," Annalise said in a tone that suggested her husband was making a fuss about not very much.

"They clean the estate every week. They clear the space between us and the estate every three months," Leonard said. "And they only take the big items away, there's always a rake of small stuff left there. And phoning the council, you may as well be talking to the wall. No one ever calls you back, they don't reply to letters. The whole system is bloody ridiculous."

"I spoke to a councillor for the Green Party. Monica Burke. She has a son in Sara's class. She was going to raise it at a council meeting," Annalise said.

"Monica with the pink jeans and the scary eyebrows? And the mustache? She's going to get a lot done."

"She doesn't have a mustache," said Annalise, trying not to giggle and failing.

"She christened her son Carson. Carson Burke. For fuck's sake. Six-year-old kid sounds like a firm of solicitors."

Annalise laughed, then made a face at her husband, and he made one back, somewhere between a grin and a grimace, and something crackled in the air between them. Their marriage seemed to thrive on tension, the spiky energy of conflict, but it seemed uneasy and sour to me. Sometimes I envied married couples. Not this morning.

"So what exactly do you want me to do?" I said. "I mean, if it's people from the estate dumping a bag of bottles after a session, or an old bike, there may not be a great deal anyone can do, even if they're caught. I can't see the Guards getting too excited. And what are the council going to do, slap a few fines on them? Kind of people who dump their rubbish in the street are the kind who don't get too fussed about being fined, they won't pay them anyway."

Annalise treated her husband to a told-you-so look and drained her glass. Joe Leonard wasn't going to be put off though.

"You know, at this stage, I don't really care, I just . . . I mean, one of the consequences of our great property boom is to fling people like us into close proximity with . . . people like that—"

"Fucking knackers, you usually call them," Annalise Leonard

offered from the fridge, where she was refilling her glass. "Skangers, scobies, scumbags."

I didn't want any wine—my head was aching from the sherry Vincent Tyrrell had given me—but it would have been nice if she'd asked. Maybe she'd gotten so used to drinking alone that it didn't occur to her.

"I don't pretend to any great fellow feeling," Leonard said. "Especially not after they broke into our car and took the spare tire, stole Sara's bike and trashed it and dumped it in our garden, ripped washing off the line and dragged it through dog shit across the way, and burned a car right out in front of our house. But that's not the point. There are five or six thousand people living in the estate. Walk through there and you'll see, for every house that has garbage dumped in the front garden, there's one with fresh paint and flowers planted. How are those people to thrive if they're being dragged down by the others?"

"The deserving poor," I said, earning myself an overemphatic "exactly" smile from Annalise. Leonard shrugged, unabashed.

"Oh, I know, that's supposed to shut down the argument. But I don't have a problem with that. I mean, if you can't clean up after yourself . . . if someone shits in the street, there's something wrong with them, we all agree. But people from Michael Davitt Gardens dump their trash in plain sight and we have to put up with it. It isn't fair."

"So what do you do? Evict them? They're council tenants. Where will they go? Into emergency accommodation, where they can do it again? Onto the street?"

"You have to have some kind of sanction. We have a social one, you know, other people will think we're pigs if we do it. We'll think that *ourselves*. They don't seem to. But we've all got to get along. I wish we didn't. I wished we lived in a middle-class enclave, like the ones we grew up in. But we don't."

For once, Joe Leonard's wife looked in total agreement with her husband, her wine-flushed face wiped clean of mockery and amusement. Most local authority estates had been built far from where the middle classes lived, back in the days when a teacher or a nurse could buy a semidetached house on a private development, days when their teenage kids viewed the prospect of "ending up" in a semi-d as a fate worse than death. But those days were gone, and young couples on good salaries were now living cheek by jowl with people they used to cross the city to avoid, and they were getting a crash course in the social policies that had left many of those people disaffected and alienated, confined to bleak estates decimated by drug abuse and criminality.

Still, for all Leonard's south-county Dublin brashness, at least he was trying to do something positive about it. Many liberals who'd be appalled by his views had the luxury of simply not having to confront the problem: they lived safely in the very enclaves he and his wife came from and dreamed of returning to, semidetached paradise lost. Who knows, if Leonard made it back there, maybe he could afford to be a liberal too.

"So what do you want, photographs? Video? I can set up a pinhole camera and record the comings and goings across the way."

"What if they see it? They'll target us," Annalise said, all irony past.

"They won't see it," I said. "It's about the size of a roll of coins, and it's wireless. I can hide it in the trellis. Connect a receiver to your VCR, you can record all the comings and goings. You'd need to keep track of the tapes yourselves, unless you want me to move into your living room. But I'll review them with you, and we can isolate any incidents of dumping where we can make out faces or registration plates or whatever, then have those sections transferred to disc."

Leonard nodded, his eyes widening.

"And that would be evidence, like CCTV," he said.

"Something like," I said. "Chances are the council might recognize faces if they're council tenants; if it's kids, we can try the local schools."

"And then?" Annalise said, her tone skeptical again; already the wine that had briefly lit her up was darkening her mood; her reddening eyes were squinting, as if hurt by the light. "We match a list of names from faces and/or registration plates, we present it to the Guards and the council and then what? We sit back and wait until fuck all happens, that's what, until a rap on the knuckles is administered. And five minutes later the Butlers or whoever it is'll be tossing cider bottles out their windows. Or through ours. And we'll still be here because we can't afford to fucking move. If it wasn't for Mummy, we wouldn't even have been able to buy *this* house."

She didn't have to direct this at Leonard for him to take it like a slap in the face; he blinked hard and grimaced, smarting from the rebuke. When he spoke, it was in that careful, steady, neutral kind of voice people who live with alcoholics often use, the kind of voice it's difficult to infer any judgment from, however self-loathing the drinker.

"I don't know what I'll do with the list of names. Maybe I'll take an ad out in the local paper. Maybe I'll nail it to the church door. I don't know. What I can't do is nothing."

His petite wife rolled her eyes at this, and drained her glass again, and smiled in a knowing way at me, inviting me to join her in her contempt for her husband, and asking, in that pouty, lip-moistening way unhappily married women who drank often had, for something else: not sex, or even the promise of it, but sexual endorsement, the reassurance that I would if she wanted me to, even though we both knew all she really wanted was a good drink. But I didn't want to give her that or any reassurance: I didn't like the way she had humiliated Leonard in front of me, and I didn't like the way she mocked his attempts to better their situation. I didn't even like the way she drank, and I was no one to talk.

I had initially thought Joe Leonard was one of those arrogant rugby guys, born to privilege and temporarily light on dough, unable to fathom how a successful school's rugby career hadn't led to greater things. But now he seemed more like one of the also-rans, the lads who cheered the winners from the sidelines, the hangers-on who believed in the dream but couldn't quite live it themselves. I felt sorry for him, but I liked his spirit.

I nodded at Leonard, and reached my hand across to him, and he shook it. He looked anxious though, and when I went into the hall he came out after me and shut the kitchen door behind him.

"I'm worried about money," he said in a low voice.

"Aren't we all?" I said.

"I mean, I don't know how long this will take, and . . . well, Christmas is here, and . . ."

He stopped, and looked at me, his tired gray eyes enlarged by his glasses, his head bowed in exhaustion and shame. I could have pretended Leonard was what I had thought him to be in the first place and taken the money; the guy he wished he was certainly would have: you don't get to the top cutting losers a break. He wasn't that guy though, and neither was I, and even though the only reason I was working this case was for the money, Father Vincent Tyrrell's cash advance meant I didn't have to test my conscience too hard.

"Give me five hundred. You're going to be running the camera yourself. If it turns out that I need to work full-time on it, we'll figure something out."

Leonard nodded, his eyes blinking hard. He gestured toward the kitchen in a you-know-how-it-is way, and I shrugged and nodded, as if most guys I knew were married to women who were drunk by lunchtime. Most guys I knew were drunk by lunchtime themselves, which at least meant they didn't have to worry anymore about their wives, who in any case had long fled the scene.

I went out to my car and opened the trunk and got an oil-smeared canvas tool bag that had belonged to my father. In it, as well as a bunch of small tools, I had a wireless covert video pinhole

camera, a half-dozen nine-volt alkaline batteries, a wireless receiver, a DC adapter for the receiver and some cable to connect it
to the VCR. I also took a bag of videotapes, closed the trunk and
went back to the Leonard house.

The trellis was about three inches deep, a crisscross lattice with
triangular holes the size of a two-euro coin. The camera was
about the size of a one-euro coin, so it was easy enough to fix it
into the trellis with the help of some sturdy Virginia creeper, and
to wedge a battery in behind it.

When I went back in the house, Annalise Leonard was sitting
at the table with her hand on her brow, shielding her eyes. The
small boy was running up and down the kitchen floor around his
father's outstretched legs, all the while chanting something about
a super-robot monkey team, if I heard it right. Sara was sitting at
the table having a jokey conversation with her mother in which
she did all the parts, both telling the jokes and supplying the
laughter.

I went into the living room and set up the receiver and its
power adapter, connected it to the VCR after a bit of faffing
about (I had to find a junction box to connect two cables together
in order to make it work), powered it up, selected a channel on
the VCR, broke a tape out of its packaging and put it in the machine and checked the sight lines. I went out and adjusted the
angle the camera was at slightly, so it had the widest view of the
dumping ground; then I went back inside and talked Leonard
through the process.

"Should I start it now?" he said.

"Do they dump in broad daylight? Better leave it until night,"
I said. "The camera batteries last eight hours. I'll turn it off when
I leave; when night falls, turn it on and mark what time it is. And
they're two-hundred-and-forty-minute tapes, so . . ."

"I'll set the alarm for four hours after I've gone to bed," he said
keenly.

"You might want to sleep on the sofa," I said.

Might want to anyway, I thought.

He walked me to the front door, smiled grimly, as if we were men setting out on a terrifying journey, and presented me with a check.

"Thank you, Mr. Loy," he said.

"Thank you," I said. "Your wife said something about the Butlers—are they people you suspect?"

"They're the most likely. There's one family in the estate, about four or five branches of them all told," Leonard said. "They're notorious around here, always up to something."

He looked around him furtively before passing a slip of paper to me, as if we were approaching the security check at the airport and the paper was a wrap of coke.

"Couple of registration numbers I think might be involved. White transit vans both. The second one of them is Vinnie Butler's."

As I was walking to my car, a blue BMW pulled up outside the house and a petite, expensive-looking woman in her sixties with short auburn hair and a fur coat got out. She looked out over the council estate with pursed lips, including me in her dismayed sweep, then clipped up the drive of the Leonards' house. When the door opened, she ignored the children who had run to greet their granny and were frolicking around her legs, instead embracing Annalise and laying her daughter's head on her shoulder as if she were a wounded bird.

THREE

The broken bicycles and trashed stereo systems were strewn around the laneways and greens of Michael Davitt Gardens, a sure sign Christmas was on its way. Some houses had gigantic inflatable Santas and Rudolphs in their tiny gardens; some had flashing lights on their roofs, or tinsel and spray snow decorations in their windows; some were boarded up with bolts on their electricity meters. The pavements were carpeted with dog shit and broken glass; pizza boxes and fast-food wrappers festooned the gates and boundary walls; old trainers and plastic bottles filled with gravel hung on cords lassoed around telephone wires. There was nothing breathing on the street save for a few sullen dogs.

The two reg plates Leonard had given me were both for white Ford Transit vans; I had already spotted half a dozen on the estate; it was the vehicle of choice for plasterers, roofers, any tradesmen who had to carry a lot of bulky materials around with them,

alongside anyone who, strictly speaking, wasn't a qualified tradesman at all, but who fancied his chances quoting low for a building job, completing half or three-quarters of it badly and then
doing a bunk, or robbing your house and driving away with all
you owned, furniture and appliances included. Their drivers cut
you off on the roads, and they let their kids ride up front in the
cabin without seat belts, let alone car seats; they felt invincible in
their white metal crates and drove accordingly. I didn't like white
Ford Transit vans and now I was parked four doors away from
Vinnie Butler's, trying not to look conspicuous in a forty-two-
year-old Volvo with RIP scraped on the hood. I might have been
many things, but at least I wasn't the cops.

Kids were drifting onto the streets: soon they'd be all over me,
or at least, my car; not for the first time, I questioned the stupidity of driving a conversation piece, particularly when I didn't
have any of the lingo: if something went wrong with it, I called
Tommy; his telephone number was the extent of my auto know-
how. I called Tommy now to see what he knew of the Butlers.
His phone went straight to voice mail, so I left a message. Tommy
was a reliable guide to the dodgier citizens in south Dublin and
north Wicklow, not least because he'd invariably had dodgy business dealings with all of them at one time or another.

I waited fifteen minutes, half an hour, an hour, reading the
same headlines over and over in yesterday's *Irish Times* and trying
to ignore the three young lads across the way from me playing street hurling with a tennis ball. That's how I almost missed
Vinnie Butler: when the ball smacked off my windshield, I turned
to see the lads scarpering around the corner; when I turned back,
Vinnie Butler's Transit van was pulling away from the curb. I
pulled out after him, drew up behind the van at the junction that
led from the estate out onto the main road, and tailed it onto the
N11 and south for a few miles until it turned off past Newtown
and headed west toward Roundwood.

Pine and fir trees flanked the road like troops massing for battle as we drove into the low winter sun's glare. I kept my distance, and when the white van took a right up a small track with a makeshift signpost reading CHRISTMAS TREES, about a mile or so from the Vartry Reservoir, I kept going until I came to a lay-by maybe three hundred yards farther up the road but still in sight of the turn. I got out of the car, produced a notebook and a pair of Meade 10 x 25 compact binoculars and made a moderate show of casting about as if I were interested in the wildlife, although nothing wheeled across the skies but magpies and sparrows.

About twenty minutes later the van piled out of the turn and I caught a brief glimpse of Vinnie Butler: burly, weathered complexion, tiny eyes, close-cropped brown hair. He tossed a fast-food carton and a soft-drink container and the colorful bag they'd come in out the window, flicked a cigarette butt after, anointed the lot with a gob of spit and hauled the Ford Transit back in the direction it had come.

My phone bleeped: Tommy had left a voice mail. He said, "The Butlers eat their young. They're a tribe of savages, Ed: cross one and ten'll come after you. The women are worse than the men, but it's not always easy to tell them apart. Vinnie is thick as shit, but he's vicious with it. They're caught up in any number of feuds over horses, cars, you name it. They sorted the last one out by burning a young one's face with acid. No amount of money is worth messing with the Butlers. Just walk the fuck away."

After that, I had little option but to check out what Vinnie Butler had been up to in the woods. The track he had exited led up to the edge of another encampment of fir trees, their serried ranks deepening in hue with the fading winter light, and then weaved back and down toward an old corrugated barn and a set of outbuildings; I couldn't see a farmhouse, but the fields ahead were fenced and cows and sheep were grazing; I breathed a tumult of manure and aging hay and fermenting compost; in the nearest field, an old blood bay was munching steadily on damp grass. A half-dozen freshly cut fir trees were propped up by the barn.

Maybe Vinnie Butler hadn't come to dump his trash; maybe he had had legitimate business with the farmer; maybe he had come to buy a Christmas tree; after all, he had waited until he got back to the road before he tossed his lunch bag.

I turned and drove slowly back around, stopping when I reached a five-bar gate that opened onto a clearing wide enough to let a van drive through the forest; it was recessed at a sharp angle from the track and concealed by a modest platoon of pines; I had missed it completely on my way up, and I spotted it now only because I was looking for it—and because a white refuse sack clung to one of the trees. I tucked the Volvo behind the pines and climbed over the gate, which was padlocked and chained.

Well-worn tire tracks sparkled bright as metal in the hard earth as I walked through the forest. Pine resin initially chased away the farmyard aroma; after about ten minutes the fresh smell receded; by the time I reached the dump, I'd've cheerfully stuck my head in a compost heap rather than breathe the rank air that surrounded it. A hole about thirty feet in diameter had been dug and the earth banked up the sides; piled high within were bags of domestic waste: rotting food, soiled nappies, detergent and bleach and paint. A halo of flies hovered above the garbage, humming, and there was the rustle and snap of foraging birds and rats; great crows hung in the nearby trees.

On the far side, I could see the gleam of the reservoir water, and was drawn toward it. The edge of the dump was no more than fifteen feet from the shore. The reservoir supplied a substantial portion of the city's water. At least I'd have something for Joe Leonard that no council official or Guard could ignore. I took a few photographs and then climbed up the bank nearest the water to see if I could find some personal traces among the trash: a utility bill or two would be enough to nail at least some of the people involved.

I put on the surgical gloves I always carry and a set of shoe covers I'd packed because I figured the job might get dirty. I waved a scum of flies away and selected the driest-looking bag I could see, which was full of old magazines, and pulled it to one side and uncovered a bag of cast-off clothes, most of them children's; mixed in were a few broken plastic toys and two empty vodka bottles. Beside that I could see the top of a bag of shoes.

I reached down and tugged on the top shoe, thinking as I did, What's the point of this? What are you going to find out from an old shoe? Maybe I was drawn to it because it was the same make I favored; I could tell from the sole, barely worn, the mark still clear: *Church's English Shoes.* Not the same shoe; I wore black wing tips, this had a buckle, and it was burgundy, a Blenheim, I thought, no, a Beckett, the last thought before my hand tugged on the shoe and what was in the shoe, and what was in the shoe gave against my hand. I flinched and yelled out and snapped my hand back as if I'd just tugged on a live rat, and I tumbled down the banked side of the dump and let gravity take me to the shore of the reservoir. I could hear the water lapping gently, as if that could distract me from what I'd just disturbed: not a rat, a foot, visible from where I stood, a foot attached to a man's corduroy-clad leg, protruding from the mound of garbage and then slowly collapsing, like a guttered-out candle subsiding into a ruined cake.

All I could hear now was my blood pounding out a funeral rhythm in my brain, and through the beats a calm, measured voice that said: "Call the Guards. Wait until they get here. Explain what you were doing. Tell them everything. All will be well." What the voice said made sense, but I didn't listen. It didn't sound like me.

The victim was a well—or at least, expensively—dressed man, unusually lean and wiry, about five foot three, with a weatherbeaten face and blond hair, possibly dyed, aged anywhere from twenty-five to fifty. He wore a kind of gentleman-farmer costume: rust-colored corduroys, olive-green sleeveless pullover, small-check shirt, brown wool sport coat. He'd been here—or dead, at any rate—at least two days, but not much longer: rigor had departed the body, but there was no sign of the abdominal staining or distension associated with further putrefaction. And there was no sign so far that the rats or birds had got to him. He'd been strangled, possibly by a ligature *and* by hand: there was a clear furrow around his neck, but a mess of bruising also; his eyes had been closed and it looked as if his mouth had been cleaned: there were no bloodstains. If I had to guess, I'd've said he'd been murdered elsewhere and the body had been dumped here within the last few hours—or possibly the last few minutes, courtesy of my friend in the white Transit van. I found four further things of note. The first three were a tattoo, a shredded slip of paper that looked like a betting slip and a small leather pouch full of coins. The fourth thing gave me such a fright I found myself back at the water's edge again, gasping for breath, the air cold in my pounding chest.

I repositioned the body in as haphazard a manner as I could and covered his face with the bag of children's clothes and walked back along the gleaming woodland track through the darkening trees, shivering now, my steps quickening, keen to see a trail of smoke from a chimney, to hear a human voice, to warm myself at the fires of the living. When I reached my car, the blood bay spotted me and came pounding up to the nearest point of the fence, champing at the wire, long tail swinging like a pendulum, seemingly as anxious as I was for animal contact. I went down and pulled grass and weeds and offered them from my hand; the horse feasted eagerly, steam rising from her coat like breath in the cold air; I inhaled her deep, musky smell, let her old teeth gnaw my outstretched palm, relished every snort and whinny. When I withdrew from the gate, and she realized there was nothing more to come, she wheeled around and took off back to her spot at the bottom of the field, the clump of her hooves on the hard winter grass like mountain thunder, thrilling to the ear.

Still shaken, I drove fast out of the forest of pines and down to the road and back onto the N11 and stopped off at the first pub I came to. It was a sprawling, anonymous car park of a place, the kind of pub you need a map to find the toilet. A rough-looking Sunday-afternoon crowd of all ages was resentfully half watching an English Premiership game that could have been of little real interest to them, Wigan and Reading, perhaps, or Bolton and Portsmouth, the adults all drunk and surly, the kids bored and restless; the remnants of seasonal turkey-and-ham lunches littered the tables amid the full and empty glasses. It wasn't a very nice place, but I was very glad to be there, among the living.

I ordered a double Jameson and a pint of Guinness and a tur-key-and-ham sandwich and found a quiet corner with a view of the car park and no view of a TV screen, and while I drank the whiskey with a little water, I took out a notebook and wrote down everything I had seen. Then I rang Dave Donnelly and told him some of it, including the need to get someone onto Vinnie Butler urgently. I told him it looked like the body had been killed elsewhere, then cleaned up and moved to the scene. I didn't tell him I had moved the body and I didn't tell him I had searched it, although I knew he'd assume I had. I didn't tell him about the tattoo either—he'd find out about that when the crime scene unit examined the body. The tattoo was on the man's left forearm: two symbols recently, and amateurishly, carved; they'd barely scabbed over. One resembled a crucifix, the other looked like the ancient Greek letter omega: †

Dave went through the motions of reefing me out of it for not staying with the body until the scene had been secured, but his heart didn't seem in it: I guess from his point of view, having me connected with the murder would be an inconvenience. I needed to be free to dig for the scraps he'd need in working the case; in return, he'd feed me what he could, and look the other way when I stepped outside the law, provided I didn't do it in too visible a way. In case I didn't understand the latter point, Dave signed off on it.

"Just don't get that O'Connor woman involved, all right Ed? Thought you had more sense than to trust a fucking journalist."

"Sure about that, Dave? Far as I can remember, the way she wrote you up on the Howard case was one of the main reasons you got your big promotion to the Bureau."

"Your memory's playing tricks with you then, Ed. Knock off the gargle and cop onto yourself, would you?"

You couldn't slam a mobile phone down, but Dave ended the call so abruptly that it felt like that's what he'd done.

The other thing I didn't tell Dave about was the shredded betting slip I'd found stuck inside the corpse's trouser pocket, as if it had been through the wash. I prised it out and bagged it and pieced it together now. It had a mobile number written on it, faded but legible. I rang the number, and a hoarse male voice answered.

"What can I do you for, friend?"

There was a hubbub of voices in the background, and the rasp of a P.A. saying, "Winner all right. Winner all right."

"Was that the last race?" I said.

"That's the last done now, friend," the man said. "All off-course accounts to be settled in the morning."

"Did Fish on Friday place?"

"Did she what?"

He barked out a loud, derisive laugh.

"Best guess is she's still out there, friend. Maybe she'll be home for Christmas. Would you like to bet on it?"

I ended the call. Fish on Friday was one of George Halligan's horses, running at Gowran Park. The dead man had the mobile number of a bookie at the same race meeting in his trouser pocket. And when I'd held his face, back in the forest, his jaw had hung open, and his mouth gaped red down his throat, and I saw the last thing I had decided not to tell Detective Inspector Donnelly. His tongue had been cut out.

FOUR

I had another large Jameson before I left the pub, but it didn't do a lot to get the chill out of my bones. By the time I reached Michael Davitt Gardens, there were marked and unmarked Garda cars flanking the white Ford Transit van; kids climbed on walls and shinned up lampposts and neighbors stood in their doorways and gardens and watched as the crop-haired driver with the red face was led into a squad car. I drove on and parked around the other side of the estate, across the road from the closed gates of the Leonard house. The blue BMW was still parked outside. I called Joe Leonard on his mobile and he came out and sat in my car and I gave him a potted account of what had happened, up to the arrest of Vinnie Butler. Part of me felt relieved, as if the discovery in the woods had restored pride and dignity to us both: a trivial litter problem had become, or was at least on nodding terms with, a murder case. I don't think Leonard saw it that way.

"If they charge him for murder, will they let the dumping offenses slide?" he said.

I looked to see if he was serious. He was: deadly.

"Probably," I said.

"Well, in that case, I'll keep the camera rolling, Mr. Loy. You'll keep me posted if there are any developments, won't you?"

I said I would, and he got out of the car and crossed as far as the BMW, stroked the blue hood with his hand, then came back and leaned into my window.

"I know you didn't see us at our best this morning," he said quietly, blushing and looking back quickly and furtively at the upstairs windows of his house, as if his wife and her mother might appear in one of them to spy on him, characters all in a not terribly comic opera.

"It's just that I . . . I had a run of bad luck a few years back . . . a dot-com start-up, and . . . and we lost our house, repossession, right when the boom was taking off . . . and, well, it's been hard getting started again . . . the kids were so young when it happened. And Annalise was pretty angry . . . still is, really, don't suppose you can blame her, I asked her to trust me . . . we lost so much. We'd be sitting on a lot of equity now, instead of . . ."

He gestured around at his surroundings. I made a face intended to suggest that these kinds of things happened (which they did) and that often it was no fault of the person to whom they happened (which it wasn't) and that I was sure nothing but good would come of it eventually (which it might). I caught sight of my expression in the rearview mirror. It didn't reassure me. But Leonard didn't notice, or didn't mind; he simply wanted me to hear him out. I nodded and shrugged in a what-can-you-do sort of way, and he thanked me—for what, I couldn't tell—and straightened up and shook my hand and crossed the road, stopping to stroke the hood of the BMW again as he passed.

ACCORDING TO FATHER Vincent Tyrrell, Patrick Hutton's last known address was a town house in Riverside Village, a private estate by the Dodder River in Sandymount. Before I left the pub I had tried the two Patrick Huttons I could find in the phone book. One was a plasterer; the other was the senior executive solicitor at South Dublin County Council. Neither had been a jockey; the plasterer sounded amused at the suggestion, the solicitor mysteriously outraged, as if I'd accused him of being a sex criminal, or a DJ. Now I was driving north toward the city, the roads clogged with traffic on the last shopping Sunday before Christmas. I crossed the railway line at the Merrion Gates and took Strand Road for about a mile, then turned off into Sandymount. There was a video store on the green that offered Internet access, so I parked by O'Reilly's pub and waited in line for the single computer terminal behind two Italian students.

When it was my turn, I entered Patrick Hutton's name in a search engine. Amid the university professors, secondary school headmasters and orthopedic surgeons, I found a few references to Patrick Hutton the jockey, chief among them the following short piece in the *Irish Independent* in December 2004.

REWARD OFFERED FOR MISSING JOCKEY

Trainer F. X. Tyrrell is offering ten thousand euros for information about the whereabouts of Patrick Hutton, the Wicklow-born jockey who apparently vanished seven years ago. Hutton, who rode over a dozen winners for Tyrrell during 1996, including the Arkle Chase at Cheltenham on By Your Leave, dropped out of public view days before he was due to ride for Tyrrell at the Leopardstown Christmas Festival, and hasn't been seen since. Anyone with information should contact Derek Rowan, head man at Tyrrellscourt.

There was a small black-and-white head shot, but it was difficult to pick out any distinguishing features: like models, with whom they have a lot in common, jockeys all tend to resemble one another at first or even second flush. There were a few contemporary reports of races Hutton had run; the only other item of interest was a short account of a meeting at Thurles in October 1996, where By Your Leave finished last in a field of nine in the third race, and the subsequent inquiry at the Turf Club, where the question of Hutton deliberately stopping the horse was raised, but then dismissed.

I spent some time trying to find out a bit more about F. X. Tyrrell. There was plenty on his achievements in racing and breeding, but relatively little on the man himself: one marriage, which lasted ten years; no kids; usually accompanied in public by his sister, Regina. Legendarily reluctant to speak to reporters, so little was known about his life away from the track and the stud that it was logical to assume he didn't have any. I copied down one quote from an interview, the only utterance of his that involved a subordinate clause: "It's a simple game: it's all in the breeding, all in the blood. If the bloodlines are right, the animals will be right, provided they're given the nurture they need. Blood and breed, that's the beginning and end of it."

It was dark by the time I got to Riverside Village; the Christmas decorations were more discreet and tasteful than they had been in Michael Davitt Gardens: hardly surprising, as an 800-square-feet three-bed went for nine hundred thousand here in Dublin 4; number 20 had a lighted candle in the window and a holly wreath on the doorknob and a red 1988 Porsche 928 in the drive. My phone rang as I pressed the bell; when I checked the number and saw the 310 area code, I realized it was my ex-wife again. Nine in the morning in West L.A. and she could think of nothing better to do than call me. I felt a momentary stab of panic, but that gave way to the sad knowledge that there was no longer anything between us to panic about, and then to anger at her unwillingness to leave me the fuck alone. And that gave way to genuine panic, because when the door of number 20 opened, there was the dark hair, the pale skin, the great dark eyes, the long legs, the slightly crooked, wide red lips of my ex-wife standing before me.

I WAS SITTING on the black leather couch in the living room. I had asked for a whiskey, and was told I could only have one if I drank a cup of hot sweet tea first, so that's what I was doing while the woman who looked like my ex-wife sat on the black leather chair across from me. Her name was Miranda Hart, and whether she was uneasy or excited at having a strange man in her house, or both, I couldn't tell; her way of dealing with it to was to laugh a little, and smile a lot, and chew her gum vigorously; she was doing all three now.

I hadn't exactly fainted, but I had swayed a little out there on the doorstep, unsteady on my feet, clutching the door frame as the woman I thought was my ex-wife tried to shut the door on my hand, and then my scalp had sparked with sweat, and my tongue felt too large for my mouth, and I knew I was going to be sick. And had I not managed to blurt out Patrick Hutton's name, I would never have been let past the door, let alone allowed to use the bathroom to throw up, and then wash my face, and now sit by the fire in the living room with the dark burgundy and racing-green walls and the dark wood floorboards and the paintings and framed photographs of horses and jockeys on the walls and ask my questions. Because Miranda Hart was Patrick Hutton's widow.

She sat in a pair of skinny jeans and black boots with low heels and a black wraparound top over a dark wine-colored camisole with six silver bracelets on one slender wrist and seven on the other and no wedding ring. Her nails were painted dark red, but they were bitten and the varnish was cracked; her mascara had run into smudges around her huge brown eyes; her lipstick had smeared a little around her mouth. There was mud and straw and what looked like shredded paper on her boots. She had poured herself a large gin, and she gulped it enthusiastically now and spilled some of it down her chin, which she wiped with the back of her hand. I didn't tell her she looked like my ex-wife; instead I said I'd had a sandwich that must have disagreed with me, but she didn't seem at all interested; maybe strangers threw up regularly in her bathroom.

"So you're a private detective who used to live in L.A., and you're looking for Patrick, and you can't, or won't say who hired you," she said. Her accent was an Anglo drawl; she said *cawn't* for "can't" and gave *Patrick* such a clipped reading she made it sound like a name rarely heard outside South Kensington and Chelsea.

"That's right," I said.

"The last private detective was fuck all use. Or rather, I suppose he was a great deal of use, since he turned up fuck all."

"When was that?" I said.

"About two years ago. I wanted to have Patrick declared dead. More like, needed: I ran out of cash for a while, and couldn't keep the mortgage on this little kip up. We'd bought it together, and he'd been gone longer than seven years."

"And who insisted on the detective, the insurance company?"

"That's right. Big-arsed ex-cop in an anorak, Christ, he was a gruesome old heap, watching him get out of a chair was nerve-racking. Anyway, he went through the motions, checked Patrick's bank records and credit history and so forth, and came up with what we all knew: he vanished off the face of the earth ten years ago. Ten years ago today, as a matter of fact. And now all this is mine."

She rolled her eyes and lit a cigarette, a More, and offered me one, which I refused; I didn't think my system would be up to it yet. I finished the tea and reached for the whiskey; the fumes didn't make me gag: a good sign.

"Lucky to have the place, I suppose, particularly since we

bought before the boom. I got left some money in '92, not long after we were married. Girlfriends said, don't put Patrick's name on it, but it's just as well I did. 'Cause I'd still have a mortgage to pay if I hadn't."

"He disappeared ten years ago today?"

"Twenty-third of December, 1996."

"Will you tell me about it?"

"I don't know," she said. She took a hit of her drink, and a drag of her cigarette, and looked around for somewhere to tap the ash, and popped her gum out of her mouth and molded it into a bowl shape and flicked her ash in it and laid it on the arm of her chair.

"I don't know if I want Patrick back. That is, if he were alive and you found him."

"You had him declared dead. Do you think he's still alive?"

She laughed, as if she'd been caught out in some strange but endearing foible, like using her chewing gum as an ashtray.

"I wouldn't put it past the little fucker, put it that way."

"I know F. X. Tyrrell put up a reward for information about him."

"Yes. Well. That was very good of him. Very good of F.X., all right."

Hart's general tone was so brittle I couldn't tell whether she was being ironic or not.

"Did he find out anything?"

"The usual: people who thought they'd seen him on a ferry, or in Spain. Nothing concrete. That was before the detective had a go."

"Were Tyrrell and your husband close?"

"I don't know if anyone gets particularly close to F.X. They were having a good year together, and Patrick was getting a lot of rides; he had three or four big ones at Leopardstown. And then: gone."

"Money trouble?"

"It was all a bit hand-to-mouth. But that's just the life, he was making his way, he was only twenty-three, just the beginning. And he'd been gambling, but don't we all? Everyone in racing gambles. No one came to me with major debts after he'd gone, the kind of debts that would've made him do a runner. And they'd need to have been big, Patrick had a lot of nerve."

"There was talk of his stopping a horse for Tyrrell. By Your Leave? But the Turf Club found there was no case to answer."

Miranda Hart smiled mirthlessly and ran a weary hand through her dark mane of hair.

"The Turf Club are such dears."

"What does that mean?"

"It means they know what goes on and we know what goes on, and they agree to pretend it doesn't go on unless we're too careless about it. And F.X. and Patrick were bloody careless that day."

"What happened? What goes on?"

She drained her glass and looked at me through narrowed eyes. "You're not some asshole of a journalist, are you?"

"I may be an asshole, but I'm no journalist," I said.

That got a laugh; showing her my card got a wary nod. When I produced a press clipping I kept in my wallet (penned by a crime reporter who owed his career to the quality and frequency of the Garda leaks he received, and who showed his gratitude by toeing diligently whatever line the Garda Press Office drew for him) featuring a quote from the Garda commissioner himself deploring the rise of "self-styled" private detectives and disparaging their "questionable personal ethics," and using a photograph of me as Exhibit A, Miranda Hart gave me a grin of what looked like kindred outlaw approval. I got up and fixed her a fresh drink, and took a hit of mine. Miranda Hart kicked off her boots and wriggled around until her long legs were splayed with one hanging over the arm of her chair.

"How much do you know about horse racing?" she said.

"Enough to lose betting on it. Not much more."

"Well. First of all, it's not an exact science," she said. "The favorite doesn't always win. If he did, you wouldn't have much of a sport, or a chance to bet. So that gives owners and trainers a certain license. If a horse with a good record is coming back after a rest, or at the beginning of the National Hunt season, no one will be too surprised if he loses a few races he was tipped to win. Maybe he's carrying an injury, maybe he's lost his edge, maybe he hasn't warmed up yet, maybe the jockey isn't giving him the best ride."

"And what's actually happening?"

"The horse is being stopped. So that the odds can drift up, and his owner or trainer or a whole bunch of interested parties can have a big punt in a month or two, when it's barely fancied and the price on the horse—and maybe the prize money—are better. Best to do with a horse that's just made a name for himself, because it could always be a flash in the pan, as far as the authorities—and the punters—are concerned. Harder with an established mount, but you can still get away with it, because there are so many legitimate excuses: one trainer will push a horse to run off an injury, another will insist on rest; if either of those horses is stopped, the trainer is covered."

"So the entire game is corrupt."

"Of course it is, darling. Not all the time—there are the glamour races everyone wants to win fair and square—but quite a lot of the time. And that's just the day-to-day; we haven't even mentioned doping, or when big gamblers or bookies bribe jockeys to throw races."

"And that's what Patrick Hutton and F. X. Tyrrell did with By Your Leave? They deliberately set out to lose the race?"

"Of course. It was evens at Thurles, and the Christmas meeting at Leopardstown was looming, so they wanted to get the price up before then. Unfortunately, By Your Leave was such a great goer, and Patrick ended up being way too obvious. So the whole thing got a little sour. And Patrick got the blame."

"Not from the Turf Club."

"No, from the punters. The footage of it was pretty clear, you could see Patrick checking his placing and holding the horse back when the two front-runners had bolted. A furlong from home and he's still at it, as if By Your Leave could have made up the ground."

"Sounds like he was deliberately drawing attention to what he was doing."

"That's what some people said. That the row was between him and F.X., that Patrick wanted to give the horse a decent ride, that he wasn't happy to be instructed otherwise. And the Turf Club would have caused too much scandal if they'd found anyone at fault. And of course, punters forgive and forget, they know this kind of thing goes on, Patrick would have lost the ride for Leopardstown, but he would have been back on winners soon enough, and everyone would have been happy."

"And how did By Your Leave fare at Leopardstown that Christmas?"

Miranda Hart shook her head and looked at me gravely.

"By Your Leave never made it out of Tipperary—fell at the last fence. The going was unseasonably firm, and the horse broke her right ankle. Which might have been okay, but having unseated her rider, she took off at the gallop she'd been straining after all day. By the time the Tyrrellscourt lads caught her up, she'd broken the leg in thirty-four places. There was nothing anyone could do."

I thought I saw tears in her eyes; the death of the horse seemed to matter more to her than the fate of her husband.

"So what happened after that? Did Tyrrell and Hutton fall out? What did Patrick tell you?"

"Do you know racing people, Mr. Loy? They're not exactly what you'd call chatty. They're certainly not introspective. I wasn't looking for a blabbermouth. I have gob enough for two. Patrick never talked about work in any detail. He'd say, 'Not a bad horse,' or 'Lucky today'—that's what he talked about most often, when he talked: luck."

"It sounds like he ran out of it at the last."

"Maybe. He walked out on F.X. before he had the chance to be sacked. Refused to talk about that either. Said there were a few trainers in England who'd made inquiries, he'd take Christmas off, talk to them in the New Year."

"Refused to talk about that. To his wife?"

She shrugged again, flicking her hair back and pouting as she did so. It was very much her habit, but it had also been a tic of my ex-wife's; I remembered now how incredibly irritating I used to find it in her; I found it weirdly alluring in Miranda Hart. She moved to stub her cigarette into her chewing gum and overturned her drink onto the crotch of her jeans. She climbed out of the chair amid a fusillade of *fucks* and *shits,* then stalked into the kitchen and returned with a few tea towels. She wiped the gin off the chair and the floor, and began to dab between her legs with a cloth, then thought better of it.

"Clumsy fucking cow. I'm sorry, Mr. Loy, I'm soaked here, I'm going to have to get changed, have a shower. And I'm going out, so . . ."

She looked toward the door, and I nodded and stood up.

"Well, thanks for your time," I said. I gestured at the mud and straw on her boots. "I take it you're a racing person yourself."

She grinned in a side-of-the-mouth kind of way and shook her head.

"I run a riding school for Jackie Tyrrell, up in Tibradden. It's a far cry."

"From what?"

She looked toward the door again, then smiled carefully at me.

"I used to ride, Mr. Loy. I grew up near Tyrrellscourt, I worked in the yard as a girl, I had a few amateur races. I was as good as Patrick. Better, some people thought. Then, after he took off, or disappeared, or whatever the fuck he did . . . I don't know, it was as if I were to blame. Like I'd been a curse of some kind. Blame the black widow, y'know? F.X. cut me off, and other trainers followed suit. I got a bit of yard work with another trainer, but I wasn't happy doing that anymore. So I kind of drifted off track, in more ways than one . . . rented this place out and just . . . let things slide, y'know? Got into a few . . . situations. And then F.X. and his wife split up, and Jackie called me. I needed to get myself together by then, so I jumped at the chance. Jackie helped me with the house, everything."

"F. X. Tyrrell's wife. All very cozy."

"His ex-wife. They parted amicably, there were no children. Why is it so cozy?"

"The person who hired me to find Patrick Hutton was Father Vincent Tyrrell."

It was as if someone had flicked a switch, or pulled a cord, in Miranda Hart's back: her shoulders slumped and her head dropped and something like a howl came from deep inside her. When she turned her face to me, I saw black eyes stained red and soaked with the black mess her tears had made of her makeup. She was shaking her head now, opening her mouth and trying to get the words out; I could see red lipstick stains on her teeth. Finally, she managed to coordinate palate and lips and tongue long enough to be understood.

"Get out of here," she said. "Get the fuck out of here, or I'll call the police."

FIVE

sat in the car and tried to work out what I had seen in Miranda Hart's eyes when she heard Vincent Tyrrell's name, the split second before she fell apart on me: what combination of fear, anger, shame or guilt. The tears were real, the emotion convulsive, hysterical even, but Miranda Hart looked like she was capable of putting on quite a show if she put her mind to it. At least, that was what I figured by the end of our encounter, once my entire system had gotten the message loud and clear that she was not in fact my ex-wife.

Next, I listened to the message my ex-wife had left on my phone, and then I did something I hadn't done for maybe three years: I called her, and asked how she was, and how her little boy was doing; I spoke to her like I should have a long time ago. She told me she still felt bad about Lily, our little girl, especially at Christmas, thinking how she might have turned out, and I told her so did I, and she said every year on a Saturday a couple of weeks before Christmas she went to the Third Street Mall and bought all the gifts Santa would have brought and then on the Sunday she went to seven forty-five mass at St. Clement's and donated the toys to the church's Angel Toy Drive for needy children and orphans. She started to cry then, and I sat and listened, and wondered whether remembering our dead child by giving toys to poor kids at Christmas was better than remembering her by getting drunk and feeling sorry for yourself and trying to blame other people for pain that was nobody's but your own. I decided that it was.

We sat on the phone for a long while after that, after she had stopped crying, not saying very much, until she said the call must be costing me a fortune, and I said there was no need to worry, because I was a millionaire, a line we used to use before any of this had happened, and she laughed then, and told me she missed me, and I thought that was a good time to send her my love and wish her a Merry Christmas and end the call.

I sat for another long while then, until I was able to catch my breath, and I could see straight. I wiped my face with a handkerchief and got out of the car and walked along the path by the Dodder River toward Londonbridge Road and smoked a cigarette and breathed in the cold winter air. Every so often I had the sense that I was being followed, but the only people I spotted were shoppers trudging home laden with bags. In any case, if Leo Halligan wanted to take me, he would, and there wasn't an awful lot I could do about it.

When I got back to my car, a taxi was pulling away from outside Miranda Hart's house. I hadn't spotted her getting in, but I didn't have time to think, so I followed it down into Ringsend toward the city. I kept close, reasoning that she might not be in it anyway, and even if she was, she probably wouldn't expect to be followed. In any case, the traffic was so thick that I couldn't afford to let the cab out of my sight. Town was seething with drunks and merrymakers, shoppers and gawkers, young and old spilling off the pavements and jostling in the streets. We passed Trinity College and headed up George's Street and around onto Stephen's Green and in fits and starts rolled along until I saw the cab pull in outside the Shelbourne Hotel. I passed it and looked back to see Miranda Hart, wearing something shiny and black over something shiny and silver, clip up the hotel steps and flash a smile at the doorman. A car horn honked behind me; I cut down Merrion Street and found a parking space on Merrion Square. There was a brusque voice-mail message from Dave Donnelly on my phone, and I called him immediately, ready to take my medicine: I was on bad terms with too many Guards to fall out with Dave; he probably figured out I had examined the body in the woods, and wanted to bawl me out over it.

He didn't.

"Ed, I want to talk to you."

"Sure, Dave. Harcourt Square?"

Harcourt Square was where the elite National Bureau of Criminal Investigation was based. DI Donnelly wanted to be seen with me there like he wanted to be caught drunk driving.

"That's funny, Ed. I'm still out in fucking Wicklow here. How about your place? When can you make it?"

"I'm on something now, but I don't know how long it'll last."

"It's seven now. Say eleven?"

"That should be fine. What's it about, Dave?"

"It's about those bodies."

"What bodies?"

"The one you found, and the one we found earlier."

"Are they connected?"

"I'll see you at eleven."

The Shelbourne Hotel was built in 1824 and every so often they closed it and refurbished it and put a bar where a restaurant had been, but it was pretty much the same now as always, except smarter, although there was a tendency, if you got drunk here, to forget where the toilets were. Or so I was told; having left for

L.A. when I was eighteen, I had only crossed the door for the first time a few months ago, to confirm to a Southside Lady Who Lunches that her suspicions about her errant husband were well founded. She took the photographs, wrote me a check and told me she'd double it if I joined her in a suite upstairs for the afternoon. Maybe I might have if she hadn't offered to pay; she had gambler's eyes, and a sense of humor, and a good head for drink. Next thing I knew, she had taken her husband for ten million and the family home in Blackrock and she was photographed on the back page of the *Sunday Independent* at an MS Charity Ball with new breasts spilling out of a dress twenty years too young for her getting very friendly with a member of the Irish rugby squad. Well done everybody. Another one for the PI scrapbook. Wonder what the Garda commissioner made of that.

I didn't have to look too hard for Miranda Hart; her silver dress blazed like magnesium ribbon amid the deep red and dark wood tones of the Horseshoe Bar. She had piled her dark hair high on her head; her black eyes flickered and her lips were the color of blood. Six foot in heels, she wore her dress calf length and cut high on the thigh; one of her stockings was already laddered. I was trying to get a look at her companions before she saw me, but she was restless, laughing quickly and nodding impatiently and chewing her gum and smoking and drinking and casting her gaze about the bar as if she expected me.

When our eyes met, her face turned to stone for a second and I thought she would start to scream; instead she turned her lamps full on, mouthed "Darling" at me and beckoned me over with the hand she held her glass in, flicking some of its contents over a fat red-faced man of sixty or so with a wispy strawberry-blond comb-over who affected to find this as hilarious as he appeared to be finding everything else. A well-preserved, shrewd-looking blonde in her fifties turned around to take an appraising look at me as the barman brought me the pint of Guinness I'd ordered. I had to remind myself that none of them, and nobody else here in this opulent Christmas melee, none of the lush young women or their overweight, red-faced partners in candy-stripe shirts and blazers or the older horsey types in tweed and corduroy and their sleek beige-and-ivory women groomed within an inch of their lives, not one of them had paid a cent for me, and I owed them nothing in return.

I carried my pint across to Miranda. Her party had grabbed banquette seats around a small table. Miranda kissed me on both cheeks, and in the ear farthest from her friends, said, "Sorry about that earlier. I *do* want you to find Patrick. I can pay you."

"I'm already getting paid," I said. "But thank you."

We were cheek to cheek, the room a clamor of laughter and jostling voices. Her bathroom had been full of Chanel No. 5 and I could smell that on her now, but faintly; her own scent overpowered it. Deep salt with a tang like oranges, it had gotten under my skin in her house; now I almost felt like the sole reason I had trailed her here was to breathe it again. She smiled at me, and opened her mouth; she still had lipstick on her teeth and I could see her tongue shift her chewing gum to one side. I laughed, and took a drink of my beer.

"What's so funny?" she said.

"You are," I said. "Is there any situation in which you don't chew gum?"

"That would be for you to find out," she said. "Mr. Private Investigator."

The shrewd-looking blonde, who was wearing cream and gold and the slightest hint of leopardskin, said something pointed to the comb-over and he exploded in a fit of convulsive laughter, his hair slipping in a long unruly strand down his face. She looked at him pityingly, like a mother would glance at her obese child when no one else was looking, then raised an appraising gaze, and her glass, to me; I saluted her in the same fashion and we both drank.

"Jackie Tyrrell," Miranda said quietly. "It's our works do. The fatso is Seán Proby."

"The bookie?"

"The father. The son, Jack, runs the day-to-day now. Seán is the figurehead, on TV telling war stories. He was a great comrade of F. X. Tyrrell's. They made a lot of money for each other. Then they fell out."

"Over what?"

"Whatever came to hand. F.X. falls out with everyone sooner or later. You can be my date, if you like. We're going to the Octagon for supper."

"Did you not have a date?"

"Are you worried he might show up and want to fight you?"

"I only like fighting in the morning. At least then there's a chance the day might improve."

"Scaredy-cat."

"Are Proby and Jackie an item?"

They were cackling with each other on the banquette, hand in hand. Miranda did an eye-rolling silent laugh at my question and shook her head at me.

"Oh dear God no. Seán bats for the other side, darling."

"Despite being someone's father. This is all getting a bit too sophisticated for me. Why did you go to pieces when you heard Father Vincent Tyrrell's name?"

Jackie Tyrell, who had been giving a very good impression of a drunk, stood bolt upright and apparently sober.

"We can't be late," she barked in a highly polished accent with a trace of Cork in it. "Gilles will sulk. What's his name?" This last to Miranda of me.

"Ed Loy," I said, extending my hand.

"Ed's writing a book," Miranda announced. "About horse racing and the Irish."

"Oh God no," Jackie Tyrell said. "That book gets written every year. It's always a fucking *bore*. *You're* not going to be a fucking *bore*, are you?"

"Compared to you?" I said.

She looked me up and down as if she had been offered me for sale.

"At least he's tall," she said to Miranda. "Not a skinny little boy. He's actually like a man, Miranda."

"Thank you," I said.

"Don't get smart with me," Jackie Tyrrell said. "I'm hungry."

On his feet now, Seán Proby was pumping my hand up and down and laughing uproariously; the more I tried to retrieve my hand the tighter he held it, and the harder I struggled the louder he laughed; there we were like two clowns in hell until Jackie Tyrrell punched him sharply in the arm and he came to and released his grip and beamed genially at me, now apparently sober himself.

The Octagon was a converted meeting hall around the corner in a lane off Kildare Street that had been painted white and gussied up with a lot of stained glass and indoor trees hung with fairy lights and gauze. People sat at several different levels on a succession of balconies and mezzanines. The staff were Irish and French and they made a big fuss of Jackie and Miranda; I heard Jackie speaking in immaculate French to Gilles, the maître d', and Gilles instructing a wine waiter to bring Mrs. Tyrrell "the usual." The restaurant was full of the same kind of people who had been in the Shelbourne, and I quickly discovered why: the prices were absurdly high, but the food was very straightforward: onion soup and egg mayonnaise, pork belly and Toulouse sausages, steak frîtes; none of your two-scallops-on-a-huge-white-plate nonsense. Thus Irish people could indulge their aspirational need to get all fancy and French, and sate their ferocious desire to spend as much money as possible, while getting a huge amount of meat inside them.

Jackie waved a hand at me.

"I'll order, unless you have some particular preference." She said *preference* in the sense of "disease."

"Go ahead," I said.

The usual turned out to be two bottles of Sancerre and two

bottles of Pinot Noir. Jackie ordered food for us all, and said, "Just pour," at the wine waiter.

I was trying to have a quiet word with Miranda, or maybe I was just trying to get as close to her as I physically could; I hadn't had much to drink but I felt like half my brain had shut down, and the other half was focused only on her scented flesh. But Jackie was beady and restless and in need of entertainment.

"You're very tall for a writer," she said. I shrugged. I was pretty sure that some writers had to be tall, and if so, that I could be one of them.

"How far are you into your book?" she said.

"I'm nearly finished," I said, wondering why Miranda had gifted me this spurious identity. When I tended bar in Santa Monica, I used to get a lot of writers. Some got paid for it, some were published, some were only writers in the sense that they didn't have a job, or a job they wanted to own up to. And whenever I asked them how they were getting on, they all said they were nearly finished, even the ones who evidently had never written a word and never would. It struck me occasionally that it might have been better to wait until you *were* finished before you went out to a bar. But then I wasn't a writer. And I had the sense that Jackie Tyrrell knew that.

"Well in that case, it's too late for us to tell you anything, isn't it? You must know it all by now."

"Well, actually, it's at this stage—when I think I know it all—that's when meeting the experts is really useful. Now I know what questions to ask."

Jackie drank half a glass of Sancerre in one and stared at me deadpan.

"Ask me then. The questions. Now you know it all. Go on."

A hush fell around the table, and I could see Seán Proby and Miranda Hart looking excited, as if Jackie Tyrrell were the Queen and she'd just put me on the spot.

"Do you breed, Jackie?" I said.

"Not as a rule, but with you, I'd make an exception," she said, and blew me a kiss. She sat back and poked Seán Proby in the ribs, and he dutifully exploded with laughter again. I looked at Miranda Hart, who leant in and said quickly and quietly, "They were at Gowran Park, they've been going since lunchtime."

The starters came, and we ate in silence. Jackie put her face down and shoveled onion soup and bread into it. At length she re-surfaced, flush-cheeked and panting. Little beads of sweat dotted her mysteriously unlined brow, and frosted the tiny soft hairs above her upper lip.

"I don't breed anymore," she announced. "I used to look after that side of things for Frank. The Tyrrellscourt Stud. Still going strong. I've a good eye for a horse still, though. I'll go on a trip with him, when he's buying. As long as he's buying."

"No one is allowed to call F. X. Tyrrell Frank except Jackie," said Seán Proby, the first coherent utterance he had made in my hearing.

"Well, no one does, at any rate, " Jackie said. "Maybe no one wants to."

"How was Gowran today?" Miranda said to Proby.

"Not bad," Proby said. "Nothing like a small country meeting. Jack was working, of course; I was merely Mrs. Tyrrell's lunch companion. But we did all right."

"The bookies always do," snapped Jackie.

"The Tyrrell horses underperformed nicely," Miranda said.

Jackie smiled thinly at this.

"Leopardstown's the main event," she said. "The ground was too firm today anyway."

"Did Jack of Hearts place?" I said.

"Won the first by four lengths at six to one. Held up well," Proby said.

"Why the interest?" Jackie said. I had the impression she was playing with me.

"It just caught my eye."

"I thought it might be because of its owner. You know who owns it, of course."

"Do I?"

"I think you do, Edward Loy. After all, when you're not writing books about horse racing in Ireland, which I would say is all of the time, you hire yourself out as a private detective. And a while back you had a hand in putting away Podge Halligan, the drug dealer, also the brother of George Halligan, who owns Jack of Hearts. Miranda, why did you think it necessary to fabricate an absurd identity for Mr. Loy? A writer, of all things. Everyone knows writers are all badly dressed overweight cantankerous faux-humble alcoholics with a chip on each shoulder and a grudge against the world. And that's just the women."

Miranda looked like a schoolgirl hauled before the headmistress; she stared at her plate in silence, her face burning.

"It was my idea," I said.

"And gallant too. Tall and gallant. We don't see many of you round here anymore. You're not gay, are you?"

Seán Proby shook his head.

"Absolutely not," he said.

"Seán's my gaydar when it comes to men. Are you working, Ed Loy?"

"He's looking for Patrick," Miranda said, her voice thick with emotion. She choked back what might have been a sob, then muttered an apology and fled to the loo. The waiter came and took our plates. I watched Jackie Tyrrell closely, but her expression was blank; she gave nothing away. When the table had been cleared, and Seán Proby had gone outside for a smoke, she smiled keenly at me.

"You know about Patrick Hutton and the Halligans?" she said.

I shook my head.

"Patrick and Leo—" she began, and then stopped as cutlery arrived for the main course. She repeated the names when the waiter had gone, her eyes dancing, then stopped again as Miranda came back to the table, eye makeup freshly and thickly applied.

"I'll tell him about that myself, Jackie, if it's all right with you," Miranda said, quite sharply to my ears.

"But of course, my darling, of course," Jackie said, all charm.

"He was my husband, and I think I'm best placed to know what's important and what's just rumor and innuendo, don't you?"

Jackie Tyrrell gave Miranda Hart what looked to me to be a very fond, warm smile, and leant across and touched her hand.

"I do," she said softly. "And you are. Nobody but you."

Miranda blushed again, and nodded; in removing her hand from Jackie's, she managed to upset a full glass of white wine over both of us; by the time we had that cleared up, the main courses had arrived. I ate steak frîtes with béarnaise sauce, washed down with two slow glasses of red. I could drink a lot, and generally did, but I had no head for wine; in any case, I wanted to study these people at the periphery of the Tyrrell family closely: there was history between them, and I'd need my wits about me to pick up on it.

As we ate, Seán Proby launched into a boilerplate account of the invention of Steeplechase: how in 1752 Edmund Blake and Cornelius O'Callaghan had raced from Buttevant Church to St. Mary's Church, over jumps, steeple to steeple; how National Hunt, as it was now called, was the true Irish horse racing, involving as it did not just skill and discipline and courage but passion and spirit and a sense of adventure. The flat wasn't racing at all, he sniffed.

Except as a means for bookies to separate punters from their cash, Jackie pointed out. Proby seemed keen to continue with a survey of National Hunt's premier meeting, the Cheltenham Festival, but Jackie reminded him that I was not in fact writing a book and if I had been I would at least have known about bloody Blake and O'Callaghan and bloody Cheltenham and could he stop boring the arse off everyone and eat his dinner like a good little boy.

She then began to talk about her riding school, her tone derogatory of her clients and dismissive of the school's worth.

"No reflection on Miranda, her teaching is second to none; if you want to know your way around a horse that lady is the one to teach you. But honest to God, these spoilt little South Dublin brats, as they zip into the Dundrum Shopping Centre in their '06 reg Mini Coopers Daddy bought them for their seventeenth birthdays, all they care about is shopping and fashion and grooming; riding's an unwelcome distraction from the beauty salon and the shoe shop; the whole thing's wasted on them."

Miranda beamed at her satirically.

"There speaks Jackie Tyrrell, who went to finishing school in Geneva. Dressmaking and deportment and Italian and place setting and flower arrangement."

"Quite right too. Made a real woman of her," Seán Proby said.

"Miranda doesn't agree. About the girls," Jackie said, seemingly reveling in any exchange that approached the condition of a row.

Miranda shrugged wearily: this was evidently something they rehearsed on a regular basis.

"Girls were always interested in hair and makeup and clothes. They just didn't have the money to do anything about it back in our day. Now they do."

"Too much money," Jackie said severely. "Too much money in the wrong hands. What do you think, Ed?"

"I'd always be in favor of wealth redistribution," I said. "The problem is, how to dole it out, and who decides?"

"I decide," Jackie said, and then, straight-faced: "Ed, do you think teenage girls should be taught to ride?"

Miranda and Proby burst out laughing at this, and Jackie Tyrrell shook her head sadly, like a prophet without honor at her own table. Champagne arrived, and we drank a toast to the riding school (in which Seán Proby had some kind of interest) against her protests, and to Christmas. Then Jackie, unprovoked and with no challenger, launched into a long and involved defense of the Irish Revenue Inspectors' tax exemption for the bloodstock industry, inviting my support on the grounds that, as a creative writer, I benefited from a similar dispensation. I tried to remind her that I wasn't, in fact, a writer, but she and Proby were drinking Calvados by now, impervious to any music but their own. Occasionally she would scribble something on a napkin, briefing herself for her rhetorical assault against illusory foes. It was after ten; it felt much later. I offered Miranda a lift home. She was on her feet before I'd finished speaking.

I offered Jackie Tyrrell some money for the dinner, but she forced it back into my hand and pulled me down until we were eye to eye. Her face was fixed in a comedy leer; her breath was a yeasty cloud of alcohol; I thought she was going to kiss me, and didn't see what I could do if she did, but when I looked her in the eye, she fixed me with an unexpectedly clear gaze.

"Call me. We need to talk," she said quietly, urgently, and then pushed her from her and yelled with flattered laughter as if I'd propositioned her. I waved good-bye to Proby from a distance, not wanting to risk giving him my hand again for fear I'd never get it back.

"See you racing!" he bellowed twice as we were leaving.

When we got out into the night, the rain was falling softly. I opened my coat and turned to Miranda Hart to see if she needed it. She snaked her arms inside it and around my neck and pulled my mouth down onto hers and kissed me; she smelled of oranges and salt; when I opened my eyes, all I could see was the shimmer of the streetlights in the rain. I thought for a second they were stars.

"What happened to your gum?" I said.

Her tongue snaked quickly out of her mouth with a little wad of chewing gum on its tip, then vanished again, to be replaced by a smile.

"Come home with me," she said. "And I'll show you how I did it."

She reached up to my mouth and wiped it with her hand. It came away red with her lipstick, and she waved it in front of me and grinned.

As we walked down Merrion Street to my car, amid weaving groups of happy and belligerent and bedraggled drunks, shiny and sodden in the damp night, I straightened the bills Jackie Tyrrell had crushed into my hand and put them in my wallet. Among them, I found her business card. On one side was printed: *The Jackie Tyrrell Riding Academy for Girls, Tibradden Road,* along with her phone numbers. On the back, in red ink, she had printed:

PATRICK AND LEO RODE TOGETHER

SIX

I saw Miranda Hart to her door and touched her arm and made to leave. She grabbed my hand and pulled me close and kissed me again.

"I can't stay," I said.

"I don't want you to stay all night," she said. "Just long enough."

She held on to me with one hand while she worked the key in the lock. It occurred to me that if I was going to stop sleeping with clients, or with women implicated on some level in the cases I worked, now would be the time to start. But I didn't. What's more, I didn't want to. Miranda Hart dragged me into the darkened living room and pushed me onto the couch and fell on top of me; she was wild and ardent at first; then, after a while, there were tears in her eyes, and she said,

"Maybe this is not such a good idea," and I said,

"Now she tells me," struggling to get the words out, and then,

"Do you want to stop?" and she said,

"Fuck no, do you?" and I said,

"No I don't," and she said,

"Come on then. Come on, come on."

It wasn't how I thought it would be, at once gentler and more passionate; afterward, she cried a little. When she asked me what I wanted to drink, I said, "Gin," and she said, "Good idea." I'd be late for Dave Donnelly, but I couldn't leave, not just yet. What's more, I didn't want to. We sat in the living room, both on the sofa, half dressed, the light from the kitchen bleeding into the dark, reflecting off the glass doors at the other end that gave onto a small garden. I could see her chewing, and shook my head in wonder. Where did she keep it? It was a gift that passed all understanding.

"Sorry about that," she said.

"Sorry about what?" I said.

"You know. The make-up-your-fucking-mind, the tears, the all-round crapness. Being messy. Behaving like a girl. I thought I could just . . ."

I took her hand and held it.

"We all think we can just . . . and sometimes we can, and sometimes it doesn't work out that way."

"Just the day, you know? You coming around asking about Patrick . . . the very day he disappeared. How weird is that?"

"Maybe Father Tyrrell planned it that way."

Something close to a shudder rippled through her body.

"You were going to tell me. What is it about Vincent Tyrrell that frightens you so?"

She took a gulp of her gin, pulled herself into a corner of the couch, and brought her knees up to her chin.

"He came around here that day. Ten years ago. It wasn't a Sunday, it was the middle of the week. Everything was a bit

chaotic here, after the whole By Your Leave thing. A lot of drinking, a lot of . . . well, I wasn't the most . . . I could have been a lot
more sympathetic to Patrick, put it that way."

"You thought he'd made a mess of the situation."

"I thought he'd been unprofessional. I mean, the rules of the
game: jockeys do what they're told. And maybe sometimes you'll
stretch that, you'll leave it a bit later than you've been told, you'll
take an earlier lead, but it's all forgiven if you win. But what Patrick did, to make such a song and dance about stopping a horse,
it was really stupid. I mean, what was the point? Everyone knows
what racing is like. And it wasn't as if it changed anything."

"Didn't he ever try to explain himself? To you, at least?"

"No."

"Miranda, I can't help you if you're keeping something back."

"I'm not. I swear to God. Look, it wasn't as if we had a big
discussion, we didn't work like that. I didn't know I wasn't going
to see him again."

"Was he going to find it hard to get another trainer to take
him on?"

"I was worried he might. But I was wrong; he'd been riding
well that year, and once the hue and cry had died down, he'd
have got another job easily. I was . . . I was horrible to him, really,
put him through a whole guilt trip. I suppose I thought . . . you
know, that Tyrrellscourt has such a reputation, it's been number
one for so long, I thought he'd been at the very top and thrown
it all away. And what were we, twenty-three or something? It
was ridiculous, we were just starting out. And the last time I saw
him . . ."

Her voice faltered and she began to tear up again.

"The last time I saw him was in the morning, I'd made him
sleep in the spare room. He'd brought me up a cup of tea, and
begged me to talk to him, to forgive him. He said he'd make it all
right. I remember, I was lying on my side away from him, and he
sounded so sad . . . so desperate . . ."

"Can you remember anything he said?"

Miranda took another long drink of gin, this time tipping the glass too far up and spilling it down both sides of her chin.

"Fuck it!" she said. "Don't laugh at me!"

"You have to be the clumsiest person I've ever met," I said.

"Patrick used to say that too. He said I'd never make it as a jockey, my body'd never cope with the injuries, I got bruises enough walking around a room."

She drained her gin and wiped her mouth and passed her glass to me. Her lipstick was smeared all over her mouth like some crazy lady from an old black-and-white movie, Joan Crawford with the sirens howling, and I laughed again, and she glared at me, and I pulled her toward me and put my arms around her, and she punched me a couple of times in the chest and then put her head on my shoulder.

"I was such a cow to him."

"You didn't know you were never going to see him again," I said. We sat for a while like that, as if we'd known each other forever, until I began to wonder whether it was Miranda Hart I was embracing, or the ghost of my ex-wife. Maybe Miranda felt the chill; she leapt up and sat by the fire, where the embers were smoldering, and tried to poke and then to blow them back into life. There was red in the turf and she coaxed it into flame and put another couple of sods on top. When she turned around, the flames danced in the silver of her dress, and her dark eyes flashed red and I found that I couldn't breathe.

"You look like you've seen a ghost," she said. I nodded.

"Someone who hurt you very badly. Someone I remind you of, someone who maybe looks a little like me."

I nodded again, dumbstruck.

"And now, at last, you're beginning to get over her. That's all right," she said, smiling. "I wanted you too." Then her mouth set hard.

"Now, I think you'd better ask your questions, and go."

I hadn't touched my gin, and found I needed it badly. I felt like I'd been slapped, and for no good reason, and I didn't like it. Miranda Hart was the kind of woman who could sense your weakest spot and reach straight for it. And she could see I wanted something more than what she had given.

"Jackie Tyrrell told me Patrick and Leo Halligan rode together. What did she mean by that?"

"What do *you* think she meant?"

"That they were both jockeys who came up together at Tyrrells-court. That they were lovers. What's the truth?"

"Leo didn't have the talent, or the temperament, to be a jockey. Because he was a fucking lunatic, and not in a good way. But I'm sure you know that, if you know his brothers. He was at a reform school near the stables. St. Jude's. So was Patrick. F.X. made a point of taking a couple of lads from there once they'd done their time, as apprentices. They were set to work in the yard; they both graduated to working the horses in the mornings. They'd be given pieces of work. Patrick took to it; Leo didn't. Leo was too smart. In every sense: too quick, too cunning, so sharp he'd cut himself."

"Were you there at the same time?"

Miranda nodded.

"I grew up in the village, a couple of miles downriver. I was the daughter of the local publican. The Tyrrellscourt Inn. Adopted, they never made any secret of that. They tried to make a lady out of me, too, but I was up at the stables any chance I got. My mother died when I was twelve, and they thought sending me to an all-girls' boarding school in England would give me a female influence, and encourage me to show willing. Except the school was in Cheltenham. It just meant I got to the Festival every year of my teens. Finally Jackie made a deal with my father: as long as I finished school, I could come and work at the yard. They didn't say I had to pass my A Levels though, and I didn't."

"Jackie made a deal with your father? Why did she do that?"

"I guess she always looked out for me. She picked me up more than once when I fell. And her and F. X. Tyrrell couldn't have kids—or didn't, I don't know, same difference. I suppose she stood as a kind of mother to me, though it didn't seem that way back then. More like a big sister. We'd go on the tear together, all that. She was a bit trapped down there in Tyrrellscourt, working up the nerve to get out."

"And were Patrick and Leo lovers?"

She smiled, her eyes glittering, as if to say: *Some people might think that an insult, but I'm not one of them.* I knew then that I could fall in love with Miranda Hart, if I wasn't careful. And I wasn't, as a rule.

"Were they? I don't know. The school had a reputation that way. And there's a bit of it in every stable. Like a jail, the hours are so long, you've no money, you're confined to camp most of the time, and you don't get enough to eat. All these young boys are dieting all the time, and they're at the horniest time of their lives, and dieting, extreme dieting, can make you absolutely obsessed with sex. It always does me. So. Can't say I'd blame them."

"Did it have any effect on your marriage? I mean, do you think he was gay?"

"I don't know. I don't think so. He didn't shy away from his . . . marital duties, as they used to say. But maybe, in another life . . . put it this way, what age are you, forty, forty-two?"

"Something like that."

"I bet you had a girlfriend when you were twenty-two, twenty-three, you drank a lot together, or got high, whatever, you laughed and cried, you said you loved each other, you fucked a lot, but even at the time, you knew it probably wasn't forever. Maybe that's the way it was with Patrick and me. We should never have got married, I don't know why we did: to get away from my family, and his lack of one. Maybe that's why. We were so young. And now . . . you know, we could run into each other on the street, and we probably wouldn't know what to say. So for all I know, he could be anything . . . ."

She grimaced then, and waved a hand in the air, as if conceding that she had merely given one version of many, that there was probably rather more to her marriage than youthful folly, certainly more than she was willing to tell me. She turned her dark head and looked into the fire. A glow of red flickered through her hair, which she suddenly shook forward and then swept back; the shadows and light bounced off the glass doors and played around the room.

"Get us another drink, would you Ed?"

I went through to the kitchen and fixed a gin; we'd been drinking it with lemon juice, which she had made up fresh and leavened with sugar syrup and orange juice. When I brought her the drink, her dismay that I hadn't made myself one was palpable.

"Not thirsty anymore?"

"I can't stay. I told you that."

She nodded, and turned her gaze back to the fire.

"Do you have a photograph of Patrick?"

She didn't move.

"Miranda, you said earlier you wanted me to find him. If you still mean it—"

She got to her feet and left the room. I looked around at the pictures on the walls, but they were all action or parade-ring photographs of Hutton in full livery; he looked like a jockey, all right, but so did all the others. When Miranda came back with a photo, I glanced quickly at it, long enough to see it was a full face shot, not so long that I began to compare it to the man I had found dead and mutilated on a dump earlier that day. I didn't want to be the bearer of that bad news, not yet.

"Can you remember the name of the private detective you hired to find Patrick?"

"Don . . . something. Kelly? Kennelly? I can find out."

"Let me know as soon as you do. Last thing. You said Vincent Tyrrell came to see you the day Patrick disappeared. What happened?"

"He told me Patrick had made a confession. To him, as a priest, the sacrament. And he couldn't, of course, disclose anything he had said. But he was very . . . it was as if he knew something about me, something I had done, or something about the way I lived . . . and that whatever it was, I should be ashamed of myself. All his insinuations . . . like I was, I don't know what, a whore, worse than a whore, some kind of . . . corrupter . . . I couldn't really follow it back then. I was angry, I threw him out, what right did he have—but I must have run it through in my head a thousand times since. That whatever had happened to Patrick, the reason he disappeared, it was all my fault, and it was somehow up to me to work out why."

"And have you?"

Miranda shook her head, aiming for a laugh that came off as a muted wail. She picked up her drink from the mantelpiece. I could hear the ice clinking, her hand was shaking so much.

"There was something about Father Tyrrell . . . the scorn for me, the contempt in his eyes . . . it was so belittling. As if I had . . . yes, he used the word *betrayal* . . . as if I had betrayed Patrick somehow. But he wouldn't say how."

She took a long, steady swallow of gin. Her use of it seemed medical, sacramental.

"The other thing was, he said something like, 'Well, he's better off now,' or 'It's probably for the best.' I thought he was just trying to placate me, because I was screaming at him, you know? I was mad at Patrick anyway, and now he'd made it even worse, setting this creepy fucking priest on me. I mean, confession? Who goes to fucking confession anymore? Old ladies. Children. Nuns. All the people who don't need to, who have no sins worthy of the name. So I really lost it with him. And I chose to remember it as, you know, well, he tried to bully me but I let him have it. And he scuttled off mouthing platitudes, you know, not to worry, all will be well. But that wasn't what happened. He knew Patrick wasn't coming back. And he was basically saying, he's well shot of you."

She drank again, emptying her glass. My phone announced the arrival of a text message: it was from Dave Donnelly, asking me where I was. I got my coat, and held Miranda Hart close, and headed for the door. Miranda stopped me in the hall.

"I did love Patrick," she said. "I wouldn't want you to think . . ."

"I don't," I said. She was shaking, face flushed red. I went to hold her, but she put up her hands and shook her head.

"No. Just, so you don't think . . . I may not have wanted to go back over any of this again, but . . . don't think I didn't love that man. Don't ever think that."

There were tears in her eyes. I nodded, and waited for the rest.

"There's one last thing," she said. "That morning—ten years ago today—when Patrick was leaving—when I wouldn't listen to him, or look at him—the thing he kept saying was, he wouldn't be a Judas. That was the last thing I heard Patrick say.

"'I won't play the fucking Judas for anyone.'"

SEVEN

The rain had turned to sleet by the time I made it back to Quarry Fields: a tricky drive in a '65 Volvo with no windshield wipers. Dave Donnelly's unmarked blue Toyota Avensis was parked outside my house, and Dave was sitting on the edge of the brown leather couch in my living room, drinking a cup of tea.

"Make yourself at home," I said.

"I'd need a Hoover."

"You're welcome."

"Or what is it these days, a Dyson?"

"It's in the press under the stairs."

I got myself a can of Guinness from the kitchen and a glass and joined him.

"How'd you get in?"

"You gave me a key."

"Why did I give a cop a key to my house?"

"The night we went out. When I got transferred to the Bureau. Remember?"

"We had a few drinks?"

"We had *all* the drinks. Dublin town ran out of drinks. And you said you had the last of the drinks back here."

"For some reason, it doesn't stand out in my mind."

"And I fell asleep on the sofa. Great sofa, mind."

"You can sleep on it without orthopedic consequences."

"You can what?"

"Without fucking your back up."

"This is not the sofa I have at home. This is why my back is fucked up."

"So there you were, asleep."

"And you were off first thing. I don't know, an early house. A woman. A client, even. And you gave me the key to lock up after."

"Case closed. Glad we got to the bottom of that one."

Dave half laughed, then looked at the floor, his low forehead furrowed in a scowl. He was a big-boned thickset crop-headed man who had lost two stone in weight quite suddenly, and it made him look ill. He had looked ill in a different way before, what with the high color and the bad temper and the bursting out of his ill-assembled, badly fitting suits and anoraks, like he was about to explode with exasperation and righteous anger at any moment, but it was a reassuring kind of ill. Now he looked ill as if he had a disease. But he didn't have a disease, he had a new job that seemed to be absorbing every ounce of energy he had, and then some.

Dave had been detective sergeant with the Seafield Garda for twenty years; a few months after he was promoted to inspector, the Howard case broke, and a web of murder, child abuse, sex trafficking and drug smuggling was uncovered, with DI Donnelly conveniently placed at the center of it all. That's when the

National Bureau of Criminal Investigation came calling. But it wasn't plain sailing at the Bureau: the Howard case had been front-page news for days, and Dave had attracted a swath of publicity which Garda Headquarters had encouraged (in part to deflect the credit away from me, a strategy that suited me just fine); his high-profile transfer (SUPERCOP TO SHAKE UP BUREAU) had been met with perhaps understandable resentment from his new colleagues, most especially Myles Geraghty, a pugnacious blockhead with whom we'd both had our tussles in the past.

I got a bottle of Jameson and two glasses and made them up two-thirds to a third water and gave one to Dave and he drank it down as if it was a cup of milk.

"What's on your mind, Dave? You wanted to talk about the bodies?"

"Yeah," he said, his mouth set in a grimace. "Talk is about all I can do with them."

"What's up?"

"Myles Geraghty is up. Up his own hole. He wants me out, and he's going to freeze me out until I get out. I was first to the scene in Roundwood yesterday, because the desk sergeant there called me, because he knows me, and he was having trouble getting through to the Bureau, some problem with the phones in Harcourt Square, fucking amateur hour. I called Geraghty on his mobile, left a message. Rounded up some of the other lads. When he finally gets there, he bollocks me out in front of them all for trying to run the show myself, for being, yes indeed, a 'glory boy.' What is it about this fucking country? The young fellas I train at football, I've one good striker, doesn't score from every chance, but he's averaging two goals a game, unbelievable, but you want to hear the fucking cloggers on his own team, the team he's winning games for, lads who can barely kick a ball let alone pass it, they're all glory boy this and glory boy that, same as when we grew up. No lads, here's what it is: he's good at football and you're shite. Glory boy. Fuck sake."

I poured Dave another drink and passed it to him; he raised it to his lips, then shook his head and set it down.

"Ah no way, Ed, the first was enough."

"So what happened, are you working the case?"

"Just about. I'm coordinating the incident room in Bray."'

"DI Donnelly speaking, can I help you?"

"Fuck off."

Dave subsided again, not even angry this time, just deflated. In a quiet, introspective voice I didn't know he possessed, he said, "I can't go on like this, Ed. I'm not sleeping. There are calls on my mobile at all hours. When I answer, I can hear someone breathing on the other end. Thought it was someone I sent down, I changed the number, same story again. Geraghty's behind it, I know he is. And at work one morning, there was a loaded gun on my desk with a Post-it stuck to it reading 'Can't Cope, Supercop? Give it your best shot.' Nobody knew anything, of course; everyone was shocked. But I could see people smirking, laughing behind their hands, Geraghty winking. I can't handle it, Ed."

Dave let his head sink into his hands. I looked at him in astonishment and dismay: Dave had always been so solid, so captain-of-the-school dependable, I guess I'd taken his strength for granted. It was like watching a cardboard cutout become real before my eyes. I wasn't sure I needed another real person in my life, but then, I had been surprised when he'd chosen me to celebrate his transfer with. Carmel had often told me he didn't have many friends, but I'd never really thought of myself as one, let alone his closest.

"Maybe I should just walk. I could take the pension, get out early, go into business with Carmel's brother. He's got a car showroom in Goatstown. Awful gobshite, but he's coining it there."

"What does Carmel think?"

"About going in with her brother? She'd like the extra change. But she knows what being a cop means to me."

"No, I meant the phone calls. The weight loss. The stress."

Dave shook his head.

"We don't really work on that level," he said. "I've always been . . . I don't bring the job home, you know? Because Carmel doesn't want to know."

"I'm sure she'd be sympathetic—"

"No. Our deal is, she has a stressful job raising four kids. She doesn't need me coming home crying like a baby. If I want to change jobs, fine, so long as the money's still coming in. But to talk to her the way I've talked to you . . . she'd consider it weak."

"Sounds like the 1950s round your house, Dave."

He shrugged, and rolled his neck, and flexed his still-massive arms.

"It's how we started out. I was the one in charge, the one to make things safe, the one she could rely on. I think how you start out . . . it colors how you proceed, you know?"

"You sure she still feels the same way?"

"I still feel the same way. End of story. Don't ask me about Carmel, all right?"

"All right."

Dave lifted his head and, in what seemed like a determined effort, cracked a smile.

"Fuck sake, look at us, like a pair of fucking 'oul ones, commiserating. Come on to fuck. It's fine, everything's just *grand*. Come on."

Dave got up and drank the second whiskey and clapped me on the shoulder. It hurt.

"Where are we going?"

"To see dead people."

We drove south on the N11 as far as Loughlinstown and came off at the exit for St. Colmcille's Hospital. The hospital mortuary is at the far end, past A&E and the main entrance. Dave asked me to bring a hat and a scarf; the only hat I had was a black fedora Tommy Owens found in a secondhand store, which he insisted I have because it made me "look like a proper detective." It didn't, it made me look like a sinister old-style priest, a detail Dave lit upon when we parked the car. He found a set of rosary beads in the glove compartment, and gave them to me, along with the black leatherette-bound Toyota manual.

"You're a priest, Ed," he said.

"Thank you, Dave," I said.

The door was opened by a red-eyed, unshaven hospital porter who didn't speak English; he was joined by a young uniformed Guard who recognized Dave immediately. Dave took the Guard aside and chatted briefly to him. I held the rosary over the book and kept my eyes down.

Dave came back and said, "This way, Father."

The Guard nodded respectfully as I entered, and I acknowledged him briefly with a low priestly half wave, half blessing and a rattle of beads. We passed through a carpeted reception area with a screened-off corner for grieving families to identify their next of kin. The porter led us through double doors to a cold room with two bodies on hospital gurneys. Each body was covered with a white cloth. There was another room ahead where the autopsies were conducted, and a refrigeration room to one side. A life-size wood-and-plaster crucifix loomed above us on the wall. The porter nodded and withdrew behind the double doors.

"What are we doing here, Dave?" I said.

"The state pathologist has done the preliminary examinations at the scene. The second body meant it was too late to start the autopsies tonight. They'll begin at eight in the morning. They brought them here because they finished late, they're starting early, and it was nearer than the city morgue."

"Okay. What are we doing here?"

Dave Donnelly's mouth was set; his eyes were burning and his hands began to shake.

"The first body," he said. "The one Geraghty insisted on telling the press bore all the hallmarks of a gangland killing."

I nodded.

"I ID'd him straight off—not by the contents of his wallet, by his face. He was Don Kennedy. He was my sergeant when I was starting out, down Kildare way, twenty-five years ago. He was like a father to me. Stood godfather to Paul, my second eldest. He got out in '99 or so, did a bit of private work, missing persons, insurance claims, that sort of stuff. I didn't see much of him anymore. Godparents don't seem to matter so much when your kids get older. But he never forgot a birthday. Look at him. He was strangled. And someone cut his tongue out, Ed. What do you think of that?"

What did I think? I thought Don Kennedy was the private detective Miranda Hart had hired two years ago to find Patrick Hutton.

"Because I know your body had his tongue cut out too, Ed. The Bureau may be trying to edge me out, but the incident room is in Bray station, and I have a lot of friends there. Your man was strangled and he had his tongue cut out too. What do you think? Coincidence?"

"There's no such thing, Dave. You know that."

"And so do you."

He took the sheet partly from one of the bodies to reveal a large male head with an unruly thatch of gray hair. The strangulation marks around the neck were similar to those on what Dave had called "my body." Dave lifted the sheet now on the blond gentleman farmer with the Church's shoes I'd found upended in a dump. I looked at the face, wondered how closely I wanted to work with Dave and decided I needed him at least as much as he needed me.

I took the photograph Miranda Hart had given me from my coat pocket and showed it to him. The hair was blond, whether dyed or not I couldn't say, but the face looked very similar: same lined skin, same sunken cheeks, same tiny point of chin. I took a latex glove from my jacket and fitted it over one hand and pointed to the vivid blue of Patrick Hutton's eyes in the photo. Dave nodded. With index and middle fingers, I tugged the corpse's eyes open. They were far from vivid, but they were blue. We weren't in a position to be definitive, but as far as we could tell, the dead man was Patrick Hutton, missing for ten years, dead for forty-eight hours. Without thinking, I turned to the crucifix on the wall and blessed myself. When I looked back, I saw Dave doing the same. I don't know if Dave was thinking about the Four Last Things. I couldn't tell you if I was either. Maybe we were just two spooked Paddies in the house of the dead. But we both had faith in this much: after violent death, there must come judgment.

EIGHT

Dave didn't say a word on the drive back. The sleet had stopped, and when we got out of the car in Quarry Fields, the air was fresh and crisp, and a star-flecked fissure had cleft the sky. The ground was snapping underfoot as we walked up the drive.

I checked my phone. Tommy had sent me a text message, all in capitals: WATCH OUT! LEO'S AFTER YOU! I figured having a high-ranking Garda detective as my guest was a reasonable precaution against anything Leo Halligan might do.

I brewed a pot of coffee and we sat at the kitchen table. Dave started by saying that Aidan Coyne, the Guard who'd been on duty at the mortuary, had worked with him at Seafield, that he was a good lad and that he wouldn't breathe a word to anyone about our visit. It was known in Bray station that Dave had served with Don Kennedy, and nobody was very happy about how Dave had been sidelined in the investigation. And there was always resentment when the National Bureau of Criminal Investigation started throwing their weight around with the local force, especially if Myles Geraghty had anything to do with it. Dave had told Aidan a version of the truth: that he wanted to say a few quiet prayers for a fallen comrade.

When the coffee was ready I poured two mugs. I had put the heat on, but Dave was shivering, and he asked if he could have some Jameson in his. That struck me as a good idea, so I had some in mine too. We drank for a while in silence. I knew he was waiting for me to spill all I knew. I was happy enough that we had made a deal. We just needed to check the small print before we took it any further.

"Dave, I'm not looking for a partner here. I want to be free to do things the way I would do them. And if that means withholding information, or taking a risk by following a hunch—"

"Or riding the arse off one of the chief suspects, or all of them; yeah, I know how you work, Ed."

Dave guffawed in what struck me as a rather forced manner, and I pretended to, hoping my laughter would spare my blushes, or his; I'd never heard him make that kind of remark before, and he didn't seem relaxed about having made it. I wondered briefly if Dave had been the one tailing me tonight. Not that Miranda Hart was a suspect. I didn't even know what the case was yet—another reason I didn't want anyone looking over my shoulder.

"Don't worry—you won't have to answer to me. I'll feed you whatever you need, and you can go your own way."

"If I didn't trust you, Dave, I'd think I was being set up. You're not setting me up, are you?"

"Ed, this fucker Geraghty is a bad cop. He's a rotten cop. I don't want to tell you what I know about him, but let's just say anything that can publicly embarrass him, any way I can trip the cunt up, anything to help push him out the door and I'll be happy."

"I don't get it, Dave. What's in it for you? I mean, say we get to the killer, or killers, before the Garda investigation does. We've still got to hand it over. I can't arrest murderers myself. And no one's going to give you credit for conducting some kind of maverick case. Quite the opposite."

"Well, let's say that's my lookout, and leave it at that," Dave said bluntly, in a tone that brooked no further discussion. He laid a spiral bound reporter's pad on the table and looked at me expectantly.

A cat or a fox set the security light on in the back. I stared out at the two bare apple trees in the center of the garden, male and female, their branches nearly touching and never quite. I wondered briefly about Dave and Carmel, then as quickly put them from my mind: they had been rock solid since school, one of those partnerships where you could never see the join—however much Dave tried to portray the marriage as if it were something from the Dark Ages. Carmel was forever asking me around to the house, but the truth was, the warmth and energy and happiness they had built there always left me feeling desolate and bereft. No, those trees were a gloss first off on my parents' ill-fated match, and latterly on the sorry chronicle of my own romantic history.

I didn't tell Dave that Vincent Tyrrell had hired me. But I went through most everything else: the likelihood that Don Kennedy was the PI Miranda Hart had hired at the insurance company's behest to find Patrick Hutton; the fact that Hutton and Leo Halligan had been apprentices together at Tyrrellscourt after their joint stint at St. Jude's reform school (Dave lifted his head from the pad for that one, his eyes wide, especially when he heard that Leo was fresh out of jail); the death of the racehorse By Your Leave; the consequent rift between Hutton and F. X. Tyrrell and its significance in Hutton's disappearance; Hutton's emotional declaration that he wouldn't play the Judas for anyone; the bizarre and formidable force that was Jackie Tyrrell and her insinuation, barely countered by Miranda Hart, that Halligan and Hutton had a sexual relationship; the omega and crucifix tattoos on Patrick Hutton's forearm.

Dave stared at his pad in silence when I had finished. He looked up and shook his head, smiling at first. Then the smile faded from his broad face, and his mouth set, and his eyes hardened and flickered like jewels, and I had a reminder of what it felt like to sit across from him in an interrogation room. It didn't feel very comfortable.

"I went to the scene myself, Ed. I knew Geraghty wouldn't like that, so I didn't tell him. But I went there anyway, and I did what I guess you probably did: I gave the body a quick once-over and then I called it in to Bray station, along with the tip-off about Vinnie Butler. Bad enough a private cop risking the contamination of a crime scene, but a real cop? Why would he do that?"

"I don't know, Dave. Why did he do that?"

"Because he knew that the private cop wasn't really to be trusted. He knew that if the private cop found something really juicy, he'd keep it to himself. And he wanted to find out just what it was the private cop was holding back."

"And did he?"

"There had been a piece of paper—a note, I'd say—in the victim's left trouser pocket. There were still shreds of paper adhering to the pocket fibers, which suggests that it had been freshly removed; there were mild ink stains on the pocket fabric, from which, as with the paper shreds, we might infer that the note had been through the wash with the trousers."

"Do you do this for a living?"

"What was written on the note?"

"The mobile phone number for a bookie who had a pitch at Gowran Park racecourse today."

"Do you know which bookie that was?"

"Not yet. But I still have the number."

"Anything else you want to tell me?"

"I didn't want to tell you that."

"If I told Geraghty you'd interfered with the body—worse, you'd stolen evidence—what do you think he'd do?"

"I have an idea what he'd do with me. What would he do with you?"

"He'd probably blame me for knowing you."

"There you are. Not to mention what he'd do if he was told you had given the scene a surreptitious one-two first."

And there we were. He had me, but I had him. MAD: Mutually Assured Destruction, they used to call it when it came to nuclear missiles. Safe as houses, unless one of us actually went mad. Dave wasn't looking completely sane to me. He topped his coffee up with Jameson, laughing gently and nodding in private agreement with himself. Then he clapped his hands and almost winked.

"So what did you make of this Miranda Hart then Ed? Is she a looker, is she?"

It suddenly occurred to me that Dave might have formed as idealized a picture of my single life as I possibly had of his married one. I threw him a look I was more used to getting from him. The look said: *Cop yourself on, you tool.* It landed right between his eyes and spread crimson across his face.

"All right," I said. "Each man had his tongue cut out. Do we have any other points of comparison?"

"One: they were connected in life, in that Kennedy tried to find Hutton. Must have done a certain amount of digging. Two: they were both killed and mutilated elsewhere, and then cleaned up and deposited where they lay in the past couple of days. Three: they were killed in exactly the same way, strangled by hand and/ or ligature. Four: they were mutilated in the same way, tongue cut out. Five: they each had a small leather bag or purse full of coins."

"Did Kennedy have any tattoos?" I said.

"Not in the obvious places. I didn't get time to search the whole body. Nothing else was found on him."

"What do you make of the tattoos on Hutton's forearm?" I said.

Dave shook his head. He had copied them in his notebook. He opened it to that page, and we studied them in silence for a moment.

†

"Omega is the last letter in the Greek alphabet," I said. "From alpha to omega: from beginning to end."

"From life to death."

"And the crucifix represents death."

"And life everlasting."

"What do you make of it?"

"I don't know. A serial killer who's into symbols and whatdo-youcallit, tarot cards and all this? That's grand for American films, Ed. In real life, I'd say it's all my hole."

I almost laughed out loud. That sounded more like the Dave Donnelly I knew, a man who assumed everyone else needed knocking off his perch, and considered himself the man to do it. If he were a T-shirt, it would read: WHO THE FUCK DO YOU THINK *YOU* ARE? That could have accounted for some of the tension between him and Myles Geraghty: they were both cut from the same cloth. Apart from Dave's not being a complete and total prick.

"Still, when was the last time you came across a tongue cut out?" I said. "That's a lot of work, and a lot of mess."

"Not if the victim's dead first. No blood to speak of then."

"But you take my point? Two in the same day? And both strangled too?"

Dave nodded.

"It's not rock solid, but it would be a hell of a coincidence if the MO was used by two different killers. And what is there no such thing as?"

"And the fact that they were dumped within a mile or two of each other—does that not suggest the killer's trying to tell us something?"

"That's the other thing I've never got about those films and all: why the killer wants to tell the cops anything. I mean, if he's happy being a mad fucker who goes around killing people, why would he want the cops anywhere near him?"

"Because it vindicates him as a person. The artistry of his killing spree is mythologized among the community at large, thus validating his ego. He is the superman, the cops humans every whit as petty and puny as his victims."

Dave was giving me the "cop yourself on, you tool" look. I shrugged.

"Hey, this stuff isn't just in the movies. These fuckers are real, and they're out there."

"I know, and it usually goes back to something that happened in childhood. Mammy never bought me a bowwow, boo hoo hoo."

"You know who you sound like, Dave? The man who, after I'd just witnessed a murder-suicide, and been advised that counseling was available to me, told me that what I really needed was a good boot up the arse. Your friend and mine, Myles Geraghty."

Dave reacted as if I'd slapped him; he leapt to his feet and wagged a finger across the table at me, his lips quivering as he attempted to form words and failed, his face red and contorted with rage; then he stormed out of the room. When he came back in a few minutes later, he was shaking his head as if in amazement at the behavior of someone else entirely, our mutual friend with the short temper. He sat and made a show of looking through his notes.

"I'll tell you this much," Dave said. "Myles Geraghty will go a long way out of his way to avoid bringing this within a country mile of F. X. Tyrrell."

"Why so?"

"Are you kidding? The queue to be F.X.'s best friend in the tent at the Galway Races, you should see it. All the politicians and the big rich. This is the man whose horses beat the Queen's, for fuck's sake: this was one of Ireland's heroes in the dark days when no one had an arse to his trousers: he stuffed the English every Cheltenham, an equestrian IRA man in a morning suit. No one will want Tyrrellscourt anywhere near this."

"And maybe they'll be right. We've got Leo Halligan connected to it, and he's got form in this area, doesn't he?"

"Leo's a bad lad all right. Do you remember him, Ed? He was in our school."

"I know, but he was never there, was he?"

"He was always on the hop all right."

"I remember he went away to reform school for stabbing Christine Doran."

"That was bad."

"He was funny though, wasn't he? He was a brilliant footballer."

"He was a good footballer. He was a brilliant boxer."

"Fly, wasn't he?"

"He went up to welter for a while, but he couldn't keep the weight on."

"It was weird, even though we were all scared of him, everyone kind of liked him, far as I can recall. I did at any rate," I said.

"I wouldn't say 'like.' He wasn't a fucking psycho like Podge, or a slick cunt like George, but yeah, he was . . . for a dangerous bollocks, he was kind of normal, wasn't he? How did he pull that off?"

"I think, because you didn't feel he was gonna take you out for looking at him."

"Yeah. Mind you, Podge would, and then he'd come after you for sorting Podge out."

"Speaking of which. Did you see the Volvo? The RIP?"

"Was that Leo? Of course, there was all this, when he got out, he was gonna get you for sending Podge down. I'd've thought it would be a relief to them to have him locked away, he was becoming a liability."

"It all comes down to blood with the Halligans."

Dave looked at his watch.

"Time I headed back to the station, see if we've had any calls."

"What's the story with Vinnie Butler?"

"He's a Butler," Dave said, as if that were explanation enough. When I shook my head, he expanded, covering pretty much the same territory Tommy Owens had in his voice mail, if in greater detail: the Butlers were a large extended family scattered around north Wicklow and the Dublin border, into all manner of burglary, extortion, fencing and low-level drug dealing. They also spent a great deal of time feuding with each other over a variety of perceived slights and betrayals, real and imagined, one branch of the family doorstepping another with machetes and shotguns and, most recently, a jar of sulfuric acid: Dave told me the young girl whose face the acid was flung in was fifteen and pregnant; she was burned so badly she lost an eye.

"Geraghty set a couple of his boys on him, but I don't think he was dumping anything more than refuse. State of the body for one thing; Vinnie Butler couldn't keep *himself* that clean: half an hour in the back of his Transit the corpse would have decomposed. Geraghty's probably pining for the days of the Branch and the Murder Squad, when they'd have fitted up a gouger like Vinnie for this no bother."

The National Bureau of Criminal Investigation had been formed from the ashes of the Garda Special Branch and the Murder Squad, elite outfits that, like many elite units within the Guards, had quickly become corrupt and unmanageable; they had been disbanded, and then after a decent interval, the NBCI was formed. Geraghty and many of his colleagues had been Branch or Squad men; now stewing with resentment, they were tipped into a Bureau they felt was beneath them but loftily consented to dominate. A lot of Dave's problems probably stemmed from the tension between the old elite and new officers keen to make a name for themselves.

At the doorway, Dave turned and looked me in the eye.

"All right, Ed?"

"All right, Dave. You?"

It was as if a shadow passed across his face, or rather, as if I'd been squinting in the sun's glare and was temporarily blinded when it passed behind a cloud: when I could see again, everything had changed. I'd never seen a grown man look so like an anxious, lonely child.

"We're having some people round tomorrow night, Ed. Christmas Eve. Will you come?"

I was worried Dave might cry if I said no.

NINE

There was a message on my phone from Jackie Tyrrell, very grave and businesslike and, if I hadn't known otherwise, perfectly sober, asking me to call her urgently, no matter how late. It was half one, which didn't strike me as especially late, particularly if you were an alcoholic, so I called.

"Ed Loy, about time."

She sounded irritable and impatient, as if it was half four on a Friday afternoon and she was trying to clear her desk for the weekend and I was an employee who knew well what a trial on her patience I had become.

"I want you to come up here at once. I've a few things you need to hear."

Her voice had dwindled to a shrill bark. I have the normal portion of resistance to being spoken to like that, plus an extra serving on the side. I said nothing. I could hear her sighing, and then the clink of ice in a moving glass. When she spoke again, it was in a more conciliatory tone, as if there was nothing done that couldn't be undone with some goodwill and understanding on both sides.

"All right, I've been sitting here obsessing about it all, I've probably entered the argument at a more heated level than was wise."

"What argument?"

"The whole . . . look, there is nothing to be gained by raking over the whole business with Patrick Hutton, believe me. It can only cause Miranda needless upset. It happened ten years ago, it's ancient history, Miranda desperately needs to get on with her life. Let the dead bury the dead."

"That's interesting. How do you know Patrick Hutton is dead?"

"I don't. I simply assume . . . if you vanish off the face of the earth like that, chances are you're dead. But for all I know, he could be on the Costa del Sol, or in Australia. As good as dead, one way or the other."

I heard the clink of ice in her glass again. I kept silent. She clearly wanted to talk; whether she had anything to tell me remained to be seen.

"Look, I don't want to talk on the phone. You'd better come up here. You can be trusted, of course."

The last without a glimmer of uncertainty. I could be trusted how? To lie to the cops? To keep rich people's secrets and carry their bags? To do what I was told, provided the price was right? No harm in letting Jackie Tyrrell believe I was corruptible. As long as she told me all she had to tell.

"Of course," I said.

She gave me directions, I shut up my house and stepped out into the night.

In the car, the first thing I noticed was the smell: French tobacco, Gauloises, or Gitanes, mixed with a lemony aftershave. It seemed to me that I had smelt that combination before. I could always have asked Leo Halligan, but since he held the point of a blade at the back of my neck, I decided now was neither the time nor the place. I looked in the rearview mirror. Leo Halligan, rail thin in a motorcycle jacket and black shirt with dark hair gelled into something not unlike a DA, his dark eyes glittering in a chalk-white face, silver sleeper earrings in both ears, cheekbones like polished knives, thin lips drawn in the mockery of a smile. Tommy had warned me he was coming, but I hadn't paid enough attention.

"Hello Leo," I said.

"Hello Ed," he said. "No sudden moves now."

He pressed the blade sharply against my neck until the skin broke. There was a little pain and then the unpleasant sensation of blood leaking down my collar.

"Just to show you I'm not fucking around, yeah?" he said. His voice was not exactly camp, but it had a bored, eye-rolling drawl to it, as if he was exhausted dealing with the endless supply of fools and imbeciles sent to annoy him.

"I would have taken that as read," I said.

"Smart. You were always smart, Ed Loy."

"So were you, Leo. Four years for a hit on a nineteen-year-old. That's a sentencing policy to get concerned citizens onto the streets."

"Alleged eyewitness said he was bullied into making his statement by the Guards. Alibi witness ignored. No forensic evidence."

"So we're supposed to think you're innocent?"

"Do I see you in a courtroom, Mr. Justice Loy? I couldn't give a fuck what you think. Start the car."

"Were you going to wait here all night long?"

"If the lights in the house went out, I would have come in to you."

"It'd be warmer in the house. Do you want to come in?"

"No, I want you to drive. I have a gun as well."

He showed me what looked like a Glock 17 semiautomatic, a gun his brother George favored. Whatever it was, I had to assume it worked.

"Good for you. I don't."

"Just in case you were in the mood for heroics."

"Never."

"Shut up and drive. Up towards Castlehill."

I did as he said. I hatched various heroic plans along the way, supposing he was going to kill me: I could reverse the car into a wall; I could stop at traffic lights, jerk away from the blade and roll out my door; I could smash into the rear of another vehicle and trust in the public to rescue me. I didn't act on any of them, not because I thought they wouldn't work. No, the reverse adrenaline of inevitability was working its phlegmatic spell on me. If Leo wanted to kill me, he would; if I had the chance to kill him first, I could try; as it stood, he had the stronger hand, and it seemed wiser to wait and see how he played it. Anyway, he could have done me in my driveway: there wasn't a sinner about, or a light in the neighboring houses. He had something to say, that much was certain. And I was curious enough, now I knew he had a part in the Patrick Hutton story, to hear what it was.

Leo directed me up toward the old car park near the pine forest, midway between Bayview Hill and Castlehill. It was quite a beauty spot, with views stretching out to the harbor of refuge at Seafield. The stars had spread until the sky was almost free of cloud. There were usually a few cars parked late here, lovers enjoying the seclusion. But it was too cold tonight, or too late, or too close to Christmas; there was nobody to see Leo Halligan wave a Glock 17 at me to walk ahead of him up the steps and around the edge of the quarry to the ruined church on the top of Bayview Hill, or to prod me in the back of the neck with the gun if I didn't move fast enough. The view here was even more spectacular, from the mountains to the sea, past the candy-stripe towers of the Pigeon House to Dublin Bay, and then north to the great promontory of Howth; the city lights flickered as if they were reflected stars: as above, so below, a gauze of light stretched out across the dark.

Leo stopped at an open patch of grass used for picnics, just below the ruined church, hard above the old quarry, where the granite for the harbor had been hewn. With the gun trained on me, he held the knife, a hunting blade with a gutter and a serrated edge, in front of my face and, looking me in the eye, nodded and lifted his arm. I braced myself to dodge it, knowing he could shoot me anyway, thinking I should try and argue with him but scared it would sound like pleading, wondering if I should run away but not wanting to be shot in the back. The knife flew over my shoulder and over the granite wall and out into the quarry and I thought I could hear it landing but I couldn't be sure. When I looked back, Leo was holding up the Glock. He snapped out the clip and handed it to me and brandished the gun in his right hand.

"Okay, Ed?"

"One in the chamber, Leo."

"Good point, Ed. Hope that's not the last thing you remember."

He pointed the Glock at me and grinned, and I saw he had more gold teeth than white ones, and I hoped *that* wasn't the last thing I'd remember, then he tipped the barrel up into the sky and pulled the trigger. For a second, on the ground where I'd fallen, I thought he *had* shot me, classic fashion, one behind the ear. Then I realized as he dropped the gun with his right he'd brought his left around in the mother and father of all haymakers and laid me out like a drunken girl. And there he was now, crouching above me, bobbing from foot to foot, fists up, gold teeth flashing.

"Come on," he said. "Come on."

The last person to say "Come on, come on" to me was Miranda Hart. My face was deep between her legs and my hands were slipping inside her torn stockings and stroking her firm, yielding, scented flesh. She had wanted me to stay, and if I had, I'd still be there, drinking gin and lemon juice, fucking in the fire's glow. Instead I had spent time in a morgue with two dead bodies, I had tried to deal with a friend who was apparently having a nervous breakdown and now I was getting to my feet on top of a hill in subzero temperatures at two in the fucking morning so a pawky little maniac could beat the living shit out of me with his bare fucking hands. Come on, come on. Jesus.

Leo was about five seven, and he couldn't've been more than eleven stone, which meant I had eight inches and fifty pounds on him, but none of that seemed to count because of three things. The first thing was, he was so much faster than me: he had popped my nose and cut my right eye before I had my guard up. The second thing was, he was wearing those rock-and-roll skull and serpent's-head rings that worked like brass knuckles. And the third thing was, when I finally got a rhythm going and managed to block a few blows and land a few digs of my own, he suddenly reared back and swung into this Thai kickboxing maneuver and slammed me in the jaw with the sole of a red leather cowboy boot that, had it been the heel, would have broken it.

Where the fuck was Tommy Owens? It was all very well his mother dying, but somebody needed to get my back: warning me wasn't enough. I was reeling like a skittle, finding it hard to keep my head up, and Leo was grinning now, scenting blood, and steadying himself to finish me off, and in my lack of strategy came my opportunity: it wasn't that I wasn't falling apart, or that my limbs weren't having trouble acting on instructions from my brain, but my judgment was unimpaired: I could see exactly when and where I was about to be hit. All I needed was one last great surge from the nervous system, one final synapse flash of a reaction. It came as the heel of his red boot came straight for my nose and I managed to sidestep the blow and to catch Leo's calf before he regained balance—he had overstretched himself, reasoning justifiably that I was a dead man walking—and pulled back and swung the eleven-stone man around and around by the legs, sensing the humiliation and unwilling to stop, having felt pretty humiliated myself in the past few minutes, until he suddenly shot out of my hands and crashed on the gravel near the ruined church and I was left with a red cowboy boot in my hand. Leo was up in a flash, his biker jacket in large part protection against the spill, a few lacerations down one cheek the only evidence of harm. He seemed far more concerned by the fate of his footwear. As he reached for it, I retreated to the wall above the quarry and held the boot out into the abyss.

"They're handmade, Ed. Imported from Texas."

"I don't care. One will do you. You can hop away to fuck."

"They cost three grand."

"My heart pumps piss. You could have killed me. A fistfight's one thing, but you could have killed me there, with the heel in the head."

Leo shrugged.

"You sent Podge down. What else could I do? I've always had to look out for the kid. And clean up his mess."

The kid. Podge Halligan, the steroid-swollen, heroin-dealing sadist who had raped Tommy Owens. Like George, sometimes you could mistake Leo for a human being. But the Halligans were all brothers in the blood, and however plausible an impression of enlightenment any might occasionally give, I guess each was just a version of the same savage when it came to it.

I extended the red boot to Leo, my hand low, and when he reached down for it, I sucker-punched him with a southpaw uppercut I must have been practicing in my dreams, and laid him out cold beneath the stars in the shadow of the old ruined church.

HE WASN'T OUT for long, although he didn't look too chipper when he came to: on top of the broken nose, he'd lost a couple of teeth. My nose had stopped bleeding, and I could see out of my eye; a drink would be a help. I found Leo's Glock where he'd dropped it but I wouldn't give it back to him, not yet, at any rate. We walked down to the car park, an uneasy truce between us, where lo and behold, Tommy Owens in his green snorkel coat was sitting on a wall by the Volvo, a cigarette in his hand, his ability to confound second to none.

"All friends now, I hope," he said. "Did you shake hands?"

Leaving Leo to tend his face, I walked Tommy to the edge of the pine forest.

"Did you know I was up there, Tommy?"

"I've been following you all night," Tommy said.

"Well. I'm glad to hear it. You know though, Tommy, when some boy threatens me with a knife, and then leads me up a hill at gunpoint, that's a good time to make your move. Especially when that boy is Leo Halligan."

"I knew you'd be able for him, Ed. Better to sort it out now than have it hanging over you. And I knew Leo'd play fair. Nice eye."

"Whose fucking side are you on?"

"Yours, Ed. And mine, of course."

"Tell me the truth then. How'd you know Leo was after me?"

"Father Tyrrell. Leo came to see him this morning. They had breakfast together. I reckoned it must have had something to do with whatever Tyrrell wanted to see you about."

That was what I had smelt in the presbytery: French cigarettes, not cigars, and Leo Halligan's lemon scent.

"What did Leo say to you?"

"Just, I have to straighten Loy out, Tommy. I'm not going to hurt him badly, because he'll come in useful. But I have to straighten him out."

"Why didn't you tell me that before I saw Tyrrell?"

"Because Leo didn't tell me until *after*, after he had scraped the RIP on the Volvo. I'll sort that out for you, by the way. So I followed Leo then, caught him staking out your place, texted you."

I said nothing. Tommy shrugged.

"You never asked for my help. You never leveled with me about the case. I mean, I'm not on salary here, am I Ed? Don't take me for granted here man, I'm looking out for you out of the goodness of my own . . . so don't fuckin' start, all right?"

Fair enough. Tommy still wasn't telling me everything he knew, but I couldn't expect miracles. I nodded, and walked quickly back to Leo, snapping the clip back into the Glock and sliding a round into the chamber as I went. When I got close enough, I fired in the general direction of Leo's precious red cowboy boots.

"Fuck sake, watch where you're pointing that thing!" Leo said.

"Very difficult to predict where the bullet will go at close range, as we all know," I said. "And the waiting time in A&E over Christmas is even worse than normal, might not make it home until New Year."

"So what do you want?" Leo said.

"Breakfast with Vincent Tyrrell," I said. "What was that about?"

"I got a tip-off. Last night. About Pa Hutton, Patrick Hutton. I called Tyrrell, he agreed to meet."

"Who tipped you off? And what did they say?"

"I don't know who it was, a woman, very southside, maybe even upper class, you know, Anglo type of thing. She didn't say who she was."

Miranda. Or Jackie.

"What did she say?"

"She said, 'You were there. In Tyrrellscourt. It's all going to come out now. The truth at last.' "

"Did she mention Patrick Hutton by name?"

Leo Halligan shook his head.

"She said, 'Ask Vincent Tyrrell. Vincent Tyrrell knows.'"

Leo's hand went in his jacket, and I brought the Glock up. He carefully took a pale blue pack of Gauloises and a brass Zippo from his jeans and lit a cigarette. He offered the pack around. I took one, and so did Tommy. Then Tommy found a naggin of Jameson in the depths of his snorkel coat, and we each had a drink. Silence reigned for a while, an almost contented calm. Perverse camaraderie in the middle of the night, flanked by a petty criminal and a stone killer on the top of Bayview Hill: I almost laughed at how good I suddenly felt, at the adrenaline surge that reminded me who I was, and why I did what I did, and all the while at the anger I could feel building, anger that was never very far below the surface.

"And how did you get Patrick Hutton out of that call?" I said to Leo.

"There was nothing else for me to get. Pa and me were friends, you know? We . . . we were good friends, yeah? So that was what Tyrrellscourt meant to me, above anything else."

"So you called Vincent Tyrrell."

"Me and Father Tyrrell go back. I told Father Tyrrell Patrick Hutton was coming back to haunt everyone who knew him."

"Why did you put it like that?"

"I thought it had a nice ring to it. I thought it might scare the cunt. Anyway, he asks me to meet him for breakfast, fuck sake, like we're a pair of suits, you know? And then he was all, oh, I can't tell you anything, the sanctity of the confessional, all this. So I said, I remember you, baby, back in St. Jude's Industrial School. I remember."

"What do you remember?"

Leo Halligan grinned.

"That's for me to know. That was it, end of."

"Do you know how he disappeared?"

"All I'll say is, you're not going to find the answers up here. To any of it. You're going to find them down in Tyrrellscourt."

He flashed his eyes at me, with the lubriciousness of someone who knows way more than he's telling.

"Anyway, coming out, I met Hopalong here, Mr. Fucking Sacristan, honest to fuck, I thought I was going to burst me shite laughing. So when he said Tyrrell had asked you down, I decided to stick around, added a little design feature to your car. I was gonna string it out awhile for you. You know, leave a dead cat on your doorstep, potshot through your living-room window. Just like a regular psycho. But it's too cold, and I couldn't be arsed, to be honest with you," Leo said.

"All because of Podge."

Leo shrugged.

"Did you know that, Tommy? Leo was after me because I helped get Podge sent away. You remember Podge, don't you Tommy?"

"No, Ed."

"Ah you do. Very well. Very very well, in fact."

"Stop, Ed."

"You know Tommy did a little work for Podge? A little courier work in the old import-export trade. And then they fell out, as fellows in that trade will. Over a gun. A Glock 17, in fact, this very model. And you know what Podge did to Tommy here?"

I could see the unease on Leo's face.

"He raped him, Leo. More than once, far as I could make out, although once would be enough for most of us. Did you know that? Or are they too scared to tell you just what kind of a maniac your kid brother is? It's not as if you don't really know."

Leo stared at the ground and shook his head. Maybe I imagined it, but I thought I saw shame in his face. I was probably wrong. I often imagine people are ashamed when they're just a little self-conscious, or indifferent, or plain bored. I could feel the anger rising like acid in my chest, singeing the back of my throat. Leo started to say something, very quietly. Then he cleared his throat and said it out loud.

"George didn't tell me that. But even if he had. Podge is my brother."

He looked up, his face a riot of opposing emotions: there was shame there, or at least embarrassment, and what looked like compassion for Tommy, but mostly there was defiance, the mark of the loyal blood code by which he lived. I had a certain respect for that. But I remembered Tommy after Podge had raped him, remembered the weeping shell of a man he became, and the anger within me erupted. Against my own best interests, against the interests of the case, against everything but the heat of the moment. I had my own blood code too, and sometimes I had to be true to it.

"Well, in every way it counts, Tommy's my brother, Leo," I said, and my hand was on the barrel of the Glock and I brought it up and smashed the butt against the bridge of Leo Halligan's nose, once, twice and again, just to make sure it was broken.

TEN

I offered to drive Leo to the A&E in St. Anthony's. He told me to fuck off, among other things, and made his way down the hill on foot. George Halligan lived on the other side of Castlehill, ten minutes' walk away. Tommy joined me on the trip to Jackie Tyrrell's house up among the pine forests off Tibradden Road. The M50 was quiet, and we made the journey in twenty silent minutes. The house, at the top of a gravel drive about half a mile above the road, was a Victorian Gothic detached redbrick-and-stone villa with stained-glass windows and a bell tower, set among bare oaks and elms; within view was the stone farmhouse with paddock and stables that served as the center of the riding school.

I asked Tommy if he wanted to come in. He said he'd wait in the car, "and keep an eye out." When I opened the car door, he put his hand briefly on my forearm, and went to say something and either couldn't form the words or thought the better of it, and looked me in the eye, and nodded: a Tommy Owens apology, or a Tommy Owens thank-you, or a conflation of the two.

"What's the story with Leo?" I said. "History there?"

Tommy flexed his narrow jaw and winced as if his teeth ached.

"It's nothing. I'll tell you about it later man."

"You've got to start acting in your own best interest, Tommy," I said, as sternly as I could. Tommy nodded gravely, but I could see he wasn't going to let it go.

"I could say the exact same for you man," he said finally.

The ensuing silence held for about ten seconds, and then we both burst out laughing.

The hall was of double height and featured the kind of Christmas tree you'd expect to find in some corporate HQ: maybe sixteen feet tall, it blazed with light amid the dark marble-floored room. The Brazilian servant (I always ask now: the Philippines and Brazil are the biggest suppliers of staff to the rich Irish, for reasons I don't pretend to understand: perhaps because they tend to be smaller, they don't have to be given rooms, but can sleep in cupboards or on shelves instead) led me up the stairs. I asked for a bathroom first, where I looked at the damage: an eye that was red and closing, and a bunch of welts and cuts across my face. I'd seen worse in the mirror. They'd be hilarious company tomorrow. I washed them with lavender-scented liquid soap and dabbed at them with towels soaked in hot water. The maid led me into a white reception room the size of the ground floor of my house; it didn't look particularly large in the context of Jackie Tyrrell's.

Jackie Tyrrell had changed into wide black silk trousers and a fitted black top with just enough cleavage and black lace on show to ensure I would pay attention. Good for her: a healthy dose of vanity was one of the vital signs of life, particularly in a woman. I joined her on a white couch with a weathered gilt wood finish that I recognized as being French and very expensive; there was a matching occasional table where she sat; the room was full of similar pieces in assorted configurations. Late Romantic orchestral music played through speakers I couldn't see.

Jackie knelt up on her knees beside me as I sat down. Her eyes were clearer than before, her manner softer, flirtier, almost kittenish; it was as if she had drunk herself, if not quite sober, then mellow.

"Your *face,* my God," she said.

"You should see the other girls'," I said.

"What happened?"

I shook my head.

"Lassie slaps. Handbags at ten paces," I said.

She looked at me for a moment, an appalled expression on her face, then agreed to see the funny side.

"Their *nails,* was it?" she said, in an effortless Dublin accent.

"Going for my eyes, they were."

"Fucking bitches. I *hate* those fucking bitches so I do."

She poured me a drink from a pitcher of iced liquid the color of tea; it had the warmth of tea but more of a kick.

"Sidecar," she said.

"Brandy, lemon juice . . . triple sec."

"Cointreau. Same difference. *Sláinte.*"

"Up."

I looked at Jackie as she drained the dregs of her glass and poured herself another. She couldn't drink like this every day, unless her face was a latex mask. I looked closer. No, it was the very moist, unlined skin of a woman in her early fifties: the folds around her throat showed the first signs of the next phase. Could Botox replenish your skin to such an extent if you regularly put away what she seemed capable of drinking? My face must have been an open book.

"This is a special occasion, Ed. I go for months without touching a drop. I assume that's what you're wondering? Why I don't have a face like a neon prune?"

"Forgive me."

"It's quite all right, I take the compliment whenever I can.

Always take the compliment, girls. I do like to drink though, so I'm being a bit of a glutton today. Tonight. This morning."

"Good morning," I said.

"Nice morning," she said.

I drank up, and she refilled my glass. The music changed: low, brooding, ominous phrases filled the room.

"I know this," I said. "*The Isle of the Dead.*"

"Rachmaninov. You're not supposed to like Rachmaninov, you know."

"Are you not? Who says?"

"The Musical Powers That Be."

"Yeah? Fuck *them.*"

"How do you know this? You're not secretly an expert cellist and a gourmet chef and a published poet and all those other things detectives are supposed to be while preferring not to go on about it?"

"No. But I was a barman."

"And like cabdrivers, barmen are in possession of absolute knowledge."

"No. I worked in an Irish pub in Santa Monica called Mother Magillacuddy's."

"Jesus."

"Well, I was young. Anyway, Irish music at the weekends, the rest of the time, we could play what we wanted. And there was a music student who worked there, a violinist. And this was one of her favorites. We used to blare it on a Monday night at all the people who didn't want to admit the weekend was over."

"I thought that was Sunday night."

"Amateurs want the weekend to keep going on Sunday. Monday is pros' night, real terminal cases. Hence *The Isle of the Dead . . .*"

"And this little violin case. Did you get anywhere with her? I bet you did. Tell all."

"You first. Fun and all as this is . . . you didn't by any chance call Leo Halligan on Saturday night, did you?"

"I wouldn't know how to go about calling Leo Halligan. I

thought he was in jail," she said, sounding indignant at the very suggestion.

"He's out of jail now. And you're not exactly a million miles removed from him. His brother was in the parade ring in Gowran Park today, you could easily have asked him for Leo's mobile."

"So don't get airs, missus."

"Something like that."

She raised her glass, as if to concede the point.

"Was F. X. Tyrrell there today?" I said.

"Of course. So everyone thinks he's taking it seriously, and not just a way of setting the odds adrift for Leopardstown. He and George Halligan were chatting. More than once, as it happens."

The music had become higher and more insistent, delirious almost, woodwinds and swirling strings. Jackie had an "ask me, go on, ask me" glint in her eye.

"What do you think that was about, Jackie?"

"*Well* . . . there was talk . . . a lot of talk, at the time . . . back when Patrick was racing for Frank—"

"You guys were still married then?"

"The wheels were coming off, but the train was still rolling. Anyway, there was talk about Patrick and Leo Halligan—"

"How they rode together. Miranda didn't really deny it either."

"Yes, but there was more to it. I mean, sexwise, you're gay, you're straight, you're somewhere in between, who cares? Miranda didn't, she was always playing games back then anyway, it wasn't as if she was a little girl whose heart was rent in twain. No, what it was about was, Leo Halligan—acting for George— bribing a whole bunch of jockeys of the day to . . . well, to anything from holding a horse up to doping horses and all points in between. And obviously Patrick's . . . special relationship with Leo put him center stage for all this."

"And what, the idea was that Leo was just fronting for George, that he was using Hutton to get the scoop on F. X. Tyrrell's horses?"

"That was one possibility. Another was that Patrick and Leo were working together, Patrick a willing and devious agent in it all."

"And then what, at Thurles, F. X. Tyrrell wanted By Your Leave held back, and Patrick was under orders to win, so he compromised by making it clear he was acting against his will?"

"That's what some people were whispering behind their fans."

"And not long after, he vanishes. Jesus!"

I involuntarily plunged my head into my hands. I had known Leo Halligan had a crucial role in this story, and all I had had to do was remain patient with him. After all, who required the most patience? Devious little sociopaths like the Halligan brothers. Now I find he could be the key to the whole thing. And how patient had I been with him? Patient enough to break his nose. Twice.

"Done something you shouldn't have?" Jackie Tyrrell grinned.

"Everything, all the time," I said. "Can you draw a line to connect F. X. Tyrrell and George Halligan?"

"Not back then. Now—I don't know. How respectable has Halligan become?"

"Very, if you go by appearances. But he's still a gangster, we think he's still moving big shipments of coke into the country. Is there any reason why F.X. would want to be involved with that business?"

"The gang business?"

"The illegal-drugs business."

"Not that I can think of. I mean, he has more money than he knows what to do with. A life in racing . . . if you stay in the saddle . . . is not without its compensations. As you can see."

"What about . . . Miranda said you had no children . . . were there any issues there? That might have led to an extortion opportunity?"

"Was Frank gay? Was I his beard? God, no. No, he . . . oh dear, I really would rather not talk about this. I don't think Frank was gay. I never saw any evidence of it. I suppose he just wasn't the most . . . demanding man. I mean, he simply didn't have much of an appetite for . . . 'that sort of thing' . . . and what we did have wasn't particularly . . . anything . . . for me, at any rate . . . and then that dwindled to nothing much. I suppose it sounds odd . . . but when you work as hard as we did, dawn till dusk . . . no, it still sounds odd. But I wasn't terribly experienced, and I mustn't have had much of a sex drive back then . . . we just . . . did without, by and large. It wasn't a good thing, it certainly didn't help when we began to drift apart. But Frank was very good about that, he set me up here, he paid all the bills. Very amicable, isn't that what they call it? Well, it was. How could it not be, really? There was no blood, no sex, no passion. That's what causes all the trouble. Isn't that right, Ed Loy?"

"I imagine you're right," I said. "I understand that to be the case. I wouldn't know, myself. So you weren't aware of any extortion attempts? Any way in which he could have been blackmailed by a gangster keen to beat the bookies? Not to mention launder vast sums of drug money through the Tyrrellscourt coffers?"

"No."

"What about Miranda? She told me she dropped out of sight after Patrick Hutton disappeared, went through what she called a few . . . 'situations'. You've been something of a mentor to her, haven't you, you persuaded her father to let her work at Tyrrellscourt in the early days, you offered her work up here when she resurfaced. What happened to her in between?"

Jackie shook her head.

"I don't know. I think she might have been in London. She didn't stay in touch. Her parents were dead, she had no living relatives . . . and I had left Tyrrellscourt, I was keeping my head down, working hard to make a go of this place . . . for a time, it seemed as if her disappearance and Patrick's might have been connected. And then she just reappeared, out there on that doorstep. She never really told me what had happened. I thought drugs, maybe a miscarriage, but that was all guesswork on my part. I was just happy to have her back, and if no questions asked was the deal, that's how it had to be. I've always . . . I love Miranda, like a daughter, you know? Like the daughter Frank and I never had. And with grown-up daughters . . . well, you've got to be careful. You've got to keep your distance."

"Leo Halligan . . . I didn't really get a lot out of him . . . but he said if I wanted to know what happened to Patrick Hutton, I wasn't going to find the answers up here, I'd have to go down to Tyrrellscourt," I said.

What happened then took me aback. Maybe because I had gotten to like Jackie Tyrrell, I had somehow forgotten she was involved in the case, and was therefore likely to have something to hide. Maybe it was because my judgment was skewed on account of the booze. Whatever it was, you're always waiting for the shutters to come down, but when they came down for Jackie, I couldn't quite believe it. She nodded, and inclined herself away, and did something tight with her lips that I hadn't seen before.

"I guess he meant, I'd have to talk to F. X. Tyrrell directly."

"You'll be lucky," she snapped. "Why would he talk to you? More likely to have you arrested for trespassing. Of course, there's someone there who'll be only too happy to fill your head full of whatever fairy stories pass for reality in her mind."

"Who would that be?"

"Regina Tyrrell."

"F.X.'s sister."

"That's right. She runs the hotel, and spa, and golf-course complex down there. And she runs Frank, if you're to believe her."

"Does anyone believe her? Did you?"

Jackie Tyrrell looked at me and there was smarting pain in her eyes, a vulnerability I hadn't seen before.

"Let's just say, the person who felt most amicable of all about my divorce from Frank was Regina."

Jackie stood up and brushed imaginary lint from her black clothes, all business.

"Wait here. I'll get you a photograph of Frank. And then I'll tell you a thing or two about Regina Tyrrell. You can listen to your little girlfriend's music again, if you like," she said, handing me a Bose remote control. "Point it anywhere."

I clicked the search button back until I located *The Isle of the Dead,* pressed Repeat to keep it coming, turned up the volume and sat back. That was how I awoke, having spilt tea-colored sidecar all over the white French couch. It took me a while to get my bearings, in fact to get my eyes open and myself upright and in focus. It was about half four, and there was no sign of Jackie Tyrrell, and no photographs. *The Isle of the Dead* was still playing; something I hadn't noticed before was that this recording had tolling bells on it; they added to the atmosphere. Was there a Rachmaninov piece called *The Bells?* I couldn't remember. I switched the music off and went out onto the landing, thinking I should check the bedrooms. Maybe Jackie'd just crashed out somewhere. She'd had more to drink than I had, which was saying something. On second thoughts, better not to creep around a strange house late at night; I didn't want to frighten anyone.

As I walked downstairs, I realized the bells I had heard on *The Isle of the Dead* were still tolling, even though the music had stopped. In the hall, by the left-hand corner behind the Christmas tree, I spied an open door and behind it what looked like a servants' passageway; the sound of the bells seemed to be coming from that direction. I went in and followed down a corridor of blue tiles and ocher walls to the stairwell of what was evidently the bell tower. Right on time, I saw a rope fly up like a slithering beast, and the bell toll again, and down on a rope to meet me came the body of Jackie Tyrrell, hanging by the neck, her legs frozen in a grotesque dance, her eyes bugging, her tongue cut out of her gaping mouth, blood staining her face and her chest. I tried to do something, and may have done it; what, I can't remember: cut her down, or hold her, or breathe life back into her, something that would help deny or assuage the horror of what I had just seen. I recall the impulse, but not the act, for between the two, I felt a blow, and I tumbled into shadow, and then came darkness.

PART II

CHRISTMAS

*Then Judas, which had betrayed him, when he
saw that he was condemned, repented himself,
and brought again the thirty pieces of silver to the
chief of priests and elders, saying, I have sinned
in that I have betrayed the innocent blood.*

And they said, What is that to us? see thou to that.

*And he cast down the pieces of silver in the temple,
and departed, and went and hanged himself.*

*And the chief priests took the silver pieces,
and said, It is not lawful for them to put into
the treasury, because it is the price of blood.*

—Matthew 27: 3–6

It was above all else a matter of taking the long view. He had hoped that things would come together sooner, that the investment he'd made in people who could be relied upon, or, failing that, leaned upon, would have brought him dividends before now. But he never let himself mistake slow progress for none, never for an instant wondered if perhaps he had been wasting his time, never succumbed to the worst sin of all: despair. Despair was for women and children and for men who were no better, and he had no time for it. Never had, never would. Say what you like about the Catholic Church—and he'd said more than enough in his time, and with good cause—it had given him an excellent grounding in his own personal insignificance, his utter abjectness. Faced with what had been repeatedly beaten into him—an infinitisimal prospect of redemption—he had cheerfully abandoned any efforts in that direction, adopting instead the serviceable motto: may as well be hung for a sheep as for a lamb. Ever after, nothing he had done had caused him more than a moment's remorse; no memory, however distressing in theory, had lingered much past the second drink. Sometimes, even he thought his mind should have been a shade more troubled. But it wasn't. And there was nothing you could do about your mind, was there?

ELEVEN

*I tossed and turned on a bed of straw, and the rustle roared in my ears
like the sound of the sea from a conch; I was awake but felt asleep, or
asleep and dreamed of waking; a door creaked, and the bolt shot back and
forth, and then a sound of doors swinging back and forth, crashing like
gunfire, and then the bolt run back, the door held fast, creaking, and the
rustle of straw again, rustle rustle, and then human voices soft, like straw,
no, like paper, whispering, entreating, yielding, the slightest breaths rus-
tling like paper, and the color of paper, white, a blinding white, the sound
so crisp in my ears . . .*

I was in a daze when I came to, and even by the time I got to
Harcourt Square it was clear I was in no fit state to be questioned,
so after a great deal of swabbing and scraping and photographing,
I was shunted into a cell and left to sleep off the roil of shock and
fear and drunkenness that clung to me like muck sweat to a frightened animal. I didn't think I could sleep after what I had seen,

but in fact no sooner had my head hit the hard bunk than I fell into a coma that was interrupted what could have been no more than a couple of hours later by a Guard pushing in a beaker of hot liquid that might have been tea or coffee and could be still for all I know and a toasted waffle clogged with chemical-smelling jam that almost made me throw up as soon as I smelled it, and then, as I kept on smelling it, did. I was on my knees, vomiting steak frîtes and red wine and whiskey and gin and brandy and lemon juice into a metal toilet with no seat that stank of pine detergent and someone else's piss so that each time I threw up, the air I sucked into my winded lungs was so foul I immediately began to retch again. Eventually, this too passed, and I sat on my bunk, bent over and humming a tuneless drone to myself and trying to reconstruct what had happened between the time I saw the hanging body of Jackie Tyrrell and now.

I'd been out cold, that much I knew; I could feel the hot, tender egg that had been grafted onto the back of my head; the gentlest pressure on it sent my belly lurching out of my mouth. My hands were streaked with mud, or rust, and there were reddish-brown stains on my shirt and streaks on my trousers and on my shoes; it came to me that I was covered in blood, and that that blood could only be Jackie Tyrrell's. I flushed red-hot then, and tears sprang into my eyes, and I jammed my fist into my mouth to stop myself yelling. If only my head wasn't pounding so hard, I could think clearly about what had happened. The only thing I could summon up was music, *The Isle of the Dead,* its insistent rhythm rolling through my head, and then the bells, the tolling of a bell, and then I flashed on upsetting the sidecar over myself and Jackie Tyrrell's good white couch, and I smelt my shirt and licked my hand and tasted brandy and felt the sweetest of relief and an obscene prayer on my lips: Thanks be to fuck. I knew I was badly in need of a cure, but I didn't think I would get one so soon.

Superintendent Myles Geraghty had found someone to press

his brown suit, and someone else to cut his unruly thatch of salt-and-pepper hair, but his gut was still poking out between the flaps of his yellow shirt, if perhaps not quite as far as it had, and his tie looked like he'd eaten his breakfast off it. He seemed in excellent form, which didn't fill me with reassurance. I had sat in the interview room in silence while a uniformed female Garda got the video camera ready; now Geraghty was here, and silence was no more.

"Ah, the hard! Good to see you again Edward Loy, and the compliments of the season to you, and tell us this: how's the old private dick, ha? Getting out and about, and in and out, is it? Are you winning, are you? Pulling the divil by the tail says you, ha? Pull the other one, it's got bells on!"

There was no reply needed to any of that, so I didn't make one. Geraghty took a long shrewd look at me, all faux bonhomie gone, and I met this full-on. He had a good poker face, a mask that meant he could play the fool but was very far from being one. It was impossible to tell what he had on me, but given the circumstances in which he'd found me, I'd be feeling pretty bullish if I were him.

Geraghty nodded to get the tape rolling, and sat down across the table from me and asked me my name and I said, "Solicitor."

"D'you get that changed, by deed poll? Or did you get married, and take the little woman's name?"

"Solicitor," I said again.

Geraghty made a face.

"Jasus, you could be out of here by lunchtime if you just answer the few questions."

I made a face at that, my "d'you think I cycled up the Liffey on a bicycle?" face. Geraghty nodded at the uniform, who turned off the tape while he bounded from the room, returning a few seconds later with a tabloid newspaper, which he handed to me. It was folded to the crossword, which had been half completed in a laborious hand.

"Six down, 'Clown, foolish person,' seven letters, begins with *B* . . . Buffoon?"

"Front page, please," a smiling Myles Geraghty said with the oily poise of a backbench politician at long last elevated to office.

The front page of the *Irish Daily Star* said, OMEGA MAN SLAYS TWO—SERIAL KILLER ON THE LOOSE, and showed a blurred photograph of a much younger, slimmer Don Kennedy in a Garda uniform. Inside there were photographs of the two crime scenes with technical officers in protective white suits going about their work, and an inset shot of a Myles Geraghty dark of hair and hollow of cheek, as he'd maybe looked the day he made his confirmation, who was "heading up the investigation." There was talk of "the killer the Guards are calling the Omega Man because of the macabre way his victims are mutilated," but no further detail about Hutton's tattoo, and a lot more high-energy ventilating of not very much information. The severed tongues didn't get a mention, nor had Patrick Hutton been identified yet.

"Very good," I said. "Congratulations, that's quite a case you've got."

"I assume you were working a case. That's what you were doing up in Mrs. Tyrrell's house."

I nodded.

"I think we can help each other, don't you?"

"Well, I believe in helping the Guards. That would be something of a motto of mine. Of course, you don't want to blunder in and get in their way. Stand well back until invited."

Geraghty looked around at the uniform, and signaled to her. She went to put the camera back on, but he shook his head and pointed to the door. When she had gone, he turned back to me, a grin on his face.

"Well, here's your invitation. Last time you and I met, I probably went a bit hard on you. Don't know me own strength sometimes, and you'd just lost your girlfriend, and your mother, couldn't have been easy. And I know at times like that, it's not easy to forgive someone who crosses you. But fair play, you got the results that time . . . and we all saw what you did on the Howard case. I mean, I know you got a lot of stick about it in the papers, with the commissioner having a pop, and the Garda Representative Association advising its membership not to cooperate with private detectives in general and you in particular, but for officers who'd been around the block, I'm telling you, it was a beautiful piece of work. Not just the Howards themselves, what a fucking collection, but Brock and Moon and the Reillys, kaput! And no fucking trials to worry about—"

"I never—"

"I know you never, that was what was so beautiful, you got them to do it themselves. Last man standing, Ed Loy. Jasus, in here we talked about nothing else for weeks, we were drawing diagrams to keep it all clear: Dublin mountains, Fitzwilliam Square, Shelbourne Road, he's off again!"

Despite myself, I was a little flattered. A case usually ended with justice of a sort, but with most of the survivors' lives in tatters; very rarely was anyone in the mood to offer thanks, let alone praise. Myles Geraghty might have been a buffoon, but he was a senior policeman, and if what he had said was a quarter true, well, the respect of your peers is always something. Then, just in time, my brain came to, and I began to see where this was going, mere seconds before Geraghty leant in and spelled it out for me.

"And we all felt the credit should have gone where it was due, instead of to people who, if we're to be scrupulously fair, did not deserve it. Now I know he's a friend of yours, and fair play, loyalty is what I look for in my officers too, I don't expect you to tell tales out of school, but the least we should acknowledge is that you're the man, Ed Loy. You and Lee Harvey Oswald both: ye acted alone, ha?"

I nodded, understanding what the game was. It looked like Dave had good reason for his fears: Geraghty was clearly out to undermine him. Geraghty took my nod as an assent, and continued.

"Good man. Because here's the thing: I don't believe you had anything to do with Jackie Tyrrell's murder up above. I want to hear what you were doing there, sure I do, down to the last detail, but I know there's no reason for you to kill her. And even if there was, you wouldn't have . . . all the other stuff."

"What other stuff?" I said.

"You first," Geraghty said. When I stayed silent, he went on.

"Because of course, I have enough to keep you here all day, and maybe charge you and all, keep you in over Christmas, even if we drop the charges then. A lovers' tiff, a drunken spat, private detective and a rich divorcée—who do you think's going to give a shite? So if you want to get out and get back to your case, you better let me know what's going on."

"What do you mean?"

"You and Donnelly, what are ye cooking up? What's he been telling you?"

"Nothing, what?"

"He was at your house last night. He was seen leaving."

"What, are you having him followed?"

"He was just . . . an off-duty officer spotted him, happened to be going the same way, saw him entering your house."

I waited to see what more there was. If there'd been a tail on Dave, if they'd followed us to the mortuary . . . no, they'd've stepped in then and there. Wouldn't they? Maybe they'd arrested Dave last night, after he left my house the second time. Maybe they were questioning him alongside me.

And if they were? What was I going to do, grass him up?

"I'll tell you about the case I'm working. Dave Donnelly's visit was . . . a personal matter."

Geraghty flinched as if I'd slapped him; his tiny eyes flared up.

"What's that supposed to mean?"

"I mean, it was a private matter. Between two old friends. You know, there's something on your mind, you drop around a friend's house, ask his advice. Trouble with your neighbors, or your kids. Or your wife. Type of thing. And of course, to make sure I'd be at the party he's throwing tonight. He said Carmel really wanted me to be there."

Geraghty was sucking his teeth and his nostrils were flaring; when I said the word *wife* I thought I saw him flush; by the time I mentioned Carmel, he was nodding briskly, as if this were a file whose contents he had already read.

"Better take me through the case you're working then," he said quickly, reaching to switch the video camera back on and not meeting my eye the while.

I told him about Father Vincent Tyrrell asking me to find Patrick Hutton. There was no reaction from him to this, which I took to mean that they still hadn't identified the body. I told him about Miranda Hart and Jackie Tyrrell, about the meal at the Octagon with Seán Proby, about getting a late call from Jackie Tyrrell, about the ten-year-old controversy surrounding F. X. Tyrrell's Gold Cup–winning horse By Your Leave and the race meeting at Thurles where the horse met her death. There wasn't a single thing I said that couldn't have been discovered with an Internet connection and, possibly, five minutes' chat with a racing journalist, or failing that, with one of the standing army of punters all over the city who divided their time between pub, bookie's and social welfare office, with the exception of the late-night drink with Jackie Tyrrell. Once he had established that Jackie had called to invite me over, and I had assured him that our conversation was largely about Jackie's anxiety that Miranda not be hurt in the process of finding Patrick Hutton, he was nodding as if our business was done.

"And were Mrs. Tyrrell's anxieties really enough to get you driving into the mountains in the middle of the night?"

"Well, I hoped I'd get more from her than anxiety, hoped she had something to tell me about Hutton's disappearance, something nobody knew but her. I hoped in vain."

When I'd finished, Geraghty looked at his watch, snapped the tape player off and stood up.

"As I say, Loy, we don't think you're in the frame for Mrs. Tyrrell. I've got an important case. You're free to go. Just make sure you're available for further questioning . . . and watch your step, am I clear?"

"I think so," I said.

But Myles Geraghty was far from clear, and as I walked down Harcourt Street to Stephen's Green and into the thick of the last hurling wave of Christmas shoppers in the icy morning, I set to wondering why. Geraghty had hoped to flatter me into dishing the dirt on Dave, but as soon as I suggested Dave was concerned about his wife, he backed off so quickly he was practically helping my coat onto me to get me out the door. Did he have a crush on her? There couldn't be anything going on between them, that was inconceivable, Carmel'd never have an affair, full stop. Still, Dave had not looked happy the other night, and he was a tough old bastard; maybe a few hard chaws in the Bureau were giving him a hard time, but all that "anonymous phone call, loaded gun" malarkey, it may have been happening, but I couldn't see it getting to him like that. You never really knew what went on in someone else's marriage, no matter how well you thought you knew them. And you were better off that way, as far as I was concerned.

When I got to the taxi rank on the Green, I texted Dave and asked him to call me when he could. There was a message on my phone from Tommy Owens:

Took the car before the cops arrived. Call me when you're out. T

I called him, and he told me he had ten mass in Bayview to get through, and that after that, we were taking a trip down to Tyrrellscourt. He told me why, and I told him he could drive.

But first, I needed to see a priest.

TWELVE

I took the Dart out to Bayview: it was as quick as a cab, and a lot cheaper, and the direction I was going, no one else was: the northbound trains were jammed with last-minute shoppers heading for the city center. The railway line hugged the coast; the bay sparkled cobalt in the bright winter light. I ran through the case in my mind. The only people who knew the man on the dump was Hutton, apart from his killer or killers, were me and Dave. But Geraghty would make the face soon enough, or someone on his team would; no more than the rest of us, Guards were desperate men for the ponies.

It was a little after ten when I got to Bayview. I bought the rest of the papers and had breakfast in a café off the main street. All the tabloids led on what they had been instructed to call the OMEGA MAN, and the broadsheets too, apart, inevitably, from the *Irish Times,* which preferred an EU directive on the regulation of wind farms and a Christmas Eve message of peace and goodwill from the Irish president for its leads. There was little new in any of the stories; Myles Geraghty's picture was ubiquitous in all; maybe he was employing his own publicist. When Dave's number came up on my phone, I stepped out onto the street to answer.

"Dave, what's shaking?"

Before he'd talk, I had to give him a full report on what I knew of Jackie Tyrrell's murder, and on my time with Myles Geraghty in Harcourt Square, the latter severely edited to omit any mention of Carmel, or of Geraghty's grudge against Dave.

"Makes sense Geraghty didn't waste his time with you, even for sport. The State Pathologist's reports are nearly done. Word is, Kennedy had a crucifix and an omega symbol carved into his back, at the base of his spine. And one of the boys on the scene up in Tibradden, one who's loyal to me, gave me more on Jackie Tyrrell: she was hanged, and her tongue was cut out, but she also had an amateur tattoo, the same kind as Hutton and Kennedy: a crucifix and an omega."

"So Geraghty's right, this is a serial killer."

"It looks like. Both Don Kennedy and Jackie Tyrrell had links to Patrick Hutton. Now they still haven't identified Hutton."

I thought about that. The Guards were better placed to conduct a murder investigation than I was, especially one on this scale. Keeping information from them didn't sit easily with me, particularly if that endangered people in Hutton's circle. In the end it was Dave's call.

"Strictly speaking, neither did we, Dave. We think it's Hutton, but jockeys look a lot alike. I say we keep it that way for now. We don't know what the killer wants. I'm heading down to Tyrrells-court today. I think whatever this is about, it has its roots down there. But look, if you want to tell Geraghty who you suspect it might be . . ."

There was pause during which Dave digested that one. He sounded like he was chewing on a twig.

"We'll play it our way for now," Dave said gruffly. "I have enough friends at court to keep the information coming, so I'll get it to you as I hear it. You might like to let your lady friend know what's happening though. I hear they questioned all the employees up at Tibradden this morning, then let them go. They start first thing up there."

"Will do."

"And Ed, listen, about last night, in the house . . . you know—"

"It was very cold, wasn't it? Did you find that?"

"I made a bit of a mountain out of a molehill."

"And now you have to live on top of it. You'll need a hat. Maybe even a scarf."

"Thank you."

"Thank *you*."

"Leo was connected to Hutton. You don't figure him for the murders, do you? Now he's out, revenge type of thing."

"Not if one of the dead is Hutton himself. They were friends, maybe more than friends."

"But—"

"Look, Dave, I'm a private detective. I find missing persons. Solving murders, that's just not my job. What you want to do with murder, you want to get the Guards in."

MIRANDA HART WAS distraught.

"I can't believe it. Who would want to murder Jackie?"

"She said you were like a daughter to her."

"And she was like a mother to me. Oh Jesus, Ed—"

"Miranda, are you at home?"

"Yes. I'm not long here, I was up in Tibradden, but everything's canceled for the day."

"I want you to pack a bag and get out here. In fact, I'll have you collected."

"Why?"

"Because I don't think you're safe. Jackie Tyrrell is not the only one dead—"

"What, is this the Omega Man that was in the papers? Who else is dead? Patrick? Have they found Patrick? Is he one of the bodies out in Roundwood?"

"They don't know. But the deaths seem to be connected . . . look, I'm sending someone for you. We'll talk soon. Okay?"

"Okay."

I FOUND TOMMY in the sacristy, brought him up to date with the case, gave him Miranda Hart's address and asked him to pick her up. Before he left, I checked over some recent church history with him.

Father Vincent Tyrrell was sitting at his table with a fountain pen and a lined pad in front of him and a cigarette in his hand, exhaling two blue plumes of smoke into space, or at *The Taking of Christ,* which was directly ahead of him. I had knocked on the presbytery door and it gave against my fist. I announced myself and he told me to shut the door behind me. He sounded like he wished he had done that in the first place, and turned the key. He didn't look at me when I joined him at the table.

"Of course, Judas had his part to play," he said. "Had he not betrayed our Lord, who would have? And if Jesus had not been betrayed, maybe He would never have been taken. And who would have died for our sins then? Who would have been our redemption?"

"Peter did betray him. I'm sure others would have as well. Seems to me there was quite a queue. When powerful people want someone dead, they generally get their way."

"That is true. Maybe too much is made of Judas, and his blood price. Maybe we're falling for the great-man theory of history."

"I heard that was back in vogue."

"Maybe it is. I don't keep up. It's better not to. Stay where you are, and everything comes back to meet you. Provided you wait long enough.'"

"This all sounds to me like an Easter sermon, not a Christmas one."

"You're right, of course. Incarnation, not redemption. The beginning, not the end."

"On the other hand, we know that the last words Patrick Hutton had to say to anyone—to anyone who's prepared to talk—were something like, 'They won't make me play the Judas.'"

Tyrrell brought his steely-blue eyes around to meet me. A faintly appalled smile played around his tiny mouth, as if he had just learnt afresh what fools these mortals be.

"That would have been Miss Miranda Hart who told you that."

"Yes. But you could have told me that without violating the secrecy of the confessional. You could have told me you visited her that night—after you'd heard Patrick Hutton's confession—and insulted her, impugned her character and generally scared the living daylights out of her. You could tell me about it now."

"Could she not recall in detail what I told her?" Tyrrell said, as if astonished that his words hadn't seared themselves verbatim on Miranda's brain. "Well, I don't think I can remember either. I may have spoken abruptly—as I remember it, I may have held her responsible for . . . well, for some of Patrick's . . . misfortune. No doubt I was harsh. I believe the young lady . . . gave as good as she got, that night. I was sent from the house with a flea in my ear."

"Of course, you knew her before, didn't you? You knew Patrick before. And Leo Halligan, your breakfast companion of yesterday morning."

Tyrrell smiled in what almost looked like delight.

"Well, I must say I feel vindicated in my choice of sleuth; nothing seems to have slipped past you yet. Am I to take it from the marks on your face that you managed to rendezvous with the unfortunate Leo?"

"You are. And the unfortunate Leo told me to ask you about

your years at St. Jude's Industrial School. See I thought he must have got that wrong. I thought you were here all along. But I checked it out with Tommy, and he said no, you'd gone down there for a few years. How did that happen? Did you run into a little trouble up here?"

"Nothing of the sort," Tyrrell said, his cheek beginning to pulse. "I went down to Tyrrellscourt, I . . . it was at the request of Francis . . . my brother . . . he wanted masses said in the house regularly, more often than the local priests could manage, or were willing to, and the archbishop at that time was a great racing man, he was reared not far from Tyrrellscourt, and he arranged it that I could serve there, and that if and when things changed, I would find a place again in Bayview."

My bewilderment must have been obvious.

"It's not unusual at a racing stables where there's a good number of staff for the local priest to come and say mass before big meetings, and bless the horses, and so on. Or at least, it wasn't. And Francis went through a phase of taking this very seriously indeed, and wanted . . . no exaggeration to say, he wanted his own priest. And for a time, he got one."

"This was before you two fell out."

"Yes, this was . . . this would have appealed to me. I was wearying of parish work, of the pastoral round of wayward youths and despairing women and their shiftless husbands. It had . . . I suppose it had another kind of pastoral appeal, that of paradise regained. The childhood we had shared, among horses, always horses. I missed the horses most of all."

"And when would this have been?"

"Much of the nineties: 1990 until '98, I'd say."

"You were there for the By Your Leave episode then, you were at Tyrrellscourt when Patrick Hutton vanished."

"Oh yes."

"But I thought Patrick Hutton came here, made his confession here."

"I never said that. I said he made his confession to me. But he made it in the chapel at Tyrrellscourt."

"All right then. Tell me about St. Jude's Industrial School."

Again the muscles in Vincent Tyrrell's face quivered, again he brought them under his control, all apart from a rogue eyebrow that continued to pulse like an insect caught on a pin.

"It was no longer an industrial school, that's the first canard to shoot down. It had been, well into the eighties, under the Christian Brothers, and a number of . . . incidents took place there, many of which have now been dealt with by the Residential Schools Redress Board. St. Jude's closed for a short while, and reopened in the nineties as a boys' home, under the joint auspices of the departments of education, health, and social welfare. The Church played no official role there; indeed it was no longer actually called St. Jude's, although that's how everyone in the locality referred to it; as a local priest, I paid the occasional pastoral visit, at the center's request."

Industrial schools had become part of the folklore of what might be called the secret history of Ireland, which had only in the past twenty years or so begun to be told: unruly, unmanageable children, or simply those whose parents were unable to cope, whether psychologically or financially, were effectively detained in schools controlled by a variety of religious orders who subjected their charges to a catalog of abuses, ranging from the basic contempt and casual disregard that was the lot of the poor anywhere in Ireland in those days, to physical beatings and psychological torture, all the way up to continual and brutal sexual abuse. The religious involved were not all equally culpable, and many had been raised in similarly harsh conditions, but it is impossible to find excuses even for those who claim they knew nothing of what went on; that said, it was a social and a national scandal as much it was a church affair: we were very happy to have someone else to look after the losers and misfits, the weak and the halt, happy to close our eyes and ears to the tales they told, to dismiss them as the hysterical and obscene ravings of a negligible class of people.

"Leo Halligan certainly suggested there was more to it than that."

"Leo would. Leo has an eye to the main chance. As soon as Leo saw there was money to be made in compensation from abusive clerics, Leo counted up the number of priests he had met in his life and multiplied it by a thousand."

"But you knew Patrick Hutton there too."

"I met Patrick there, and then he came across to Tyrrellscourt as an apprentice, the pair of them did."

"Miranda Hart told me F.X. made a point of taking boys from St. Jude's on as apprentices. Did he rely on you to choose them?"

"Not in every circumstance. But I recommended Patrick and Leo, yes."

"And would you have been aware of the relationship between them?"

"I was aware that they were friends. What you're suggesting—"

"That they were lovers."

"Yes. I don't believe any such . . . nothing like that. Really."

Vincent Tyrrell looked appalled at the very notion of homosexuality, or at least, he wanted me to believe he was. He shook his head, looked at his watch and lifted up his pad.

"Blank page, Edward Loy. If I can't have it finished, I like at least to break the back of the damn thing by lunchtime. Otherwise it's a joyless meal, and no wine either."

"I wanted to ask you about Regina. Your sister."

"I know who Regina is. What about her?"

"Are you close? Is she close to F.X.? Where does she fit in the family?"

Vincent Tyrrell's face reddened. He stood up and started to shout.

"Why on earth should I answer that? I didn't pay you to . . .

who the hell do you think . . . What gives you the right to ask all these questions?"

I stood up now. The days when I sat in my seat while an angry priest shouted at me were done.

"You did. I don't know what you intended. Maybe you don't know yourself. Maybe you wanted Patrick Hutton to remain a mystery. Maybe you wanted me to throw a scare into Miranda Hart. Maybe it has something to do with Leo Halligan, something neither of you is willing to tell me, and you hoped I could somehow brush it under the carpet for you both. But it's too late now. You see, you didn't ask me to find Patrick Hutton. You didn't ask me, in the event Hutton was dead, to locate his killers. You just told me his name. And you paid me. Way too much, as it happens. And now I can't stop until I know the truth. Maybe you thought you were clever just giving me a man's name. But it looks like it's enough to build an entire world around. And I won't stop until that's what I've done."

Vincent Tyrrell had retreated behind the supercilious smile that had served him so well, the smile that didn't know whether to mock or pity the rest of humanity. I wanted to wipe that smile off his face.

"You know your former sister-in-law was murdered this morning? And nobody thought to ring you, not your brother, nor your sister, not the Guards, nobody. You charged me with having a footfall too light upon the earth for comfort. Well, it takes one to know one, Vincent Tyrrell. You have no one belonging to you who cares enough to tell you one of your family is dead. How did that happen?"

I don't know how I thought I'd feel when I succeeded in wiping the smile off his face. Not very good would have been my guess, to reduce an old man dying of cancer to a pale, twitching frame of flesh and bone. I made a gesture with my hands, something approaching an apology but not going all the way, and made for the door.

"Maybe I shouldn't have been so hard on Miranda Hart. But it would have been impossible to tell the child the truth," Tyrrell said.

I opened the door. Father Vincent Tyrrell stopped me with what he said next.

"By Your Leave was an experiment. Very unusual. Something of a freak, you know. If you get to talk to Francis face-to-face, ask him what he thought he was doing. If you don't, ask someone who knows about close breeding."

Tyrrell was standing behind me now; I felt his breath on my collar, and then he tugged my arm with his claw of a hand and spun me round to face him. He was smiling again, a gleeful, more than half-mad smile I wanted to look away from but couldn't.

"By Your Leave. That is all you know on earth, and all ye need to know," he said. And then Father Vincent Tyrrell kissed me on the mouth.

THIRTEEN

Back in Quarry Fields, I showered, shaved and changed into a fresh white shirt and a clean black suit. I had fallen into dressing like this when I arrived back in Dublin but my luggage did not; I was dressed for a funeral and, once I'd taken off my tie, I found no great reason to dress any differently afterward. Occasionally I felt a little overdressed, but that was rare in the city of suits Dublin had become; mostly it suited my purposes, whether to curry favor with a headwaiter or at a reception desk, or to impress a client, or simply to remind myself in the hours when I was flagging to keep my shoulders back and my head held high. I looked at my face in the mirror: it was drawn and sallow, but something in the eyes was different; the ghosts of the past had lifted, and there was light instead of darkness; for the first time that I could remember, as I heard the front door slam and the creak of floorboards below, I had a glimmer of a future, by which

I meant a woman. The fact that the woman bore an uncanny re-semblance to my ex-wife was a detail that appeared lost on me.

In the kitchen, Tommy Owens was making tea. He greeted me with a shake of the head and a look of appalled fascination, as if to say he'd seen some gobshites in his time but I could be their king. I didn't much care though, as Miranda Hart was by then in my arms, her tears wetting my cheeks, holding me as if she'd never let me go; what was Tommy next to that?

"Is Patrick dead? Is he one of the bodies they found?" she said.

Tommy looked at me keenly.

"I think so," I said. "I can't be sure."

She was shivering, in coat and scarf with her gloves still on.

"We need to talk, Ed," Tommy said.

"Let's talk then," I said. "If we're going down to Tyrrellscourt, Miranda can help us: she knows the place inside out. There's nothing to say she can't hear."

Tommy and Miranda exchanged glances, and I got the im-pression that Tommy had already had a go at her on the journey here.

"Ask her about Leo Halligan," Tommy said. "The phone call."

I shook my head.

"What's up, Ed?" Tommy said. "Gauze on the lens, is there?"

Miranda Hart understood immediately what was happening.

"Ask away, I've nothing to hide. I don't need kid gloves," she said to Tommy.

"Did you ring Leo Halligan on Saturday night?" he said.

"I didn't even know he was out of jail," she said.

"But you'd've had his number," Tommy said.

"I used to have his number, years ago. That was another life, as far as I was concerned, until—"

"Until what?" Tommy snapped.

"Until Ed came around yesterday asking questions about Pat-rick, about the Tyrrells, about the whole bloody thing. And now there are these dead bodies . . ."

"One of them is Don Kennedy, the private detective you hired to find Patrick two years back."

Miranda Hart shook her head.

"And Patrick, and now Jackie . . . good Jesus, what's happening?"

"That's what we need to find out."

"Someone—a woman with a posh accent—called Leo and told him that the story of Tyrrellscourt was about to blow, and that Vincent Tyrrell knew the full story," Tommy said.

"Do you want me to draw you a fucking map? That wasn't me," Miranda said to Tommy.

"Maybe it was Regina Tyrrell," I said.

"Regina Tyrrell doesn't have that kind of accent," she said in that crisp, faux-objective way women take care to use when slighting one another.

"What kind of accent does she have?" I said.

"Oh, you'll find out. You'll find out soon enough."

She colored after she'd said this, and looked down, and I wondered again what had passed between her and Tommy.

"Tommy followed a car that left Jackie Tyrrell's house last night," I said. "The bells had begun to toll, and the car screeched out from the stables, an old Land Rover with UK plates. Tommy followed down the N81 past Blessington and then west toward Tyrrellscourt. He lost it somewhere in the approaches to the village."

"We hadn't reached the stables," Tommy said, shamefaced still that he had lost the car. "By the time I got to the entrance, there was no sign of the Land Rover."

"Derek Rowan was head man at Tyrrellscourt ten years ago. He always used import secondhand Land Rovers from England," Miranda said. "I don't know if he's still there. If it's not him, it may be his son, Brian; Derek was training him up."

Miranda Hart's tea bag was beside her cup; she had been smoking, with her gloves still on; Tommy looked on in disgust as she doused her cigarette in the tea bag and dunked the lot in her half-empty cup.

"We'd better get moving," I said. "Christmas Eve. No one will want to talk to us if we don't get down there soon."

"No one will be in a fit state to talk to us," Tommy said.

I began to talk Miranda through the eccentricities of my heating system when Tommy interrupted me.

"Ed, if your one is really under threat, your gaff is not the place to be. The killer knows you're on the case, knocked you unconscious last night; if he's looking for her, your house is going to be the first place he comes."

"You're right. We'll find a hotel—"

"She can stay at my place," Tommy said. "Plenty of room, nobody there, quiet road."

And with instructions not to answer the door to anyone, and an unconcerned look around at what a not very apologetic Tommy accurately described as "the state of the place," she stayed there.

Before we hit the road, Tommy retreated to the car to let us say good-bye. And after we'd kissed, Miranda Hart said, "Please, Ed, promise me, you'll try and understand . . . no matter what you hear."

And I promised to try.

WE TOOK THE Tallaght exit off the M50 and kept on the bypass until it became the Blessington Road; the hills were white on all sides while the low December sun scorched our eyes; skeletons of forests changed places with service stations and new building developments until we cut off west toward Tyrrellscourt through the open plains of Kildare.

Tyrrellscourt had long been associated with F. X. Tyrrell and his prodigious stable of prizewinning racehorses, and with the Tyrrellscourt stud, the jewel in the crown of the Irish bloodstock industry. More recently, the Tyrrellscourt Country Club, a luxury hotel with golf course, leisure center, gymnasium and spa, had opened, with elaborate fanfare in the press; apartments with life membership of the club were made available at prices in excess of seven figures; all had been snapped up the day they were released. Celebrities flocked to celebrate their weddings there, and an EU gathering of some description had reached its climax with the assorted heads of state stomping around the Tyrrellscourt fairways in a variety of garish leisure wear.

The third thing Tyrrellscourt had become famous for, quite at odds with the first two, was the number of people who went there to disappear. The guitarist of an obscure late sixties English rock band, part of the Canterbury scene, hadn't been seen since, following the breakup of the group, he got on a train at Victoria Station, headed for Brighton; thirty-five years later, following sightings all over the globe and a persistent rumor that he was now an obscure novelist nobody knew anything about either, an English music magazine tracked him down to Tyrrellscourt, where he had been living with his Dutch wife running a candle-making business. The group subsequently re-formed and made quite a lot of money before breaking up for roughly the same reason they had in the first place: because they couldn't stand one another. But this aspect of Tyrrellscourt, its ability to give shelter and succor to a variety of misfits and n'er-do-wells of one kind or another who couldn't cut it in the new thrusting entre-preneurial Ireland, or simply refused to play by the new rules of the game, was particularly vivid given that the shiny happy face of the country club was so often used as a brochure to advertise the extent of the Irish success story. It was a script that could have been designed with Tommy Owens in mind; in fact, it turned out he'd been disappearing down here for years. Maybe they'd been running a bus from Hennessy's bar.

"I won't go on about the country club, except to say they got the fuckin' name right, and the stables is what it is, yeah, but if you want to know what Tyrrellscourt's about, then McGold-rick's is the place to go," Tommy said. "There are others places, Sheehy's and the Big Tree, but McGoldrick's has the best mix. And that's the point, the mix, know I mean? Up in the country club they're all prancing around in their Pringle and Lacoste like the cunts they are, a fucking kindergarten for the nouveau riche whose mammies won't let them play outdoors. And the horsey fuckers have work to do, fair enough, they're at the gallops and so on, and they have a couple of older restaurants they go to, salmon *en croûte* and Black Forest gateau they're serving, like a fucking geezer theme park, sixties cuisine for the hundred Irish cunts who've been rich since then. But everyone passes through McGoldrick's, not just the people I know: all the jockeys come there, and they're fucking mental bastards. And even middle-class people want some action after a week of golf and spa treatments and Chardonnay. Because everyone knows if you need something extracurricular, McGoldrick's the place to go."

"When you say all the jockeys go there—"

"When they can, when they're not in training, or wasting; they get a night out, they go mad."

"So there'd be boys who knew Patrick Hutton?"

"Chances are. Boys who'd say they knew him. Anyone riding in Leopardstown probably won't be there. But you never know, they do what they please, jockeys."

"Tommy, what happened between you and Miranda?"

"What do you mean, Ed?"

"I'm saying, fair enough to ask her about the call to Leo, but there was a real edge between you two. Why?"

Tommy grimaced.

"I'll tell you over a drink."

"Why can't you tell me now?"

"Because you're not going to like it. And when you don't like something, you do better with a drink in your hand."

I pressed him a little further, and when we reached a set of traffic lights, he turned to me and said pretty much the worst thing Tommy could say about anyone.

"Ed, I *know* her."

THE VILLAGE IS on a slope, and at its top, you can see the Tyrrellscourt gallops stretching out below in two lazy figure-of-eights for the horses' round and straight work. Driving down along the main street was like one of those posed features in a color supplement about "The Subcultures of Our Time": there were new-age crusties and tree huggers with multicolored sweaters and tights and those strange cropped-pate and pigtail haircuts with dogs on strings and petitions to save the whale, and the world; there were older hippies in saris and denim and leather, with mustaches and ponytails and nature shoes and raddled complexions; there were horsey, country types in Barbours and yellow and crimson and lime cords; there were obese white-faced teenage Goths in long leatherette coats and vast black T-shirts and six-inch steel-inlaid wedges; there were the usual complements of cheerful or surly layabouts, faces weather-beaten from standing smoking outside the pub or the betting shop all day; there were clutches of stripe-shirted men with mobile phones and oblong glasses thrusting their entrepreneurial way into the future; there were spiked-fin rugby boys and primped and groomed OMIGOD girls; there were slender, fine-boned blond women from Poland and Lithuania with their crop-headed sinewy men; there were 'oul ones with walking frames and tartan shopping trollies getting the last of the Christmas messages, and 'oul fellas with papers rolled tight beneath their arms, transporting their custom from one pub to another.

It was Christmas Eve in Tyrrellscourt, and everywhere there was tinsel and holly and flashing neon and twinkling fairy lights; last-minute bargains were being bruited from shop doorways, and the queues from the two butchers for turkeys and hams together ran the length of the town. At the bottom of the main drag the road forked in two, and there was a central meeting place with benches and flower beds and a great Christmas tree, and throngs of folk were gathered to gossip and idle and pass the compliments of the season back and forth. An accordion-playing trio from Central Europe was providing musical backing to the festive hordes; as we passed, they finished "Hark, the Herald Angels Sing" and kicked into "Carolan's Welcome," a traditional tune from the seventheenth-century blind Irish harper. I began to laugh at this point, and Tommy turned to me.

"You know when Yanks say to you, 'Oh, you're so lucky to live in Ireland,' like it's some fucking Celtic theme park full of *characters* and *crack* and *gargle*? And we're like, no, it's just like anywhere else, except with rain? Well, sometimes that's what Tyrrellscourt is like. It's like visiting Ireland for an Irish person."

We braked suddenly as a BMW Estate pulled out of its parking spot, and then Tommy smartly rolled the Volvo into its place and killed the engine. He flipped a half-smoked roll up from his shirt pocket to his mouth, lit it and exhaled with a grin.

"Of course, by half three, the light will be dying, and the freeze will be kicking in, and half the town will be pissed, and the other half will be getting there, and the blood will be up and the knives will be out, and all of this fucking . . . *Brigadoon* will just . . ."

Tommy held his hand out to the color and bustle of the town, and raised it in a parting wave.

"*See ya . . .*"

EVERYONE PASSES THROUGH McGoldrick's, Tommy said, so it only seemed right that we did too. It had a traditional frontage and an old mahogany bar with snugs on either side; double doors led through to a larger lounge and restaurant area; at the end of this another set of doors gave onto a vast room that looked like an old warehouse: girders had been painted pillar-box green and floorboards had been waxed and tossed with sawdust and old suitcases and books and vintage bicycles and typewriters were stacked on shelves and in alcoves; lunch was being served from an open kitchen that ran the length of one wall by young staff with the striking looks and excellent manners of Eastern Europeans to tables filled with Christmas Eve revelers, mainly families with supernaturally excited kids. We retreated to the lounge, which seemed to have a more upscale buzz to it, judging by the high-maintenance sheen of its predominantly female clientele. Without even having to look at each other, we found ourselves back in the bar, perched on two bar stools and ordering pints of Guinness and bowls of Irish stew. The graying ponytailed barman, whose name was Steno, gave Tommy a high five and made fun of his short hair and close-shaven face; evidently Tommy had established a minor reputation down here for himself. I wondered if I should tell Steno about Tommy's recent career move to the Church. Better to keep that in reserve, I decided. The bar's customers were on the horsey Barbour side, chomping brown bread and pâté and drinking hot ports and yelping about Leopardstown.

"Later in the day, it all gets a bit . . . looser," Tommy said.

The foaming half-poured pints sat by the taps to settle, and I nodded to Tommy to get on with it, and he nodded at the pints, so we waited until Steno had topped them up and gave them another couple of minutes and at last set them down in front of us, the swirling brown now solid black, the heads creamy and firm. We tipped them back. I don't know about Tommy's, but mine tasted like the first pint God made.

"All right then, Tommy, I have the drink; now, tell me what you know about Miranda Hart."

Tommy grimaced, then raised his eyebrows to heaven resignedly.

"All right, Ed, but don't go blaming the messenger."

"Just get on with it, will you?"

"Right, I used to come down here a fair bit, '98, '99, things weren't going so well with Paula, better than before they started to go really badly but still, anyway, I was down here, doing, I never told you this, a bit of work for Leo Halligan. Don't get the wrong idea, Ed, only Leo wasn't the maniac everyone thought he was, and no one thought he done that young fella, he was covering up for someone else, or something else, and there was a lot of talk that he was happy to do the time, get himself out of the way. Anyway, I was doing a bit of work for Leo—"

"What kind of work was this, Tommy? For a Halligan brother? Painting and decorating, were you?"

"You were away, Ed, so you missed a lot of . . . when George and Podge Halligan were getting going back in the nineties, Leo was down here, trying and failing as a jockey. Not as if he was morally opposed to his brothers, he just had a different plan. After that plan didn't work, he hung on down here, and he became a kind of . . . I don't know, he was like, at the center of a whole bunch of guys, jockeys, a bookie or two, even a few racing journalists."

"At the center of them how?"

"He'd be buying them dinner, drinks, comping them to events, you know, gigs in Dublin. Lining up women. And a little dope, a little blow, a few E's."

"And you were his distribution network for the drugs, yeah?"

"Yeah."

"And so what was it all about? Was it some kind of charitable work maybe? These horse-racing professionals were all-work-and-no-play merchants and Leo stepped in to modify their work–life balance? Or, having given all their lives, they decided it was time they got something back."

"You may laugh."

"Some days, I do little else."

"Leo may be a Halligan, but being gay is like a passport across the classes. And racing has a fair bit of that as well. So you'd be surprised who you'd've seen down here. And Leo was always setting up the jockeys to go to these charity balls for MS and the Hospice Foundation and whatever, photographs of them in the *Sunday Independent* with a bunch of orange-faced models. He knew all these guys who trot around after the ladies who lunch and, you know, go with them to all these events their husbands can't be bothered going to anymore. And they're all hoovering up blow any chance they get, so it worked out nicely, all very respectable."

"Meanwhile."

"Well, I don't know, I mean, I have no evidence, no proof. But the story was, it was all about race fixing. Leo was working with George at this stage—George has a place in the Algarve, and a lot of the jockeys were flown out there on golfing holidays, they were given presents, sometimes cash, sometimes cars or whatever. George has been running a book for ages for people who can't bet legally, usually because their money isn't clean. So the jockeys were holding up horses mostly, in some cases maybe doping them."

The Irish stew arrived, and for once, it actually was Irish stew—mutton, potato and onion in a white sauce—and not the brown beef concoction that often masqueraded in its place. I fell on mine in a spasm of lunchtime-after hunger; Tommy peered at his disapprovingly, pushed it to one side and ordered two more pints.

"I need to be back for midnight mass; plenty of time to let these metabolize," he said.

"What was in it for the journalists and the other bookies? The same?"

"Sure. They knew when to bet, when to lay off. And the journalists could mount a defense of any jockey that made it look too blatant. Every trainer keeps a tame journo or two."

"Any bookies we know?"

"There was only really the one: Jack Proby. Well, and his old man, Seán, of course. But Jack was the main man, Jack was into everything, Jack—"

Tommy stopped suddenly, and then stared across the gantry at a bottle of Irish Mist, as if it had asked him a question. His face flushed.

"Is this how the girl gets into the picture?"

He nodded, grimacing.

"Spit it out."

"She was with Proby, but . . . well, she was doing a lot of coke, and then she got into smack, and . . ."

"And what?"

"She turned into a total skank, you know? She'd go with anyone. And I think the idea was to pimp her out, because she was a gorgeous-looking woman, but she got too messy for anyone to deal with. Too messy for anyone to pay money for. She got barred out of here, and pretty much everywhere else. And it was really humiliating for her because she was known in the town, you know? Her old man used to run the Tyrrellscourt Arms and all. It was almost as if that was why, you know, *because* she was known that she was doing it. I mean, she didn't have to. Even on smack, blokes'd queue down the street for a woman like that."

"What happened to her father?"

"He died not long after Miranda left school, I think. And the Tyrrells bought the pub, it's now a kind of gate lodge to the country club."

"When you say you think the idea was to pimp her out . . . whose idea was that? Leo's?"

"Actually might have been Jack Proby's. He was a piece of work, that guy . . . it was like, he was doing these drugs and taking these holidays and all against his will, you know, he was always beefing about it, the coke was cut with bleach, the champagne wasn't vintage, know I mean? Like he was being held hostage somehow. And I think he took it out a lot on Miranda. Mind you, I couldn't swear to this, Ed, I mean, I was doing a lot of drugs at the time."

"Could you swear to any of it?"

"I don't know whether Miranda Hart was being forced, or whether she was using her own free will, but I know people paid her money for sex down here. I know that for a fact."

Fair play to Tommy, he lifted his face to mine so I could see the shame in his squinting eyes and the fear whipping around his mouth. Tommy Owens never lacked guts, even if sometimes it took him quite a while to remember where they were. I took a long drink of my second pint.

"When you say you know for a fact that people paid Miranda Hart for sex, Tommy . . . just how do you know that?"

"Because I was one of them."

FOURTEEN

I didn't want to listen to Tommy's explanations or excuses, and in truth, he didn't seem in much of a hurry to offer any. We drank in silence for a while, and then I told him I'd see him later and left. I wasn't sure exactly how I felt about what he had told me, but I wanted a break from having to look at his face while I worked it out. Everyone's allowed a past, and if we weren't able to forgive and forget much of what went on there, our lives would run aground on banks of grievance and resentment. That's what I told myself, not what I felt in my chest or in my gut.

The crowds were dwindling with the fading of the light, and a north wind dug deep into the bone. I pulled my overcoat tight around my throat and walked back out of town until I came to the gates of the Tyrrellscourt Hotel, Health Spa and Country Club, and what must have been the Tyrrellscourt Arms, a double-fronted stone bungalow maybe a hundred and fifty years old. It now functioned as a dedicated tourist office for the club and also for the stables and the stud, with brochures and a range of merchandise.

A uniformed security guard came out at my approach and asked me if I was a resident. I said no, but I had business with Regina Tyrrell. When the guard found out I didn't have an appointment, he wouldn't even lift the phone. He said Ms. Tyrrell was seeing nobody that day, and I said she'd see me, on account of how my business had to do with her brother Vincent. He was still reluctant, but when I said Ms. Tyrrell hadn't heard from her brother the priest for a long time but would obviously be anxious to on a day of such pain and distress for the family, he went back inside and made the call; when he came out and gave me the go-ahead, I wondered what she had said to him; he looked like he certainly didn't envy me my errand.

Hardy souls were still playing on the golf course I could see; the brochure assured me there was another course somewhere to the rear of the hotel, which loomed up ahead, white and sprawling, like a château that couldn't stop growing, with its multiple bow windows and its Italianate campanile. Landscaped gardens and a three-tiered lawn led up to the grand main entrance; signposts pointed the way to the wings and annexes that housed the tennis and squash courts, the spa, the swimming pools and the gymnasium; as I stood on the threshold, I heard the competing roars of a car and a river; the car was a steel-gray Bentley Continental Flying Spur, and it swept its cargo of laughing blondes past the main entrance as if it could spot the checkered flag; the river was the Liffey, which sprang from here and flowed on into Dublin and out to the sea.

The lobby was the usual nightmare mismatch of expensive styles and fittings common to every luxury Irish hotel: We Can Buy What We Like, And We Will, it screamed. Expensively tanned and scented guests wandered about exuding the relaxed ease of the rich; they seemed absurdly vivid and I an impostor, a monochrome man in their Technicolor world. The cute Scottish redhead at reception directed me to a function room jammed with highly excited children and their parents; in the middle, a red-suited Santa Claus was doing his thing. Regina Tyrrell spotted me immediately; I guess since I was the only man in the room not wearing deck shoes or a cardigan, that wasn't too hard.

The first thing I thought when I saw Regina Tyrrell was how much she looked like Miranda Hart, which is to say, how much she resembled my ex-wife: the same coal-black eyes and hair, the same long legs and rangy frame, the same imperious bearing. She was older, of course, but she didn't look it, or rather, age to her didn't look like any kind of burden; she was carrying maybe ten pounds, which showed on her body in a series of pleasant curves and helped to keep her face supple and smooth; she wore a black trouser suit and a square-cut black top. Her hair was cut short rather than piled high; her expression grim and resourceful, as if she'd taken all that life had thrown so far, but didn't expect it to stop anytime soon. Without a word, she indicated that I should follow her up a flight of stairs to a pale pink office that looked out over the rear of the complex. Before I had a chance to take in the fading view, she sat behind a white desk and began to talk.

"I haven't spoken to Vincent in thirty years, out of choice. What makes you think I'd want to talk to anyone who'd have anything to do with him?"

Her accent was melodious Dublin in its Sunday best, not lazy or glottal-stopped, not affected; unusual to hear it these days spoken by anyone of status, especially a woman; it sounded intoxicating to my ears.

"I don't know. Why would you? And yet, here we are."

She turned on a pink-shaded desk lamp and looked past it at me and shook her head.

"She said you'd be cheeky, all right."

"Who did?"

"Miranda."

"I got the impression you two didn't speak either."

"We don't. But given the night that was in it . . ."

She blessed herself, and I noticed the silver cross at her throat.

"Miranda said you were there."

"I found her. And the murderer—at least, I assume it was the murderer—hit me on the back of the head and knocked me out."

"Francis is in shock," she said. "He went up to Dublin this morning to identify the body."

"What else did Miranda tell you?"

"What are you doing for Vincent?"

"He asked me to find . . . no, that's not right, he didn't ask me anything. He gave me a name. Patrick Hutton."

I looked closely at Regina, but there wasn't any visible reaction. There should at least have been a flicker. I looked around the room. The walls were pale pink, the furniture pink and white, the strawberries-and-cream drapes ruched and tasseled; two gold chandeliers hung from the ceiling; the carpet was white. It was a room decorated by a twelve-year-old girl: all that was missing was the stuffed toys. I looked again at the impressive woman before me. Sometimes I felt I could spend a lifetime trying to work people out until they added up, and at the end they'd still be the strangers they began as.

"Did Miranda not tell you that?" I said.

Regina Tyrrell set her lips in a wry smile.

"Miranda said there were things she couldn't tell me. She said it might be harmful to the work you were doing. She said any of us could be next. I asked her was the second body that had been found Patrick's. She said that I should ask you. And she said it all in this hushed voice, as if she was in a crowded bar and the bad guys were listening. As if she was in a movie. Such a drama queen, our Miranda, always was. I think the bit she liked most was ringing me up and then not telling me anything. Her knowing something I didn't know. She liked that all right. Was it Patrick?"

"They haven't identified the body," I said. "But it sounds like it could be."

"It makes sense. What doesn't make sense is the rest of it."

"That's why I'm here," I said.

"To ask me questions? To poke your nose into our family affairs? What makes you think we should welcome you with open arms?"

"I'm not used to that kind of welcome. But what Miranda said was true: there seems to be a pattern to the killings, and any of you could be the next victim."

"And what about the Guards? Why aren't they here?"

"They're conducting their own investigation. A lot of it would depend on forensics, on what they can deduce from the crime scene. And since they've got three to examine, that is probably where the bulk of their focus lies at the moment. They'll get here presently."

"And how do you know Vincent?"

Every time she spoke his name, it sounded like the twist of a knife in her guts. I explained about growing up in Bayview with Tyrrell as the parish priest, and about Tommy's unlikely job as sacristan providing the connection between us. At this, she visibly relaxed, as if reassured that I wasn't acting in some sinister manner on Vincent Tyrrell's behalf. She got up from her desk and walked to the window.

"It never looks the same, does it, twilight?" she said. "Or maybe it's that your eyes never quite get used to it. You look, and everything seems unfamiliar, and by the time you've adjusted, the light has changed, and what you saw is past, or the moon is down, and everything is equally visible in its glare, and none of it makes sense."

As I joined her, I could see a half-moon popping out like a cymbal crash and shedding its silver everywhere. There was another golf course out there, with dramatic bunkers and water features; below it ran the river; in the distance I could see high walls and bare trees ranged around a neo-Gothic mansion; beyond lay the gallops of Tyrrellscourt stables.

"Maybe that's what trying to really look at your life is like, look at your own family," she said. "That moment between twilight, when everything is strange and mysterious, and moonlight, when you see everything plain, and nothing stands out: everything is clear and nothing has any meaning."

Maybe I was so struck by her image that I forgot what we were doing, or maybe I had spotted something by the walled house that distracted me; when she next spoke, it was as if to a man who had made his own way to the dining table without waiting for her to lead.

"What I'm saying is, maybe an outsider's eye is just what we need, Mr. Loy."

She went back to her desk and sat down and turned the light off. Her face in the shadows immediately looked older, gray and tired, her great dark eyes pools, inviting strangers at their own risk.

"Tell me about the family, then. Tell me about the Tyrrells," I said.

"I don't know about the Tyrrells. But I can tell you about myself," she said. "My mother died giving birth to me. I think that was hard on the boys. I never knew any different, but boys need a mother if they're to avoid . . . a certain kind of coldness. Anyway, I grew up here, went to the local school, boarding school in Dublin."

"Is that where you got the accent?"

She grinned.

"I got the accent in Dublin, but not at boarding school. Everyone told me to get rid of it. Maybe that's why I hung on to it. Too late now."

"I like it a lot."

"Listen to you. Say anything so you would. Say mass if you were let."

She laughed, an uneasy laugh, and it struck me that, beneath the brittle sheen, she was an uneasy woman. Maybe when you sat opposite a detective, only fools and knaves weren't. Or maybe she had a lot to be uneasy about.

"So this would have been sixties, seventies?"

"Left school in '74."

"F.X. would have been running the show here by then?"

"For ten years. Francis trained his first winner at nineteen. Won the Gold Cup the following year, '65. And on and on."

"And what about you? University? London?"

"Nah. I came back here. I missed it like mad. And the horses. I was one of those pony girls. In boarding school up in the Dublin mountains . . . Jasus, Mother Borgia, that was the mother superior's name, Mother Borgia, you wouldn't believe it now, but back then . . . anyway, I hated the place, all these snobby southside bitches, but there was a riding school nearby, and a couple of local lads who'd sneak me in and sneak horses out . . . oh, we had such a time of it. I think that's where I got the accent. And of course, it gave the nuns conniptions, it went against everything they stood for, which wasn't education at all, it was how to arrange flowers and give a dinner party and get into a sports car without showing your knickers so you could nab some young businessman and make him a fragrant wife. And certainly not be letting him down in front of his boss talking like some common-as-muck Dublin Chrissie. We've got over that now, at least. Anyone in this country with a few bob in his pocket's as good as anyone else."

"And anyone without a few bob?"

"Let them go out and work for it. That's what the Poles and Latvians and all are doing, and fair play to them. If there's a generation of Irish too lazy to work, that's a shame for them, but what are we supposed to do about it? Sponsor them to drink all day and go to the shops in their pajamas?"

"So you came back to Tyrrellscourt, and trained?"

"Not really. You have to be . . . touched by God to be able for that."

"Touched by God?"

"Laugh if you like," she said. "But it is a kind of vocation. I've often watched Francis during the day, inspecting the horses and the lads in the morning before work begins, checking the earth and watching the sky, supervising the feeds, right the way to patrolling the yard at night, listening for a restless horse, the wrong kind of cough, and all in silence: there's a kind of devotion to it, it's . . . I used to think he was like a monk. Only the horses had called him, not God."

"Your brother Vincent said much the same: the horses knew F.X., they didn't like Vincent at all."

"Good sense they had," she said, the wistful look she had had in talking about F.X. curdling when it came to her other brother.

"What caused the falling-out between you and Vincent?" I said.

Regina simply shook her head. Whatever it was, I wasn't going to hear it from her. She looked quickly at her watch, and I pressed ahead before I was cut off.

"So you didn't have a similar vocation?"

"No. The only thing I can compare it to is a musician. The kind who, they make the records, they give the concerts, they have the career, but the only time they're truly alive is when they're playing, is in the music. And F.X. was like that, at race meetings, he'd be hiding behind the horses, and when they won, there were no fists in the air, no big shite talk to the crowd like some of the knackers you see masquerading as trainers these days, it was just a quiet nod, the sense that this was as it should be. And I loved to play piano, classical, my favorite thing now, but if you think you can play the piano, and then you hear a Barenboim, a Rubinstein, well if you're not a total idiot, you understand immediately what you don't have. And to try would be futile, really. But you want to do something, you believe in what's being done. So I did what I could. I ran the house for him. I took night courses in bookkeeping so I could keep an eye on the money. I took cookery courses so when owners came to visit, they could bring their wives and children. I made sure the gardens were kept up. And I dressed up and went with him to Cheltenham and Aintree and Leopardstown and all, chatting to the Queen Mother and so forth."

"Like a wife."

"It wasn't unusual where we came from. Eldest son inherits the farm—"

"Youngest becomes a priest, unmarried sister comes home and keeps house for the brother—"

"Not unusual at all."

"She never married."

"Nothing like that," Regina said sharply. "There was more than one fella, over the years. But none of them . . . I don't know, unless you're going to settle for less. And I had all this, I didn't need any man's money."

She gestured toward the window, and then around the room.

"This house was in ruins, some 'oul dacency sisters were hanging on for dear life, until they gave up the ghost. We got it for a song in 1970. Francis put the whole thing in my name, I had the idea for all this."

"Well done," I said, and meant it.

"And so that was another thing, you're a successful woman, you attract gorgeous-looking fellas with expensive tastes and no funds, and you scare off the me-Tarzan types. So what can you do?"

"What did you do when Jackie Tyrrell appeared on the scene?"

Regina sighed and shook her head at that.

"What did I do? I invited her down here, you know. Jackie Lamb. She was in school with me. And she'd been writing to me, all this very flattering stuff, she was working for one of those Irish women's magazines, wanted to do a feature, sisters are doing it for themselves, all very exciting. So down she comes, and it's soon very clear she has F.X. in her sights."

"And were you hurt by that?"

"Hurt? What do you mean, hurt? I told you, there was nothing like that. Do you think I was after her?"

"I didn't mean about her. I meant, hurt that your brother . . . there must have been a very strong bond between you both. It can't have been easy to bring another woman into that."

Regina Tyrrell looked at her watch again, and lifted her hands up and almost clapped them.

"Four-thirty. Sun over the yardarm. Miranda said you drank."

"I do."

"Don't we all?"

"Does F.X.?"

"Of course he doesn't."

Light spilled from the far end of the room as Regina opened a white wood door that concealed a fridge freezer and produced a bottle of Tanqueray and a bottle of Schweppes tonic. She found glasses and brought the drinks to the desk and we drank in near darkness. I thought of asking her to put the light on, but then found I didn't want to.

"I wouldn't say I was hurt," Regina said. "But it was hard not to feel excluded. I mean, she was at the races instead of me. Literally. And of course, she had the finishing school thing going on, and the magazine and all, these lady writers who were friends of hers up in Dublin, gossip columnists and what have you, giving her great write-ups for the frocks. So yeah. But like I mean, I just moved in down here and let her get on with it. There was a time she was up and down to me three times a day, how does this work, when does Francis like his dinner, all that. Felt like his ma so I did."

"You said F.X. doesn't drink. Jackie Tyrrell said there were a lot of things F.X. didn't do."

"Really. I wouldn't know."

"Because it seems odd on the face of it that they never had children. She said—"

"Yeah. She said that to me too. And says I to her, there are things a sister shouldn't really have to know about her brother, and that's one of them."

"No curiosity?"

"No thank you. Did she tell you all this the night she died?"

"She did. I was the last person who saw her alive. Apart from her killer."

"What did she say about me?"

"She said you run all this, and you run your brother too."

Regina laughed mirthlessly.

"That's the way Jackie saw everything. It was all about control."

"And what is it all about for you?"

The question seemed to catch her unawares. In the pale light I thought I saw something like vulnerability, even fear, cross her face.

"The future. It's all about the future."

I forbore from asking the obvious question—what kind of future could the Tyrrells have when the current generation was too old to provide another?—but I felt it lay heavy in the air between us.

"She also said you were glad when she and Francis got divorced. And that she was going to tell me a thing or two about you," I said.

"And did she?"

"That was the last thing she said to me. The next time I saw her, she was dead."

Regina's hand went automatically to her throat, and she shuddered, whether in sympathy or out of relief, I couldn't tell.

"What kind of relationship did you have with Miranda Hart?" I said.

Regina shrugged.

"I didn't really get a look-in. Jackie was hugger-mugger there. I liked her as a teenager, she used to haunt the yard, drive the lads wild. In every way. Reminded me a bit of myself at that age. When her mother died, her father sent her off to boarding school in England, and she came back talking like Lady Diana, Jasus, that was something to hear. Jackie kind of adopted her then, bought her clothes and all. Had her show-ponying around the place. I never thought Miranda had what it took to carry that off. Her name is Mary, you know."

"Mary?"

"Yeah. I think she took some stick from the gels in Cheltenham over that, about being a little Irish colleen, holy Mary, all this, so when she got back here for good, she was Miranda, with the yah accent. Jackie bought into the whole thing, and it stuck. 'Course everyone knew she was Paddy Hart the publican's daughter Mary, but if she says that's not who she is anymore, who's to say different?"

Regina's tone was jaunty and high, as if discussing the amusing caprices of a neighbor's daughter. My next question not only put a stop to that, it retrospectively undermined any gaiety she had supposedly felt at Miranda's adventures.

"And what happened with Patrick Hutton?"

"That was just an unsuitable, a wrong marriage, I told Jackie from the very beginning, she should and could have stopped it, but no, I was being petit bourgeois and lower middle class apparently, the snotty Cork bitch, she thought it was *wonderfully brave.* I honestly think she pushed it out of spite, because I got Francis to try and intervene. If he's good enough to ride for F. X. Tyrrell, she said, he's good enough to marry a publican's daughter. As if all the Miranda stuff, the airs and graces she'd taught her, was for nothing, or worse, a game to keep herself amused, like the girl was a doll, a toy to be played with. I felt sorry for the child . . ."

She stopped, and raised her glass, and sighed, as if she'd said too much.

"She was adopted, wasn't she?" I said, in as pointed a manner as I could manage.

"Are you asking me what I think you're asking me?" Regina said.

"She's the image of you," I said.

"No, is the answer," she said. "Fuck's sake, I see the black eye, I'm not surprised, questions like that."

"She had a rough time of it after Hutton disappeared."

"A lot of which she brought on herself," Regina said. "Ah, she lost the place altogether, I don't know what happened to her. Drink, drugs . . . I suppose you heard she was little better than a prostitute there for a while. It wasn't as if she needed money."

"Did she not? She was renting out her house, I know."

"She inherited the Tyrrellscourt Arms when her father died sure. Ninety-two, was it? And she made a lot of money out of that."

"She sold it to you, didn't she?"

"For a quarter of a million pounds. That was before the boom, when two hundred and fifty thousand would have got you pretty much anything you wanted in Dublin. That little place in Riverside wouldn't have been more than sixty then, if that. I never knew what got into Miranda. She got over it, at least. Jackie gave her work, helped undo some of the harm she'd done."

Regina looked at her watch again.

"Now. Christmas Eve. I have family commitments."

"Just one last thing," I said. "Patrick Hutton. Didn't you ever wonder over the years what had happened?"

She stood up and shook her head.

"No," she said. "But I always hoped he was dead, to be honest with you. I hoped and prayed he was dead."

I couldn't hold her gaze, and looked out the window, to see that the Range Rover that had been parked near the walls of Tyrrellscourt House when we came up here had gone.

FIFTEEN

egina Tyrrell walked me down to the lobby. At reception, a tall slim girl of about nine or ten with long dark hair and dark eyes was waiting. When she saw Regina she ran to her and kissed her.

"Karen, meet Edward Loy. Ed Loy, Karen Tyrrell. My daughter."

I shook the girl's hand, trying to fix a smile on my face. Her daughter? Behind the girl stood a slim male figure in his sixties, immaculate in tweed jacket, cavalry twill trousers, polished tan brogues, Tattersall shirt and cravat; only a small swollen belly betrayed F. X. Tyrrell's age. His weathered face had the same prominent cheekbones his brother's had; his eyes were smaller, but the same deep brown as his sister's; his lips were fleshy and loose. He had the quiet, watchful, half-sad, half-amused air of a man well used to having people report and defer to him; Regina, while not exactly going that far, seemed to genuflect an apology in his direction, which he dispelled with a half smile.

"I'm sorry for your loss, Mr. Tyrrell," I said.

He nodded to acknowledge my sympathy, and again to deflect it, gesturing toward the child. Everywhere in the lobby people were trying not to stare at F. X. Tyrrell and failing; they probably would have done so anyway, but with shy smiles on their faces; a glance at the pile of *Evening Herald*s at reception explained why they weren't smiling today: OMEGA MAN KILLS TRAINER'S EX-WIFE, screamed the headline. I quickly scanned the story. They still hadn't ID'd Hutton. When I turned back, it was to Karen Tyrrell alone; Regina had drawn F.X. off down the steps to one side, and they were locked in conversation. Karen smiled at me, and I smiled back.

"Do you have any children?" she said.

I couldn't really explain, not to a child.

"Yes," I said. "A little girl. She'd be about your age now."

"I'm nine," Karen said. "What's her name?"

"Lily," I said, and then heard myself saying: "She lives with her mother. In America."

"I live with my mother too," Karen said. "And Uncle Francis, but he's never there, and even when he is, he isn't. If that makes sense. Sometimes I don't make too much sense, Mum says."

"It sounds sensible to me," I said. "A lot of men are like that."

"I wouldn't know. My dad's dead," she said gravely.

"I'm sorry," I said.

"I suppose. I never knew him. I don't think Mum knew him very well either. She doesn't even have a photograph of him."

Karen had been surveying the come-and-go around the room while we talked; now she looked up at me through eyes widened to express her bemusement at the scant trail her father had left. Her gaze left me reeling, and I felt as if it was setting me a challenge which, if met, could solve the mystery of the Tyrrells and of the killer who could be on their trail. For Karen Tyrrell's eyes were not identical: one was brown, and one was dark blue.

Regina joined us and told me her brother was waiting to speak to me outside the hotel. I found him by the far end of the building, looking back toward his stables. He didn't turn as I stood alongside him, barely moved a muscle.

"Did Jackie say anything about me?" he said quickly.

His voice was quiet but perfectly pitched, the kind of voice you listened closely to for fear of missing a beat. A king's voice.

"She said several things."

"What were they?"

"Why do you want to know? It was a private conversation."

F. X. Tyrrell made a sound in his throat, a sound like a dry branch snapping.

"Just answer my question."

"No, I don't think I will."

Tyrrell still hadn't moved, but I could hear his breath coming quickly through his nose. He started to say something that sounded like a threat, then stopped himself and changed course.

"She was my wife, Mr. Loy."

From another man it might have been a plea; F. X. Tyrrell made it sound like a command.

"I know that. But you weren't the subject of our meeting. Jackie spoke mainly about Miranda Hart, and Patrick Hutton. You know your brother has hired me to find Hutton?"

F. X. Tyrrell turned around and faced me, his small eyes blazing.

"A brother is loyal or he is nothing. I have no brother."

"Father Vincent suggested I should ask you about close breeding."

I don't know what reaction I was expecting; what I got was a weary shake of the head.

"Father Vincent should stick with his discipline, and let me stick with mine," he said. "Tell my sister I'll be waiting for her."

I found Regina Tyrrell in reception. She whispered to Karen to wait with Uncle Francis, and Karen gave me a little salute somewhere between a nod and a curtsy and made to go; then came back and reached up and kissed my cheek and whispered something in my ear, and half skipped, half danced across to join her uncle, who was standing by the door.

"Great kid," I said. Regina Tyrrell nodded as if that was beyond dispute, and looked at me impatiently, and I gave her my full attention.

"I have a proposition to put to you, Mr. Loy," she said.

"I already have a client," I said. "Your brother Vincent."

"We could pay more."

"He's paying plenty. Besides, I don't know that F. X. Tyrrell took to me."

"F.X. will do as I ask. We have our own security people, of course, but there are so many staff, here, and at the stables, and it would be good to have someone who's on top of the case. Not that I believe our lives are in danger, but . . ."

"I'm sure the Guards will offer some people."

"That would be good for business. Guards clumping around."

"I can't do it. There is someone . . . he's a little unorthodox . . . but I'd trust him with my life. Indeed, on several occasions, I have."

"He'd be under your control," she said.

I nearly laughed at the notion that Tommy could ever come fully under anyone's control.

"That's the general idea," I said. "I'll try and get him to you this evening."

We discussed money, and when she didn't haggle, I got suspicious. I was suspicious anyway.

"Ms. Tyrrell, do you drive a Range Rover?"

"I do, as a matter of fact."

"Could I see it?"

"It's right outside. Francis drove Karen over in it."

"So you don't use it exclusively?"

"I usually do. Francis borrowed it today. His has something up with it."

"He drives one as well?"

Regina nodded, already looking bewildered and a little bored by the questions. She nodded at me to follow her, conferred briefly with a trim blonde in a black trouser suit not unlike Regina's who was presumably the duty manager and joined F.X. and Karen at the door. The Range Rover was outside and they climbed into it. I copied the number of the UK registration plate into my notebook. When I looked up again, Regina Tyrrell was standing before me, her face uncertain, her eyes wary.

"If you see Miranda . . ."

"Yes?"

"You will see her, I expect?"

"I expect so."

"And she's safe?"

"I hope so."

"Tell her . . . tell her . . ."

The engine of the Range Rover started, and Regina shook her head, and a wave of what could have been irritation at her inability to find the right words, but looked darker than that, looked like pain, rippled across her face. She turned and almost fell into the car, which took off immediately. I followed on foot down the drive.

On the way, I checked my messages. Tommy had left a voice mail saying that he'd met someone who knew Leo and Hutton in St. Jude's, that he was still in McGoldrick's and would I be okay to drive back to Dublin. And I got a message from Joe Leonard, he of the uneasy marriage and the garbage dump on his doorstep: a picture of him and Annalise and the kids with Santa hats on and the legend: *Merry Christmas from the Leonards!* So maybe I had a satisfied customer somewhere.

I walked back into town thinking about Karen Tyrrell. Ten years ago Regina would have been forty-two or forty-three, reaching the end of her fertility; many single women who get pregnant by accident at that age keep a child they would have aborted ten years previously: some go out with the intention of getting pregnant by an anonymous one-night stand. But nine years ago would also bring us back to the aftermath of Patrick Hutton's disappearance; nine years would be long enough for someone who'd been made pregnant by Patrick Hutton to have his baby, almost a year after his disappearance. That would help to explain Miranda Hart's less than fond tone when she mentioned Regina. It might also go a long way toward accounting for Miranda's self-destructive trawl through Tyrrellscourt in the period after Hutton's disappearance: hard enough for your husband to disappear, but knowing (assuming she did know) that he had impregnated another woman, an older, richer woman whose family had in a sense informally adopted Miranda and Hutton both: that must have felt like betrayal. *I won't play the Judas for anyone,* Hutton said; perhaps he already had, with Regina Tyrrell, and when Miranda found out, she made sure the Tyrrells got to see the ugly consequences on the streets of their own town. Maybe that accounted for Regina's dismissive attitude to the marriage: not because she considered Patrick Hutton unworthy of Miranda, but because she had been in love with him herself. I called Dave Donnelly, and a couple of minutes later he called me back.

"Dave, I want you to see if you can get hold of Don Kennedy's case files. He looked into Patrick Hutton's disappearance a couple of years ago, so that Miranda 'Hart could have him declared dead."

"What am I looking for?"

I thought for a minute.

"Birth cert, baptismal cert, anything official. Hutton seems to have been a man without a past. And anything else that Kennedy turned up . . . I mean, he cleared the way for the insurance company to sign the house over to Miranda, but any time you do a trawl like that, you always uncover other stuff. Anything, even if it feels like gossip to you."

"Want to explain?"

"Not sure if I can. Just feeling my way."

Dave ended the call, and I kept along the road.

My thoughts turned to my own little girl, and the lie I had told, and how I felt about telling it. It hadn't been about me: it was to spare Karen Tyrrell's feelings. Not that she needed me to. Kids don't live in quite such dread of death as adults do. But it reminded me of the relief I had felt when my daughter was born, that I was no longer the center of my own world, she was. I had moved contentedly away from center stage in my own life. I remember the initial vertigo, and then the thrill, the rush to embrace the natural feeling that a new generation is more important than your own. And the grief of her death was accentuated and prolonged by my revulsion at having to deal with myself and my own feelings: it felt like indulgence, or worse: I made myself sick. A month ago, I wouldn't have told a lie about Lily, even to say she would have been nine, instead of five, let alone that she was alive when her ashes lay scattered in the ocean at Santa Monica under an indifferent sky. But I told it, and I was glad I had, and Karen Tyrrell's kiss on my cheek had made me feel closer to Lily than three years of drinking and fucking and fighting had. I said a prayer, or something like a prayer, offering it up to the clear, starry sky, then slipped and nearly fell on an early frost outside McGoldrick's pub. I righted myself, hand on cold railings, my breath pluming in the freezing air, relieved to be upright with blood in my veins, the living voices from the pub swirling around my head; relieved to be among the living, with the memory of what Karen Tyrrell had whispered still fresh in my ears: *Don't look so sad.*

Before I went inside I played a hunch. I called the bookie whose mobile number I had found in Hutton's pocket.

"Yes, friend?" came the reply.

"Jack Proby?" I said.

"Who wants to know?"

"Edward Loy. I'm a friend of Miranda Hart's. I'd like to talk to you about a horse called By Your Leave."

"Yeah? What are you, friend, some kind of journalist?"

"No, I'm some kind of detective. Friend."

"Well, I'm kind of busy at the moment. How did you get this number anyway?"

"If I told you, you'd have to kill me."

"That's very funny, friend, but I'm here at home with my family and I really don't appreciate—"

"I hear you, friend. That's what I'm calling about actually, the unappreciated. The jockeys who disappear because they won't carry out orders. The women who sell their bodies because the men they love are scumbags who'd rather pimp them out than care for them. The men whose fathers are gay and vulnerable to blackmail, who end up working for gangsters to keep the family secrets. Unappreciated, every one. We really should do something for them, don't you think? In this season of goodwill."

"What do you want?"

Proby's voice had lost the hail-fellow-well-met tone; now he sounded edgy and dangerous, like a rat in a trap.

"Where do you live?" I said.

"Foxrock," he said.

"Foxrock? Nice up there."

"I worked for every penny," he said.

"So do most people. They just don't seem to end up with as many pennies. A shame, isn't it?"

"Keeps me awake at nights."

"I'm sure it does. I'll see you at midday tomorrow down in Seafield. The West Pier."

"Tomorrow's Christmas Day—"

"So it is. Where are my manners? Merry Christmas. Friend."

It was called pushing the boat out. The cops would be all over this case soon, if they weren't already. But what lay beneath it might never come out in their investigation. It would in mine. Call it justice. Call it curiosity. Whatever it was, it came down to this: I needed to know that nine-year-old girl had a future, one in which she would not be betrayed. And I wasn't convinced that, without my help, she would.

TOMMY OWENS WAS sitting on the same stool he'd been on when I left the pub, but it was as if a carnival had erected itself around him: face painters and street performers in clown costumes; folk musicians wearing bad hats; bearded bikers in leathers and their women in lace and feathers; three Santa Clauses and several drunken helpers in green-and-red elf costumes and, holding the line at the bar, a phalanx of little old men in jumpers of all ages, drinking seriously and devotedly and steadfastly resisting the temptations of excessive gaiety, even if one or two couldn't resist a stray look in the direction of the drunken elves, particularly the one who kept threatening to get her tits out unless one of the Santas promised to "do" her in his costume. Steno the barman, who had a reassuring aura of calm authority, finally brought this seasonal tableau to a close by ejecting the offending elf, but she was accompanied off the premises by one of the Santas, although possibly not the one she favored.

The lounge was calmer and tonier, with a crowd that looked bored by their money and keen to get rid of it; you could sell a lot of blow here tonight, and someone no doubt was. In the warehouse, it was as if everyone we had seen on the street earlier today was crammed inside; indeed, when I pulled open the double doors, three people stumbled back into the lounge; Noddy Holder was shrieking "It's Chriss-miss" on a jukebox as I made my way back to Tommy. I assumed he had been drinking all this time, but in fact he was stone-cold sober, or as stone cold as Tommy ever got; he nodded at me and introduced me to the short, slightly built guy on the stool next to him, who wore an olive-green flight suit and looked like a shaven-headed heroin addict: his taut flesh was mottled and pocked; his drawn cheeks had tight vertical folds like stiletto scars; his tiny eyes were recessed deep beneath heavy brows: dark blue and bloodshot, they glowed like hot coals.

"Ed, Bomber Folan. Bomber, Ed."

Bomber promptly stood up and left the bar. Tommy got to his feet to follow.

"Come on, Ed, we've a trip to make. Bomber's driving."

I followed reluctantly. If I had learned anything over the years, it was not to do business with anyone called "Bomber," and especially not to get into a vehicle with him. Besides, I wanted a drink. I needed a drink.

Outside, Tommy grinned.

"The expression on your face man."

He started to laugh. I didn't like being laughed at, especially not by Tommy Owens. Coming on top of what he had told me earlier this afternoon about Miranda Hart, I liked it even less. Without pausing for thought, I hit Tommy a dig in the mouth that send him skidding on the frosted ground. The smokers in McGoldrick's porch stiffened and a murmur of interest ran through them. Bomber drove up in a Jeep that looked like it had been fashioned from a corrugated iron shed and some old scaffolding. He jumped out and came at me, his hands up.

"No, Bomber, it's all right."

Tommy was on his feet, wiping blood from his mouth. He brought his face close to mine, close enough that I could see the anger in his eyes.

"Fair enough, Ed. I probably would have done the same. But you left before I could explain. Earlier."

"Explain what?" I said, knowing already I was in the wrong, and fearing it was only going to get worse. Tommy looked around at Bomber and nodded him back to the Jeep.

"I paid Miranda money. But I didn't get my money's worth. I didn't . . . she was so out of it that it wouldn't have been right. And anyway, I . . . I was never into that, into paying for it . . . I was kind of goaded into it . . ."

"You don't have to tell me this, Tommy," I said.

"I do, actually. Because you're the only one who . . . who

even half believes I'm . . . you know . . . and the look on your face today when I told you about your one . . . I didn't want you thinking I'm some kind of fuckin'—"

"I don't, Tommy. All right? I don't."

Tommy nodded, and I put my hand on his shoulder. He looked me in the eyes, and I thought I saw tears in his. And then he hit me, a smack to the left cheek that dropped me to my knees and left my head jangling. I laid my palms on the cold ground to steady myself, and then I got slowly to my feet. The smokers were all beaming at the prospect of what this pair of out-of-town clowns might do next.

"Gonna have that drink now," I said.

"We'll wait for you."

I went back inside and Steno poured me a double Jameson and I added a third of water and he nodded approvingly at me as I drank it down like breakfast juice. The adage about being able to choose your friends but not your family ran through my mind. It wasn't true though, or at least, not as you got older. Unless you were the choosy type, or you went on a lot of cruises. No, you were stuck with your family and you were stuck with your friends, and you'd better just make the best of it. I thanked Steno, who had the solemn confessional gravity I prized in a barman, or at least the appearance of it, and went out to join Tommy in the back of a Jeep driven by a man called Bomber.

SIXTEEN

Bomber was a good driver, given the vehicle, and he had been a promising jockey until the heroin whose ravages still showed in his face had worked its way mercilessly through body and soul, calling a halt to his burgeoning career. Now he "did something with scrap," Tommy assured me. As we crossed a humpbacked bridge across the river at the far end of town and the suspension rattled and clanked like a mechanical press, I concluded that one of the somethings with scrap he did had become the Jeep we were sitting in. We turned in along the river and pulled up briefly outside a set of high iron gates. Bomber unlocked the padlock and uncoiled the chain and opened them and we drove up the short gravel drive to a large granite building with a slate roof that looked like a cross between a church and an asylum. The windows were all boarded up, with the exception of one stained-glass pane high on the rectangular bell tower; the grounds were overgrown; broken glass and beer cans and the dead embers of fires lay strewn about.

"St. Jude's," Tommy said.

Bomber, who hadn't spoken and didn't look like starting anytime soon, produced flashlights from a toolbox in the Jeep and gave us one each. He set off up the steps and unlocked a further three padlocks and set aside three iron bands and pushed the door open, and we followed him inside.

We found ourselves in a blue-tiled entrance hall. Bomber used his flashlight to guide our eyes. On the turn of the stairs, the Blessed Virgin Mary stood in matching blue; facing us, Christ hung from the cross, minus a hand but otherwise intact. Bomber set off down a corridor to the left, flashing the light from side to side to illuminate classrooms still filled with desks and blackboards. Cobwebs hung like lace curtains and dust clung to every surface, but the classrooms were intact, as if their occupants had stepped out in a hurry, expecting to return at their leisure. At the end of the corridor Bomber flung open a heavy oak door and waited for us to pass through. We were in a small chapel, with rows of plain wooden pews and, near the altar, individual mahogany chairs with padded seats and matching kneelers. Bomber hoisted one of the kneelers on his shoulder, wheeled around and headed out of the chapel again, turning at the door to indicate that we should follow. I looked to Tommy for some explanation, but he wasn't talking either.

We followed Bomber upstairs past the Blessed Virgin Mary and onto the first floor, where we filed through a spartan dormitory; the beds were separated into small cells by means of wooden partitions; a small locker stood adjacent to each bed, with a chamber pot beneath. Bomber had paused by one of the cells; he shined his flashlight on the side of the locker nearest the bed, where the occupant had carved some hieroglyphics; I crouched down close to see what they were. Bomber stared at me until I nodded to confirm that I had understood what I had seen; then he was up and off, through a communal bathroom and down a carpeted passageway paneled in dark wood. He stopped outside a door, nodded to us and went in.

The first thing I saw was the reproduction of Poussin's *Last Supper,* one of the paintings Father Vincent Tyrrell had hanging in his Bayview presbytery. Then I took in the thick-pile red carpet, the burgundy-and-gold-flock wallpaper, the luxurious eiderdown on the queen-size bed, the red velvet seat on the mahogany carver chair, the gilt-framed mirror above the marble fireplace, and the image of the Sacred Heart watching it all, although His light had been extinguished. Bomber's light was burning bright: he waved his flashlight and fixed his eyes on us as if to check he had our full attention. We nodded, and then he presented what amounted to a kind of grotesque pantomime. He took a black scarf from his pocket and wrapped it around his eyes, then he took the kneeler and set it down so that it faced the Sacred Heart; this left him with his back to us. He knelt down and rested his elbows on the arm rail of the kneeler and brought his hands together ready for prayer; he raised his flashlight toward the Sacred Heart and brought forth the first sound I had heard him make. I thought he was cawing like a crow, but soon it was clear he was making a sheep's baa. After a bit of this, he clapped his hands together and blessed himself, then bent down until he was on all fours, with his head beneath the kneeler; he brought his hands up to hang from the kneeler's rail, and with his rear end extended toward us, proceeded to squeal and roar and scream, like an animal in pain. He rocked back and forth on the kneeler until it tumbled over and brought his head crashing down on the floor, where he stayed, whimpering now, like a dog that's been beaten too much.

After a while, he picked himself up and turned to us, his face wet with tears and snot and smeared with dust and blood where he'd torn his forehead. He came toward us then, the beam of the flashlight pointing up from beneath his chin; in its glow, amid the falling dust, he looked like his skull was smoldering; when he took his blindfold off, his tiny blue-black eyes burned like red Christmas berries. He came up close and opened his mouth wide, and showed us exactly why we hadn't had a word out of him. Like Patrick Hutton, like Don Kennedy, like Jackie Tyrrell, Bomber's tongue had been cut out. His work done, Bomber smiled, and almost bowed.

As it had begun, so it ended: Bomber picked up his wooden kneeler and put it on his back and made his way down the stairs and out into the night. While he replaced the bars and padlock on the doors, Tommy Owens and I lit cigarettes and smoked them as if they were the eighth sacrament. The moon was down, and you could see across the road to the riverbank. From the upstairs windows too, from the dormitory cells, you would have seen the river flowing, keeping its secrets all the way to Dublin and out into the sea.

"Monasteries, convents, fuckers always arranged it so they'd have themselves a nice view, didn't they?" Tommy said.

I nodded, hearing Bomber moaning to himself as he fumbled with the locks, and suddenly found myself shaking with rage, my head hot and pounding; I walked down the drive and crossed the road, shouting something at the sky, I don't know what, nothing like a prayer, and stood by the river until Tommy came out and Bomber locked the gates and gave us a lift back into town. He dropped us off at the Volvo and nodded solemnly to me, as if we had made a deal; I felt like we had too, but the difference was, he seemed to trust me, whereas I was far from sure I could say the same. I held his gaze though, and he gripped my hand and used it to roll up his sleeve, and show me the tattoo he had on his forearm. The runes were familiar to me now; I had already seen them carved on the nightstand in the dormitory cubicle Bomber had singled out; they had been tattooed or carved into each of the murder victims; now here they were on Bomber's arm: †

"Your tongue," I said. "Who did it to you?"

He grinned, and threw his hands in the air, and pointed at me, as if I should know.

"What does the tattoo stand for?"

He grinned again, and this time flung his arms wide as if to embrace the world around. Then he got back in his rickety vehicle and drove away.

Tommy wanted to set off for Dublin, but I didn't want to leave before I had more information on Bomber, so we sat in the car and Tommy told me what he knew.

"His name is Terry Folan. Bomber Folan, they called him. I got to know him slightly down here, he used hang around at the fringes of that crowd Leo and Jack Proby ran with. There was smack going around, not through me, I don't know who was dealing it, Miranda Hart would know. Folan had come through St. Jude's in the nineties, just after Leo and Hutton, and then he'd been given a start as an apprentice in Tyrrellscourt stables, too. He was given a few rides, he moved up, he was still around when Pa Hutton vanished, the odd ride here and there, and then it all started to fall apart for him, he was drinking, he couldn't keep the weight off, he was just doing yard work and then not even that. He used to be one of the drunks in McGoldrick's and then he was barred from there. You'd see him stumbling along the main street, you know, half ten in the morning with a can of Dutch Gold and a rough sleeper's tan? That was as much as I knew, '98, '99 that would have been, I dropped out of sight here then. Paula wanted me home. Those were the days, right Ed?"

Paula was Tommy's ex-wife, and the divorce had been far from amicable; the *marriage* hadn't been very amicable in the first place. After years of Paula's utter disdain at his uselessness, Tommy cheated on her at a party with a drunk woman who Tommy thought was in love with him; he then made the mistake of telling Paula, whereupon she promptly threw him out, and then proceeded to sleep with everyone either of them had ever met, and to make sure everyone else knew about it. When the drunk woman sobered up, she told Tommy that it hadn't been love, not even lust, just drink.

"Steno filled me in on what happened then, insofar as he knew. Apparently Folan befriended this old scrap-merchant character, Iggy Staples, who lived out of town a couple of miles, he . . . lived on a dump, was how Steno described it. It's actually Staples collected scrap but he never really did anything with it, he lived off his pension in a cottage that was falling in on top of him. Anyway, Bomber used to go up there and sleep, there was enough shelter, he'd pull together some kind of shed for himself. And Staples got used to the company, enjoyed it, and when he died, hadn't he left the place to Bomber."

"And what about the keys to St. Jude's? Is he the caretaker?"

"It's not a good question to ask around here," Tommy said. "Even Steno, the first time I asked, he just walks off, didn't see him for an hour, piano-stops-playing type of thing. There's a lull in the afternoon, he asks me through to the warehouse, you know the restaurant there, they're changing over from lunch to dinner. The way he put it, St. Jude's is a scar on the town? Like, everyone knew what was going on there, but nobody did anything. And there wasn't just one Bomber Folan, every year there'd be casualties, a lot of them'd go to England, but a lot stayed, and those that went away usually came back, because they weren't fit for anything, and there they'd be, Tyrrellscourt's standing army of drunks and drug addicts, of misfits and losers, getting barred from the pubs and shambling round the streets, a living reproach every one to the town's puffed-up image of itself. Eventually they got St. Jude's closed down, there was one more scandal . . . no, I know what it was, your friend did a documentary on it. Your woman, the dykey one."

"Martha O'Connor?"

"That's right. And all these stories came out, even into the nineties, some of the laypeople were abusers—"

"Vincent Tyrrell? He was there in the nineties for a while, when Leo and Hutton were there."

"It wasn't in the program. I don't think Father Tyrrell . . . I mean, he's a bollocks, but I'd never have put him down for that."

"'The dykey one.'"

"What?"

"Is that how we talk?"

"It's how I talk. I've nothing against them. Which is more than they can say for me."

"Tommy."

"All right Ed, Jasus, you're very fucking Californian sometimes, do you know that?"

"How'd Folan get to be the caretaker, if that's what he is?"

"Nobody knows. Steno said no application has been made for the property, so nobody even knows who owns it, the Church or the state or what. But that Folan has the keys to the locks, whether he appointed himself to put them on, or whether he's carrying out duties for the owner, nobody knows."

"And what about the tongue?"

"No one had really seen Folan since Staples died, about five years ago. He'd come down to the town for groceries, and for his dole, but that was it. Then, about two years ago, he kind of presents himself, the head shaved, in the bar in McGoldrick's, drinking the few pints, not saying a word. At the end of the night, he opens his mouth and shows the whole pub why he's so quiet. Pleased by the reaction he gets, and away with him. After that, he's in regularly. I got talking to Steno tonight, told him why you were in town, he said Bomber's our man. When he came in, he remembered me. He actually can speak, he has enough of his tongue left for that, and to eat with. Anyway, I talked him through the whole thing, Pa Hutton, Leo, immediately he's nodding, he's got something to show us."

"And what a show," I said.

"Poor fucker."

"What do people think happened? To the tongue, I mean."

"They think he did it himself."

"I want to see where he lives, Tommy."

Tommy started up the engine.

"It's on the way back," he said.

Maybe half a mile after the turnoff for the country club, there was a narrow mud boreen indented with car tracks. It curved back toward the town for maybe half a mile, climbing as it went, then dropped suddenly toward the river. Tommy stopped the car before the drop, and we got out. To one side, you could see the golf course sweeping down from the rear of the country club; on the other, there was a steady incline; nestled in the valley between the base of the hill and the river, I saw a couple of mobile homes, old cars and car parts, a mound of assorted scrap metal and wood, a stone cottage with a light burning and the Jeep Terry "Bomber" Folan had been driving. The light from the cottage spilled onto a small fenced-in paddock around which a horse was steadily pacing.

On the journey back, I checked the plates of Regina Tyrrell's Range Rover with those on the one Tommy had seen leaving Tibradden the night Jackie Tyrrell was murdered. They weren't a match. I told Tommy that Regina Tyrrell had tried to hire me as her inside man, and that I had offered her him in my place; among other things, that'd give him a chance to check out F. X. Tyrrell's Range Rover, and see if Miranda Hart was right about Derek Rowan or his son driving the car. Tommy looked taken aback, then flattered, then got all serious and businesslike about it.

Then he said, "I'll still have to do the four masses tomorrow morning, Ed."

"Maybe the Omega Man will suspend hostilities for Christmas Day," I replied.

Tommy didn't know whether I was being serious or not. Neither did I. My mind was still reeling at the dumb show Bomber Folan had presented to us. A shrink I went to for a while after my daughter died, until he refused to see me unless I could at least be sober once a week for the hour-long session and I decided that that was not going to be possible, told me that in London during Jacobean times, people used to go to Bedlam to look at the lunatics in the way rich socialites used to swing by Harlem during the jazz age: it was what the smart set did. Eventually playwrights caught on to this, and inserted scenes with lunatics into their plays, in much the same way blackface sequences found their way into Broadway musicals, I suppose. I'd never seen one of those plays, but I thought of them tonight when the man with no tongue simulated anal rape in a red room beneath a picture of the Sacred Heart of Jesus.

I kept coming back to the fact that Bomber Folan had resurfaced two years ago, around the same time Miranda Hart had Don Kennedy investigate the disappearance of her missing husband, in order to have him declared dead. And now there were three dead bodies, all with close connections to Miranda Hart, all with the same tattoos, all with their tongues cut out: Folan had the tattoo, Folan had no tongue, Folan must at the very least have been known to Miranda Hart, even if it was just a case of sharing the same smack dealer.

Folan had put on a show tonight for my benefit. His parting gesture was to intimate that I should know who was behind all of this. The tattoo, the abuse, the tongue, they all seemed to be connected. If I were Myles Geraghty, I'd put Folan in a cell and beat the shit out of him until he confessed. When I saw his house, I was tempted to go down there and try that tack myself. I had too much information and not enough, the ideal time to take it out on someone weaker than you.

I called Martha O'Connor. She might have brought me too much publicity in the past, but if anyone could be relied upon to know what had happened to whom in which industrial school, she could. Martha was somewhere noisy, getting pissed and having a nice time. I was happy for her, and I said so. Not convincingly enough, however; soon she was giving out to me for being a kill-joy and a scold.

"It's not as if I go out every night, you know," she said. "Or any night, come to think of it."

"I know. I'm sorry. Are you with Fiona Reed?"

"Mind your own business YES and I think she's really into me," Martha said, or yelled. Fiona Reed was Garda Superintendent in Seafield, and she didn't like me, but I was convinced if she and Martha made a go of things, it couldn't do me any harm. "Are you the last man working, Ed Loy? Take a break."

"You're one to talk."

"If I can do it, you can. Even in the trenches, they stopped shooting for a day or two."

"Yeah, that just occurred to me. About someone else, though."

"The Omega Man?" Martha said, sharp as a tack, and abruptly the party noises faded.

"Jesus, Martha, what did you do, kill everyone?"

"I stepped out of the room. Is it the Omega Man? What do you need?"

"I don't know what you're drinking, but I'd ask for my money back, it's obviously not working."

"That's funny, Ed. I'll make a note in my diary to laugh when I've time. What can I do?"

"I need to see a documentary you made about St. Jude's, or that St. Jude's featured in. The industrial school."

"Yeah, when? Now? Now is not great, but—"

"Martha, you're on a date."

"We don't all think with our dicks, Ed Loy."

"I'll give you that one, for Christmas. Tomorrow sometime. I know it's Christmas Day—"

"Big swing. St. Jude's, Tyrrellscourt, Jackie Tyrrell, F. X. Tyrrell, Father Vincent, how does it stack up so far?"

"Is a highly ranked police officer leaking you her best stuff?"

"Not as often as I'd like. What time? She's going to her mammy's for dinner, I'm home alone all day."

"Maybe two, two-thirty?"

"The turkey twizzlers are on me."

IN TOMMY'S KITCHEN there was a turkey and a ham, vegetables and fruit and a Christmas pudding, sauces and mustards, pickles and cold meats, cheese and wine, a bottle of Tanqueray and a bottle of Jameson. Tommy looked at them and shrugged his I've-already-said-what-I-had-to-say shrug.

I went upstairs. She was asleep in the box room. More than ever, she reminded me of my wife: how vulnerable a woman was when she slept, how it was then that you saw the little girl in her. I thought of everything Tommy had told me about Miranda Hart tonight, and all I felt was pity, and sadness, and an urgent sense that I could help her, and that she needed me to. I shut the door behind me and made my way out into the night.

SEVENTEEN

I dropped Tommy off at the church for midnight mass, and headed back up toward Castlehill. Dave lived on a quiet road down from the Castlehill Hotel in a semi-d he bought back when he first graduated from Templemore with the help of some money an aunt of his in America had left him; he couldn't have afforded to buy a third of it on his current salary. I didn't want to go to Dave's party for any number of reasons, chief among them that it would be full of cops who wouldn't want me there, a feeling one or two of them would relish making plain. Another of the reasons I didn't want to go opened the door to me: Myles Geraghty, making himself at home. He clapped me on the shoulder as if we were the best of buddies and let out a loud roar.

"It's Sherlock fuckin' Holmes, lads, as we live and breathe."

"Language please, Detective Geraghty," snapped Carmel, snaking an arm around my waist and tugging me into the house.

They continued their exchange in mime over my head, which Carmel had tucked into a cleavage on full merry-widow duty tonight and stoked with some musky aroma. When she let me up for air, something in her eyes was reckless, almost delusional; maybe she was just another party hostess flying high, but I wondered: Carmel had always had a sexy, flirtatious look that said you'd missed your chance with her, but only just; tonight, it looked like the "only just" had been set aside. She still had a great body, long-legged and rangy, but the dress she wore would have been cut too low and hemmed too high for a twenty-eight-year-old, and her heels put her maybe half a head below me, and I'm six two when I don't slouch. I certainly didn't object to the view, but it's not one I'd have relished in a wife; I saw Dave eyeing her as she danced me toward the kitchen and poured me a glass of lethal-looking punch; he had the fixed, glassy smile of a man whose car has just rolled back off the viewing platform and tumbled into a quarry while he waits for it to explode. Carmel told me I'd missed the prospect she had lined up for me, but that we had to have a good long talk; this having been established, she clipped off to more urgent business: swaying about drawing hungry looks from every man in the place, or so it seemed.

The party had wound down, but the dwindlers were determined to stay until the bitter end, despite the unwritten rule that if you're in another man's house after midnight on Christmas Eve, you'd better have a red suit and a big sack. The Guards had neither; indeed, a Guard I recognized from Seafield with no lips and no manners seemed hell-bent on proving he had no wits either: ranting lachrymosely and aggressively about how Christmas wasn't what it used to be, and of course it never had been, he had to be physically restrained from breaking to Sadie, Dave's angelic five-year-old, who was skipping about in a turquoise-and-lavender tutu with a magic wand, the news that Santa Claus didn't exist. Dave did the physical restraining himself, and he looked to me like he'd have enjoyed doing a lot more of it. The lipless Guard resumed after a brief pause with an ill-tempered, sanity-taxing tirade about how contemporary Christmas songs weren't fit to shine the shoes of the immortal classics of the genre, by titans such as Mud, Wizzard and Gary Glitter.

In the living room, the source of the inferior contemporary sounds, Dave's three boys, who were between ten and fourteen but looked like they'd been fed on beef three times a day since birth, were trying out their rucking and mauling techniques on a couple of Guards who wanted to show what good sports they were to three young female Gardaí who had drunk themselves to the land where the only response to any event is to shriek with laughter. The shrieks only got louder when Dave's eldest lad tried a handoff that was more like a punch, causing a Guard's nose to flow and his temper to fly a long way from where the good sports play.

In the back room, a few older hands were putting on a different kind of show for their juniors, and after sinking the punch and finding some whiskey and hearing the Butler family being discussed, I felt emboldened enough to insinuate myself onto the edge of it.

"They're a blot, a fucking plague all over north Wicklow, and there's nothing you can fucking do with them," a thickset ginger-haired comb-over said.

"Are they all one family?" a spotty young fella said.

Comb-over led the older hands in a burst of hollow laughter.

"You could say that," he said. "Put it this way: Old Man Butler wasn't fussy about where he dipped his wick. He didn't mind if you were his cousin. He didn't mind if you were his sister. He didn't mind if you were his *daughter*."

"He didn't mind that at all at all," said a skinny cop with a hook nose and floppy gray hair in a side parting.

"Oh, he liked his daughters very much," said Comb-over.

"He liked his granddaughters too," added Hook Nose. The young Guards were appalled and delighted by what was obviously a practiced routine.

"He was an equal-opportunities shagger," Comb-over said.

"'Twas the granddaughters that did for him though," said a crinkle-haired Galway man with a big mustache.

"What, his granddaughters killed him?" a round-faced young smiler said.

"In a manner of speaking," said Comb-over, who smoked a pipe, and would have strung this one out until New Year's if he'd been let.

"One of the daughters caught him with the granddaughter," Hook Nose said. "Not in the act, but in the bedroom, very cozy. She reefed him out of it, sent him home with a flea in his ear. Then the young one, she's what, twelve, thirteen, doesn't she tell her ma her elder sister's been going in the bedroom with Granda for years now. The sister gets home, the ma gets it out of her, she hasn't been riding him, she's just been sucking him off, as if that wasn't as bad. And Ma goes fucking mental."

"There was three Butler sisters in the Michael Davitt," said Mustache.

"And Vinnie," said Hook Nose.

"Well they were hardly gonna get Vinnie involved, sure wasn't Vinnie as bad as the old man?" said Comb-over.

"So the daughters took the old man down the seafront there in Bray, in and out of any pub or hotel he wasn't barred from, started at the harbor, ended up by the amusements, in full daylight this was, the wintertime, and they filled him full of drink and bullshit, bygones be bygones, nothing to forgive, sure nothing happened anyway. And the women were watching what they drank. And then they set off up the hill a little way and around the cliff path, work up a thirst for more, Da, they said, night falling fast. And when they got to the sheerest drop, little pick of a man at this stage, and two of the women twenty stone each, didn't they pick him up and fuck him down onto the railway tracks."

"And what happened?" said Spotty.

"Into the station with them," said Hook Nose. "They told me

Old Man Butler had committed suicide. I asked them why he'd done that, he didn't seem the type, and they said that he'd finally seen the error of his ways, and then they each produced a statement detailing what he had done to them over the years. And what he'd begun to do to their children."

Hook Nose stopped talking, and drained his drink, and Comb-over passed him a bottle of Paddy.

"It didn't make pleasant fucking reading, I can tell you that for nothing," he said.

"You took leave, didn't you?" Mustache said.

"Ah, I needed a holiday anyway."

"But . . . how do you know they murdered him?" Smiler said.

"Because they were fucking boasting about it all over Bray that night. 'We killed our da, and we'll kill you if you fuck with us.' And Vinnie comes in three days later, the last to fucking know as usual, and he wants to press charges," said Comb-over. "They've told him they did it, they've told half of Wicklow they did it, and the other half know they did it anyway. So we prepare a file, and we send it to the DPP to see if they'll take it to trial, and he comes back with his decision: Not In A Million Years."

"It'd be a grand 'oul story," Hook Nose said, "like in a film or something, only for the fact that the daughters are fucking savages too, and they've raised broods of savages: junkies and dealers and whores. Every night there's joyriding or robbing or fire-setting or some fucking shenanigans up there and it's always the Butlers."

"What do you do though?" Smiler said. "I mean, there's always gonna be families like that on a council estate, families that drag the rest down. And the only sanction you have is to evict them. And then what do you do with all the evicted families?"

"They used to go to England," Mustache said. "That's where Old Man Butler came back from. With three brothers, you know what they were called? Seán, John, and John Junior. And Old Man Butler was called Jack. Fuck's sake like. They all had the same fucking name. Making a show of us in front of the Brits, thick fucking Paddy can't even think to give his kids different names like."

"Seed and breed, seed and breed," Comb-over said.

"When the blood goes bad, it's a hard job to put it right," Mustache said.

"It's the job of generations," Hook Nose said.

"It's not our job lads," Comb-over said.

"But seriously, what do you do?" Smiler had drunk himself earnest. "I mean, if it's one or two families, and you get them out, what do you do with them then?"

"Is this a social services or a waste management problem?" Comb-over said.

"Burn them," said Hook Nose.

"Bury them," said Mustache.

"Recycle them," Spotty chirped, staying up late with the big boys.

They all looked at Smiler.

"I mean, it's just such a tragic set of circumstances," he said, sticking nervously to his guns. "There must be some way make an intervention, to break the cycle, to rehabilitate . . . some of them, at least," he said. "The children?"

Hook Nose and Mustache looked up at the ceiling and piously intoned the word *intervention*. Comb-over exhaled a cloud of smoke from his pipe, then leant through it and jerked his chin at Smiler.

"In our day, son, a Guard was supposed to marry a nurse, not fucking turn into one."

EVERYONE WAS TALKING about the Omega Man case, and everyone stopped talking about it whenever I got close. I decided it was better if I made good my escape. I was at the front door when Dave appeared at the top of the stairs and tiptoed down them. He raised a finger to his lips, then went around the rooms, turned the music off in one and brought the noise level down in the others, then reappeared at the kitchen end of the hall and unlocked the door that led to the converted garage. Dave had wanted this space to be a den, or a home office; Carmel had argued for a family room, or somewhere she could start one of the business ideas she had had but never pursued; eventually it had become a garage with plasterwork: old computers, a canoe, a cutting machine for dressmaking, a swingball set, a turntable, two VCRs, the kids' old schoolbooks, Dave and Carmel's old schoolbooks, you name it. Dave locked the door behind him and found a chair without turning on the light; I sat on a railway trunk in the dark.

"Thanks for coming, Ed," he said in a low, anxious voice.

"I wouldn't have missed it. What's up?"

"Sorry about the cloak-and-dagger, it's just—"

"Sure, I understand. What have you got, Dave?"

"The latest from the postmortem. Hutton's body was frozen. It still hadn't completely thawed out. It means establishing a time of death is much more difficult, maybe impossible. They probably have to mess with entomology, what bugs were frozen when. But that'd take days in normal time: over Christmas in Ireland, it could be March. Both Hutton and Kennedy were killed elsewhere and moved to the scene. Each was strangled by hand: there are scars consistent with fingers digging into the neck; there's some matter that may be fingernail debris, from which DNA might possibly be extracted, in the event that we ever get ourselves a suspect."

"And all of this applies to Jackie Tyrrell as well?"

"Except it seems as if the killer was wearing gloves this time: there are fewer finger tears at the neck. And one more thing. The bags of coins found on Kennedy and Hutton. There was another on Jackie Tyrrell's body. Same kind of bag each time, leather pouch with a drawstring. And there were thirty coins in each, thirty single euro coins. Remember your gospel?"

"Judas. Thirty pieces of silver. That's the last thing anyone re-members Patrick Hutton saying: 'I won't play the Judas for anyone.' And the tongues cut out: Does that mean the betrayal lay in tell-ing someone something? In confessing? Or in not speaking up?"

"Either way, some kind of betrayal."

"And now someone is making people pay for that betrayal."

I thought of Father Vincent Tyrrell kissing me on the mouth this morning. After I'd gotten over the shock, I had thought it seemed at once deliberate and cryptic, a statement I was to inter-pret—a Judas Kiss?

"We still have no ID on the body, Ed."

"What do they make of the tattoos?"

"They've got hold of a few people from Trinity College, a pro-fessor of art history and someone who works in heraldry—they're both writing up reports. But I don't see it that way."

"How do you mean?"

"Well, a serial killer works at random, right? And then he does something to tie it all together, he only kills young women, or gay men, or whatever. And if he uses symbols or leaves tags, it's a kind of taunt to the cops: I'm smarter than you. Come and get me if you think you're good enough."

"Yeah?"

"But in this case, the victims are linked: they're all connected to a horse race in 1997, to a stable, to a town and to a family. So there's a different kind of logic going on. It's like the killer is saying, understand why I'm doing this. I have a plan, and it has a logic, and you better work it out before . . ."

Before Miranda Hart is murdered, I thought. But the face I summoned up was not Miranda's, but Regina Tyrrell's daughter, Karen: I could see her eyes, one blue, one brown, shimmering in the dark.

"I laid it out for Geraghty, Dave. I gave him enough to con-nect Kennedy and Jackie Tyrrell, which gives him Hutton—not an ID, but at least the lead."

"He doesn't want to see it that way, Ed. He wants his own serial killer, with biblical quotes and runic symbols. And he has enough evidence tending in that direction to ignore anything that doesn't."

"And he lacks a wise senior colleague he trusts who'd be better able to advise him."

"Something like that."

"What about Vinnie Butler?"

"They're running forensics on his van. He denies everything, including even being at the dump, but you'd expect that. My gut tells me no, but you never can tell with the Butlers."

"Anything on Don Kennedy?"

"There was a team trawling through his home office today. They've sealed it over Christmas, but I've got the key. I'll slip out tomorrow."

"Okay. There's an industrial school in Tyrrellscourt, St. Jude's, I think it figures in this, too. I'm seeing someone tomorrow about it."

"Not your one off the telly? Fuck's sake, Ed—"

"What do you want? She's the expert. And fuck it, you might need the publicity badly this time, when you get the killer and Myles Geraghty insists on taking all the credit."

There was a long silence, and I could hear Dave breathing deeply, as if trying to keep a lid on something. When he spoke, it was in a tremulous, quavering voice, as if he was trying to sound happy about something and not making out too well with it.

"Sadie pegged out in my arms, she's the only one in the house who still believes in Santa. I made a doll's house for her, I was up nights most of November building the fucking thing. I always do November off the booze. Good to have something to do then. Otherwise you start noticing all sorts of stuff you wish you hadn't. But you should have seen her little face tonight, Ed, I swear, looking at them when they sleep . . . you'd swear there wasn't a thing astray, not a single thing in the world."

Dave did the breathing thing again, then got up and unlocked the door.

"Better leave it awhile before you go."

"Sure," I said. "Thanks, Dave."

I sat in the dark for five or ten minutes, and then I looked out, and saw no one in the hall, and made it to the front door again. I could hear low murmurs from the living room, and I thought I'd make a quick escape, but then I remembered Carmel had taken my coat and put it upstairs, so I went up to get it. As I climbed the stairs, I thought I could hear a noise from the master bedroom. I figured the boys were in there watching TV. I found my coat in one of the boys' bedrooms. I stepped out onto the landing and the door to the master bedroom flew open and Carmel stood there, panting, her hair all mussed up and her lipstick smeared, and I had an intense flash of my mother in a doorway just like this one, in the house in Quarry Fields that was more like this than not; in the room behind my mother was a man putting on his clothes: the man who killed my father. In the room behind Carmel, who was smiling desperately, even though we both knew there were tears in her eyes, was a man adjusting his shirt: Myles Geraghty.

I'd parked around the corner near the hotel, and that's where Carmel caught me up; I could hear her shoes clipping up the road after me; she must have kept her heels on, was the lurid thought, and image, that came unbidden and unwanted into my head. I didn't want to look at her, but she tugged on my shoulder and spun me around. Her eye makeup had melted into two black smears across eyes prickling with what looked like desperation.

"Ed, please don't . . . it wasn't what you thought . . ." she said, the words fading in and out of range on the ebb and flow of her emotion.

"Don't dem . . . all right, Carmel, what was it, then? Are we gonna agree to pretend it wasn't what we know it was? Don't—"

"Don't *demean* myself? Is that what you started to say? Having *demeaned* myself already, I shouldn't *demean* myself by lying about it?"

It was as if I'd hit her; the desperation flared into anger and defiance.

"That's about right," I said.

She hit me then; she was shaking with rage and unhappiness and she hit me a few times across the cheek, but her heart wasn't in it, and I grabbed her wrist and hoped she'd subside, but she didn't; she wrenched it off me as if I had assaulted her.

"Don't you judge me. You're no one to judge me, you fucking . . . you've the morals of a beast in the fields, Ed Loy, you'd fuck your own shadow."

"I'm not judging you."

"You fucking are. The look on your face—"

"What do you expect? Dave's my friend, and you betray him, fine, you're right, I'm no one to judge, but you could pick your moment, Carmel, and you could pick your man: Jesus, of all people, Myles fucking Geraghty, talk about rubbing a man's face in it, do you not know what a nightmare he's made Dave's life since he joined the Bureau?"

"No, I don't know, how would I know? Do you think he talks to me about it? Any of it? Of course he tells you, men only, noble beasts grunt out your pain to each other, then down the next whiskey and get on with things, don't tell the little woman, she'd only get upset, or worse, think you were human."

"He said if he brought his troubles home, you'd think he was weak."

Carmel's face nearly gave, she looked so hurt; she twisted it into a snarl and a harsh laugh.

"Weak? Christ, he thinks that of me? And he *said* it to you? Who's betraying who, Ed? Who do you think I am, Lady Mac-fuckingbeth? Let me tell you about Dave's mother's funeral: after the removal, I found him in the garage, crying his eyes out. I went to him, arms out, you know. *He backed away from me.* He left the house, he drove around, I don't know where, he came back when I was asleep, that was the last tear he let me see. I'd think he was weak? I'd think he was a human being. It's got worse since you came back. He thinks you're . . . I don't know what, he's always sniggering like a teenager about what you get up to . . . it's as if he thinks you're cool, that's what it is."

"I'm not cool."

"Do you think I don't know that? Misery knows misery. I *see* you, Ed Loy. The same fucked-up woman in one guise after another. The booze, the fights. You're so in love with your own fucking pain, you need to keep the wound fresh and flowing to feel half alive. Don't take Dave down with you. He's got like that: the job is everything, but he can't talk about it, what he goes through, what he suffers, he removes himself from my life, from our lives. Absent. And then he shows up, expecting us to be like a family in a movie, he wants me to fuck him, the kids to adore him. Frolic along the beach with a big furry dog. We don't even *know* him."

Carmel was shivering, maybe crying. I took off my coat and tried to put it on her shoulders, but she wouldn't let me. She pushed me away, and then hung on my lapel, her hand on my shoulder. I knew that nothing like this happened for no reason, that making a family wasn't easy, that Carmel and Dave were very far from the couple I'd idealized. But I'd seen her with Myles Geraghty, and I felt it in my gut, and I couldn't let it go.

"I hear all that, Carmel, and fair enough, I don't really know what it's like . . . I was only married a short while, and I didn't make a great go of it. But . . . sorry, I can't get away from this, in front of all his colleagues, and if they didn't see, you can be fucking sure they'll be told, Myles Geraghty. I think Dave knows something is going on—"

"Of course he *knows*. There's not much point to it unless he knows. Do you think I *like* Myles Geraghty? Do you think I want to do this? Turns out it's all I have, after fifteen years of kids, these legs, these tits, and I won't have them for long, not in this shape anyway. Getting old, Ed, and I don't want to wait around to die.

I've tried talking to him, tried warning him. Nothing. Calls for desperate measures. Rub his face in it? Yes. Demean myself? Yes. What next? I know what you'd do. Walk away. School of Ed Loy says, just walk away. But you don't put twenty years into what I've built up to walk away. You can't."

A breath at the corner, a foot snap on frost, and there was Dave. Carmel turned to him, and nodded, and turned back to me.

"I'm sorry if what I said hurt you," she said.

"That's 'Happy Christmas' in Irish, is it?"

"Some things are more important than who fucked who. You know that."

I thought of my daughter, how she hadn't been mine, not in blood, yet I called her mine and always would and knew it to be true. I nodded, and Carmel gave me a kiss, and walked up to Dave and put an arm around his waist and put her head on his shoulder. Dave raised his hand in the air, and I returned his salute, and they walked back down to their house, and their family, and their life, about which, it turned out, I knew next to nothing.

The roads had frosted up, powder bright in the moonlight; I drove back slowly, wondering how this would affect the Leopardstown Festival: Irish racing did not like firm ground, and would cancel a meeting rather than risk the horses.

When I got back to Quarry Fields, I found Tommy Owens's key on my kitchen table and Miranda Hart in my bed. Better than the other way round, I remember thinking as I got in beside her, trying not to wake her, but not trying too hard. She awoke, and her breath smelled of oranges, and the rest of her smelt just as good.

"Merry Christmas, Edward Loy," she said, and for a while, it was.

EIGHTEEN

The door creak again, and the rustle of straw, of paper, and the bolt run with a crack, and her dark head turning, Miranda Hart, and then the bolt again, or the sound of it, like a pistol shot, like the slam of a door, my Spanish girl, my ex-wife, now the rustle of straw, the pistol crack, the turning head, my mother, dark-headed, too, as she was when I was a boy, rustle, crack, door, turning head, Regina Tyrrell, fear in her eyes, and another, someone else, I can't make out his face, rustle, crack, door, head turn: Karen Tyrrell, one eye blue, one eye brown, and the hand closing on her, the hand about to touch her, I can't see his face, Karen, Miranda, Regina, my wife, my mother, rustle, crack, door, the turning head, the reaching hand . . .

I woke up alone, bathed in sweat, with Carmel Donnelly's words burning in my ears. *You're so in love with your own pain. The same fucked-up woman over and over again.* It didn't have to be that way. I wouldn't let it be that way. I went out on the landing, and smelt breakfast being cooked downstairs, bacon and eggs, or something that good. I remembered how I'd felt yesterday, before the trip to Tyrrellscourt, when I heard Miranda's footfall and felt the promise of a future. But as I showered, it all came back to me: not just what Tommy had told me about her operating as a prostitute, not just the drugs, not just Bomber Folan or Jack Proby, but what it all amounted to: that she knew so much more than she had told me. What I saw in the bathroom mirror as I shaved was not promise; it was resignation, and something worse than that: betrayal, and the fear of betrayal. The Judas Kiss.

I didn't think I owned as many pots and pans, plates and cooking utensils, as Miranda Hart had used to make a breakfast fry; she emerged from the debris with two plates as I sat down; I wanted to greet her smile with something more than the polite nod I managed, but found that I couldn't. We ate in silence. Miranda broke it.

"I suppose Tommy told you, did he?"

I nodded.

"Well, he probably remembers it all better than I do. I was pretty far gone, most of the time. What did he say?"

"That you took money for sex. That you were available to a whole circle of men that formed itself around Leo Halligan and Jack Proby. He said he didn't know whether you were doing it of your own free will or not. That you were doing so much heroin you maybe didn't even know yourself."

I found myself trying to make it easy for her. To her credit, she didn't want that. She popped some gum in her mouth, lit a cigarette and exhaled.

"No, I wasn't forced. The opposite. I was with Jack Proby at the time, nothing serious, just for laughs—funny how relationships that are just for laughs quickly run out of them—and we were doing a lot of drugs, too much coke, and then I got into smack to take me down, I couldn't sleep, and then I needed the coke to get me back up, and that became a cycle. And that became expensive.

And it had gotten so I didn't much care what I did—I can't quite explain how that happens, but when it does, it seems so simple and so realistic, you know: there's a rich golfer, or a trainer, or a jockey, why don't I just fuck him for five hundred quid, or spend the night for a grand. I won't feel anything anyway, the smack guaranteed that, so why not make a profit, you know?"

"And what was this about? This was all after Patrick disappeared: Was it a kind of grief, a distorted mourning for him?"

She bowed her head, and I thought she was crying. When she looked up at me, there was laughter in her eyes.

"I'm sorry, I shouldn't laugh, it's just . . . I didn't really give you the full picture before, Ed. Not sure that I should have, worried I'd scare you off. 'I really like you, come in for coffee, but first listen to my life as a smackhead and a hooker.' Above and beyond on a first date, don't you think? But . . . I don't know, is the answer. I don't know what happened then. What I can tell you about is what happened with Patrick. What happened to By Your Leave."

"I thought you already had."

"That was a version."

"Let me try my version," I said. "Patrick Hutton was getting paid by Leo Halligan, possibly fronting for George, possibly acting on his own, to hold various horses back, dope them or otherwise interfere with them. At Thurles that day, Leo wanted a winner; F.X. wanted to lengthen the odds for Leopardstown; Hutton was caught between them, so he made it obvious he was holding the horse up to throw the blame onto F.X., but also to show Leo he couldn't be bossed around."

"Sort of, but not quite. In a way, Patrick did exactly what he was told to that day; he just did it too well, too publicly, he brought down too much attention on the sport. And on the fix. In truth, at this stage, F.X. and Leo were pretty much in league. F.X. didn't feel you could hold a horse like By Your Leave back, it was better to use her as a flagship for the other Tyrrell rides, you know, let her win, to hell with the odds, and let the glory drip through to the other horses in the stable. And Leo agreed. But this particular race, George had a lot of money laid against By Your Leave. So the word came down to hold the horse back." ·

"And Hutton rebelled?"

"Patrick was a hothead. He was a bit of a fucking eejit. In fairness to him, it was never going to be easy, unless you out and out doped the horse, and they'd heard she was going to be drug-tested. But Patrick didn't even try."

"Why would F. X. Tyrrell put up with this? What did George Halligan have on F.X.?"

Miranda grinned, and stubbed her cigarette out in some bacon rind. I stared at this picture, trying to remember where I had seen it before.

"Leo was a busy boy in those days. F. X. Tyrrell picked him and Patrick from St. Jude's to be apprentices. And then he wanted extra services. Well, Patrick wasn't into that. But Leo was."

"And F.X. was, you're saying."

"Oh yeah. Did Jackie not tell you?"

"She just said it never really happened for them."

"And that's the reason. She was probably being loyal. She knew what was going on. Leo and F.X., Leo and Seán Proby, too. And Leo got it all on film. Photographs of F.X. and Leo in some position or other. Shots that wouldn't look well on pages three to ten of the *Sun* during Cheltenham week. So F. X. Tyrrell belonged to the Halligans. Still does, I imagine."

"And so what do you think? Did the Halligans get rid of Hutton for rocking the boat?"

"I don't know. They could have. Not because Leo wanted it, but George might have decided to cut him out. Either way, he had become a liability. So the Halligans gave the word that F.X. could cut him loose."

"So George Halligan controls F. X. Tyrrell?"

"To a certain extent. I mean, the thing about George is, he's not stupid. It's like, if you have a restaurant and you can eat free there. Well, if you go every night, if you bring all your friends, if you take the piss, there's not going to be any restaurant. So George played it cute, a few scores here and there but nothing that's going to make the headlines, or push F. X. Tyrrell over the edge."

"And do you have anything to add to how you parted, you and Hutton?"

"It was . . . more emphatic than I told you. On my side, I was so fucking pissed off, we could have had it both ways: we knew what Leo had on F.X., and we knew which races were crooked; plus, we had the Halligans offering to make side deals with us. We had an insurance policy, all we had to do was play it smart."

Miranda seemed to wake up in the middle of saying this, wake to the realization that it made her sound like a cheap chivvying little piece of work. Again, to her credit, she held her hands up.

"I imagine this makes me sound pretty bad," she said.

"I imagine you wouldn't make yourself sound like that if it wasn't true."

"It's just, it was hard to draw the line. If a jockey pulls a ride for his own trainer, why is that better than pulling it for a gangster? It's the same thing, just a question of degree. And if you get more money from the gangster, and if your trainer is already in league with him . . ."

She shrugged, and flicked her hair, and pouted the way she did, and I could feel my heart breaking. I'd built her into a princess, and she was just a tramp on the make. Merry Christmas, Edward Loy.

"Ask me anything else, please. I really want to . . . to set the record straight, Ed."

She looked at me, unblinking, as if nothing had changed. And maybe nothing had. Maybe Carmel Donnelly was right, and I had fallen for another fucked-up woman I couldn't possibly have, or didn't want in the first place. I still didn't want to believe that.

And I tried not to, right up until she heard me ask the next question.

"Did you ever come across a guy called Terry Folan? Bomber, most people call him."

"No," she lied, so quickly I almost didn't hear her. "No, I don't . . . I don't think so, I . . . or maybe . . . *Bomber* Folan, that rings a bell . . ."

She said a lot more in that vein, until she arrived at the lie she was happy with: that she vaguely remembered him riding for F.X., and that he could have been around afterward, hanging out with Leo in McGoldrick's. At that stage, I was on my feet. I told her I had to go, I had to meet someone, and she asked me if I'd make it up to Tommy's for the Christmas dinner she was going to cook today, and I said I wouldn't miss it, and she kissed me and held me in the way you would if you loved him, or if you wanted him to love you, and again I tried to believe in her, and got my coat, and just when we were at the door she asked me if I still had the photograph of Patrick Hutton she gave me. It was the only one she had. No, it wasn't that, it was quite special to her, in a way she didn't want to tell me. Or wouldn't. Or hadn't made up yet. I said I didn't have it anymore. I don't know if she believed me, or pretended to believe me. I pretended I didn't care anymore. I left her at Tommy's, looking so beautiful and so forlorn I couldn't bear the sight of her. I think she knew what had happened; she couldn't figure out how. I wasn't sure I could either. I just knew that the next time we met, we'd be on opposite sides. You think you're never going to fall in love with anyone again, and sometimes the only way you know you did is because she's just broken your heart.

At Tommy's doorstep, after I'd said I wouldn't come in, and she said it was a sin to waste all that food, that she'd been looking forward to spending the day with me, and I looked at the ground as if that was any kind of answer, and she nodded, and suddenly there was fear in her eyes, real terror, and she looked as if she was about to howl with it.

"I can't tell you any more," she said.

"You know more than you're telling me."

Her eyes welled up with tears, her beautiful eyes.

"I can't . . . it's not my fault . . . I'm sorry, but I just can't . . ."

I shook my stupid head.

"Well, I'm sorry too, but neither can I."

I waited down the road from Tommy's until the taxi arrived to pick her up, and I tailed it until I was sure she was on her way back to Riverside Village. Then I drove to the Church of the Immaculate Conception in Bayview, and found Tommy in the sacristy and took him through what I thought had happened.

"Who's going to cook our Christmas dinner then?" he said, which was better than "I told you so," but not much.

I called Regina Tyrrell and apologized for not having been in touch, and checked that she still wanted an extra man.

"Do you think we need one?"

"I think you do, yes."

I quoted her a price for Tommy and Regina agreed to it while he looked goggle-eyed at me.

"Time you took yourself seriously," I told him.

"You first," he said.

I gave Tommy the key to my house and asked him to pack some surveillance equipment in the boot of his mother's car before he left for Tyrrellscourt. Then I gave him Leo Halligan's Glock 17. He flashed a look toward the door to the church, then stowed the gun beneath his cassock and nodded gravely to me, as if to say he appreciated the trust I was showing in him. I didn't tell him I had no other option.

When I left the sacristy I saw Vincent Tyrrell watching me from the altar; he seemed insubstantial to me, like a wraith; I wondered if I'd see him alive again.

———

WHILE I WAITED on the pier for Proby, I called Jim Morgan, a cardiologist I'd worked with on the Howard case. Once he'd gotten over his dismay at being phoned on Christmas Day, and once we'd established that eyes were not his area, he listened to my description of Karen Tyrrell's eyes, and suggested that it was possibly a condition known as heterochromia, that it was possibly genetic, and that if I wanted to move beyond the possible, I should find an opthalmologist and spoil his Christmas lunch.

Jack Proby was about my age, skinny and tall with boyish floppy hair in a seventies center parting and a seventies mustache to match and a mouth full of teeth that wouldn't've shamed a pony and acne scars on his long face. He stood at the start of the West Pier in a fawn cashmere coat over a navy suit and tan Italian shoes, looking like a hotel lobby was his idea of out in the open. The wind off the sea was cold enough to give me second thoughts too.

"The Royal Seafield know me," Proby said. "We can get in out of this."

The Royal Seafield was a Victorian seafront hotel of indifferent quality, but they did know Jack Proby, and admitted him even though the hotel was open only to residents, which is how I found myself drinking a large Jameson in a bar on Christmas Day, apart from Good Friday the only day of the year you cannot get served a drink in Ireland. Proby drank the same.

"How's it looking for you at Leopardstown tomorrow?" I said.

"What the fuck do you care?" Proby said. "Business, friend." His accent was educated northside, lazy and drawling; his voice was hoarse as a rule: it sounded like someone had cut him. I looked for a scar, but he wore his collar high.

"All right: Are you still tied to the Halligans because of what they've got on your old man?"

"What have they got?"

"Photos of him and Leo Halligan. Photos his family wouldn't like to see. Let alone the great Irish public."

Jack Proby suddenly looked like his collar was a size too small for him; he worked his neck around and blinked his eyes and sniffed.

"What is this? Is this blackmail, friend? 'Cause I tell you, if it is—"

"It isn't. It's tell me what I want to know and don't be a fucking prick."

"Because I know some important people in this town—"

"See, you've won already. The only important people I get to meet hire me to clean up the mess they make because they spent too much time with corrupt moneygrubbing scumbags like you. And afterward, they don't want to know me. The feeling's mutual, mind. Believe me, I've places I'd rather be today and all. Anywhere tops the list."

Proby, calculating I'd got the market in aggression tied up for the moment, nodded his consent, as if to a waiter.

"All right," I said. "To be honest, I don't much care if you're feeding the Halligans tips or if they're feeding you the inside on Tyrrellscourt horses—"

"George Halligan is a legitimate player now, friend, he has horses in half a dozen stables, not just F. X. Tyrrell's."

"That's what makes our system so great, isn't it? Any murdering drug-dealing scum-sucking savage can call himself an entrepreneur and be forgiven. Business washes us all clean. But I'm not one of the ruthless boys in a hurry, impatient to get on with making and building and storing up wealth for the winter months. I'm one of the laggards, the stick-in-the-muds who are always looking back, endlessly worrying about some sticky little detail everyone else is too busy going forward to be bothered with."

Proby looked at me as if the whiskey had gone to my head. Maybe it had. Get a refund if it hadn't. Proby signaled to the waiter for more. I shook my head, but he pointed to himself. He leant forward, all confidential.

"Look, I'm not proud of the life I led for a stretch there, in the late nineties . . . I ran with a pretty wild crowd . . . did a bit of this and that . . . but I swear, I was never a pimp."

"I know."

"You know?"

"Miranda told me. Mind you, she tends to lie."

The waiter brought Proby his second whiskey and he drank half of it back in one, and within seconds, seemed to turn into himself. He was that kind of drinker.

"She's not lying about that. We were both strung out for a while . . . I came out of a failed marriage, and she, well, there was the whole Patrick Hutton thing, you know? She was still freaking out about all that. But it was, it started off as, just a great time down there, party town, coke, champagne, all this bread, and I was doing some work for the old man, but it was so easy to keep George Halligan sweet. We had enough of the jockeys to spread the fixes to lay it so the betting patterns were never noticed. It was a fucking operation. Coining it. Beautiful, so it was. And then came heroin."

"Whose idea was that?"

"I don't remember. Because I asked myself that, like with some mad fucking bird you wake up with, you know, retrace your steps, locate the fatal moment, don't do this at home, kids. But I can't . . . eventually it was that ponytail guy who ended up barman in McGoldrick's, unbelievable, only in Tyrrellscourt would a smack dealer be taken on as head barman, what's this his name was?"

"Steno?"

"Steno, the very fellow. Anyway, we got into it, and after a while, you start running low on readies, no matter who you are, drugs cost a lot of bread, so Miranda decides to sell her stuff. I didn't like it, I argued against it, I was supposed to be her boyfriend, for fuck's sake, but . . . I was out of it anyway. What was I gonna do?"

Proby shrugged and finished his whiskey and immediately waved up two more.

"And why do you think, was there any other reason for her to get into heroin? Apart from it being there?"

"I think . . . well, I think after the whole thing with the baby, she found it hard to get back on track."

"What baby?"

"She had a kid . . . I can't really remember the order of events back then . . . but she had a kid and gave it up for adoption . . . would it have been before Hutton took off? Or afterward? I think afterward, yeah, that's *why* she gave it up, *because* he took off."

Proby nodded stupidly, already drunk. He beamed as the fresh drinks arrived. I still had half of my first.

"Weird to do something like that in 1997, '98," I said. "Lots of women raising kids on their own then."

"Not Miranda. Not her scene at all," Proby said.

"And you don't know who were the adoptive parents?"

He shook his head, then held a finger up.

"Tell you what I do remember. Who introduced smack to the Tyrrellscourt scene."

"Who?" I said.

"Patrick Hutton!" he said delightedly.

"Patrick Hutton vanished after By Your Leave was put down at Thurles. Before Christmas 1996."

"Oh no. No he didn't. No, he was around, because he was around when the kid was born, except he was smacked out of it then. Wasn't racing, wasn't anything, just . . . hanging around town for it. And after *that* he disappeared. Kaput! I don't know if they were still happy families, but I remember the three of them being around. And then it was just Miranda."

Proby nodded, seemingly relieved to have sorted that out. I

took out the photograph Miranda had given me and showed it to Proby.

"Patrick Hutton," I said.

"Patrick Hutton," he said. Then he peered at the photograph again.

"Except, that isn't Patrick Hutton."

"I'm sorry."

"That isn't Patrick Hutton. That's the other guy."

"What other guy?" I said, but his name was on my lips, had been from the moment Miranda asked for the photograph back.

"The jockey F.X. got in to replace Hutton. Only he didn't last long. He lost it completely, became a kind of wino. Bomber, they called him."

I could have prompted him, but I waited. He was the kind of drunk whose wits accumulate as the spirit level rises. He studied the photograph again, then lifted his weak face in triumph.

"Terry Folan," he said. "Terry 'Bomber' Folan. One for the road? Come on, it's Christmas."

IN MY CAR, I called Miranda Hart on her mobile and landline and left remorseful messages on each; the trip to Martha O'Connor's place took me past Riverside Village but there was no one home and the Porsche was gone. I stood by my car and swore quietly. If the body I had thought was Patrick Hutton was Bomber Folan—and I had been led to believe that by the photograph Miranda Hart gave me—then there was a good chance Bomber Folan was really Hutton, and either Miranda Hart was in league with him, or she was in his power. Bomber/Hutton was obviously a disturbed individual; if he was responsible for the killings so far, it was clear he had some kind of plan; it was entirely possible Miranda had been drawn into this plan out of fear, either for her own safety, or the safety of someone she prized. Jack Proby had told me Miranda had had a baby, with or without Hutton:

that child would be about nine or ten now, and might well look like the girl Regina Tyrrell was raising as her own; I had thought Regina was Miranda's mother, they looked so alike; equally Karen Tyrrell could be Miranda Hart's daughter. Was Bomber/Hutton threatening Miranda's child in order to make her an accomplice to the murders? I called Tommy and left a message on his voice mail asking him to set up surveillance on Bomber Folan/Patrick Hutton when he got established at Tyrrellscourt. Then I got back on the road.

NINETEEN

Martha O'Connor lived on two floors of a Georgian house on Bachelor's Walk on the North Quays, within sight of O'Connell Bridge. There was an antiques store on the ground floor, and a hotel named after an American military cemetery next door, and African immigrants pushing children in buggies on the streets and on the riverside boardwalk; I wondered if the rare pleasure of having the streets to themselves on Christmas Day compensated for the harsh winds whipping in off the Liffey. An Internet café with cheap dialing rates for Africa and Eastern Europe was open down toward the Ha'penny Bridge. When I left Dublin in the early eighties, this stretch of the quays looked like a disused set from a Hollywood studio, the false fronts of a western ghost town; now it was peopled and dressed and animated; even on Christmas Day, it exuded the kinetic energy of a living city. It was bloody freezing though, and I leant on the bell for far too long until I heard Martha O'Connor's voice.

"Sorry, *Messiah* on full," she trilled in her Oxford-inflected tones.

Martha O'Connor had silky short hair like an English public schoolboy; her long fringe hung in her eyes, which were free of makeup, as was the rest of her pretty, youthful face; she typically wore what she was wearing today: jeans and a baggy jumper or sweatshirt which covered up as much as it possibly could; big-boned and wide-hipped, she carried more weight than she looked happy with; to my eyes she always carried it off well. I had never been in her apartment before, and admired it as she brought me into the front room whose three great sash windows looked out over the Liffey and south across the city to the snow-capped Dublin mountains; the wall to the rear had been knocked through, as had the kitchen partition, so that the entire floor made one great open-plan living space. The period plasterwork on the high ceilings was intact, but the furniture and decor was spare and modern.

"Good digs," I said. "Can I be your boyfriend?"

"You come with the wrong bits. Have you been drinking already? Jesus Ed Loy, you're falling apart."

"Business. Seriously, how'd a pointy-headed journo like you afford a place like this?"

"I didn't. My mum and dad bought it for a song in the eighties, when it was a total shambles; thinking ahead, I'd just been born; it was left to me when Daddy died in '99, by which time it was already worth ten times more; *now . . .*"

Handel's *Messiah* blared in the background, a melodramatic underscoring of the unspoken truth between us: that both Martha's parents had been murdered, and that I had helped solve the case.

"Just lucky, I suppose," I said, and Martha laughed.

"Well, yes, and it's vitally important for pointy-heads like me to have a nice place to begin with, preferably one you bought before the boom, or even better, with the mortgage paid off. That way, we can bemoan the dreadful property bubble and sneer at everyone's obsession with house prices and cheerlead for a bust in the market so that ordinary people can afford houses in the areas they grew up in and be impeccably liberal and PC about it all at absolutely no cost or risk whatever to ourselves."

"Not just a pointy-head, a self-loathing pointy-head. Is that cooking I smell?"

"It is cooking. I figure the kind of woman who falls for you, or on you, only knows her way to one room in the house, so I thought you might like your lunch."

"I did have a dinner offer, you know. She'd bought the turkey and everything."

"And what happened?"

I shook my head. I couldn't quite keep the brittle ball in the air; it was too soon, and I was too disturbed by what I thought I'd discovered about Miranda and Patrick Hutton. Martha vanished and reappeared with a tumbler of whiskey and a smile.

"Fiona Reed spoke warmly of you when I told her you were coming here."

"I'm sure she did. Was she here?"

"She's just gone. She's here most nights now."

"Listen to you, Anaïs Nin. How warmly did Superintendent Reed speak of me?"

"She said you were a total fucking bollocks who needed to have his legs broken. But I could tell she meant it with affection."

"Is that a diesel thing?"

"We'll do our own jokes, thank you. Me kitchen, you TV. It's all lined up."

St. Jude's was one of three industrial schools Martha looked at in the documentary, which was called *Say Nothing*. It was the least severe case, in that nobody had actually been killed and anonymously buried there, say, but it wasn't easy viewing. The basic components were all in place: half-educated Christian Brothers, some of whom had themselves been physically and sexually abused, inflicting that abuse on others; abuse among the boys themselves, as the old turned on the young; a collective disbelief among the wider community, including priests, teachers, the Guards, a justice of the peace, and even journalists on the local paper, that amounted to denial; harrowing testimony from a man in his midforties who looked about sixty, red-faced and swollen, about the serial abuse he had suffered from the age of five, by religious brothers he named and others he said he never saw; a caption ran underneath his interview saying he had hanged himself before the program was shown; a bland nonapology apology from the archbishop of the diocese with a semolina face and a prissy, sibilant voice, who barely conceded that any abuse had been committed by priests or religious at all, in such a hurry was he to condemn "the wider decline in standards among society as a whole, particularly in the area of chastity"; a wheedling excursion in self-justification and evasion from the minister for something or other, keeping the shit from sticking to the government of the day, probably, that kept insisting, eventually in a rather menacing fashion, that what we had to remember was that these events, terrible though they were, all took place in *a different time.* The St. Jude's section ended with a bunch of apparently happy boys swarming around the front lawn with the river view, and the announcement that St. Jude's was now being run as a boys' home under the joint control of the departments of education, health, and social welfare.

I finished my drink by the window, looking out at the same river and wondering how many tales of ruined lives and broken hearts it carried from its source through the hard-knock city of Dublin to the sea. Martha joined me with a refill, which by now I badly needed, and a drink for herself, and I toasted her achievement in silence.

We ate mostly in silence, too. Martha had cooked pretty much everything you could: turkey, ham, roast potatoes, sprouts, bread and cranberry sauces, the lot; there was plenty of wine, and Christmas pudding to finish. It all tasted good, and I was glad to have it. But I didn't feel like celebrating, and Martha, usually relentlessly upbeat, didn't either. Maybe it was the documentary, maybe it was the case, maybe it was just that, when you're alone, you eat your Christmas dinner at a table full of empty chairs.

Afterward, Martha made some coffee and took out a red-and-black bound A4 notebook.

"Right, that's Christmas done," she said.

"Thanks for me dinner," I said.

"Easy for you, only have to eat it once. I'll have leftovers until February. Okay, *Say Nothing* covered the first incarnation of the school, ending in the late eighties. Subsequent to that, it reopened staffed by laypeople, supervised by social workers, but there were two abusers among them, one from a care center in Wales where there had been systematic abuse."

"This would have been through the nineties."

"It finally closed in '98. That was to have been the second part of the film: how, when the Church's influence declined or was removed, the conditions in residential homes did not improve; in fact, in certain cases, they got worse."

"And why didn't you make that film?"

"Because people involved—doctors, civil servants, care workers and others—refused to cooperate, and in several cases threatened us with legal action. And there was a marked reluctance on the part of the national broadcaster, all of a sudden, to tangle with so many different forces. So what you get at the end of *Say Nothing* is basically this complete fucking lie, these happy boys gamboling about on a front lawn they were still forbidden to walk across. I could tell you three of those boys at least whose lives were ruined by the abuse they suffered during that time, after the Church had withdrawn from St. Jude's."

"Not completely though. I mean, there was still a chapel, it was still basically a Catholic institution. It had its own chaplain pretty much. Didn't it?"

Martha sat back and smiled.

"You tell me," she said.

"Father Vincent Tyrrell," I said. "But he says he had nothing to do with anything."

Martha poured herself another glass of red and looked through her notes.

"All right. The way it happened, the abusers in the nineties, they found a couple of older boys happy to serve as willing helpers. And they got to join in, too. But most importantly, they helped to conceal the identities of the chief perpetrators."

"Including people from outside the school."

Martha sat forward and looked at me keenly. "What makes you say that?"

"I don't know. Did you find people in the town would talk to you about it all?"

"No way. All they want to talk about is horses, or that fucking country club for rich Americans and golfers. It's like it never existed."

"Despite the fact that the casualties were wandering around Tyrrellscourt for years afterward, doped or smacked out of it, the walking wounded of the town."

"I know. They turn that into almost a badge of pride, you know, oh yeah, it's not just the Celtic Tiger down here, we have our share of Characters. And because a couple of burnt-out musicians from the sixties decamped there, they try and sell the whole package like, you know, Haight-Ashbury on the Liffey. A few of the people in McGoldrick's will talk, but more in general, and it always goes back to the Church, you know, it has to be some priest to blame. I mean, fair enough, the Church did its share, but it's a fraction of what went on."

"Was your film instrumental in getting St. Jude's closed down?"

"No, it was already shut. It might have thwarted any possibility of it ever opening again, but I don't know. What did you mean by the chief abusers being people outside the school?"

"Can I have a look at that last scene again, all the boys by the river?"

"I have an image of it here," Martha said, and showed me a scanned photograph of the boys of St. Jude's by the river.

"This would be about '92," she said. "And here's the legend—sorry, you have to keep turning over." On the next page, there was a pencil tracing of the photo with each face numbered, and a list of the names to match the numbers beneath it. I flicked back and forth, and quickly spotted Leo Halligan, who was fully grown then. Patrick Hutton's name was there, but his head was almost completely hidden behind another boy's: that boy had vivid eyes and blond hair, and his name was Terence Folan. And there was a fourth boy, whose face I had difficulty matching with the one I knew, but whose name rang a bell: Gerald Stenson.

"Did you come across this guy?" I said. "Steno?"

Martha nodded.

"The barman in McGoldrick's. He reminded me of a hippie from the first time 'round, actually, someone who you think must be really sweet and love and peace because he's got the hair, then you find out he deals bad acid, or he's a rapist."

"Anything concrete to base that on?"

"Nah. Except for extreme prejudice against guys with pony-tails."

"Extreme prejudice means you kill them."

"What jury's gonna convict? What did you mean by abusers coming from outside the school that's the third time I've asked and I gave you your dinner so if you don't answer you can fuck away off with yourself."

"If you give me any more publicity, I won't be able to do my job."

"So I won't give you any more publicity."

"Promise. Swear."

"I swear, if I get anything I can use that won't land me with a libel action, I'll take full credit and cut you out totally. If you had a lawyer, he'd fire you."

"I do have a lawyer."

"Where is he?"

"He fired me. It was the practice, apparently stretching back I don't know how long, but an earnest little researcher like yourself should be able to find out, for a couple of likely lads a year from St. Jude's to be taken on as apprentices at Tyrrellscourt stables."

"By whom? F. X. Tyrrell?"

"That's what I was told. But the lady who told me—"

"Wouldn't stick around to cook your dinner."

"It may have been the head man who picked them out, I don't know. But F.X. still takes credit for horses from his stables, he's still hands-on there, so there's no reason to suppose he wouldn't handpick potential jockeys."

"Nobody said anything to me directly about this. But when it emerged that there was no interest in making a follow-up film, the decision came wrapped up in a ribbon that said Bloodstock-Industry-Tyrrellscourt-Stud-National-Good-News-Story-Irish-Win-At-Cheltenham-Shut-The-Fuck-Up-You-Fat-Troublemaking-Shit-Stirrer."

"You're just big-boned."

"I have a horrible personality, though."

"F. X. Tyrrell's late ex-wife, Jackie, told me that they hadn't had much of a sex life of any kind. She put it down to a kind of neutered quality in him, an absence of a sex drive, rather than anything else. F. X. Tyrrell personally requested that his brother, Vincent, come down from Bayview, where he had been parish priest for twenty years, to serve as his own personal prelate in Tyrrellscourt: say private masses, bless the horses and the jockeys before races, take care of all that. The archbishop of the time—"

"The one who looks like a nun's granny—"

"Apparently was happy to facilitate this request, so down Vincent went to perform these arduous duties. And also to pay pastoral visits to St. Jude's."

"Is there more? You say Vincent claimed he wasn't involved in anything."

"This is a family that seems to specialize in looking the other way. It was Father Vincent Tyrrell who hired me. I didn't think he was . . . in the front line, so to speak. Now I'm not so sure."

"Is there more?"

"I was in St. Jude's last night. There was a guy who let me in. One of Tyrrellscourt's walking wounded. He brought me up to a room—a room I think belonged to, or at least was furnished by, Vincent Tyrrell, and basically simulated being raped. It was pretty grotesque."

"Who was the guy?"

"That's a very good question."

"Ed, don't fuck me around."

"I'm not. He's a strange-looking guy, I was given one name for him, I suspect he might be someone else. I don't know which is the truth, and until I do, I don't even want to tell myself, let alone you. Do you understand? Because that's how I work, I feel my way through the dark until there's a ray of light. And no light yet."

Martha took that. By her smile, she even seemed to like it.

"The impression he gave though was that he hadn't seen who had done it to him. Or that he had, but he couldn't tell anyone."

"So what, F. X. Tyrrell, facilitated by his brother, plus one or two of the older lads, was coming in to rape selected boys, grooming them or training them in or assessing them and then selecting them as apprentices for his stables."

"Is one possible version."

"Or Vincent Tyrrell himself doing it all, with the promise to F.X. that he'll pass the best ones on when he's done."

"Is another."

My phone rang. It was Dave Donnelly. At first, I thought I wouldn't answer it; I figured I deserved a day off from the Donnelly maritals; then I remembered he'd promised to check out Don Kennedy's place for case files.

"Dave?"

"Ed. You're going to want to see this yourself."

"Where are you?"

Dave gave me an address in Ringsend, and I said I'd see him there.

"There's one other thing, Martha," I said. "Tyrrellscourt. I assume that's some Anglo family from the eighteenth century or before. Is it just a coincidence that F.X. has the same surname?"

"And this would rank in priority where?" Martha asked.

"Low, I guess. But it would be nice to know."

"I'll see what I can dig up, Ed."

I thanked Martha O'Connor for the dinner, and she thanked me for the company. Part of me regretted leaving her alone for the evening, but it was overwhelmed by the part that was relieved I didn't have to stay; I suspect she felt the same way: when I left, she was clutching a box set of Barbara Stanwyck movies. Loneliness is sometimes easier solved alone than in company, and especially on Christmas Day.

TWENTY

I told Martha O'Connor I needed to see Dave Donnelly urgently, but I didn't want to see him yet; I was haunted by the spectral memory of Vincent Tyrrell on the altar that morning, afraid he would die before the light I was searching for would come. It would have been quicker to stop off in Ringsend before heading out to Bayview, but at this stage in the case, in any case, I needed the time that driving brought, the sense that as I watched the dark road, the case was smoldering at the back of my mind: when I reached my destination, with luck, another spark would be lit.

On the coast road into Seafield, I reached for the radio, and came in on a Bothy Band tune as it was starting, "Martin Wynne's/The Longford Tinker," from the first album. I'd never been much for trad growing up in Dublin, seeing it as the preserve of beardy blokes in jumpers and the women who looked like them, but a Donegal barman at Mother McGillicuddy's gave me an education that showed me the error of my ways. (He'd got the job because he used to come in every Monday night, one of the terminal cases, and demand we play "Coinleach Ghlas An Fhomhair," a beautiful, melancholic song from Clannad's second album, before they turned into a kind of musical backdrop to aromatherapy; he'd sit and drink and pretend he wasn't crying until the owner took pity on him and offered him a job on condition he didn't cry behind the bar. He was still desperately homesick, and left at the first opportunity, but not before he had he taught us all a thing or two about Irish music.)

The Bothy Band played like a runaway horse you'd just about clung on to; the delirium of pipes and fiddle on "The Longford Tinker" was euphoric and tortured, swaggering and mournful all at once; it felt like the sound track to the case, where the exhilaration of progress told an increasingly tragic tale; like any case, it was absorbing and relentless; by the end of the tune, I was thirty kilometers over the limit and had to brake hard just to get my bearings.

The church car park was locked, so I parked up near the new houses on the other side and hopped over the hedge into the church grounds. I don't know what I expected Father Vincent Tyrrell to be doing on Christmas night. At best I thought he'd be drunk on Manzanilla and full of bile. But there he was, alive and possessed with energy, darting around his table, blue eyes flashing. The table was covered with a chart made out in different colored inks. At the top was the legend:

Leopardstown Festival—
St. Stephen's Day, December 26th

Below, there were seven columns, one for each race, each with a title and a time:

FIRST RACE: 12:25—Maiden Hurdle for Five years old and upward

SECOND RACE: 12:55—Maiden Hurdle for Four years old only

THIRD RACE: 1:30—Juvenile Hurdle for Three years old only

FOURTH RACE: 2:00—Handicap Hurdle for Four years old and upward

FIFTH RACE: 2:35—Novice Steeplechase for Four years old

SIXTH RACE: 3:10—Handicap Steeplechase for Four years old and upward

SEVENTH RACE: 3:40—Flat Race for Four-year-old colts and geldings only

Each column had a list of the runners and riders drawn up like a race card, with owner, trainer and form recorded; even the jockeys' silks had been drawn in a variety of inks. Tyrrell had a series of colored pencils with which he was making what I assumed were preliminary selections; he'd compare this with a form book he had compiled himself, a black hardback journal filled with figures and swollen with clippings from newspapers and racing journals. It was the first time I'd really understood what an exile he felt himself to be: this was more than a hobby or a passion, this was the liturgy of a lifetime calling, a vocation, as Regina had seen it in F. X. Tyrrell. F.X. had been chosen, but Vincent, the younger, had felt the call too.

"Any tips for tomorrow?" I said.

"The big trainers have good selections running," Tyrrell said coldly, like a cartoon Englishman talking to a foreigner. "Noel Meade, Dessie Hughes, Eoin Griffin."

"F. X. Tyrrell."

"Indeed. And I think the worst we'll get is sleet, so the form book will be a reliable guide," he said, caressing the black-bound volume like it was holy writ.

"Did you ever . . . I wonder, when you were back in Tyr-rellscourt in the nineties, did you ever get the urge to train yourself? Did you get out among the horses? Watch the morning work? Or did F.X. not want you interfering?"

Vincent Tyrrell stared hard at me through icy blue eyes and I had to stand firm not to be reduced to a shivering ten-year-old in line for a thrashing.

"It seems to me, Edward Loy, that since I hired you, I should be able to fire you. You've been paid more than generously, and I don't want any of the money back. I think it would be best for all concerned if you'd kindly just fuck off."

I had often wondered if the word *fuck* would ever acquire force again; Father Vincent Tyrrell had just imbued it with some. Not that I was going to let him know that.

"But I've come to report," I said. "You're my client, yet you don't seem remotely interested in how the case is going. You had affairs to set in order, and the main one was Patrick Hutton. Well, the good news is, I think I've found him."

Vincent Tyrrell almost smiled. That was usual with him, the almost: his smile always looked as much like it was congratulating himself on his superior intelligence or his steely detachment from the little people or his conviction that whatever you were going to say, it couldn't possibly surprise him, as it did like a smile. Once again, I wanted to wipe that smile off his face.

"He was on a dump near Roundwood, and I had identified him to my satisfaction, and it was only a matter of time before the Guards ID'd him too. At least, that was what I thought. But of course, I turned out to be completely wrong: that wasn't Patrick Hutton at all. It was someone called Terence Folan, who was a jockey at Tyrrellscourt, too; indeed he took over when Hutton was sacked by your brother. He was at St. Jude's as well: who knows, perhaps you picked him out for F.X. I'm not really sure how that side of it was handled, but it must have been very difficult to turn a blind eye. Patrick Hutton, alive. Have you known all along?"

"She said—" he started to say, and then stopped. His eyes flickered across the table, and my mind went back to the first time I saw it, with the remnants of three breakfast plates. One of them had had two cigarette butts stubbed out in bacon rind. I flashed on Miranda Hart in my kitchen this morning, stubbing her cigarette out in her half-eaten breakfast, and in that instant, I knew she had been the other breakfast guest, along with Leo Halligan. Her elaborate fear of Vincent Tyrrell must have been, in part at least, a charade.

"She said what? That Hutton was dead? Or gone? That it would be safe? You knew people were being slain. Two men. Your brother's ex-wife? Did it not matter to you? What did Miranda Hart tell you?"

He shook his head.

"Tell me about St. Jude's, Father Tyrrell. You must have known what was going on there. I think I was in your room. The red one, with the Sacred Heart, and the Poussin *Last Supper.* That's a tasteful atmosphere in which to rape a teenager. Did you do it yourself, or did you let F.X. come in and sample the wares?"

"I'm not going to rise to this."

"What did you think you were going to achieve by digging all this up? What did Miranda Hart promise you? That everything could be buried? Or was it not her idea? Maybe she didn't have any choice in the matter. Yes, that's more like it: Patrick Hutton was back, and he had a plan. I don't know what that plan is. Maybe none of us does. We've seen what the first three installments are, but the rest of it? Who can say?"

"Have you seen him?" Tyrrell asked quietly.

"Yes, I think I have."

"How . . . how does he look?"

"He looks . . . like he's suffered a lot. He looks quite mad."

"Mary . . . Miranda . . . God help the poor child . . . she feels loyal to the creature . . ."

I didn't expect Vincent Tyrrell to astonish me, but spontaneous compassion for a fellow human being was enough to do it.

"There are a lot of questions you could answer," I said. "Is

Regina Miranda's mother? Is Karen Tyrrell Miranda's child? Was Patrick Hutton the father of that child?"

"Why is any of that any of your business?"

"I think you know why. And to know and do nothing makes you just as guilty."

Tyrrell ran his fingers over his Leopardstown chart.

"See here, the third race. Francis has Bottle of Red running, she's a fine filly, but her rider will be lucky to make it. Fillies are allowed an extra five pounds over the ten-stone-nine, but Barry Dorgan is a greedy little boy, I remember him from St. Jude's distinctly, round face full of sweets, a smiler and a crybaby. Francis has persisted with Dorgan, but to my mind it's a sentimental attachment that has no place in the game: it's unfair to the punters, it's unfair to the horse and it's unfair to the sport."

"A sentimental attachment."

"Dorgan has a plump wife and two plump babies. I think Francis is simply fond of the boy."

"Like a son."

"Well, perhaps. I wouldn't know about that."

"Neither would he. You don't deny that F. X. Tyrrell had sexual relationships with boys from St. Jude's?"

"I wouldn't deny that he had an unfortunate relationship with young Halligan, which has brought nothing but complications upon his shoulders. I wouldn't deny that. As to the others: I really couldn't say."

"Couldn't or wouldn't?"

"It all amounts to the same thing. It will come out eventually, I have no doubt. Bottle of Red, that would be my strongest tip for St. Stephen's Day. The uncertainty about the rider has seen the odds drift satisfactorily; I'd say you could get it for nine to two, even five to one if you were up early. I imagine you get up early, Edward Loy."

"Patrick Hutton—the man I believe to be Patrick Hutton—

gave the strong impression that he had been raped, in that room at St. Jude's—it was your room, wasn't it?"

Tyrrell shrugged and nodded.

"He made it clear he had been blindfolded, that he hadn't seen his rapist."

"Perhaps it wasn't rape. Perhaps it was consensual, and now he's decided to cavort as if it wasn't."

"Cavort?"

"Hutton and young Halligan were . . . well, they were about to be expelled for indecent conduct. I thought Hutton would fare well in the stables, I thought he had the makings of a jockey. I knew F.X. liked the look of him. And Leo . . . Leo was part of the deal. For Hutton and, eventually, for Francis. To the ultimate cost of each."

"Two of the care staff at St. Jude's were known abusers."

"Have you been talking to your burly lesbian friend again? No charges were ever laid, no case was ever brought. I've always found it curious, these liberals, they have a very illiberal concept of justice: they seem ready to destroy a person's life on the basis of one accusation."

All of this came from the side of his mouth as he pored over his chart. I had rattled him, but not nearly enough. I put my coat on and joined him at the table.

"When we spoke last, you talked about By Your Leave. Said it was something of a freak. What did you mean by that?"

"I told you to ask someone who knew."

"I did. I asked your brother. He said he'd stick to his discipline and you should stick to yours."

Tyrrell didn't flinch.

"Martha O'Connor—you know, the burly lesbian you're so fond of—her documentary about St. Jude's was halted because nobody wanted to speak ill of F. X. Tyrrell. I don't think anyone has the same sensitivity when it comes to his estranged brother, the Catholic priest. Maybe you are dying of cancer. You're not dead yet. I could make your last days here a misery. Given the degree to which, as far as I'm concerned, you've obstructed this case—Jackie Tyrrell might be alive were it not for you—all because of your bullshit about what you know being told to you in confession."

"But it was," Tyrrell said. "It's not bullshit at all. That part of it is God's truth."

He leant his hands on the chart.

"Very well. See here."

He pointed to Bottle of Red.

"Below the name of every horse, there's a list with the year of foaling, color, sex, and then the name of sire and dam. That's the horse's father and mother. Bottle of Red is by Dark Star out of No Regrets. Now, Francis went through a phase of experimenting with extremely close breeding. That means mating between parents and offspring, or siblings. Siblings are the most volatile in any pedigree breeding, and you have to use the very finest mares and stallions, but even then, it's discounted for everything except genetic research purposes: to breed out abnormalities, say, or uncover hidden gene types."

"And are Dark Star and No Regrets brother and sister?"

"Oh Lord, no. No, Francis has stopped all that. Or it was stopped for him."

"With By Your Leave. A thing of beauty, like a Grecian urn."

"What?"

"You said By Your Leave was all we know on earth, and all we need to know. Keats. 'Ode on a Grecian Urn.'"

"I didn't think you'd get that reference."

"Of course you did. Anyone of my age would, Keats was on the Leaving Cert English course. That was about a work of art, though, not a living being."

"That's right, and that's where it should have stayed. But Francis persisted, and to his credit, he created a beautiful, if unstable, compound. By Your Leave was too fragile for what she was asked to do, and everyone knew it."

"The reason being, she was the offspring of a brother and sister?"

"Not just that. The brother and sister were themselves got of a brother and sister. Two generations against nature. Setting himself up as God. It was an abomination."

CAMBRIDGE AVENUE WAS tucked in behind the R131 off Pigeon House Road, across from the tip of the North Quay, with big Polish and Russian vessels moored on the docks. Kennedy's house had a view of Ringsend Park, or at least, it would have had were it not for the fact that every cubic inch of the place was packed full of stuff, like a holiday suitcase. There were files, loose-leaf binders, notebooks and briefing documents for all the cases Kennedy had ever worked as a Garda detective. There were more of the same for all the cases Kennedy had worked as a private cop. There were concertina files full of tax forms, bank statements and insurance certificates. That was just the paper.

In the hall there were golf clubs, fishing tackle, gym equipment, tennis, badminton and squash gear, a racing bicycle and a canoe, all new, all unused, some still in their packaging. In the living room there was a Bose home cinema system, Bang & Olufsen stereo components, a MacBook, a MacBook Pro, an iMac G5 and three Dell laptops, all box fresh and polyethylene-wrapped. There was no room in the kitchen because the tiny floor space was taken up with a new Neff double oven; a giant Smeg fridge sat in the doorway; upstairs there were new beds resting on the old beds, and department store bags full of clothes and shoes on top. Dave sat half in the hall, half in the living room, some kind of ledger or account book with assorted sheaves of paper sticking out of it on his knees; he didn't have much choice unless he wanted to perch on the toilet, and even that had a new bathroom suite shoehorned around it.

"Hold the front page: Don Kennedy was Aladdin," I said.

Dave looked up, shaking his head, a bemused grin on his face.

"You never know, do you? You just never know about people. They're fighting out in Bray station not to catch this detail."

"Did he have a sideline as a fence? Or did he just lose his mind?"

"The mind, I think. But he had a budget to lose it on. The soul went first. Blackmail."

Dave reached back into the cornucopia behind him. Resting on a white Apple carton was a box file marked PATRICK HUTTON. He opened it and handed me a sheaf of photocopied reports on paper that had BARRINGTON INVESTIGATIONS as its heading.

I began to read.

POSSIBLE SIGHTINGS: HUTTON, PTK.
1. Sealink Ferry: 11/1/99

Inteviewed: Goughran, Derval (Miss); asserted she saw subject (Hutton, Ptk.) boarding ferry at Rosslare, and again in Mariner's Bar during sailing. Did not see subject disembark. Speculation as to whether subject may have flung himself overboard before vessel docked in Fishguard.

SEE APPENDED COASTGUARD'S REPORT
(DOCUMENT I (a)).

I stopped reading and rustled through the pages. There were another thirty-six possible sightings. I looked up at Dave.

"Did anyone see him?" I said.

"No," he said. "But that doesn't undermine the value of the reports. You should learn a lesson from them, instead of running around after trouble like a madman: the value of painstaking and meticulous work documented in full. If you followed that course, you might have a house full of brand-new consumer goods too."

"Did you notice the quality of gift his godson received increasing in value recently?"

"No, actually."

"You see. Hoarding. Never a healthy sign. Apart from the fact that he didn't get all this crap for his meticulous documentation, he got it from blackmail. Not to mention his body dumped in a shallow grave in fucking Roundwood. Did he document the blackmail too?"

"In a way."

Dave pulled bank statements from the ledger he had on his lap. All this time, he had been sitting on a chair in the living-room doorway and I'd been standing above him, wedged between the golf clubs and the canoe; it was an unlikely setup, almost comical if it hadn't felt so stupid. I looked at the statement.

"See: there was an electronic transfer every month, two thousand euros. But no way of knowing who it's from: whoever it is ensured that their name not appear on the statement."

Dave rustled through the paper.

"The payments begin about two years back."

"When he searched for Hutton."

"So it could be your one, Miranda, or one of the Tyrrells. A lot of money for Miranda to be shelling out."

Dave was trying to hold back, but he couldn't contain himself; he looked like a children's entertainer before the big finale. I was getting a crick in my neck: I wanted to see the rabbit now.

"I don't know what Kennedy asked for, but this is what he had, and whoever worked their way through the files didn't spot it; I think it was an extra copy: it was folded inside another endless report about sightings of people who may have been but probably were not Hutton in disguise," Dave said, and handed me the copy of a birth certificate. I thought I was one step ahead, which is a way of guaranteeing that life will constantly surprise you. There was the mother's name I expected, Tyrrell, Regina Mary Immaculate; there was no father, sure enough; but then there was the sex: not *F* for female, not Mary, later to be known as Miranda, but *M* for male: the child was a boy, born on the second of November, 1976, and his Christian names were Patrick Francis.

PART III

ST. STEPHEN'S DAY

FERDINAND: *Strangling is a very quiet death.*

DUCHESS: *I'll tell thee a miracle;*
I am not mad yet, to my cause of sorrow:
Th' heaven o'er my head seems made of
  molten brass,
The earth of flaming sulphur, yet I am
  not mad.
I am acquainted with sad misery,
As the tann'd galley-slave is with his oar;
Necessity makes me suffer constantly,
And custom makes it easy.

—John Webster,
The Duchess of Malfi

When everything was suddenly within reach, that was when people got sloppy and took their eye off the prize, as if it was already within their grasp, just a matter of ask and it shall be given. He couldn't understand that kind of amateur-hour carry-on. It revolted him, if he was being honest, and he liked to think that honesty was not the least of his virtues. No, when your goal was in sight, that's when you needed to buckle down and apply yourself more than ever before. Strict discipline. Self-denial. The benefits of a Catholic education. Because it wasn't going to be handed to him. He knew he was unworthy from day one. And as a result, he had schooled himself in the art of cunning dissimulation, he had studied human weakness in all its many, pitiable varieties, and he had waited, silent, vigilant, solitary. When the opportunity finally presented itself, he could be forgiven a glimmer of self-congratulation, for though it was initiated by others, it had arisen directly out of the balanced actions he had taken, the considered choices he had made. Taken as a whole, it was like a . . . like a work of art: it had integrity. It had beauty. It was, ultimately, all his own work. They couldn't deny him that now, could they?

TWENTY-ONE

I drove back to Quarry Fields, Dave Donnelly following. He had a bag in his car and he followed me into the house with it in his hand. In the kitchen, making coffee, I looked at the bag until he said something.

"I was hoping I could stay a few days, Ed. Until things . . . you know . . ."

"I'm not sure I do know, Dave. I mean, of course you're welcome to stay, but is it a good idea? What about your kids?"

Dave set his jaw in that brooding, deliberate way he had, as if I were a puny earthling who could never truly understand the colossal scale of his plans.

"They think I'm working. Emergency shift. It's not unusual."

"And what about Carmel. Did she throw you out?"

"No. No, she . . . she asked me to stay. Tears, the whole lot. She begged me."

I couldn't see Carmel begging, but then, I couldn't have pictured her with Myles Geraghty either. How much did Dave know about that?

"Maybe you should go back there," I said. "You don't want to be alone on Christmas night. Certainly not if a woman needs you to be with her."

"Carmel doesn't need me," Dave said, but he sounded, if not actually hopeful, certainly unconvinced.

"Oh yes she does," I said. "She . . . she told me she did."

"Last night? And what else did she tell you?"

Some things are more important than who fucked who.

"Dave, whatever's happened between you . . . you have a woman who wants you. And like any woman, she needs you to pay her some attention. To behave as if you know she's there, and you're as glad of it today as you were twenty years ago."

Dave looked skeptically at me.

"You almost sound as if you'd like to be in my shoes," he said. "Football practice and sleepovers and Friday-night pizza and mass on Sundays and nodding off in front of the TV and watching each other get old."

I looked out the back window at my apple trees, close but never touching; the bare limbs looked like bones in the hard wind. I looked out into the hall, where a pine stood bare and unadorned in a coal scuttle; I had forgotten, or hadn't bothered, to decorate it.

"It would have its compensations," I said.

Dave looked at me in disbelief.

"Anyway, you can't stay. No one with a woman who wants him sleeps here."

He thought about that for a while.

"You don't know what she did . . ."

I took a chance.

"Do you? Really? Maybe she needed to get your attention so badly . . . she tried before and failed . . . maybe it was your last chance . . ."

"Is that what she said?"

There was fear in his eyes. I shook my head.

"I don't know. She was upset. She wants you. I know what I'd do."

Dave was doing his best to look wounded and noble, but I think he was relieved. We talked about the case for a while, but I could tell his mind was elsewhere; on the doorstep, he looked at me as if, in some crucial way, I'd let him down. If I'd told him to leave his family, would that have suited his image of me better? Now I'd let him believe I envied him, he felt happier about himself. Just to make sure, I asked him to keep his mobile on: I told him I might need him, and I could see he liked the idea that I might. After he drove away, I rang Carmel and told her he was coming home. She started to say a lot of stuff about being sorry and ashamed, but I told her nobody wanted to hear any of that, now or ever, wished her a happy Christmas, hung up and left the house.

THE THREE MEN who took me were under orders not to hurt me; that's why each of them carried a gun. None of them wore sportswear either: with their dark leather jackets and jeans and boots, they could have been construction workers on a stag night; they certainly didn't draw the eye the way Burberry hoodies did. They put me in the back of a Mercedes Estate with blacked-out windows, one on either side, one to drive. When we got to Redlands, which is where I assumed we were going—they could have shot me on the doorstep if they'd wished—I was led to a small bungalow George Halligan had built in the grounds, a three-room den with a pool table, a home cinema system, a bar and an en suite bedroom. What more could a man want? A head butt from Leo Halligan would not have been top of my list; nor would the kicks to the head and body that followed; a cowboy boot to the liver wouldn't have made the backup list; it felt like a week before I could breathe again. Leo was breathing heavily when George called a halt; he was almost out of breath when he stopped. The off-duty construction workers got me upright and propped me in a chair; George presented me with a tumbler of whiskey and sat opposite me; Leo hovered to one side, an elaborate dressing with some kind of metal frame over his nose.

"Compliments of the season," George said in his fifty-a-day rasp. "Sorry about that, Ed, but it sounds like you were asking for it."

"I'm sure I was," I said. "Still, I didn't think Leo was such a girl he'd have to get his brother to hold me down."

Leo came at me so fast he forgot to bring his brain along; he was drawing a blade from his jacket, but before he pulled it free, I smashed my tumbler hard against the metal-framed dressing on his nose and jammed the shattered glass against his throat; the metal jarred the bone out of its setting and blood was flowing from his nose and he was screaming and gurgling, and I was on my feet now, a red mist swirling around my head.

"You see what can happen? You see?" I heard myself shouting. I had lost any sense of where or who I was. I dug the broken glass into Leo's throat. I could see George waving at his henchmen to drop the guns they had pulled. George's mouth was moving, but I couldn't hear what he was saying; it took me a while to realize that that was because I was still shouting.

"You see? When we all live like savages? Blood! You see? You see?"

I could see the panic in George's eyes as he pointed at Leo; the sudden sight of Leo's face covered in blood, of the punctures the glass had made in his throat, of the choking quivering mess of him beneath me brought me to my senses. I signaled George to kick the guns across the floor to me; when he hesitated, I jammed the glass back into Leo's throat until I heard the skitter of metal across the floor; then I let him have Leo, whose injuries looked worse than they were; it was only because I had him lying on his back that he was choking; George sat him forward and gave him a bar cloth to stanch the flow, and one of the construction workers got some ice from the bar and wrapped it in another cloth and passed it to him.

My head was throbbing and there was blood on my face where Leo had opened the eye he had blackened on Bayview Hill and the pain on my right side where he'd caught my liver hurt so bad I felt like crying, and possibly did. But I watched Leo with his face in his hands, whimpering, and George, his prematurely white head bowed over his brother, and the three construction workers, their faces registering as much shock as you could discern through their folds of beer and steroid fat, and I thought: They won't forget this in a fucking hurry. And fool that I was, I felt stupid blood pride in my victory, suppressing the ache that, worse than any physical pain, warned me that maybe the only way the Halligans could properly settle this was to kill me.

I gathered up the guns: two Glock 17s and a Sig Sauer compact. I didn't know what was waiting for me down in Tyrrellscourt, but I figured it wouldn't do any harm to be prepared for it. I popped the Glocks in my coat pockets and kept the Sig trained around the room. George Halligan gave me two looks: one included a nod to Leo and an arched eyebrow, meaning all friends now; that was George's way, but I knew I'd have to watch my back with Leo, and resolved to help put him back behind bars as soon as possible, a resolution that I suspected would find favor with his brother. The second look followed the guns into my pockets.

"I'm going to need them," I said. "I'm going down to Tyrrellscourt."

"That was the main reason we wanted to talk to you, Ed," George said, as if we'd spent the last five minutes chatting about football before getting down to business.

Leo lifted his head, and dabbed his nose: the flow of blood had diminished to a trickle. George leant in and conferred with him in a low voice. Then he looked around and directed the largest of the construction workers, who had a goatee and no neck, to fix three drinks and pass them around. George had caught me like this in the past, so I watched closely to see that the liquid, which turned out to be brandy, was all coming from the one decanter. It was, and when I had a tumbler of it, I waited for George and Leo to drink, and then I did likewise, and we got down to business, Halligan-style.

"We heard you were asking questions," George said.

"Who told you? Jack Proby, I suppose."

Leo and George looked quickly at each other.

"Yeah, Jack called me," George said unconvincingly. "You see, the festival starts tomorrow, and we don't want anything to get the way of . . . a good day's racing."

"Well, let me put your minds at rest," I said. "I don't give a damn about what deals you have with F. X. Tyrrell or Jack Proby. I don't give a damn which horse wins or doesn't, although I am always in the market for a sure thing. All I care about is that since I started looking for Patrick Hutton, the bodies have been piling up. Far as I'm concerned, if F.X. is shy about who he sleeps with, that's his lookout. And allowing for the fact that I don't like blackmailing, extorting, scum-sucking sociopaths like yourselves on any level you care to mention, you're not my problem. My problem is finding out what happened to Patrick Hutton. Allied to that, I've inherited the problem of who killed Don Kennedy, Jackie Tyrrell and Terry Folan."

"Terry Folan?" Leo said, looking up at me. "Bomber Folan?"

"That's right," I said. "Who'd you think that body on the dump was? Patrick Hutton? Or did you not think anyone else'd find out?"

Leo began to say something, then stopped himself. George looked from his brother to me and back, a Cohiba chafing against his still-dark mustache.

"Anything here I should know about, lads?" he said. We both ignored him.

"It wasn't just you at breakfast with Vincent Tyrrell, was it Leo? Miranda Hart was there too."

Again Leo went to speak, but stopped himself.

"That's why I'm here, is it? In case the inconvenient deaths of three people get in the way of a fucking horse race?"

"And if you go blundering about down there, you could fuck up quite a few fucking horse races, Ed Loy: the last thing we need is the Tyrrell horses being withdrawn because their trainer is up on a charge, Bottle of Red in particular," George barked from a blue cloud of cigar smoke. A descant of coughing followed; Leo winced and flapped a hand in front of his face.

"Fair enough," I said. "Is that what you're telling me, that F. X. Tyrrell is the killer?"

"That's just a for instance," George spluttered.

"Well, here's another: the killer takes F. X. Tyrrell out. Maybe he already has. Same result to you: no Tyrrell horse at the races."

George sat still, his black eyes vanishing into his clenched fist of a face.

"I don't think it was Jack Proby you were talking to at all," I said. "I think it was either Miranda Hart, or Gerald Stenson."

George's face didn't flicker. Leo on the other hand, finally spoke.

"I thought I knew what was going on there, but I don't. Your woman's a lying cunt, every disrespect, she's a whore and a pig and she always will be, right?"

He knew I had to take that, and I did.

"I think her and Steno are into the fucking Tyrrells for some fucking score, I don't know what it is."

"How do you know?"

"Good question. Because she told me: which almost guarantees it isn't true. Steno always was a sly cunt, mind you."

"Did she know about the bodies?"

"She knew about Kennedy. And she said she thought the other body was Pa Hutton. She said it was nothing to do with her, but she couldn't stop it. Wouldn't explain that. Father Vincent said she needed to call the cops and tell them. She said there was no way she could get out of it. All this, and of course she's crying and wailing and looking up out of her big eyes like a fucking panda, oh poor her."

"What do you think?"

"That's what I'm telling you. I don't know."

"What about Steno? He's beginning to sound like an interesting character."

Leo drew his narrow lips farther into his mouth.

"Steno was a nasty piece of work. People talked about St. Jude's, you know, the abusers on the staff. The one I remember, going around, you had to watch your back, was one of the boys: Steno. And later, when he was dealing smack, he'd take his pick of the junkies. When Miranda Hart was at her worst, that was Steno she was running around with. Pair of them suited each other."

I thought of Hutton's dumb show of rape and abuse.

"Did Steno ever attack Hutton?"

Leo looked astonished at the question.

"How the fuck d'you know that? Did Father Vincent tell you? Fuck, I don't think even he knew."

"He raped him, didn't he?"

"I always blamed him. Pa never knew for sure, said he had a blindfold on. I don't think Pa ever really got over it. Seriously, how do you know? Is Pa Hutton alive? Have you seen him?"

George cleared his throat in aggressive distaste.

Leo flung a look at George, and I thought for a moment he was going to show him what aggressive meant; then he turned back to me, his dark eyes suddenly desperate for a word from beyond the grave.

"I think he may be, yes. The more you can tell me, the closer I'll get to him. What about back in the day, you and F. X. Tyrrell?" I said. "Was F.X. interested in Hutton too?"

"Pa was never into that."

"Vincent Tyrrell said the pair of you were about to be expelled from St. Jude's for indecent conduct. He said at first, F. X. Tyrrell had his eye on Patrick Hutton."

"Father Tyrrell is a devious cunt. Father Tyrrell wants you to find things out, but he doesn't want to help you. Father Tyrrell must think you're going to get divine inspiration."

"How could he have helped me?"

"He could have told you that I was the one F.X. wanted. Sure he had a notion of Pa as a jockey, but I was the one he wanted all along."

TWENTY-TWO

One of the construction workers drove me back to Quarry Fields, and Leo sat in the backseat beside me. For some reason, the physical threat seemed to have receded, or at least that was what my gut told me. My gut had been wrong before, but this late in a case, it was almost all I had. When we got to the house, he put a hand on my arm.

"As long as Bottle of Red loses tomorrow, George'll be happy. Don't fuck that up, all right?"

I said I wouldn't.

"It might all sound very seedy and fucked up at this distance, you know, industrial schools, abuse, all this. And then F. X. Tyrrell . . . as if he came in and said, I'll have him over there, that one. But it wasn't like that, you know?"

I looked at Leo, and by reflex at the driver.

"He's Ukrainian. Fuck-all English. Apart from beer, isn't that right man, beer, beer, voddy vodka and beer?"

The driver nodded dutifully, a grim smile on his wide mouth. Leo turned his dark eyes back to me.

"It was . . . he'd chosen me, but I was willing. He was a serious guy, F. X. Tyrrell, he was a fucking legend. I mean, say you were sixteen and I don't know who asked for you, some older one, Michelle Pfeiffer, or Ellen Barkin, or fuckin' . . . your one . . . who would you have liked?"

I shrugged.

"Your one," I said, and Leo giggled.

"I can't remember her name, the English one who's always in the nip. But I mean, you would have said, fucking sure, wouldn't you? And that's what it was like, he was a charismatic guy, a suave fucker, and we were always into the ponies so he was like a fucking hero: I said, which way do you want me? I'm not sayin' there was no shit at St. Jude's, there fucking was, and it was always the weaker kids that got fucked, in every way. But I wasn't one of them. I was older anyway. And I was looking out for Pa, too, I . . . I loved the guy, you know? Mates. Not that there was anything between us, I mean, he was never that way, though I gave it a decent go . . . but we were like brothers . . . only, not like my fucking brothers . . . no need to mention Podge, I should pay someone in Mountjoy to shank the fat fuck . . . and as for fucking George, since I got out, I don't know who the fuck he thinks he is, always shitein' on about fuckin' business lunches and helipads and fucking interest rates, I've a pain in me hole listening to the cunt, I'm not coddin' you . . . I knew Pa needed a helping hand, you know, but he was a class jockey . . . so anyway, we were both getting what we wanted, that's how it was."

Leo lit a Gauloise and exhaled and sat in wistful reverie for a while.

"That was the time of my life, know I mean? The time of my life."

"And then when Miranda Hart came back from school . . ."

"Mary Hart as was. That was Jackie as well, claiming her, using her as a pawn against Regina. The politics of the house."

"And she made her play for Patrick Hutton."

"Yeah, they just, they got together, they got married, we were all working at the stables, getting our first rides, so forth. Then three things really: Patrick's career took off, and mine didn't, and F. X. lost interest in me."

"This would be coming up to the By Your Leave incident?"

"This would. Because Pa rode By Your Leave. And because . . . I was gonna lie about this even now, I was gonna say it was George's idea, but it wasn't, it was mine."

"To blackmail F. X. Tyrrell."

"Yeah. I suppose I felt a bit excluded, know I mean? There they were, on the gallops, in fucking Cheltenham, and where was I? Back up in fucking Seafield sorting out Podge's mess. Dealing to skin-popping scobies. George looking at me like I'm some kind of fucking burden. So I decided to cash in."

"You had photographs."

"I had videotape. I took it without F.X. knowing."

"Planning ahead."

"I don't know. Maybe I was. Maybe deep down I'm a double-dealing scumbag. I thought I wanted a record of it, to believe it myself, to get off on it all. So I'd never forget. Maybe I'm lying to myself. You look back on what you were like, and you can't swear to anything, can you? Anyway, I took the tape to George. I made him watch it first. That was funny, seeing him sit through it, watching him squirm. And then he got his hooks into the Tyrrells."

"A lot of money over the years?"

"I wouldn't let him take it too far. I mean, Podge never knew about it, can you imagine? Podge and his crew swarming around the country club, the whole thing would have collapsed. Nah, George took it steady. A race here and there, and the opportunity to get all the money laundered."

"That was Seán Proby, wasn't it?"

"Yeah. Well, once I had F.X. on board, I figured, may as well get stuck into Proby. I knew he was up for it, he was always pant-

ing around Tyrrellscourt hoping for action, too shy to do anything about it, so it wasn't too hard to set him up with a couple
of nice-looking young fellas and record the results. And bingo,
Proby was the route for clean cash."

"And after By Your Leave, after Thurles, you went back down to
Tyrrellscourt, dealing. What happened to Patrick Hutton then?"

Leo grabbed my arm.

"That's what I want you to find out. Steno . . . I kept in touch
with Steno, but I never trusted the cunt. You bring smack in, say
good-bye to business, it's a fucking fire sale. I mean, Pa Hutton
and me, we weren't really close anymore, not with your woman
around . . . the guy had lost it anyway, he was on heroin. And
the baby could have been anyone's, Miranda's baby, Jack Proby's,
Steno's, anyone's."

"Bomber Folan's?"

"Bomber didn't last long with F.X., fuck sake. Out on his ear,
he had no discipline, the stupid cunt. I told Steno, I said the fucking smack was more trouble than it was worth. I got out, and he
wound it down and reefed them all to fuck. And that was the last
I heard until I got the phone call on Saturday night."

Leo still held my arm; it reminded me of Vincent Tyrrell's grip
the morning I took the case. He brought his other hand around
and clasped my hand and locked eyes with me; his breath came
through his mouth in sodden gusts.

"You want to get that seen to," I said.

"Where d'you think Boris is taking me after this? Christmas
night at the A&E in St. Anthony's, fuck sake, I should have you
killed."

"Don't start that again."

"You could do with a checkup yourself."

"In the New Year."

"You think you've seen him. How does he look?"

"If it's who I think it is, he looked fit, but he didn't look well.
Not in his head. I'm sorry."

Leo gripped me harder, and tears brimmed in his eyes.

"Try and keep him alive," he said.

"I can't promise anything. He already looked pretty out of control. If he's the killer . . ."

I didn't have to spell it out. Leo nodded, then rolled up his sleeve and showed me his forearm. The tattoo there was a familiar one, a crucifix and an omega symbol: †

"I know there's all this, the Omega Man going on in the papers, like he's some Mister Evil fucker, yeah? And I read how the crucifix represents whatever, Christmas, or it's the killer pleading for forgiveness. But that's all bullshit man, it's not an omega, it isn't even a crucifix. It's, we all got them done in McGoldrick's that time, there was all raggle-taggle tradheads and eco cunts with dogs on strings and this cornrow chick used to do tattoos and we all got them, or I can remember everyone getting them anyway."

"And what does it mean?"

"No big mystery. Just T and C, a fancy way of doing a T and a C."

"T and C standing for—"

"Tyrrellscourt."

THERE WEREN'T MANY people on the road, but those that were out were mostly drunk, so I had to take it easy on the drive, which I would have anyway, since my right eye had almost closed now, and it was past midnight when I arrived in Tyrrellscourt. I had showered before I left, and cleaned my wounds, and gobbled some Nurofen Plus, and resisted the call of my bed, although not without difficulty: What could eight hours change? I asked myself, and answer came there: Absolutely everything.

An unshaven security guard in a black uniform was on duty at the gates to Tyrrellscourt House, which was surrounded from the roadside by high granite walls; I gave the guard my name and he went back into his booth and opened the gates. I drove up the long gravel drive and came to a crunching halt in front of the imposing house, whose stained-glass windows and glittering granite stonework and Victorian Gothic features gave it the look of a haunted house in a child's storybook. I could hear the whinny and snort of horses in the yard beyond. Snow was falling lightly in the moonlight as I climbed the steps of the house. Before I had time to knock, the great black front door with the stained-glass panels depicting horses in full flight opened, and the fairy tale was interrupted by Tommy Owens, standing there in tan brogues, red cord trousers, a check shirt and a sleeveless pullover, his face flushed and his hair wet. He looked at the new map Leo had kicked onto my face and shook his head, as if my brawling ways would someday drag his squeaky-clean twenty-first-century operation down. I heard piano music, and the wow and flutter of a television or computer game. Tommy looked at his watch and shook his head again. I always liked it when Tommy began to think the case was slipping away from me, and he had to pick up the slack.

"Come on," he said, his voice prim and impatient, and led me briskly across a flagstoned hall, along a corridor and down a flight of stairs. We walked through a passage stuffed with riding hats and boots and Wellington boots and red coats and Barbour jackets and dog baskets and into a darkened conservatory with walls of glass on three sides. Once your eyes adjusted, you could see right across the valley in the moonlight: to the right, the lazy S and straight green band of the gallops; center bearing left, the river and the golf course to the rear of the country club, and at the extreme left, the tip of a mobile home that was part of the old Staples property.

Tommy had a MacBook laptop set up on a low table by a cane sofa; a videotape was recording the signal from a wireless receiver not unlike the one I had set up for the Leonard family to trap their neighborhood dumpers; on a side table there was turkey

and ham and lettuce and tomatoes and French bread and mayonnaise and mustard and chutney and pint bottles of Guinness and a
bottle of Jameson and a flask of coffee. If this was an all-nighter,
we were traveling first class.

"Miss Tyrrell said if you came in at a reasonable hour, you
should go up and see her," Tommy said. "She's a class act, that
one."

"Miss Tyrrell?"

"Regina. Miss Tyrrell, I call her."

"What's with the young-country-squire outfit?"

"I needed a change of clothes. Miss Tyrrell kindly—"

"Sounds good. So take me through what you've been up to."

"Go up and see her first. She's playing the piano up there, I
think."

"Tommy, you know conventional wisdom? It's always in-
complete. Never keep a lady waiting—provided you know what
you're going to say or do to her when you meet her. I don't, and
I'm relying on you to help me."

I made myself a turkey salad roll, poured Guinness into a glass
and sat back on the sofa. Tommy looked at me in dismay.

"What do you think this is, a fucking picnic? That lady up
there is at the end of her tether."

"Really? How did that happen? She struck me as a pretty cool
customer when I met her. What's happened to get her so pan-
icked?"

"There's no one she can turn to. And the situation is sinking
in, you know? And I think someone's been talking to her."

"Who?"

"Your one."

"Miranda? Say her name at least, Tommy."

"Yeah. So . . . I mean, some of us have been . . . while
you . . ."

Tommy waved dismissively at me, as if I'd arrived in white
tie and tails with two strippers and a big bag of coke. The pain

around my right eye suddenly shot out of the gates, neck and neck with the pain in my liver. It was hard to call the odds on which would romp home first: a joint favorite photo finish was my conservative forecast. I popped a few more Nurofen, tipped some Jameson into a glass and threw the lot back. When that didn't immediately help, I turned on Tommy.

"This face came from Leo Halligan, one of your little drug-dealing friends, Tommy. Whose attack was a result of Podge Halligan, who again was a business associate of yours, just like the fucking Reillys or any other number of thugs and scum-bags whose affairs you get embroiled in and I end up dealing with, usually with my fucking chin, because you can't cope and come crying to me like the fucking . . . so I really don't fucking need—"

I stopped then, because Tommy didn't have the heart to take what I would have said, or because I didn't have the heart to say it. I put a hand in the air, and he matched it, and he pointed at the red-and-green Jameson bottle, and I poured us both whiskeys and we knocked them back and that was that. So while I ate my sandwich and drank my beer, Tommy took me through what some of us had been doing.

TWENTY-THREE

First off, they've no servants here since Christmas Eve until after Stephen's Day, they give them Christmas off, Miss Tyrrell said it was so Karen can see how Christmas should be in a proper family, without being waited on hand and foot like," Tommy said. "So security-wise, all there is is that fat fuck at the gates. I suppose if they wanted anything, they could send over to the hotel for it, but they haven't, or at least, not since I've been here; there's a big kitchen with an Aga and all in it and Miss Tyrrell was going at it there since eight this morning. I got down here just as they were about to eat and they made me join them, insisted on it. F.X. wasn't around then, I didn't see him until later. Miss Tyrrell just said Christmas Day was always a working day for him, on account of Leopardstown, and horses had gone to Chester as well: he does be out and about all day, checking up on the work, the horses, the boxes, so on. And then it's an early start, he has a lodge over near the stables so he sleeps there.

"Anyway, it was a beautiful dinner, and little Karen said grace and all, and I was dreading it, on account of it's the first time I ever ate Christmas dinner without me ma, know what I mean, and Regina—Miss Tyrrell, I told her about it and she was very . . . she understood. Wine and pudding and hats and crackers and everything. They were both giddy then, playing games and so forth, but I said I needed to get some work done. I don't know if Miss Tyrrell took me entirely seriously, but that didn't matter, I'm used to that. Anyway, she was kind, and she's a real lady. No question.

"I had the Range Rover in my sights, first off. I counted three around the stables alone. Two of them had UK plates; neither of the registration numbers matched. I had a run-in with Brian Rowan, he's head man here, getting the horses settled for the night. Big curly top, thought I was some skanger on the loose, or a bookie's spy, but he called the house and Miss Tyrrell set him straight. I went through, there's a couple of garages with horse boxes and transporters and so on, but I didn't see any more Range Rovers.

"Next thing was to set up the pinhole camera on Bomber's place. I reckoned the only way was to approach by the river; he's bound to have some way of scoping whoever comes head-on. I packed a little bag and walked the track down from here, there's a path above the river by the trees that runs the length of the golf course. Now, when you meet the lane we drove down, that leads to a bridge across the river; the Staples property lies to the other side, and there's a mesh of chicken wire and barbed wire on that side. I thought about placing the camera there, but it wouldn't really have caught anything except the coming and going of vehicles, and not even them in any great detail. But it was bleedin' freezin' out there, and the one thing I didn't pack was gloves, I did have a pair of bolt cutters though, so I used them to snip the wire, just enough to squeeze through, reminded me of robbin' orchards, don't let the gardener see how you got in and you'll always be able to go back."

Just listening to Tommy was making me feel cold. I poured a couple more Jamesons. Tommy took a hit of his whiskey, then picked up his story.

"Other side of the wire, I can't get enough purchase on the ridge to take me around to the Staples place, there's a dirty big bank sloping down to the riverbed, it's got, you wouldn't call it a waterfall, a bit of a gusher, there's a stream up on the property, anyway, I can't get around it so I've got to climb down, there's a bank of brambles and nettles, then there's elder and sycamore a bit further on, I cling to some ivy and get as far as a sycamore that's trunk is swathed in the stuff and I can scale down the ivy to the riverbed no bother.

"Getting up to the house is a bit more of a problem, because the moon has gone behind a cloud and I don't want to use a torch. I'm also in difficulties because my shoes are soaked and freezing and there's marsh stretching on as far as I go, until I find another sycamore on the Staples side. The ivy only climbs about fifteen feet, and there's a fork in the tree another ten feet up and nothing but the odd whorl and nub to get me there and the bark is all frosted now, slippier than a whore's knickers but I make it, and from the fork there's enough branches to get ten feet above the backyard, which I now see in the moonlight has a fucking fence of *palings,* so I'm there, sodden, shivering, crackling with the fucking cold, thinking, if this fucker has searchlights, or dogs, or both, I am finished, because I don't see where the extra yard of whatever is coming from. And then I think, fuck it, we're mates, he was gonna step in for me with Ed outside McGoldrick's. And then I'm, yeah, but how friendly is he gonna be, you just dropped out of a fucking tree into his backyard on Christmas night, chances are he's gonna revise his opinion of you downward.

"But to be honest with you, there's only so long you can stay up a fucking tree, by its nature it's a temporary location, so I'm ready to jump, I'm watching the yard, there's a couple of mobile homes, an avalanche of scrap, I can see lights in the stone cottage,

Bomber's homemade Jeep and another vehicle, a Range Rover looks like. And I'm watching, and I hear an engine, and lights approaching, and I've leant so far forward I feel I'm slipping, and Bomber comes out of his house and stands in his doorway and I'm jamming myself back against the bough that's above my head and sliding my arse in tight against the trunk as another fucking Range Rover bounces up into view. Out get Miranda Hart and some bloke, can't make him out, expected, it looks like, and they all go into the cottage, five minutes, ten minutes, half a fuckin' hour, great, I'm like, if I fell on the palings, maybe they'd bring me to hospital, where the heat would be on. And then I'm like, maybe they wouldn't."

Tommy stopped then because I was laughing so much; he did his best to look indignant, poured himself a fresh drink and waited until I'd composed myself before continuing.

"Anyway, if good things don't come to all who wait, something does: the three of them pile out, all business, and into one Range Rover, at this stage I'm fucked if I can remember which one is which, and off they go. I give it a minute or two before I jump, and all I'm thinking is, if I've actually frozen solid and I shatter into, you know, blocks, fragments, whatever, then that's it, much relief, I Can Do No More man, know I mean?

"I don't shatter, but I go on me ear, literally because one arm is so cramped and numb I can't bring it up to break my fall, but it's just mud and sand I fall on, so I'm grand. And I'm on my feet and moving to keep warm and moving to get the fuck out of there. First thing is, I go through what I can, the house is locked and bolted but the mobile homes just slide open. And what's important for us, there's one that half of it's like a big cold room, I mean a freezer, and there's all, there's rabbits, chickens, salmon, there's a fucking larder. And room to spare. It's the size, a side of beef or whatever you fucking call it, both sides of the fucking thing, you could keep something that size—like a body—in there, long as you liked.

"All right, that's the first finding. The second is, in the other big mobile home, there's a rake of racing cards and clippings, scrapbooks, and videos and DVDs of races, some of Terry Folan, some of Patrick Hutton, some of both. So I picked up a few to have a look at.

"Third thing, a red Porsche '88 is around the front, tucked in behind an old milk float that's marooned up in front of the house, the car that was outside Miranda Hart's house when I went to pick her up on Christmas Eve.

"Fourth thing, I checked the reg on the Range Rover left behind: it doesn't match the one I saw leaving Jackie Tyrrell's after the murder.

"Fifth thing, I better get this camera fitted and get out of there. There's no way I can get into the cottage short of forcing the door or breaking a window, but I figure if I get it set in, the stonework's crumbling all over, it's a tumbledown, get it *wedged* in a crevice above the door and we should be good.

"And then I'm, what if the camera's out of range? I didn't check it, and I didn't check the distance I've come, and maybe it's grand, but I don't know, and I haven't gone through all that to end up with four hours of white noise on a videotape. Or worse, they come back before I have the chance to set the thing up and running. Because there's one thing more I want to know, big number six, and I'm not taking the chance.

"There's a corrugated iron lean-to near the front of the property, there's aluminum beer barrels and car doors surrounding it, it's like a hide, maybe that's what he uses it for, to catch the geese and whatever. Anyway, it's cold in there man, and I'm not looking forward to it, but in I slide, trying me best to think about whatever, something good, turkey with cranberry sauce, Miss Tyrrell's roast potatoes, very nice by the way, and I still have Leo's Glock, I slide one into the chamber and wait.

"Long story short, my luck is in; five minutes later they're back to drop Bomber off again, and Miranda gets out with him, they're talking at the door, she looks like she's reassuring him, or stoking him, or whatever shit she's pulling; anyway, she's done and he goes inside; she makes off in the Porsche and then the Range Rover turns and follows. When it turns, I see the driver is the bould Steno, and when it takes off, I clock the plates: we have the UK, and we have the numbers: this is the vehicle that tore out of Tibradden like Michael Schumacher the night Jackie Tyrrell was murdered.

"After all that, I'm too cold and too wrecked for strategy, I give it a few minutes and then I bolt out from under me house of scrap and just leg it down to the road man, Bomber may be after me, but if I don't move I'm gonna be dead. And Bomber isn't after me, and I'm not dead, and I make it to the house, no, first I make it to the gate lodge, where fat fucko doesn't want to let me in, he's giving it No I Cannot Ring Miss Tyrrell At This Hour and No I Do Not Remember You and Please Walk Away Or I'll Call The Gardaí. So I lean into the booth and I shove the barrel of the Glock right up underneath his chin, shove it so hard it's scratching his forehead from the inside. And *then* he makes the call.

"And Miss Tyrrell very kindly lets me have a shower, and finds me clean clothes—I know, I know, I look like the Brit on holidays who walks into the wrong pub and ends up buried in a ditch, but it's the thought that counts. Like I said, a real lady.

"Another detail from Bomber's place. The paddock that we spied from the road, it has hurdles set out, and there's a small stable yard with a horse in it. So Bomber, or Patrick Hutton, whichever he is, is training.

"So I come down here and check the receiver and yes, we're in business. Nothing happening down there since I got back, but if anything does, we'll see it."

Tommy nodded and picked up his drink and I nodded back and toasted him: job well done. He hadn't finished yet, however. He had a DVD in the MacBook. It was a collection of races Patrick Hutton had run. He fast-forwarded through the action, freeze-framed on two moments from a postrace interview, and pointed out the salient point to me and its relevance. The man who had taken us to St. Jude's, who we thought to be Patrick Hutton, had blue eyes. That was relevant because in his interview, the salient point about Patrick Hutton's eyes was that one of them was blue and the other one was brown—"just like little Karen has," as Tommy put it. Just like little Karen Tyrrell.

TWENTY-FOUR

The piano tones were still wafting from above as I retraced my steps to the entrance hall and climbed the wide wood-paneled stairway to a landing the size of the average house, with couches and easy chairs and occasional tables laid out beneath exposed beams; I could see two corridors, and chose the one I thought the music was drifting from: the acoustics in the house were sound, and I was soon knocking on a dark wood-paneled door.

"Come in," said a woman's voice, and I did, my eyes drawn instantly toward an upright piano from where I assumed the music to be coming, assumed it so strongly that I stared in disbelief at the vacant stool and the covered keyboard, as if I'd been the victim of some devious trompe l'oeil effect. When I came to, I saw Regina Tyrrell on a couch at the foot of her bed; the music came from speakers I couldn't see; I flashed on Jackie Tyrrell's house the night of her murder.

"You look like you've seen a ghost," she said, her Dublin accent adding to my sense of the incongruous: how had she clung on to it after all these years of the Queen's horses, in this old Anglo setup? Maybe it helped her to recall a time when she was young, and her life spread out before her full of nothing but promise and adventure, a time when dressing in pink and listening to the "Moonlight" Sonata were the motifs of an overture, not an elegy.

There were three matching chairs set in a ring around the couch, which was white and gold and enough like Jackie's to maintain the sense of haunted unease I felt. I sat on one of the chairs, and looked tentatively around the rest of the room, as if fearful of other phantoms lurking there. My fears on that score were in vain. On the evidence of this and her office in the hotel, Regina's visual sense had been set in stone, and brightly colored stone at that, when she was a teenager: pink and white, ruched curtains, satins and silks; she wore pale pink satin pajamas and a matching gown; I wouldn't have been surprised to see stuffed animals on the bed. The music was in a similar vein: the "Moonlight" Sonata had given way to the slow movement from Rachmaninov's Second Piano Concerto in all its glutinous glory. I think I was with the Musical Powers That Be on that one. In contrast, Regina herself looked hard and shrewd and sanguine; her bloodred lips stained the tips of the cigarettes she smoked, and the glass of gin she drank; if she was at the end of her tether, I wondered how Tommy had noticed.

I sat for a long while without speaking. Regina didn't appear unduly bothered; indeed, she seemed grateful for the company. I looked up at one point to see that the music had brought tears to her eyes, or something had; she dabbed at them with a tissue and sat back as if hoping for more. I could think of nothing to ask except the darkest questions, nothing to consider except the most horrific possibilities. Finally, I just produced the copy of the birth certificate of Patrick Francis, born to Regina Tyrrell on November 2, 1976, and passed it to her. She looked at it, and nodded wearily and sadly, and shrugged.

"Patrick Hutton?" I said, and it was as if a wind had blown through the room, leaving everything apparently still and settled and yet altered irrevocably.

"How did you find out?"

"I didn't. Another detective, Don Kennedy, did. And somebody murdered him, either for that, or for whatever else he discovered."

Regina tipped her head back and looked in the direction of the gold chandelier at the center of the ceiling rose.

"I suppose it explains a lot. Why you mightn't have wanted him as a match for Miranda. On the other hand, it explains nothing. Why you haven't tried to find him. Why you didn't help him more when you could."

"I offered the reward. When Miranda was looking for him. It was in Francis's name, but it was my offer. And what more should I have done? He was taken on as an apprentice, his career was growing fast, if he hadn't been so bloody headstrong—"

"He was raised in an orphanage, worse, a boys' home where there had been serious allegations of abuse—worse than allegations, it had been closed down once already. A home just down the road from here, from your country house, your country club, your exclusive country life."

"I couldn't raise that child. I couldn't raise that child. His father . . . I couldn't've raised that child."

"Why not? His father . . . explain."

Nothing from Regina but the ability to meet my eye.

"So you couldn't raise that child. You could have afforded better than St. Jude's, where the kids nobody wanted were dumped."

"It wasn't as bad as it was painted, that place. The boys who came through to the yard, they were good lads, they seemed to have survived all right. I thought it would give the child a spine."

She nodded, as if she had somehow been vindicated by events, then blinked hard and turned away.

"You could have fostered him—"

"And lost him."

"Did you not lose him anyway? What did you gain?"

Regina hugged herself as if the wind was still blowing chill, and shivered.

"What is it, Edward Loy? What do you want, to tear the Tyrrells asunder? If I told you now that we've suffered enough for everything we've done, and it's not over yet, every sin I've committed has been paid for ten times over and will be until the end of time. Would that be enough? Would that make you leave, drop this and go?"

"It's not up to me anymore," I said. "There are people out there . . . some of them your children . . . they're angry. They want you to pay more, and to go on paying."

Regina shook her head, scorn in her eyes and in the curl of her lips.

"Children of mine? Who?"

"Patrick Hutton. Miranda Hart."

"She's not my child," Regina said.

"I couldn't help noticing your daughter Karen's eyes. Very unusual. Unless of course she was Patrick Hutton's daughter by Miranda Hart. He had that feature, too, didn't he? Heterochromia, is that what it's called? I suppose it's genetic. Can it be inherited?"

Regina Tyrrell's head was in her hands. I thought she was weeping, and I hoped she was too; if she was, maybe I could stop torturing her like this, and maybe she could think of something that would satisfy me, and bring the whole hateful saga to a close, make it vanish into thin air. She wasn't weeping though. When she sat up, she had something filmy glistening between finger and thumb, and one of her brown eyes was now blue. A tinted lens could give a blue eye the look of a brown. And if it could do it for the mother . . .

"Yes it can be inherited. Karen Tyrrell is my daughter," she said. "She is my daughter."

"I don't believe you, Regina. I think Karen is Miranda Hart's daughter by Patrick Hutton. And because she was incapable of looking after the child, she gave her to you. And you've brought Karen up as your own, protected her from the truth. But now it's too late, and the truth is crowding in like wind."

Regina got to her feet. Shaking one hand at me, she stretched the other out toward the door and began slowly to gravitate toward it, as if being tugged gently by an invisible cord.

"I think you better leave now, Edward Loy, or I'm going to call the Guards—"

"That's increasingly looking like our safest bet," I said. "You see, Patrick Hutton isn't dead. He's out there, living like a wild man on the old Staples place—"

"That's Bomber Folan."

"That's not Bomber Folan, Bomber Folan was murdered years ago and Patrick Hutton took his place, he kept Folan's body on ice and then made it appear on a dump in Roundwood two days ago. Alone, or with Miranda Hart, and a fellow called Gerald Stenson, Steno, another former inmate of St. Jude's. Between them, they murdered Folan, and the detective Don Kennedy, because whatever he found out when he searched for Hutton two or three years back was not something they wanted revealed. Kennedy was blackmailing someone—maybe Miranda, maybe you, maybe Francis. I don't know. All I do know is, he's not blackmailing anyone anymore. And then they killed Jackie Tyrrell; Tommy saw the car they drove from Jackie's house the night of her murder up at the old Staples place tonight, and all three of them in it: Steno, and your son, Patrick. And your daughter, Miranda."

"She's not my daughter."

"I'll take your word for it. She does look awfully like you."

"She's not my daughter. She can't be."

Rachmaninov gave way to Schubert now, a piano impromptu, the yearning, plaintive one, regret for the life not lived. Regina moved toward me, as if fixing her gaze and holding mine could insulate her from what she feared most.

"She can't be your daughter?"

"Francis promised."

"Francis promised? What had he to do with it?"

"He . . . I wouldn't stop working . . . but I couldn't . . . not have the child . . ."

"There was another child? A girl? And you wouldn't have an abortion?"

"It was unthinkable. To me. I don't condemn others, but for me . . . so Francis . . . when the time came, he arranged the adoption. I went away, you see, there was a place outside Inverness, in Scotland, to avoid the scandal, you could go there, a convent . . . they would have taken the child, too, but Francis insisted . . . said he knew the right family . . . then later on, when Miranda came in here, people used to say, you could be sisters, you could be mother and daughter, Jackie Tyrrell was never done worrying away at it, giggling away at it, all very sophisticated, as if we were some kind of small-town inbreds, and I asked Francis, was there any possibility . . . No, he said. Emphatic about it. I had to believe him, I had to. I mean . . . why would he lie?"

"Who was the child's father? The child that . . . you don't believe was Miranda?"

Regina stared at me, but wouldn't answer.

"Who was Patrick Hutton's father?"

She stared harder, but stayed silent. I felt like she was willing me to understand, imploring me to guess it. Her eyes not matching heightened her beauty and gave her a vulnerability that made me think of Karen Tyrrell; I told myself I had to keep going, for the child's sake, though every word I spoke was like a thorn in Regina Tyrrell's flesh.

"Vincent Tyrrell told me something about close breeding. He said your brother used to be very interested in it. That it was quite controversial, even with horses. He said By Your Leave, the horse that caused all the trouble for the Tyrrell family, was the offspring of two generations of brother and sister pairings."

Regina Tyrrell stared at me, her eyes glistening.

"Vincent Tyrrell met Miranda Hart before he hired me. And then he gave me one man's name—Patrick Hutton—and I've found a whole history of secrets to go with it. Who was Miranda Hart's father? Who was Patrick Hutton's father?"

Still holding my gaze, she began to shake her head.

"Was F.X. the father, Regina? Was Vincent? You were raped, you were abused by your older brother, no wonder you were ashamed, wanted to keep it a secret, it wasn't your fault, no one would ever hold it against you—"

"You cannot say such things. You cannot *know* such things. Think of the children, what nightmares they'll have if they find out."

I thought of the title of Martha O'Connor's documentary: *Say Nothing.*

"Think of the nightmares they'll have if they don't. Think of the nightmares some of them are living, or are destined to live. If Patrick and Miranda are brother and sister . . . and if Karen is their child . . ."

Regina Tyrrell was beginning to shake, the start of what appeared to be a convulsive tide of grief. She reached for my hand and fell to her knees.

"Maybe the others know the worst already. But Karen's only nine years old, for pity's sake."

"Yes," I said. "Young enough to survive it. If we're lucky."

She bent her head over my hands, as if in prayer, as if I had the power to change the past. But all I had, all we both had in common, was the desperate need to hear the truth, and to understand it. I think Regina had felt that need for a long time. And in that moment, maybe she finally chose to act on it. She stopped herself shaking, and breathed hard and deep, and looked up at me.

"All right," she said. "All right then. I dreaded this day. But I think I prayed for it too. It was always too much for one soul to bear."

And then, before she could say another word, the doorknob clicked and the door swung open and the cold relentless wind blew through the room again.

TWENTY-FIVE

Steno didn't really give a fuck about anyone but Steno. When it came down to it, that was all there was: Number One. The rest was bullshit, and he didn't mind saying that, although in truth he had learned over the years to never actually say it to anyone but himself, even if it was what everyone believed, deep down. People couldn't bear the truth, but the truth had never bothered Steno. You didn't have to be brutal about it, and if you weren't a fucking savage, you'd avoid that side of things as much as you could: it was messy, and there was a lot of cleaning up afterward, and broken bones and blood and dead bodies; the whole thing was a bit of a fucking downer. It could get you down—especially if that was all there was to it. Some of the rows he had seen in the bar, over fuck-all, if you broke it up, and Steno always had to, and asked them what it was all about, neither of them could tell you. Waking up the next day with a broken face and for what? That was short term, that was amateur hour, that was no better than a beast in the fields. Because you could brood about the blood, how it would linger in your eye line like the red sparks you see when you close your eyes at night. And sometimes, the eyes of the dead, they'd pin you so they would, you'd wake before dawn with the memory of that last look, the last hope. And to go through that for no reason, for "The fuck are you looking at?"; for "Are you calling me a liar?" No way. Not in this life man.

That's why, if you were going to get involved on that level, you needed the long view. Fair enough, there'd been times when accidents happened, and you just had to get someone from location A to location B where B was a ditch or a dump or a riverbank: that's just day-to-day, that's just business, you can't shirk when that comes around. But if you were ambitious, and Steno was, the long term made the grief worthwhile.

Not to make too much of himself—Steno hated when people did that, you had to put up with it behind the bar day in day out, stable lads who had "really" trained Gold Cup winners, salesmen who "really" ran the companies they worked for, all the drunks and losers who were going to run marathons and write books and get record deals and act in movies and be models and comedians and every fucking thing, and there they fucking were ten, twenty, thirty years later, fatter and redder and still in the fucking pub.

The usual? The usual.

Steno was happy to admit it had all been a happy accident. It was when the Halligans had got their claws into F. X. Tyrrell, and Leo was running his happy band of jockeys and golfers and tooting them up big-time, and young Proby and Miranda Hart were hanging out. Twenty of them in the back room—it was before the Warehouse refurbishment, just a lounge at the back—no one else got in: Private party sir, sorry sir. Aw, again? Private party every night sir.

Steno could see there was something happening there, the cars, the money, the action. There was a whole bunch of women hanging around that time, skinny, expensive-looking women, the kind of women who appear like thin air when there's coke around, kind of like models but not as attractive, kind of like whores but not really into the money. Steno had just started working in McGoldrick's then, and he couldn't remember how many times he had his cock sucked to let some flooze in leopardskin and lace into the back room. Not that a woman knew how to blow you. How would she? Like knows what like likes, it's only common sense. Steno had no great interest in women. No, he had no *use* for them, that was more like it. Although if he had to, he'd find a use, just like he had with Miranda Hart.

She was up in the shower now, but she was still here, wasn't she? And maybe she had screamed when he'd done her the way he wanted, maybe she'd screamed at first, but she'd *stopped* screaming. She'd stopped screaming, and she was still here. Because it was worth her while. Because she was using him, too. Just like those coke whores, when he'd got tired of their sloppy fucking lips and he told them what he wanted, the ones who really wanted to make the scene, the ones who really wanted to score, they'd deliver like pros, they'd shut the fuck up and take it. As for the others, crying and blubbering and he hadn't even touched them, amateur fucking hour. He had nothing but contempt for that kind of carry-on. One thing Steno had never done was take what wasn't on offer. Of course, you always had to work the angles to maximize what *was* offered, or even to make it available at all, but who didn't do that? Or at very least, who didn't want to? And maybe there were people going to their graves crying over not getting what they wanted because they didn't go after it hard enough, but Steno was not one of those people, never had been.

In fairness, it wasn't true to say Steno didn't have a use for women. There was no percentage in being the way Steno was, not in Tyrrellscourt; it was dangerous most places now, not to mention pathetic and embarrassing. What you did was (and Steno couldn't understand how people couldn't get this through their heads, now that air travel had come down in price, and not be going around playgrounds and schools making shows of themselves, or acting the bollocks on the Internet, those days were done) you went to Thailand, or the Philippines—parts of Africa were good, too, or so he'd been told, but Steno thought Africa might be a bit of a fucking downer—and there you were, whatever you wanted, as many, as often, as young. Twice or three times a year—last year, Steno took four trips—and that was you set up for a few months. And if you couldn't be happy with that, what kind of a sick fuck were you anyway? The odd weekend in Amsterdam didn't do any harm either, you could always get what you wanted in Amsterdam.

But you needed a wife, or a girlfriend, or—you could be "gay," but Steno had never liked any of that either, well, he liked some of it, but not the fucking public side, and they were very fucking pushy about it now, everything out in the open. What was the point of that? Steno didn't like *anything* out in the open. Anyway, in a town like Tyrrellscourt, you needed a wife or a girlfriend so that everyone would just shut the fuck up, and once Steno got his feet under the table at McGoldrick's—it was a skill he had, he had always been able to make people feel comfortable, and relaxed, not just *like* him, that was no great accomplishment, but *want to impress* him. Even that cunt Loy the other day, he'd said something about Leopardstown to Steno. Steno could see Loy didn't know one end of a horse from the other, but he was a man, and men always wanted to say something to Steno about Leopardstown, or Croke Park, or Stamford Bridge. That was how he'd got the job, when McGoldrick Senior saw him behind the bar. He could empty the place at closing time without having to raise his voice: people just knew. He didn't know what it was; it was like, some people were good with children.

Sometimes Steno wished he had been into women, because there were nights when he could take his pick. The women would see their men edging up to him and they'd draw their own conclusions. It was like a nature program Steno had seen shot at night, or in a cave, all you could see was the animals' body heat, represented by color; the shade indicated who would mate with whom: the hotter you were, the redder you were, and the redder you were, the bigger the stream of rapidly reddening females piling over to you. Steno broke his shite laughing when he saw that program. Christine asked him what he was laughing at.

Nothing, he'd said.

Well, he couldn't say, you, you red bitches in heat you, could he?

Christine had come in trying out for the back room. Steno could see immediately she didn't have what it took. But she wasn't the kind you done in the backyard by the bins either. He took her out and he took her home and they became boyfriend and girl-friend. He had to fuck her quite a lot to begin with, and she wasn't into anything "like that," and there was a point when he didn't think he was going to make it, but that point was around the same point that Steno saw there was a market for smack around the place. He had mates in Amsterdam, and they'd send a mule, or sometimes he'd pick it up himself; no one at customs ever stopped Steno. He smoked it with Christine until she got into it, and then he'd kept it coming. Then he didn't have to fuck her so much, or at all, and if he did, he'd do what he liked and she'd put up with it, long as the smack showed up. And long as you had regular bread coming in, a smack habit was as easy to handle as a bottle of wine a night; Christine had a regular job as a secretary in a solicitor's office in Blessington and she kept herself looking smart and they lived in a bungalow on the Dublin road, although Steno had a "manager's flat" McGoldrick built for him when the Warehouse refurb was taking place, an inducement to persuade him to stay. They couldn't run McGoldrick's without Steno.

Well, maybe one day soon, they were going to have to.

The happy accident occurred, as so many have, on account of smack.

After Pa Hutton blew it with By Your Leave at Thurles, he was hanging around a lot, hitting the booze hard, and Leo Halligan stopped slipping him freebies because Hutton wasn't at the races anymore, at first literally, and then majorly. Soon after, Bomber Folan was rolling around in pretty much the same condition after he'd been dumped in short order by F. X. Tyrrell. Folan and Hutton soon found smack was a perfect way of taking the edge off life's little disappointments. Leo Halligan wasn't happy at first that Steno was dealing, but it worked out all right in the end: George was keen that Podge Halligan came nowhere near Tyrrellscourt because he was a headbanger and a madman, he'd scare all the jockeys away and the Halligans' betting deal with the Tyrrells would collapse. With Steno there, George could tell Podge there was no room for him in the market. George even saw to it that Steno took a weapons delivery or two, just in case a bout of competition erupted.

McGoldrick Senior didn't much like the way superannuated jockeys from Tyrrellscourt seemed to end up haunting the pub, but Steno took a strong line there: quite apart from their being his clients in more ways than one, the town had a loyalty to those who hadn't kept up with the race—not to mention the lads who came up through St. Jude's. That's what Steno said anyway: he didn't know whether he believed it or not, and he didn't really give a fuck: he liked the way it sounded, and the effect it had on the people who heard it, and why else would you say anything? It made him feel like he was a good man, at least some of the time, and sometimes you seemed to need that. Steno didn't know why, but there it was.

Folan fell asunder very quickly. He began kipping up at the old Staples place, helping Iggy Staples out in the scrap trade, trekking down the town for his smack. Meanwhile, Miranda Hart had reappeared—there was talk she'd gone away and had a baby and given it up for adoption, or had an abortion, or some fucking thing: Steno didn't really give a fuck; at least, not back then he didn't. She was hanging out in the back room, hoovering up coke with Jack Proby, spreading herself around, and soon she needed a little taste to bring her down at nights. Steno steered clear of any shenanigans with Miranda Hart though: even if she wasn't in the loop at Tyrrellscourt anymore, she had been once, and there'd always been talk about whose daughter she might have been. He'd supply her with smack, but rarely directly; he preferred to deal with Proby: it kept the lines clear, in case there was any grief from on high.

Pa Hutton was miserable, of course: he'd lost his job, and now his woman, his wife, and possibly his child, and what did he have? A spike in his arm, end of story. Leo Halligan tried to straighten him out more than once, but there was nothing you could do with a junkie: if they want to go all the way down to hell, you can either take the trip with them, or let them fall and hope they get such a land they'll try and climb back up. Leo had the fucking nerve to have a pop at Steno once for feeding Pa the smack; Steno reefed Leo out on that one, told him if he didn't want to find himself and his playmates another powder room, he could lose the fucking career guidance counselor routine. For a poxy little faggot, he'd always been a self-righteous cunt, right back to St. Jude's days. Fucker was never done riding some young fella or other, keeping the lads awake at night grunting and fucking whooping, yet he had the fucking gall to object to the way Steno conducted himself.

Steno had no regrets or qualms about the manner in which he had stewarded the younger lads through the hazards of St. Jude's, and he could have taught Leo and any number of other whores in that school the meaning of self-control: he'd internalized the crucial lesson, which was that you exercise caution and self-discipline at all times. Steno had never played favorites, he'd never had anyone more than once, and he'd always insisted on anonymity: a blindfold properly applied, a willing assistant or two. It wasn't always pleasant; in fact, there had been times when Steno had wondered whether it was worth the grief. But fuck it: you done one, you done them all; easier that way, from a logic point of view. Easier in your own mind. And what was Leo gonna do about it? Go to the cops? (Steno knew what it stemmed from: Leo had always had a thing for Hutton back in St. Jude's, and Hutton just didn't go that way. Well, Steno didn't take no for an answer at the time: he'd used Father Vincent Tyrrell's room in the school when it was Hutton's turn, took him on a kneeler. Hutton didn't like it, and Steno hadn't much enjoyed it himself, it had felt like a duty. Anyway, he knew Leo always blamed him for that. But Hutton never suspected him, and Leo had no proof, never had. If there was one thing Steno couldn't abide, it was any kind of false accusation, no matter what the context.) And Pa Hutton and Bomber Folan didn't have to come to McGoldrick's, did they? He knew Leo had been pouring poison in people's ears about him, but there he was in the bar too. Hypocrisy, some people would call it: Steno said it was just The Way Things Are. Don't bear a grudge unless it works to your advantage.

So Miranda Hart had run out of bread, and Steno wasn't gonna give her any more shit for free, and he didn't find anything else she had to offer appealing; she'd always been a dirtbird, but she'd turned into a total skank on H; the golfers weren't interested any-more, and she was reduced to blowing drunks for twenty quid in the back lane. That's what she was doing, in the rain, when someone told Pa Hutton about it and he walked out and caught her sucking off Bomber Folan and went straight for Bomber's neck. The whole thing was over in seconds. Bomber's system was trashed by the smack anyway, so he was too weak to fight back; the worst thing about it all was, Miranda Hart kept working away down below while Hutton was strangling Bomber, as if she had lost any lingering sense of reality, and the rain teeming down on it all: that's the sight that greeted Steno, like some nightmare act from the circus in hell.

Steno had a choice to make, and he made it quickly, with the usual calculation in mind: How will this work best for Steno? Simple answer: clean it up and hold it in reserve; the alternative—the Guards, and charges, and a court case, with all the damage that would be caused to the reputations of McGoldrick's and the stables, not to mention Steno probably getting caught in the cross fire—was simply out of the question. You didn't know what caliber of man you were until tested in extreme circumstances. Steno still felt pride at how he had comported himself on that evening. He had instinctively taken leadership positions because he was hardwired to do so.

It had been the work of seconds to gather Folan up—he remembered thinking it was like handling an oversize umbrella—and bundle him in to the walk-in cold room and lock him in one of the individual compartments; they were all padlocked in case the staff got the notion that no one'd miss the odd loin of pork. Steno got hold of that particular key, and insisted on taking full charge of the stocking and maintenance of the cold room thereafter.

Steno realized that this was one of those moments that changed everything, and that if you didn't want to be led by that moment, you had to be a leader of the change. He got hold of Leo Halligan and Jack Proby and explained that there'd been an accident; he wouldn't say what had happened, just that the days of the back room were done. Proby was scared enough to do what he was told, which was to get Miranda up to Dublin and make sure she kept her fucking mouth shut. Leo took a little more convincing; eventually Steno just went into the back room and had a quiet word with each of the respectable golfers and married jockeys about what the Guards (and/or their wives and families) would be told if they didn't clear out right now and never come back. Steno could always clear a bar without raising his voice. That was Leo's back room business finished.

Pa Hutton was the one who seemed to present the biggest challenge, but as it turned out, he lit on the solution to the problem himself. Himself and Folan hadn't looked too dissimilar: same blond hair, same whippet build. The eyes were a problem, but tinted lenses would sort that out. And in any case, Iggy Staples was legally blind; he had a bit of vision, but not enough to make out eye color. Hutton, who had always been a dapper dresser, exchanged clothes with the dead man, and went forth to assume the identity of Bomber Folan, and live up on the Staples property, and the word would go out that Hutton had disappeared, and that would lay the whole thing to rest.

Hutton was eager to do it: he was half mad with guilt over Folan's death in any case, and saw the whole thing as a way to atone for his sins. To each his own, Steno reckoned, at least it meant Hutton was close at hand.

And there it lay for a lot longer than Steno expected. Steno kept in touch with everyone—isolation breeds discontent, and if there was even the slightest danger that anyone was getting the urge to confess, Steno needed to know before they knew it themselves. He tracked how Proby got himself and Miranda into clinics and off drugs, encouraged Proby to get Jackie Tyrrell to employ Miranda Hart, visited Hutton after Staples died to see that all was well, and generally monitored the level of stability surrounding the principals in the incident. And gradually they grew to trust him, he thought, or at least, to rely upon him. And all the time, Steno waited for his opening.

It came when Miranda Hart hired Don Kennedy to investigate Hutton's disappearance. The first thing Steno knew was when this fucking heap of an ex-cop lolloped into the bar, heaved his fat arse up onto a stool and started asking questions. Steno felt hurt that he hadn't been consulted, but he knew that his feelings were useful only if he could transform them into something productive. He called Miranda and assured her that all would be well, thereby reminding her that it didn't have to be. Soon Miranda was ringing him five times a day freaking out about all manner of things Kennedy was digging up. Steno wasn't sure what those things were, not at first anyway, but they resulted in Kennedy blackmailing Miranda for a couple of years, until they'd hit on the new plan.

He still wasn't sure he knew all of it—the part about Hutton being Regina's son wasn't all of it, he knew that much—but on one level, it didn't matter: the dead couldn't blackmail you. But he knew whatever it was had something to do with Hutton and Miranda. Kennedy had gone up to the Staples place and . . . well, it wasn't known what was said, but the next thing, Patrick had gone and cut out his own tongue. Steno assessed that one and came up blank, unless you just called him a fucking mental bastard like everyone else: What kind of analysis could you make of a fucker who'd do something like that? But Miranda assured him later that Hutton was sound, and sane enough up there, clean and fit and back in training she said, and Steno had seen the horse, and fair enough, Hutton had his weight down and looked capable enough, and then gradually Miranda presented him with a revised appraisal of Hutton's and her ambitions: the new plan.

The new plan. Steno had to laugh sometimes at the plan: the symbols, the tongues, the thirty pieces of silver, like one of those movies you watched on DVD, drunk with a pizza. He didn't know whether it had all been Miranda's idea, or whether it came from Hutton; the idea had been partly to throw everyone off the scent of what was really happening, but everything they used meant something too, and that appealed to Steno. Miranda had timed it to kick off when Leo got out of jail—she'd been communicating with him when he was inside, Steno believed, playing on his past loyalty to Pa Hutton—in the hope that Leo would join their enterprise. Steno had advised against this, but he was reminded yet again that working with a woman was a hazardous fucking endeavor: she'd sometimes agree completely with what you said and then go out and do the complete fucking opposite, like a monkey or a child. Leo had always been a volatile little fuck, and Steno had had no confidence that Leo would act

274 | DECLAN HUGHES

in concert with them. That shrewd evaluation of the situation turned out to be more than vindicated by subsequent events, not that Miranda Hart had thanked him. But Leo was never gonna be a tout, not even to your man Loy.

Steno still wondered whether he shouldn't have taken Loy out of the picture that night up in Jackie Tyrrell's. He conceded privately that he'd been troubled by the idea of killing them both in one go, especially since Loy did not appear to present a clear and present danger—although Steno believed he was, and that he should go down. Steno suspected that he had succumbed to the worst kind of initiative deficit; he had weakly allowed himself to be defined as a hired hand, simply carrying out orders. Steno didn't need reminders from history to understand just what a cop-out that defense was.

He hadn't particularly enjoyed cutting out the tongues; at least with Folan's, and even Kennedy's, there'd been time, and so the blood wasn't an issue: dead bodies don't bleed in any significant way. With Jackie Tyrrell, Loy was on the premises and there were servants around and he'd had to work fast; he'd started on the tongue when she was still warm, and there was a certain amount of mess. It was a bit of a fucking downer, truth be told. He wouldn't say it had rattled him, but it took all his concentration to set the body up on the ropes and ring the bells, and lay in wait for Loy and *not* kill him, and maybe that was how Steno glossed over what deep down he considered a failure on his part: despite everything, he had stuck firm to his purpose, and acquitted himself with distinction. Spilled milk under the bygone bridge, whatever: he was ready now for what was about to ensue. The beauty-and-the-beast malarkey Miranda had been running with Hutton was nearly done. Brian Rowan, the head man up at Tyrrellscourt, was bought and paid for: he'd soon be assuming a lot more responsibility at the Tyrrellscourt yard.

Jackie Tyrrell's murder hadn't been part of Miranda and Hutton's original plan, but Steno demanded it as the only adequate recompense for his services: Jackie's riding school and lands were all bequeathed to Miranda; Steno had made sure the papers had been drawn up in advance with Miranda transferring the same bequest to a company he controlled. All that remained was the final spectacular. It was that aspect once again that appealed to Steno: the *art* of it. Provided Beauty and the Beast played their parts correctly, and they would, he'd make sure of that. No, it would be spectacular, it would be public, it would bring Tyrrells-court to its knees at last—Steno just wished he could sign his name to it. Maybe that was the ultimate act of self-sacrifice. Not that Steno expected anyone else to understand that.

He looked at Miranda Hart before they got in the Range Rover, and mentally shook his head in despair: her lipstick was crooked, her hair was askew and her eye makeup was asymmetrical. What a fucking downer. It was the problem with democracy, as Steno saw it: some fucking people, no matter what you gave them or did with them, they were never going to get their act together. She smiled at him, and he could see she'd been crying. Was he supposed to feel guilty about that? Well he didn't. She looked scared. At least that showed judgment on her part. She had good reason to be scared. They all had. If there was an enterprise worth the hazard that didn't strike fear into your heart, Steno wondered what it might possibly be.

TWENTY-SIX

The door swung open and the cold relentless wind brought, first Tommy Owens, his hands on his head and his right eye bruised, then Miranda Hart, wearing riding boots and a long Barbour jacket and carrying a black Adidas sports grip, and finally Steno, who wore a broad-brimmed hat and a long coat like an Australian and had a Heckler & Koch MP5K submachine gun in one hand. I didn't check to see what he had in the other. Steno pointed the SMG at me, and I held my hands up and out to be searched. Just as the doorknob had creaked, just before the door opened, I had hidden the Glock 17 I was carrying among the cushions on the sofa. Miranda Hart appeared terrified, her hands shaking as she unzipped the grip, her lips trembling as she produced hanks of nylon cord and bags of nylon grip ties and rolls of silver duct tape. Regina Tyrrell stared at what was unfolding before her eyes in astonishment and fear, then made a rush for the door, only to be brought up short by Steno waving the MP5 at her.

"Karen," she cried. "Karen! What have you done with her?"

"Calm, calm, she's all right, she's fine," Steno said.

"Where is she?" Regina said.

"She's locked in her room. Miranda has the key. We've left food and drink there for her. It's just for a short while, until Leopardstown is done. Miranda, why don't you get things tied up with our friends here?" Steno said. "Take Mr. Loy first, if you would."

I had quickly calculated that there was no percentage in trying to make a grab for the Glock: it wouldn't make much of a show against an SMG. But it might come into its own later on. Miranda looked as if she wanted to say several things, but she didn't say any of them; instead, she got her sports grip and Steno pointed me into a chair with the SMG, and without a word, Miranda tied me up with plastic grip ties around my wrists and ankles and nylon cord around my waist, and then frisked me. When her hand passed over my mobile phone in my jacket pocket, she tensed and looked me in the eye, and I waited for her to come to a decision. It was a moment in which time seemed to slow to a crawl, in which I sensed both her power over me and her powerlessness, now that she was in Steno's thrall. And the strange thing is, in that instant, I felt so much toward her, such a mix of feelings: compassion, and sympathy, and fear for her welfare, and, despite all I knew then and all I suspected and was subsequently to dis-cover, the hope that she and her daughter could somehow escape together, and put all the bad history behind them. And even as I tried to hold the thought in my mind, it turned to dust, like all dreams that involve fighting the past again and winning this time do, turned to dust and was scattered on the relentless wind. She passed over my phone and leant into my ear.

"Please try and think kindly of me," she said, and turned to Steno.

"He's clean," she said, wafting past me, and I breathed her incense of oranges and salt, and the two things combined, the smell of love departed and the chirping of a tramp on the make, filled me with melancholy.

Miranda moved toward Tommy, but he waved her off and approached Steno.

"Steno, you remember me man," he said. "The back room of McGoldrick's, with Leo an' all. And then I was in with you the other day."

Steno looked at Tommy's ruined foot and nodded.

"Sure. Tommy Owens? What's on your mind?"

Tommy looked at me, then approached Steno and spoke in a hushed, confidential voice, as if he'd been living a lie for a long time and was relieved finally to be able to come clean.

"I'm just a hired hand here man," he said. "I mean, I don't have any loyalty to your man Loy, know I mean? And frankly, I put him together with Leo, he beat the shite out of him for no reason, I think he's losing it man. So if you're putting something together you need an extra pair of hands, all I'm saying is, I'm here if you want me man, to drive, whatever."

Steno stared at me, and I stared at Tommy. I knew Steno was trying to work out if Tommy was on the level. I was almost sure he wasn't. Almost was as good as it got with Tommy, but from where I was sitting, bound if not yet gagged, almost didn't feel like a lot. I let this curdle naturally into a glare of disgust at his betrayal; Tommy returned this with a shrug of indifferent scorn. We looked like thieves without honor. I prayed that's not what we were.

"You can drive?" Steno said.

"Sure," Tommy said.

"All right. Good to have an extra pair of hands along."

Then he poked the barrel of the SMG hard in Tommy's face, hard enough to bruise.

"I get so much as a glimmer you're not down the line with me, you're sneaking to Loy, or to the cops, you're gone, understand, and a day, an hour later, I won't even remember the hole you're buried in, let alone your name."

I had to give it to him, Steno was a scary piece of work. He threatened to kill Tommy like he was warning a lounge boy about skimming from the till, and you felt it was of as great, or as little, consequence to him.

"All right Miranda, it's Regina's turn," Steno said.

Regina sat in a chair opposite me, and Miranda fastened her to it in the same way she had fastened me, ties to wrists and ankles, cord around her waist. Both women were trembling, and Miranda kept apologizing for being too rough. Or at any rate, she kept apologizing. When Regina was secured, Steno made a call on his mobile.

"All right," he said. "We're ready up here."

Steno went to the windows and opened the curtains. Gray dawn light trickled quickly in, borne by showers of sleet that pelted against the panes.

Steno stood over me and spoke calmly to my face.

"Whatever happens next, know this: if you contradict anything I say, I'll take you out immediately. Plan A is the plan we're working, for Miranda's sake, for old times' sake: I don't claim to understand it myself, but that's the route we're taking. But if I think you're putting that in jeopardy, even for an instant: Plan B, baby."

"And what's Plan B?"

Steno almost smiled, his fleshy face heavy and still, his eyes genial and dead.

"Kill every fucker standing, and get out of here fast. And don't think I won't."

I didn't. Steno gave Miranda a Sig Sauer compact, looked like one of the Halligan cache I'd brought down. There was a knock at the door, and then Francis Xavier Tyrrell was led in by a red-faced, straw-haired man I didn't recognize, but whom I soon found out was Brian Rowan, the Tyrrells' head man. Tyrrell looked around the room, his cheeks aflame, his sharp, intelligent features quivering with quiet anger and indignation. He wore a sleeveless padded green jacket over tweeds and a brown fedora. No one spoke. It felt as if a bunch of teenagers had been having a party and the father who had expressly forbidden them such an event had arrived home.

"What the devil is all this?" he said.

Regina's emotion overflowed into tears; she spoke through them now in a rush.

"Francis, they have Karen, they're holding her."

"They have Karen? What do you mean, they're 'holding' her? What do they want?"

"They've kidnapped her, they want . . ."

Regina faltered under F. X. Tyrrell's glare. Steno looked to Miranda Hart, who beckoned F. X. Tyrrell to the open window.

"Can you see the gallops? See the rider there? How's he doing, do you think? Do you need binoculars?"

"My sight is perfect," Tyrrell said.

The room fell silent as he watched.

"Good seat. Nice action. Who is that, one of the apprentices? Brian?"

"His name is Patrick, boss."

"We want Patrick to ride today," Miranda said. "The third race, the juvenile hurdle for three year olds. Barry Dorgan hasn't made the weight for Bottle of Red. We want Patrick to start in Dorgan's place."

Miranda's voice was shaky but firm; it also, for the first time, expressed for Patrick Hutton an emotion she hadn't betrayed before, at least, not in my hearing: love. As Miranda spoke, dawn light from the window shifted slowly across her face. F. X. Tyrrell transferred his gaze to her as if seeing her for the first time.

"You're . . . you're Mary Hart, aren't you?"

"Miranda."

"Yes. Yes. Look at you child. All grown up."

There was a silence, punctuated by Regina Tyrrell's quiet sobbing; Miranda Hart looked quickly from Regina to F. X. Tyrrell and shuddered; F. X. Tyrrell shook his head suddenly, as if a ghost from his past had asked him for help and he found he had nothing left to give. Tyrrell looked out toward the gallops again, then he pursed his lips and wrinkled his nose.

"You want Patrick to ride one of my horses? Patrick? Who the devil is Patrick?"

"Patrick Hutton, remember?" Miranda said. "You remember Thurles? By Your Leave?"

Tyrrell looked out again at Hutton, and the blood drained from his face.

"I remember, yes; I remember what he did to my beautiful By Your Leave."

His face was creased with sudden pain, and then his small dark eyes blazed.

"Get out of my sight, the lot of you! How dare you!" he cried.

Nobody moved. Now there was silence, and the relentless wind, and the insistent sleet on the windowpanes. F. X. Tyrrell looked from face to face, and for the first time, uncertainty appeared on his. It was like an old play when the conspirators confront the king, and the king commands them to desist, failing to grasp that at the instant of their challenge, he has ceased to rule. He turned to Brian Rowan with his big plump farm-boy head, his shock of fair hair, his shrewd, watery blue eyes.

"Brian," he said. "Brian, for God's sake."

Brian looked at the floor, then briefly at Steno, before fixing on Regina.

"It's like Miss Tyrrell said, boss," he said. "Think of Miss Karen. Better to go along with it. It's . . . it's just one race."

The last idea was the one Rowan evidently found the most difficult to express, and it was clearly one of the major difficulties for F. X. Tyrrell as well.

"Just one race?" he said, as if the very notion of looking at the sport in that light was so bizarre he'd never contemplated it before. "This is Bottle of Red."

Regina spoke then, her tone suddenly hard and cold.

"Francis. They know . . . *everything*."

F. X. Tyrrell flashed her a look that mixed anger with real fear. Steno yawned and looked at his watch.

"Want to get moving," he said quietly, waving his MP5K sub-machine gun gently back and forth, like a wand.

Tyrrell peered at Steno as if he hadn't noticed him before.

"That's Stenson, isn't it?" F. X. Tyrrell said. "From Mc-Goldrick's? I'll have you dismissed from your post for this."

"I already quit," Steno said. Then he took Tyrrell's right arm and bent it behind his back until his wrist was at his neck. The old man gasped in agony.

"Now you go along with this, and behave yourself, and you do your thing in the parade ring, and you talk nice to the TV people with Patrick afterward if he wins, do you understand?"

Tyrrell nodded, whimpering in pain.

"And you don't call for help, and you don't tell anyone, especially not the Guards?"

"No!"

Steno let Tyrrell's arm go, and the old man dropped to his knees. I don't know if the hoarse sound he made was breathing or weeping, but I know that all the other men in the room turned away. When I looked at Regina Tyrrell and Miranda Hart, however, I saw that they could not take their eyes off his suffering. Brian Rowan helped Tyrrell to his feet and began to talk to him in a low, quiet voice as he led him out. Tyrrell's face was haggard with pain and confusion.

Steno summoned Tommy and gave him what looked like another warning. Then Steno nodded at Miranda, waved the SMG at us all and followed Tommy out.

TWENTY-SEVEN

Miranda Hart trailed after Steno. While she was gone, I thought about various ways of getting free of my bonds, but the chair was too solid to be wrenched apart, and I didn't carry a blade as a matter of course, and short of launching myself out the window, nothing else occurred to me. If I could maneuver my way to the couch, I could maybe get hold of the Glock, although how I'd aim it at anything worth shooting was another matter. Just as this thought was forming, Miranda came back. She brought a tray with a pot of coffee, cups and milk with her and offered it round.

"That'd be nice if we had our hands free," Regina said.

Miranda looked at the grips tying our wrists to the arms of the chairs and nodded and apologized, then poured a coffee for herself.

In the silence, I heard a muffled voice coming from down the hall. It was the voice of a child.

"Mummy? Mummy? Mother? I can't open the door!"

"Karen . . . oh my God, let me go to her," Regina said.

Miranda looked anxious and shook her head.

"Just reassure her, all right? Shout from here."

"Mummy? I'm locked in!"

Regina took a deep breath to compose herself, then raised her voice to a yell.

"It's all right, sweetheart. The lock's broken."

"Just find the key."

"The key won't work. We have to find a locksmith."

"Mummy!"

The child was wailing. Miranda held her face in her hands.

"It's all right, sweetheart. Just . . . find a book and get back into bed. Or do some drawing. We'll get you out soon. Okay?"

There was silence then. Miranda looked shamefaced, and shook her head at me, as if to say that she wasn't in fact responsible for this. I shook my head right back and looked her in the eye.

"One thing I don't understand, Miranda," I said. "Well, that's not true, actually, there are many things I don't understand about this case, but best to take them one at a time. What's in it for Steno?"

"You have to understand," Miranda began. "You have to try and track this from the beginning. It's all because of Patrick. And Patrick will have what he's dreamed of today, after all this time. He's been training, he's in good condition. It's the least he deserves."

"And what? Are the other horses just going to sit back and let him win?"

"You'll just have to wait and see. Live on television."

"And what then? He takes the fall? He has his Tyrrellscourt tattoo, he has no tongue, he's perfect for a clogger like Myles Geraghty. Best of all, you probably have him so he wants to confess. He's the Omega Man, he acted alone, and you all walk away scot-free? But what about Steno, what does he get? I mean,

Regina here is in the way, isn't she? Maybe the Omega Man needs to claim a fourth victim. Get rid of Regina and Miranda hits the jackpot. Karen Tyrrell is the heiress, Miranda is reunited with her daughter, and Gerald Stenson gets paid off until his dying day."

Miranda shook her head.

"You're looking at everything the wrong way round. Start with Patrick, living half-wild up on the Staples place, a bunch of scrap and a fistful of memories, some sweet, many bitter. The private detective Don Kennedy found his birth certificate. It wasn't in Lombard Street, it was at the registration office in Naas, I remember that much. Maybe because I was trying to remember anything but what he was telling me. See, Kennedy didn't come to me first, like he was supposed to. From the word go he had wanted to go and see Folan, he kept saying since Folan and Patrick were contemporaries, and in many ways had a shared history, he was a crucial witness. I kept making excuses not to go—I don't think I could have handled it. Anyway, I think he suspected Folan was Patrick, and now he had a foolproof way of finding out. He went up to the Staples place and showed Patrick the birth certificate, right there in black and white: Mother: Regina Mary Immaculate. And I can't remember what Patrick was working on at the time, I think he might have been putting up some fencing. Anyway, he had a pair of metal snips in his flight suit pocket. I don't know why, he took to dressing in flight suits when he went to live up there. Kennedy confronted him with the birth cert, and asked him what he thought. And Patrick took the snips and pulled his tongue out and snipped a good half of it off."

Regina screamed at this, and began to shake her head, wailing. While I listened to that sound, and to Miranda talking, I was aware again of Karen calling for her mother, over and over again, sometimes through tears, sometimes angrily, rattling the door or banging on it. I hoped the sash windows in her room were too stiff for her to open, and if they weren't, that she didn't do anything foolish. Regina was still wailing, keening like a banshee.

Miranda leant across and slapped her hard across the face, and she stopped.

"Listen to me," she said. "This is the beginning. This is just the beginning. Don't forget what you did to him, Regina. Don't forget you dumped your son into an orphanage, no, a torture chamber, then took him into your house while never acknowledging him. Do you know what that did to him when he found out? That you were his mother, but you had never treated him like a son?"

It couldn't have been much after nine in the morning then, but that was the point where I thought: I could really do with a drink.

"Kennedy got Patrick a doctor he knew, avoided a hospital situation where the police would have been involved. Setting me and Patrick up, getting us to trust him, so he could blackmail the fuck out of us. But you know what Patrick told me? He wrote it down, he couldn't speak at all back then. Because I kept asking, in the days and weeks after, pleading with him to tell me why he had done it. And eventually he took a piece of paper and he wrote two things on it. The two things were: 'Tell No One,' and 'Say Nothing.'

"I knew what that meant. When Patrick had been in St. Jude's, he'd been raped twice. He didn't know who the rapists were. He wasn't even sure there were two, but he thought there were, he said they smelled different. He said sometimes he thought it might have been Vincent Tyrrell, sometimes Leo, sometimes even Steno. I asked Steno and he swore he hadn't touched Patrick."

I intervened at that point.

"You didn't believe him, did you? I know you didn't believe him. Leo Halligan always thought it was Steno who raped Hutton."

Miranda looked at me and swallowed, and continued from where she left off.

"And Patrick said, they'd each said that. Each of the perpetrators—and the other boys who were victims were told the same thing too. Tell no one. Say nothing."

Tell no one. Say nothing. The secret history of Irish life.

"I asked you what was in it for Steno. Looks like you won't answer. Explain something else to me, Miranda," I said. "I can understand Folan—a row, or a brawl, or some messy accident that got covered up. I can understand Kennedy, the blackmailer. What I don't get is Jackie Tyrrell. She was your friend, in many ways your champion. You clearly revered her. Why did she have to die?"

Miranda began to nod her head very quickly, as if someone was disagreeing with her but she had right on her side, and if only they'd stop talking, she'd set them straight.

"It's the same answer to both questions. Patrick wanted to return. He wanted one last race, that was all. And I felt . . . because of how I'd treated him, the way I'd abandoned him, given up our child . . . I felt I had a lot to make up for. I felt I'd betrayed him, and I needed to atone. Patrick killed Bomber Folan years ago, and I was there. It was an accident, but Steno knew we were both involved. He cleaned up afterward, and then we were both in Steno's power. When Kennedy started the blackmail, we both wanted him to die. I don't feel guilty about Kennedy, he was a piece of filth, extorting money out of our unhappiness and shame. But I couldn't do it myself, and neither could Patrick, as it happened. So Steno did it for us."

"And Steno's price was Jackie Tyrrell. Why?"

Miranda stared at the floor.

"I said no harm could come to Regina. And . . . as you said, Steno wanted to know what was in it for him. I was . . . I am Jackie Tyrrell's heir. Her estate: the riding school, the house, everything, it all goes to me."

"And now it all goes to Steno."

"I couldn't argue him out of it," she said. "I begged him, I said I could get her to advance me enough to keep him going . . . it wasn't enough. Steno went his own way. It frightened me."

Miranda looked at me with tears in her eyes, and everything I had felt for her brimmed to the surface again. Complicity in Jackie's murder had pushed her beyond the pale; now I knew she was not directly responsible, my flexible moral code longed to find some clause that would welcome her back to the fold. Regina Tyrrell looked between us, her face closed to everything but her own pain. The sleet had picked up to hail now; it pounded needle sharp against the windowpanes; I had to raise my voice to compete.

"What else had Kennedy on you, Miranda? I mean, it couldn't've just been Regina as Patrick's mother, there must have been more to it. Otherwise he would have been blackmailing Regina, or F.X., not you."

Miranda took a page from her coat and unfolded it. It was a long-form birth certificate.

"Kennedy was a predator. He was real scum. He wanted more money. He threatened to go to Regina, to tell her what he had found out. I didn't think she knew . . . I reasoned that no one but me knew, that Regina had a better chance of . . . of bringing up my little girl properly if she didn't know either."

"I think Regina suspected, at the very least," I said.

"You can suspect, and go on living. You can suspect, and keep lying to yourself, and survive. That's what people do every day. But you might not make it past knowing. Anyway, this pig wanted more to keep the secret. I couldn't afford it. That kicked the whole thing off, really. Steno helped us then. Helped us to scare the daylights out of Kennedy until he gave us the key to a safe in his house where this was kept. Helped us to kill him. And good riddance."

"What's the secret?" Regina asked.

And Miranda Hart said: "That you are my mother. That Patrick and I are brother and sister. That our daughter, Karen . . ."

She didn't need to continue. Regina nodded her head wearily. She had said to me earlier that she had dreaded this day, but prayed for it, too. I think dread was the dominant emotion in the room, especially because of what Miranda Hart said next.

"Maybe we could have gotten past that," she said. "Maybe . . . I don't know . . . but when Patrick . . . when Patrick went to confession with Vincent Tyrrell . . . it was after By Your Leave, and all the shenanigans with the Halligans and so forth, and Patrick was sick to his stomach, he didn't like the cheating, that side of the game, he was straight as a die, really. And he went to confess his sins. And he told Vincent Tyrrell he was worried about getting another job, with a bad reputation, because his wife was pregnant. Tyrrell got very angry, and Patrick was confused: he knew he'd been in the wrong, but surely these things happened to everyone at one time or another. Surely even a Catholic priest could be more understanding than that.

"And Vincent Tyrrell told him that this child would be an abomination. It would be against nature. Patrick asked why. And Vincent Tyrrell said, because its mother and father shared the same mother, and their fathers were brothers."

All you could hear when Miranda stopped speaking was the hail against the windowpanes and the slow, steady wailing of Karen Tyrrell.

TWENTY-EIGHT

Tommy witnessed what happened in Leopardstown that day at first hand, and this is the way he told it to me:

"I was the driver, Steno in the back with Hutton. Hutton kept drizening this tune to himself, over and over, driving me mad so it was. Steno seemed as ever, you know, Mr. Chill. I was trying to get something out of him on the whole operation, find out what the plan was: giving him a lot of excitement and enthusiasm, not laying it on too thick 'cause he's obviously not a fucking plank. Telling him I'd had it up to here with fucking Ed Loy taking me for granted and paying me shit and expecting me to watch his back all the fucking time. But Steno played it cool and steady: is that right, no really, Tommy, all this. Pretty soon I gave it up. The driving was taking up all my attention anyway, the hail and the sleet, our number one weather choice, and cunts in Mercs and boy racers still pissed from the night before cutting me up in a poxy dribble of muddy water morning light, you wished you were in your bed with nothing more taxing than a trip to the pub ahead. Stephen's Day, a few bets, a few jars, and home to see what's on the box. Turkey sandwich, bottle of beer. Not this year.

"We're on the M50, heading south, Steno says to keep going on past Leopardstown, and then to cut down toward the sea, onto the N11 and down into Bayview. Father Vincent Tyrrell, I'm thinking, and sure enough, we get to the church car park and Steno nods me out. He leaves Hutton in the backseat, still singing away to himself, sounds like a Christmas carol to me, but I've heard so fucking many the past few weeks I can't remember which is which. We head into the back porch, there's a mass on, I look at Steno and he shrugs, and I'm thinking, this cunt would strafe the fucking church now not a bother on him, and then I'm like, calm the fuck down, this is a barman from Tyrrellscourt, not a fucking suicide bomber for al-Qaeda. I open the door and it's Father Lyons, home from the missions, and the beady-eyed cunt clocks me instantly, caught rapid, where the fuck were you? I can see he spots me, well, pity about him. Twenty women and three men over seventy in the church, you have to feel sorry for them, sorry for Lyons too, I mean, six masses between them yesterday, and Stephen's morning these 'oul ones and 'oul fellas are back for more. I know they're probably lonely and they've fuck-all else to be doing, but come on, Jesus knows you love Him by now, He got the message big-time on His birthday, relax there or He might start to think yiz are all laying it on a bit thick.

"We go around to the presbytery, knock away, nothing doing. Steno looks at me like I have the inside story.

"'Maybe he's gone to Leopardstown,' I say.

"'Maybe he has. Two birds,' he says.

"I don't like the sound of that.

"And we're back in the Range Rover, back up and onto the M50, heading for Leopardstown. The hail and sleet have dwindled to a scuttery rain now, and the air is warming a little, and there's a crack in the sky that, if it's not exactly blue, it's at the silver end of gray, and I can see Steno nodding out the window.

"'The day is coming together,' he says. 'The day is going to happen.'

"F. X. Tyrrell has gone ahead with the head man, Brian Rowan, in the last horse box. Always goes with the horses, Rowan says, still in awe, and Steno checks him, is he sure he's with the program, and Rowan reassures Steno he's onside, well in there, bought and paid for. Horses'll be up in the stables with all the lads looking after them, and Tyrrell too. We turn off for the course and the Garda checkpoints are already in place, waving punters into the car parks about half a mile from the track. Steno's given me some kind of official pass he's got from Rowan and they nod us through. And part of me is, why didn't I just call a halt, tell the Guards I've a madman with a submachine gun in the back, not to mention a madman with no tongue who thinks he's Lester Piggott? Why don't I tell them about you, tied to a chair in Tyrrellscourt? I could pretend I think nothing bad is gonna happen here, like it's just a sentimental old debt being paid: Hutton gets to run a prestige race, ten years after everyone thought he disappeared. What a story! But I know that's not all there is. Maybe it's that I want to know what happens next. Like it's their story, and I want to see how they play it out. And maybe it's because I still don't like talking to the fucking cops. And maybe there's a second, just a glimmer, when I roll down the window and show the Guard the pass, and he sees it's Tyrrellscourt stables, and he looks in the back and sees Hutton, and you know what he says?

"'Is that him? Is that Hutton?'

"Fuck sake, it's out already. And of course, I know Tyrrell has to tell them Barry Dorgan is being replaced by Hutton. Maybe I just don't expect everyone to remember who he was. But why not? Fuck, I do. There's lads in Paddy Power's who talk about By Your Leave and Hutton vanishing still. So it's out there, the return of the prodigal: they're building the fucking myth already. And maybe there's a glimmer: tell him. Tell him. And then he's beaming at us, his eyes twinkling with excitement, in such a fucking hurry to wave us on it would've seemed like bad manners to disappoint the cunt. In for a penny. And I thought, what would Ed do? He'd follow it to the end. Follow it to the end, Tommy, and see where it takes you.

"We park close enough to the entrance, and Steno goes off to the stables; he's got to get passes for us all. While we're sitting there waiting, I finally pick up on what it is Hutton is humming.

Rejoice, rejoice, Emmanuel,
Shall come to thee, O Israel . . .

"I join in on the chorus, and he gives me a big smile when I've done, and nods his head, like, at last, here's someone who understands me.

"Mental, totally fucking mental.

"When Steno comes back, he tells us Hutton needs to go to the weigh room, and then we can hang on in the jockeys' changing room—but not to go yet, or we'll be in there too long, and the other jockeys'll be hassling us.

"'We?' I say.

"'Yeah, you can be his valet, all right?' Steno says to me.

"Not as if I have a great deal of choice in the matter.

"Steno rolls his eyes then.

"'You'll never guess who's up there with the animals.'

"'Dr. Doolittle,' I say, before I can stop myself. Then, 'Rex Harrison, not Eddie Murphy,' as if that's gonna help. It doesn't: he gives me the base of his hand smack in the jaw and sets my teeth scraping and my head clanging like an anvil, the fucker.

"'Don't get smart with me, you mangy fuck,' Steno says, side of the mouth, all smiles, like he's chatting to a friend. 'You're still on probation. And Rex Harrison is dead.'

"I nod, trying to look sorry, which is no great stretch, 'cause after the clatter he's given me, believe me, I am.

"'Vincent Tyrrell. He knows all the stable lads of course, half of them were in St. Jude's, so he's at home up there. Him and the brother pretending they don't see each other. Said he's particularly keen to see how Bottle of Red gets on.'

"Steno seems to be directing this as much at Hutton as at me, and when I look round, there's Hutton all fired up, glaring, eyes boiling, like a bull at a gate.

"Steno fucks off then, but before he does, he takes my phone, and gives me a little warning about what he'll do if I double-cross him. I can remember it, but I'm not going to repeat it, 'cause there's a chance I might forget it one day, but not if it lodges in my head.

"We hang on for a while, then twelve-twenty, just before the first race, that's our cue. We go in and present our passes and head for the changing rooms and grab a spot. Hutton has a bag with his silks and riding hat and his whip and some street clothes. There's a bit of muttering from the other lads. But Hutton doesn't care, he just changes into his colors, cool as you like. And then a couple of lads come up and give it a bit of remember me, I was a boy in Tyrrellscourt when you were riding. Hutton smiles at them, and nods away big-time, and maybe they're a bit disappointed he's not chatting to them but they're not really surprised, and they seem to go away happy. Any jockeys I ever met, either they wouldn't fucking shut up or you couldn't get a word out of them, so maybe he's coming across as normal. I can see all eyes are on him though—the fucking head on him man, even without knowing about his tongue: he has that complexion street drinkers have, like he's been boiled. Not to mention he's the comeback kid to beat the band, a fucking legend in the making.

"We go around to the weigh room, which is on the lower deck of the grandstand just across from the parade ring. Same story here, everyone having a squint. Hutton's not bothered, the opposite actually, like he's missed it, the attention, and I have to say, it is pretty class now, all the riders in their silks, the colors, the shine of the boots, the roar of the crowd for the first race, I'm getting into it man. While he's queuing for the scales, I grab a race card, maybe I'll get a chance to slap a bet on. No time like the present. And the first thing, looking at the card for the third race, what jumps out is Bottle of Red's owner: Mr. G. Halligan. Looks like it's going to be quite a circus out there in the parade ring this afternoon.

"The weight's ten-stone-nine, and Hutton makes it with three pounds to spare, fair play, and he is in good shape, and we're off to hang in the changing room again. The boys are in from the first race, winners and losers, and Hutton gets a bit more attention and handles it the same, and then the second race is called, and we're out to saddle up. While we're on our way around the parade ring to the saddling stalls, Steno falls into line with us and tells me to get lost. I linger though, long enough to see him draw Hutton aside and slip something to him, something Hutton slips inside his silk top, something that glitters in the faint sunlight that's still trying to break through.

"The parade ring's where it's happening now. I can see Vincent Tyrrell in his dog collar and his long black overcoat and his black fedora, looking like a priest in a Jimmy Cagney movie, and there's George Halligan in his Barbour jacket and his tweed cap, looking like a cunt, basically, giving F. X. Tyrrell an earful, and there's Brian Rowan in the middle of them with one of those women George collects from Russia or Brazil who all look like they're waiting for the operation. She's a foot taller than Rowan, snow-blond hair, wearing a white fur coat, a lynx it must be, Rowan's talking into her fake tits and she's looking out across the crowd pretending she hasn't noticed every eye is glued to her.

"Mind you, there's a lot of money here today, a lot of new tits and teeth and holiday flesh and fur being waved; it's been a while since I was racing and the biggest change is, fair enough, there's the usual crowd, the old boys in their trilbies and wool coats, the country farmers, the Barbour jacket crowd, all the middle classes in their Christmas best, then there's the betting-shop boys giving themselves a day out from the bookies, scruffy lads in jumpers and jeans like, like me, to be honest, but then there's also a lot of young people, young fellas with estate-agent hair and cheap suits and young ones in skimpy dresses and high heels, like it's a night-club they thought they were going to, working-class kids out for a big day. And some politician getting his photo taken with your one off *You're a Star* on the telly. And Bono and Ali here too, someone said, up in one of the boxes, I suppose. Even a few Butlers are here, picking pockets and rolling drunks. Everyone's here, relieved the big freeze never came. Everyone's here!

"And here comes Patrick Hutton on Bottle of Red being led by her groom into the ring, and such a roar goes up you'd swear it was one of the Carberrys or A. P. McCoy, one of the crowd's favorites anyway, and you can see George Halligan is still bulling but F. X. Tyrrell has moved away from him, and George has tugged on his shoulder to turn him back, and suddenly Steno is at his side, looking as if he has every right to be there in his long coat and his big hat, looking like an Australian. George is still looking gnarly and aggravated, and then Steno prods him in the side, and George looks at him straight on, and Steno nods, and George nods back. Deal for now.

"Patrick Hutton is leaning down to listen to whatever F.X. has to say to him, taking instructions, fair play to F.X., he looks like he's making the best of it. Hutton is beaming, and there's a chant going up:

Pa-trick HUTTON, back from the DEAD!
Pa-trick HUTTON, back from the DEAD!
Pa-trick HUTTON, back from the DEAD!

"The chant builds and builds, and he's taking the horse around the ring now, and as it hits a big crescendo Hutton touches the peak of his riding hat, and the crowd erupt in cheers.

"Now I'm watching Vincent Tyrrell, who's staring at Hutton, never at the horse, always at Hutton, like he's trying to hex him or something, and Hutton looks across every now and again, and looks away as quickly. And then I get a dig in the ribs and a hand on my collar and I'm pulled out of the crowd by Leo Halligan.

"'What the fuck is going on?' he says, and I look around, and see that Steno is still in there, and I tell Leo Halligan as much as I know of what the fuck is going on. He nods at me, and then he vanishes into the crowd. The next thing, Steno is at my side.

"'We'll go down onto the turf to watch the race,' he says.

"Fair enough. Down we go, through the tunnel beneath the private boxes, and Madigan's bar is heaving with half-dressed young ones, it's like one of those Club 18–30 holidays. Out we come and it's good to feel grass beneath your feet, even if it is sopping wet. The grandstand is behind us, with the Dublin mountains towering above, but we head down past the line of bookies' pitches, and Steno salutes Jack Proby of Proby and Son, who doesn't look very pleased to see Steno.

"It's not the best place to watch a race if you want to get the whole picture, but it's the business if you want the atmosphere, and the atmosphere is only brilliant. Bottle of Red was favorite anyway, and the Hutton thing has added a whole other level, the chant's going around in waves:

> Pa-trick HUTTON, back from the DEAD!
> Pa-trick HUTTON, back from the DEAD!
> Pa-trick HUTTON, back from the DEAD!

"Rocking back and forth from the grandstand down to the barrier and back, impossible not to get caught up in the motion of it, absolutely classic.

"There's a field of thirteen, and Hutton keeps the horse back all the way around the first time, buried in a pack. Contrariwise and Vico Fancy lead from the off, and you just know they're not going to have the legs to make it, and when they're on the road side for the second time, they fall away, and Hendre takes up the lead and holds it until they hit the last jump and turn into the final furlong and here comes Bottle of Red, Hutton has to use the elbows a bit, he's boxed himself in, but he breaks out and he breaks clear and now he's coming, past Columbine, past Kelly's Hero, past Dodger, and as they turn he's neck and neck with Hendre, Hendre and Bottle of Red, and then Hutton lets her go and it looks like he was holding her back all along, and Hendre has nothing left and Bottle of Red, Bottle of Red, Bottle of Red by a mile, and the chant would raise the hairs on your neck:

> Pa-trick HUTTON, back from the DEAD!
> Pa-trick HUTTON, back from the DEAD!
> Pa-trick HUTTON, back from the DEAD!

"'Beautiful!' Steno yells in my ear, and I'd swear there were tears in the fucker's eyes.

"'Parade Ring, come on,' he says, and we boot up there. Some courses have a separate winners' enclosure; at Leopardstown, the horses go back round to the parade ring they started in.

"There's a huge crowd gathering, and Steno brings me into the parade ring, maybe to keep me close, maybe to use as a shield. Means I get a perfect view of all that happens. There's TV reporters going around with those huge microphones and cameras and everything, and Hutton rides the horse in to great applause, and someone is talking to F.X., asking him about Hutton's return, and Hutton tips the hat to even greater cheers, and F.X. mutters something about there being much rejoicing for the one who was lost, and Hutton dismounts as the groom rushes to hold the horse, and as Hutton approaches F.X. a blond female reporter spots Father Vincent Tyrrell and draws him into the group of three for the camera and asks him about the parable of the prodigal son and Vincent Tyrrell says yes indeed, Luke chapter fifteen, but of course there are all manner of prodigals, why he and his brother, Francis, haven't spoken in ten years, not since the day Patrick Hutton disappeared.

"I can see Steno edging closer because Hutton is freaking out now, looking wildly around him, like a robot malfunctioning, whatever the plan was, this wasn't it, and Vincent Tyrrell is still talking, and someone to one side of the camera is signaling to the reporter to cut the interview dead, but the reporter won't, she seems mesmerized, so does everyone, and no wonder: while Hutton is shaking his head and blinking and F.X. is standing stock-still like he died ten years ago and forgot to tell anyone, Vincent Tyrrell is saying that the prodigal son is of course at root a story about the father, not the son, and he should know: Patrick Hutton is Father Vincent Tyrrell's son.

"Patrick Hutton is shaking his head, and suddenly he has a long knife in his hand, and the crowd in the ring turns to flee, and Hutton steps up to F. X. Tyrrell and the knife flashes in the light, but before he can use it, Vincent Tyrrell is in front of F.X., protecting him, and Hutton steps back and stares at them both for a moment, shaking his head some more, then Hutton brings the blade up and slashes a gulley deep across his own throat. Blood shoots from it, and there are screams everywhere, and Hutton topples to his knees and then to the ground, and Father Vincent Tyrrell goes down to him, and as the cries go out for doctors and ambulances, the priest who was his father whispers a last confession in his son's ear, and above them, like he's been turned to stone, in the parade ring at Leopardstown Racecourse in the shadow of the Dublin mountains on St. Stephen's Day stands Francis Xavier Tyrrell, the trainer of the winning horse."

TWENTY-NINE

The screen went black after Vincent Tyrrell's admission on live television that he was the father of the winning jockey of the 1:30 at Leopardstown. In their confusion, which they no doubt shared with the viewing public, RTE replaced the racing altogether with a concert of Christmas music from Vienna.

"Why did Vincent Tyrrell say that? What was he thinking of?" Miranda cried.

"What were you expecting Hutton to do? Kill F. X. Tyrrell live on air?" I said.

No sooner had I formed the words than I realized that yes, that was exactly what had been planned for Tyrrell. Miranda's phone rang, and she took the call out in the hall. When she came back in she was crying, but through her tears her words were hard with rage.

"That was Leo. Patrick is dead," she said. "He wanted to die.

He killed himself. But for nothing. F.X. is still alive. Patrick went for F.X. and Vincent saved his life. No one can put an end to the Tyrrells. Oh God, poor Patrick."

She shook her tears away, apparently uncertain what to do next.

"The Guards will be coming, then," I said. "By now, F.X. will have told them Regina and Karen are being held hostage."

"Yes," Miranda said. "They'll be coming for me. There's not a lot of time left."

"You can say you were forced into it by Hutton and Steno," I said. "That's certainly how Vincent Tyrrell must see it. The victim. That's what you were. A tragic set of circumstances, the child of incest, an incestuous marriage, a child of your own who . . . nobody could have anything but sympathy for your plight, Miranda."

"You know that's not exactly how it happened. Real life kept intruding, getting in the way. I've never looked for anyone's sympathy. I've never been anybody's victim. And I'm not going to play the part now."

Miranda suddenly burrowed in the sports grip she had brought and produced a Stanley knife. With it, she cut the ties binding Regina to her chair and then cut mine. There had been no sound from Karen's room for a while. I assumed Regina would go to the child instantly. Instead, as if set free by the silence, Regina suddenly spoke in a voice that she had kept silent for a long time, a voice that seemed to come from a younger place within her, and what she said carried the intensity of a dream.

"It was in the stables," she said. "The last one, you could see the river from there. And the paddock with the trees, and the two ponies sometimes. There was always the rustle, but not of straw. Francis was an innovator there, straw could carry all manner of bugs and ticks and rot, parasites and spores that would cause the horses illness. Francis pioneered the use of shredded paper. It was so white there, the bright white that fills up a room, like when you wake up and it's been snowing, and everywhere there's soft bright light, like the first day. That's what it was like in all the stables, but most especially this one. There was a ledge above the door, and you could see the river from there. That winter, it snowed. A thick blanket. Makes the sound different in the air, as if you don't have to speak so clearly. As if everything was understood.

"I was always in love with Francis. He was my daddy and my brother, my protector and my friend. I would have done anything he wanted."

"Did he force you?" Miranda said, seemingly unable to bear Regina's fond, elegiac tone applied to an event that was to have such devastating consequences for her.

Regina smiled, a sad smile that chilled me to the bone. She shook her head.

"No. No, he didn't force me. I'd like to say he did, because it would give you comfort, and me at least an excuse, and maybe a shred of dignity. Later, the other one did, or more accurately, they both did, but that's to jump ahead. No, Francis didn't force me. The reverse. It wasn't in his nature, I know, he wasn't disposed that way. But I kept after him. I had decided that he would be the first."

Miranda groaned in anguish and disgust.

"That's how I thought. And I kept it going, hints and caresses and invitations, I'd give him rubdowns after the day's work with the horses, so he'd see how well I could run things here, how I'd be a credit to him. And one day, in the snow, in the white of the stable, in the white of the snow . . . the rustle of the paper now, so soft in your ears . . . like music it was . . ."

It was Miranda's turn to retreat now; I could hear her trying to control her breath.

"A few months, that's all it was. A few days within a few months. He brought it to a close. We both knew it was wrong, but I didn't care. And then . . . and then I was pregnant. I never knew . . . the nuns in Scotland said they'd look after the child, but Francis insisted he knew the right family. I never dreamed for a second it would be the Harts at the Tyrrellscourt Arms. It was almost . . . it was almost like it amused him. Like it was a game for him. And of course, I suspected, everyone assumed it, for heaven's sake, are you two sisters, are you mother and daughter? But I didn't want to believe . . . couldn't let myself believe . . ."

"Why did he do that, Regina? Why did he place her so close to you?"

"To punish me. Just as I had punished him."

She said the words blankly, without affect.

"What about Hutton? What about Vincent Tyrrell?" I said.

Regina's face clouded over.

"That's where it got . . . I never . . . oh God forgive me . . . it was Christmas, Vincent was staying here . . . I was drunk, and a bit . . . maybe I was talking loose . . . flirting with Francis, who wasn't responding, and with Vincent, who was . . . I got angry with them both, and stormed off . . . and Francis came, and said, why didn't I . . . if I slept with Vincent, I could be with him again . . . so I did. It wasn't even . . . I'm trying to make it better now on myself, saying I was drunk, I knew what I was doing . . . I knew damn well what I was doing. I don't know why I wanted it . . . still don't . . . Francis was all I ever wanted . . ."

"But you went with Vincent just the one time. How did you know Hutton was his child, and not Francis's?" I said.

"Francis had an operation, after Mary . . . after Miranda was born, a vasectomy. So nothing like that could happen again."

"And then when the boy was born, you said you couldn't raise him."

"The child of a priest? I couldn't. I wouldn't. I let him go. Francis persuaded me it was the best thing. I was young, starting out, I didn't need that. Didn't need it."

"But you stayed here all those years, and let them both come back into the house, and saw them come together—"

"I did everything I could to block that match. Everything. I . . . and don't forget, I didn't know Miranda was my daughter—"

"But you suspected. Why didn't you act on those suspicions?"

"I don't know."

"And then there was a child."

"There's nothing wrong with the child," Regina said. "She's had every test, every . . . they found no disability, nothing. And Francis . . . I don't think he enjoyed a day of peace after those children were born. Neither of us did, really. It was a kind of torture to him, knowing what he had done, never quite being able to forgive himself. I think . . . I think what we made was a kind of sacrifice, to live through it together. And I was blessed that Karen was given to me. Unworthy as I was."

"Why?" I said. "What possessed him? To experiment with human lives that way?"

Regina shook her head, all tears spent for now.

"He once told me, out in the stable, he said he thought the purest blood might make the finest offspring. That if it could work for horses . . ."

"But it doesn't work for horses."

Regina nodded.

"And you went along with him," I said. "Why?"

Regina looked at me with what almost looked like pity in her extraordinary eyes and shook her head. Again, when she spoke, it was in a voice that seemed to come from the very depths of her soul.

"You don't understand. No one could understand who wasn't there."

"Who wasn't where?"

Regina turned her gaze on Miranda as she spoke.

"My mother died when I was born, I told you that. But I didn't grow up here. I was taken into care, placed in a home. It was just the two boys and Da, in a small tenant cottage out the road a few miles from Tyrrellscourt, two rooms, that's all they had. Francis was fourteen, Vincent twelve. Da was a farm laborer, drinking a lot, and . . . well, other things. With both of them. Until Francis stood up to him. Francis put an end to that. Francis turned him out. And our da was never seen again. And Francis worked every hour God sent on farms in the area, his eye for a horse quickly noticed, training for this owner, then that one, and the winners began to come, and then the Derby in '65. Sure he became a hero in the town, more. He found this place, it was in a tumbledown condition, the family had left for England during the war and never come back, and he set us up here. Came and got me, told me my place was with him, was here, at the heart of the Tyrrells. Made sure I went to school. Sent Vincent for the priesthood."

"And was your name Tyrrell to begin with?"

Regina almost smiled, a rueful flicker, as if still bewitched by the family mythology.

"We . . . we *became* the Tyrrells," Regina said. "Francis called himself that after he got rid of Da. And then he had his name legally changed. The town had been on its knees until Francis came. So anyone who tried to call us something else was quickly silenced. And soon, no one even wanted to. It was as if we had been expected. As if F. X. Tyrrell was a king in exile, come home at last to regain his throne. Without him, what would anyone around here have been? And what would I have become, a charity girl scrubbing floors and scalding laundry in an orphanage?"

She looked at me as if there was any answer I could give her, other than: What have you become now? Her story had explained everything and nothing. I turned to Miranda, who was staring at Regina with tears in her reddened eyes, the Sig Sauer Compact suddenly flashing in her hand, a droning, humming sound coming from the back of her throat. She looked like she was ready to do something rash. I edged forward to the sofa to get the Glock 17 I'd hidden there, much use it had done me.

"Miranda?" I said.

"What?"

"Let me get this straight: Patrick was supposed to kill F. X. Tyrrell first, is that right?"

"That's right. First F.X. Then himself. He had a confession. That he was the Omega Man. He takes all the blame."

"He'd never killed anyone before, had he? Not intentionally, not in cold blood. How was he supposed to do it this time?"

"Because it was F. X. Tyrrell."

"And why should that have made a difference?"

"Because Vincent Tyrrell told us that F.X. had raped Patrick in St. Jude's. He said F.X. had been a frequent visitor there. He said that's largely why he was asked back to Tyrrellscourt in the nineties: to facilitate F.X.'s visits again."

"That can't be right," Regina said. "Francis always told me . . . that after you were born . . . and after Patrick . . . never again. That would be his way of atoning."

"His way of atoning," Miranda said, her scorn like a whip. "What about F.X. and Leo Halligan? You must have known about that."

Regina shook her head.

"I . . . since Karen came here, I suppose I . . . I've kept my head down. I've see as little of Francis as possible. I haven't wanted to know . . . about anything."

Regina was shaking, her face like a mask; she looked helpless and old, her last illusions carried away on the relentless wind.

"His way of atoning," Miranda said, rolling the words around in her mouth like sour fruit. "His way of atoning. What could that be? What could that possibly be?"

I had the gun now, and came up with it loose in my hand, not pointing it at her, just ensuring she could see it. Miranda saw it, and looked at me, and smiled.

"I'm sorry, Ed. I'm so very sorry. It was hard to know what to do. I know I've done wrong. I thought I could survive. But not everyone can be a survivor."

She turned to Regina.

"Please, just one thing. Don't tell Karen the truth. In this instance, it's better if she never knows. Do the right thing. Tell no one. Say nothing."

Miranda Hart put the barrel of the Sig Sauer compact in her mouth and pulled the trigger.

THIRTY

Regina ran to Miranda and fell to her knees and howled, and pulled Miranda's body to her and clung to it as she never had, as she never would, the daughter she had found and lost in a day. I located the key I was looking for in Miranda's sports grip. I tried to tell Regina I was going to check on Karen, but she couldn't see or hear for grief. I shut the door behind me and went down the corridor to the child's room. I checked my appearance in the window opposite to make sure that I wouldn't scare her, and I saw that the snow had finally come. I knocked, and identified myself, and turned the key in the lock and opened the door.

THEY NEVER FOUND Steno. They had a witness (Tommy) who saw his Range Rover leaving Jackie Tyrrell's house the night of her murder, and they reckoned they had enough forensic evidence from that messy night to make a case. They had Vincent Tyrrell as well, to testify to all manner of things he had been told by Miranda Hart, but they didn't think Vincent Tyrrell would stand up in court. But they had no Steno: he never returned to his house, or to Tyrrellscourt. No one has seen him since.

When I say they, I mean DI Dave Donnelly; Myles Geraghty had taken two days' Christmas leave to go to a race meeting at Kempton Park, where his brother-in-law had a horse running in the George VI Steeplechase. Tommy had called Dave as soon as Steno had fled from Leopardstown. Dave was the man on the spot, and thanks to Tommy, and eventually, to me, he had enough inside information and witness testimony to close the case. I made sure Martha O'Connor got a blow-by-blow account, and suggested to her that if anyone wanted to run a story ridiculing the "Omega Man" theory, that would be no bad thing. Martha's paper ran it front page every day for a week, until I almost felt a little sorry for Geraghty. And the brother-in-law's horse came home eighth in a field of nine.

Dave and Carmel are still sharing a home, and to the best of my knowledge, a bed, although I'm happy to say my knowledge of that is strictly limited to Dave having grunted, "Everything's grand thanks," as a way to close the subject down. He's taking the family to Disneyland at Easter, the news of which was certainly enough to cure me of any residual envy of family life.

Nobody told the truth about F. X. Tyrrell, out of respect and solicitude for Karen Tyrrell, but that doesn't mean that people didn't know, in the way news like that always spreads to those it needs to and to some it doesn't, in Ireland at any rate. Tyrrell did not hang himself for shame, but he was found dead within six months anyway; nobody at the stables or the stud farm would work with him; no one in racing wanted to know him; his life's achievement as a trainer and a breeder had been irrevocably disgraced; the very thing that had kept him alive, the only thing he had ever really loved, was the thing he could no longer work with: horses. His doctors said it was a burst aortic aneurysm. But, insofar as I have any insight into the opaque character of the man, I believe he died of a broken heart.

Vincent Tyrrell did not have to be quietly retired from his parish; his cancer did that work for him. I visited him in hospital not long before he died because I had so many questions that only he could answer: what kind of hold had his brother possessed over him that Vincent should sire a child with his sister, or enable F.X. to abuse boys in Vincent's care? What had happened in that cottage after their mother died, the two boys alone with their father? Did Vincent save his brother's life to make him suffer more? Or did he hope his son would kill him first? Had he been leading me by the nose all along? I didn't get any answers. I don't know if I expected any. Maybe there were none to be had. In the end, it was a not-at-all sacred mystery. It was the last breath of a dying breed. It was the price of blood. I left Father Vincent Tyrrell dreaming over the day's racing in *The Irish Field,* working the race cards with his fingers like rosary beads.

Regina Tyrrell, fearing that Karen would be taken away from her, left the country with the child. I don't know where they are. Every time I think of them, I recall F. X. Tyrrell's belief in the bloodline, his creed that blood and breed are the beginning and the end. I hope his granddaughter can find a future that will prove him wrong.

After a lot of digging, Martha O'Connor discovered that the Tyrrell family name had originally been Butler. And after some digging of my own in registration offices in Wicklow and Kildare, I established that John Butler, F. X. Tyrrell's father, was a distant cousin of the Butlers that settled in North Wicklow. The Butlers that eat their young, that settle disputes with sulfuric acid, the Butlers Tommy Owens called "a tribe of savages."

The Butlers had an eventful Christmas also, as did the Leonards. On Christmas night, Joe Leonard came out of his house to chase off two young men in sportswear and hooded tops who were messing around with his mother-in-law's blue BMW, the car he had seemed so in awe of. The men were joined by two others, and they refused to stop. Instead, they picked up their attack, kicking the vehicle and scraping the bodywork with keys and knives. When Joe Leonard put himself between them and the car, they kicked him and stabbed him and left him bleeding in the street. Joe Leonard died later that night in Loughlinstown Hospital. The whole incident was recorded on one of the tapes Leonard had hired me to set running to find out who was trashing his neighborhood. The tapes were admitted as evidence, and the Guards were able to get a case brought against the men, who weren't men at all: three of them were fifteen and one sixteen. They were too young to be named, but three of them were from the extended Butler family. None showed any remorse; they all felt Leonard was reckless and foolhardy for trying to defend his property. Dave told me what the sixteen-year-old said.

"What the fuck did he have to get in our way for? I mean, he should have known. Family man, he shouldn't've been taking risks like that."

He said that over and over again, each time with mounting rage.

I went up to see the Leonards. I went to the removal, and to the funeral. All I can remember are the weeping children clinging to their mother, and their mother not being able to walk very well, and my wondering was it from grief, or from the fact that the kids were clinging to her, and wondering why I was wondering. I still have the picture on my phone of the Leonards wishing me a Merry Christmas. I find I look at it almost every day.

KAREN TYRRELL STOOD at the far end of the room with her back to me. She faced a big sash window that looked out across a paddock to the river. She was working at something, and when I got closer I saw that it was a painting. She had a table by the window, and around it on the wall, sketches and oils of the same view: the paddock, always with two horses, and two trees just far enough apart that they never touched, and the river. The river was altered in the paintings so that its flow caught the eye: it seemed as if the horses, and the viewer, yearned to be taken by the river, to be caught up in its current, to escape, while the trees stood upright, implacable, season in, season out, shedding and sprouting and never touching. I watched for a while as she worked, very deliberate, very careful, incorporating snow into the scene as it fell in real life. I set my face to try to feel as little as possible, to think of nothing but the picture she worked on and the scene it represented. There were no horses in the paddock today, but there were two in Karen Tyrrell's painting, of course. I stood and watched that little girl work, oblivious to the horrors that had taken place in her house that day, to the legacy of horror she had inherited, stood and prayed that the Guards would get here before she asked me what had happened, and if not, that I would find the heart to know what to say.

She turned around, and I almost gasped at her tear-stained face, at the dark hair, her mother's hair, at the startling eyes, one blue, one brown, her father's eyes, at her clear, confident gaze, as if we were at the very beginning of things.

"Where's my mother?" she said.

If you enjoyed *The Price of Blood*, don't miss

ALL THE DEAD VOICES,

the next Ed Loy thriller
from Declan Hughes.

CHAPTER 4

The door to my apartment opened onto a hallway that led directly to the small kitchen; the bathroom lay to the left; to the right were the two great rooms with high ceilings that I lived and worked in. My office was to the front; it didn't have a glass door with my name on it, or a rolltop desk, and the whiskey was Irish, and in plain view, not hidden in a filing cabinet, but I had done without an office before, and it had somehow helped to make everyone's problems my problems at a time when I had enough of my own to be going one with; I hoped an office would serve as a kind of clearinghouse for me, impersonal walls within which the dark secrets and thwarted passions of the cases I worked might disperse, or at least be safely caged. Hope springs infernal. There were three big sash windows and a sofa and two armchairs, in case an entire family wanted to hire me, which had happened a few times, with successful but never happy results. There was a pale oak desk and a dark-stained captain's chair that I sat in, the windows behind me; across the desk there was a Lloyd Loom leather chair with a cane back which women liked to sit in; there was one sitting in it now.

Anne Fogarty was about forty but looked thirty-five, or maybe she was thirty-five and looked her age. It was hard to tell these days, when twenty-one-year-olds were so primped and groomed and orange-faced they often looked like startled fifty-five-year-old millionaires' wives with too much work done. She looked well to my eyes, whatever age she was, in indigo jeans and a tight purple wraparound top that exposed just enough flesh at eleven in the morning to keep my gaze determinedly level on her twinkling brown eyes, which was no hardship. Her lips were full and painted red, and her slightly prominent teeth were crisscrossed with metal braces; her wavy hair was dyed honey blond with the ghost of dark brown roots showing; it fell in wayward bangs to her lightly freckled neck and brushed against the chain that held a glittering silver crucifix at her throat. She wore several silver and jeweled rings, but her ring finger was bare with a tan line wide enough for a wedding ring; as I was looking at hers, I saw her notice mine. I saw her notice my ear also, and something like pity, or horror, shuddered across her face.

She laid a pale green file on my desk, took the cup of black coffee I offered her, sat back and told me why she was here.

"My father was murdered in 1991. At the time, my parents' marriage was effectively over. They were staying together . . . 'for the sake of the children' is, I think, the expression, even if the children were old enough to work out for themselves that all was not well in the land of Mammy and Daddy. I was fifteen when it happened, and my sisters were seventeen and fourteen. But whatever we thought was going on, we didn't know about my mother and . . . I'm sorry, this is such a jumble, I should tell you what happened first. It's all in the file, newspaper clippings, accounts of the trial."

"I'll read the file later. But it's always good to get it straight from the source. Any way it occurs to you to tell it is fine," I said. "Was your mother having an affair?"

A flush of red rippled across Anne Fogarty's face and sparked in blotches on her chest. She laughed in embarrassment, and almost upset her cup of coffee in her lap.

"I'm sorry, was that too direct?" I said.

"Not at all. It's just strange to hear it spoken out loud. For too long the words have been boxed up in my head. My sisters don't want to know about it anymore. And the Guards are happy that they know the truth. But they don't. Which is why I'm here, Mr. Loy."

She smiled at me then, bravely, I guess you'd have to say, and I saw a history of suffering in her eyes, and of strength too, the strength to carry a burden by herself a long way after everyone around her has cast it off and wishes she would too. I smiled back, because I thought it would reassure her, and because I wanted to anyway.

"Yes, my mother was having an affair . . . and while Daddy wasn't exactly happy, he put up with it. He sort of had to. He had been first in the infidelity stakes, casual stuff with secretaries and women he met in the pub, and then Mammy found out and was heartbroken. They were childhood sweethearts, and Ma thought it would be roses all the way, the anniversary waltz in their eighties. And it didn't turn out that way. And after the hurt—she spent about a year of my childhood in bed, I was twelve—we didn't know why, we understood in retrospect—at least, I did.

"Aisling, my older sister, just gave up on Ma, she had no patience for women who 'suffered with their nerves,' as it was called back then. And it fell to me to look after Midge, that's what we called Margaret, she was still the baby, and Midge never transferred her affection back to Ma afterward. I'm not sure Ma tried very hard to win it back either. When she got out of the bed, it was like she'd shed a skin: she was cooler, more distant—she wasn't 'Mammy' anymore, she'd become . . . her own person. I've understood it better since I've had my own. I don't think it's an unusual situation, the man has a few flings, the woman finds out, and she can never quite put her heart together again the way it was. And then she met Steve Owen, and fell in love with him."

"But you didn't find out about this until later?"

"Until they arrested Ma and Steve for Daddy's murder."

"They charged them both?"

"No, they went ahead with Steve. A jury found him guilty. The conviction was later found to have been unsafe. He was released on appeal after five years. The appeal-court judges criticized the Garda investigation, and the trial judge."

"And what did the Guards say?"

"Officially, that the investigation remained open. But they leaked to every journalist in town that they weren't looking for anyone else in relation to the murder of Brian Fogarty."

"And your mother—"

"Ma died in '94, three years after Steve was sent to jail. It was like her heart had been broken one time too many."

We finished our coffee and sat in silence for a while, as if to mark with due respect the sadness of the story she had just told me. Before I had time to ask her about the circumstances of her father's death, she continued.

"Daddy was a tax inspector. The Revenue Commissioners. Worked there all his life, after a commerce degree in UCD. We lived in a semi-d in Farney Park in Sandymount. It was nothing then, but of course, it'd be a mental price now, even with the market on the slide. The neighbors were teachers and civil servants, shopkeepers and salesmen. The lower middle classes, years before they became paper millionaires. Anyway, Da was working at home one morning—he used to do that sometimes, I think it started because he was worried about Ma when she had her whatever, her breakdown. And then he got into the habit of it, he'd work the morning at home, always gone by the time we got back from school for lunch. Only this day, he wasn't gone. Not entirely."

Anne Fogarty made that smile people make when grief, however seasoned it is, brims of a sudden and threatens to spill, a smile that's both urgent and painful all at once.

"Did you find the body?" I said.

She shook her head, her smile intensifying until it looked like it had been painted on her face and left to dry.

"Midge. When I got home, she was sitting on the doorstep, covered in blood, crying like a baby. I had to walk past her to see what it was, she couldn't get the words out. He was lying on his face at the end of the hall, just at the kitchen door. The back of his head was all red and black. There was blood on the floor, blood on the walls. He'd been beaten to death. The Guards said he had his back to his killer. They deduced from this that Daddy must have known him. To trust him, to turn his back on him. But it could have equally meant he was being forced along at gunpoint, couldn't it?"

"I suppose so. Why would he have been forced along at gunpoint? Who would have pulled a gun on him? Was there money in the house?"

"No, it was . . . it was to do with what Daddy was working on. He used to have a thing about ill-gotten gains, how in Ireland, crime always pays. He'd talk about it at the kitchen table, criminals buying property after bank raids, Provos with holiday homes, heroin dealers coining it, living like kings. This was in the days before the Criminal Assets Bureau, there was no will to do anything about these people. Individual Guards wanted to act against them, and so did legal people within the DPP's office and social welfare inspectors, and some of Daddy's colleagues agreed that targeting criminals' wealth was the way to go. But there was no cooperation between the agencies, no joined-up thinking.

"Daddy used to compile these—dossiers, he called them—present them to his superiors, and wait for them to take action. But nothing ever happened. He got so frustrated about it. He'd leak stuff to journalists, but they were hampered by the libel laws, they could only refer to the individuals in code. And it wasn't as if everyone didn't know who they were. Finally, he sent letters to three particular individuals setting out what he reckoned they were worth in assets, what that amounted to as income, and what their tax liabilities were."

"He sent them letters," I said. "Signed letters?"

"Yeah."

"And you knew this back then? The day of his death?"

"Not that he'd actually sent the letters. Mammy only told me that later. But it was like . . . the Guards, as soon as they heard about Steve, that was it, it was him and Ma. They wouldn't consider any other possibility."

"You say your mother told you the letters had been sent. How did she know? She was having an affair . . . were she and your father even speaking?"

"They were keeping up appearances. They were still great friends, actually, even if the romance had come to a halt. Friends and comrades. They always talked, you know, at dinnertime, big debates about politics, the Irish language, what have you. Rows, you might say. But that's when it all used to come out, who was getting away with what. Mammy told me he had made copies of the material he sent to each individual. She gave these documents to the Guards that day, she knew instantly who the main suspects should be."

"So what happened?"

"There was no proof that he had ever sent the letters. And obviously, they carried no force, no legal force. The defense tried to use them at the trial, but they were ruled inadmissible. And of course the names never got out. The boyfriend did it, with the connivance at least, if not the active participation, of the wife."

"Rule of Domestic Murder Number One. What happened at the appeal?"

"Steve was convicted on circumstantial evidence—he was in the area, because that's where he lived and worked, he was a teacher in Marian College down the road, he had the opportunity, he had no alibi."

"Motive?"

Anne Fogarty shrugged.

"A crime of passion. Ma wouldn't leave Daddy. Allegedly, Steve was upset. He testified that he hadn't wanted her to walk out, but . . ."

"But what?"

"But they had a letter . . . letters . . . between Steve and Mammy . . . where they'd live when they were together, how happy they'd be . . . how they couldn't wait to be free of Brian Fogarty . . . how nice it would be if he were to disappear . . . how Steve couldn't bear it much longer . . ."

Anne Fogarty's voice cracked then, and she exhaled loudly and looked at the floor. I rounded the desk and rescued her cup, which was rattling in its saucer, and refilled it with hot coffee and brought it back to her. She lifted the cup to her lips and drank and raised her eyes to mine and nodded, and I sat down again.

"It was the way lovers talk. We two against the world. They were looking toward . . . four years or so, when Midge was out of school, when we were all grown up."

"You sure?"

"There was a day . . . a couple of days . . . when I wasn't sure. When I hated Mammy, and wanted to believe she and Steve had done it. But that passed."

She held my gaze to assure me that it had. In her dark eyes I could see the embers that still glowed, the smoke of doubt that would never quite disperse.

"So it wasn't as if the Guards had taken a personal set against

Steve Owen," I said. "There was enough in the letters to give them cause to believe he and your mother conspired together, or at least, had considered it."

"Only if you ignore the other evidence. That's what the judge said at the appeal, that the nature of Daddy's work, even if unofficial, should have been considered. And it emerged that he had registered the letters he sent the three suspects, that the receipts had been collected as evidence, and that that evidence had mysteriously gone missing for the original trial."

"The finger pointing where—at the prosecution or at the Guards?"

"The finger wagged back and forth, but left everyone off the hook. 'An administrative error 'was how it was phrased. I think the Guards on the scene found the receipts on him that day, in his wallet or among his papers, bagged them without appreciating their significance, and when the defense asked if there was any sign of them, they deliberately vanished them."

"Why would they do that? To protect one of the recipients of the letters?"

"The men to whom the letters were sent were Bobby Doyle and Jack Cullen."

"Bobby Doyle?" I said. "The same Bobby Doyle who's behind the Independence Day Bridge?"

"The very same."

"I know he made a settlement with the CAB in '98," I said. "But I thought that was just for unpaid taxes. Crime the conventional way. A house on Clyde Road, a couple of hotels and shopping centers, and now Independence Bridge, the most prestigious building project in the history of the state. He's done well, hasn't he?"

"He's done very well. He started off as a slum landlord on the northside in the late eighties. That's what the settlement was about, undeclared rental income. Before that he'd been in America. And before that . . . well, he's been talked of as one of the businessmen who's sympathetic to Sinn Féin, and there's no evidence to say he's anything else."

"But you wonder—what? Before he went to America?"

"He's from the North. Was there throughout the seventies. But there's no record of his family, where he lived, what he did. No one seems to know very much about him."

"And you think . . . what?"

"I don't know. He was one of the names on the list, is what I think. And Jack Cullen—"

"I know a little about Jack Cullen. I know Jack Cullen was in the IRA. Still is, insofar as it exists in any meaningful way. And I know what he does now. What about the third man?"

"The third man you know well, Ed Loy. It was in the papers, you grew up with them all. You sent his brother to jail. The third man was George Halligan."

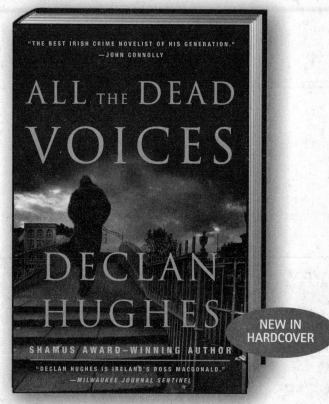